Dear Readers,

The Ultimatum is my third book in a series that began with *The Challenge* and *The Dare*. While each book stands alone and contains its very own hero and heroine, I hope that if you enjoy this book and have missed any of the others, you'll read them, too.

Every time I finish a book, I think making that particular story come to life was the most difficult one yet. And *The Ultimatum* was no different. My heroine, Dr. Allara Calladar, comes from a culture that is different from any I had yet envisioned. And due to her biology, she looks at the world in ways that are unusual—not just to twenty-first-century humans, but also to her enemy, a Rystani star pilot who lost his homeworld to her people. Writing *The Ultimatum* taxed my brain. And yet that's also part of the fun of creating new worlds, new societies, new cultures—and letting my imagination run free. And once I finally finished the book, I was glad I pushed the envelope, especially after my editor approved the story.

So what's up next? In May 2006 look for *Midnight Magic,* an anthology with Rebecca York and Jeanie London where I'll introduce you to the heroine of *The Quest,* a July release from Tor romance and the fourth book set in the future.

I always enjoy hearing from readers and you can reach me through my Web site at www.susankearney.com

As a thank you for purchasing *The Ultimatum*, I have a free gift for you. When you visit my website, click on the Member Section. There, you'll find a free screen-saver to download and games to play. Enjoy!

Best,
Susan Kearney

"Filled with sexy love scenes, wild adventure, and characters that are unforgettable, this is a 'don't miss'!"
—*Loves Romance*

PRAISE FOR *THE CHALLENGE*

"Looking for something different? A futuristic romance: Susan Kearney's *The Challenge* gave me a new perspective . . . love and sex in the future!"
—Carly Phillips, *New York Times* bestselling author of the Chandler Brothers series

"Sizzling sex and rousing adventure easily combine to produce a truly spicy and fun futuristic tale. The multi-talented Kearney's story sparkles with excitement and thrills."
—*Romantic Times BookClub Magazine*

"The sexual tension and scenes in this book are hot, hot, hot, and sure to delight readers who enjoy the mix of romance and futuristic elements."
—*The Romance Reader's Connection*

"A one-sitting read, purely enjoyable and very enthralling. Ms. Kearney brings this story vividly to life and makes a reader think. One hundred percent recommended for readers who love sci-fi/futuristic romance. I hated to see this story end."
—*Road to Romance*

"*The Challenge* is well written and riveting and worthy of recommendation to all but the most reserved reader."
—*Romance Reviews Today*

"*The Challenge* is a gripping story, from beginning to end. Tessa and Kahn have intriguing layers and the supporting characters are very engaging. The action never lets up, and when things turn romantic, the pages steam with heat. So, if you want to experience a sci-fi romance, but are not quite sure, give *The Challenge* a try. If you love sci-fi, then this book should be on your auto-buy list, along with the sequel, *The Dare*."
—*A Romance Review,* Five Roses

TOR BOOKS BY SUSAN KEARNEY

The Challenge
The Dare
The Ultimatum
The Quest*

*forthcoming

For a special sneak preview of *The Quest*, turn to the
back of the book!

The Ultimatum

SUSAN KEARNEY

tor romance

A TOM DOHERTY ASSOCIATES BOOK
NEW YORK

This is a work of fiction. All the characters and events portrayed in this book are either products of the author's imagination or are used fictitiously.

THE ULTIMATUM

Edited by Anna Genoese

A Tor Book
Published by Tom Doherty Associates, LLC
175 Fifth Avenue
New York, NY 10010

www.tor.com

Tor® is a registered trademark of Tom Doherty Associates, LLC.

ISBN 0-765-35448-9
EAN 978-0-765-35448-8

First edition: February 2006

Printed in the United States of America

0 9 8 7 6 5 4 3 2 1

For my husband Barry—with lots of love.
Thanks for putting up with me for twenty-five years.

Prologue

"**M**ama. Don't leave me." Dr. Alara Calladar sat beside the pallet she'd made for her mother in her bombed and caved-in laboratory and gently held her hand. "Please don't go."

"I have . . . no choice." Her mother opened her eyes and the cloudy haze of pain that had been there for days suddenly cleared. She gripped Alara's hand with fierce strength. "You must go on without me."

Alara's throat tightened but tears spilled over her cheeks. She might be a woman fully grown, she might be the most educated woman scientist on Endeki, but she still needed her mother. But her mother had closed her eyes again, leaving Alara alone, trapped in the cave in.

What the *krek* had happened to cause the blast in their home above them? She still didn't know.

Four days ago, she and her mother had entered

Alara's underground laboratory to check her latest experiments. While her mother wasn't a scientist, she'd been a teacher, and she often helped Alara clean the lab, answer calls and pay bills, but mostly she encouraged her independence.

They'd been chatting about a play they both wanted to see when with no warning, the basement floor had shuddered like a quake. Only Endeki didn't have quakes or seismic tremors like so many other Federation worlds. Instinctively, mother and daughter stumbled toward one another. Fell. Part of the roof caved in. Dirt and powder rained down, sending up clouds of dust, but thanks to the suits every Federation citizen wore, they could filter the dirt from the air and shield their bodies from the debris.

In the darkness, Alara had crawled to her toppled desk, found an emergency light and discovered that huge beams blocked the stairs and their exit.

Digging out from beneath the debris proved an impossible task. They'd been trapped down here for days, and while their suits kept them warm and clean, they had to conserve their emergency lighting. They had no food and only a few mouthfuls to drink, and air was in short supply.

Yet, even suffocating would have been better than watching her mother die cell by cell, listening to her draw each tortured breath. Due to the unusual connection between Endekian husbands and wives, her mother had instantly known that her husband, who had been in the house above, had died in the blast. And her father's death had set off a physiological chain reaction in her mother's cells. Alara could describe the process in scientific terms. But her knowledge couldn't prevent the inevitable—her mother's death.

Alara couldn't imagine what her mother must be feeling. Although the marriage had been terrible for years, her mother must have once loved her father. As for Alara's own feelings, she could only rage at her father for putting her mother through hell while he'd been alive. If his demise wouldn't soon cause the death of Alara's precious mother, she wouldn't have minded his passing. She doubted she'd ever forgive his many cruelties to his wife and daughter.

Her mother had always tried to protect Alara, and her impending death was no different. She'd kept the truth from Alara for two entire days, suffering in silence, bravely enduring the agony of every organ and tissue failing, until she could no longer conceal her pain.

To lose the woman who had brought her into the world hurt so much that Alara didn't know how she would go on without her—if she survived the cave-in. That all of Alara's education, all her science couldn't stop her mother's biological reactions made her feel helpless, trapped by biology she hated.

"Did you hear that?" Her mother's eyes opened again.

Drawn from her grief, Alara listened and smoothed back her mother's hair and tried to make her voice cheerful. "Rescue workers are coming. They'll get us out."

Despite what had to be immense pain, her mother offered a weak smile. "Knowing you will live, I can die . . . with peace."

"No, Mother, please. We'll heal you."

"It's not possible for me." Her mother licked her dry lips and spoke with more strength than she had in days. "But you . . . you must continue your research . . . so other women won't die for no reason."

Alara could barely speak through her sorrow. "I can't it without you."

"Promise . . . me . . . that you'll never forget . . . that you'll never give up . . ."

Alara choked on the words. "I promise."

1

She needed a man. But she sure as *krek* didn't want one.

Dr. Alara Bazelle Calladar shoved aside her test samples and rubbed the bridge of her nose. Success had once again eluded her. And success would mean freedom from the Endekian biology that drove the females of her species to have sex—whether they wanted to or not—or face a painful death. She'd hoped to find a remedy soon, but she wasn't going to succeed today, not in time to prevent her own elevated hormone levels from driving her away from work and into the arms of a man, any man, to satisfy her biological compulsions. Instead she was left with no answers and too many blasted urges.

Just once, she longed to give in to frustration and smash something. But the only items at hand were the DNA maturation receptacles that housed her experiments, materials too precious to sacrifice in a fit of temper.

"Alara." Her assistant and good friend, Maki, interrupted her thoughts, the voice echoing through the com system. "You have a visitor."

"I'm busy." *Busy* was code for putting off whoever was interrupting her work until another day, a day when she wasn't so frazzled. Under normal circumstances, her research was difficult, but during the beginnings of *Boktai,* Alara's elevated hormone levels made unclouded reasoning as elusive as a Denvovian sandworm that'd grown wings. As if in anticipation of mating, the pathways that transmitted reflexes to her brain had fully engaged. Due to increased blood flow to her tissues, her lips already tingled, her breasts were tender.

"He's . . . insistent."

"He?" Alara snapped her head up from the array of test samples, too few of which showed any sign of promise. Science required patience and normally she had plenty. But with her metabolic rate rising, just the mention of a man caused her heartbeat to escalate, her patience to dwindle.

"Oh, he's one hundred and ten percent male," Maki practically purred, and Alara imagined how the man would preen at Maki's compliment. He'd no doubt entered the reception area, puffed up with the confidence of a blowfish, certain he was wanted and worthy of female attention. Very likely, he wasn't—though only a few of the women on her planet were enlightened enough to notice. Endekian men treated their women no better than their favorite canine, and they would never change—not until women no longer had to offer up their bodies to them on a regular basis in order to stay alive.

But while it took a lot of male muscles to impress Maki, she still wouldn't have interrupted unless she believed the man important.

Alara swore under her breath, annoyed that in her current metabolic state, she would react to the unidentified male just like every other Endekian woman whose hormonal system demanded sex. After she lost control of her psi and failed to filter out his male scent, she'd inhale his pheromones, and she'd find him irresistible—even if he turned out to have no more charm than a sand flea, no more brain cells than a slime slug, no more sense of humor than a Terran terrorist. In the early phase of *Boktai,* her enhanced senses would enflame, deepening her desires, quickening her yearning, until she transformed into a *rintha*—an undiscriminating female who required sex with every needy cell in her body.

Alara welcomed the temptation of a male in her lab and in her life as much as she'd welcome a political debate over the ethics of her research. Both were irritating, painful—but a fact of life. She had no use for men—not until she had no choice. In fact, the few rare males who deigned to enter her laboratory were often those who sought to discourage her from continuing her work.

Why wouldn't they? Since Endeki had come into contact with worlds in the Federation, their women had discovered something amazing. On other planets, women were not trapped by their bodies into having indiscriminate sex. They chose their partners for a variety of reasons—attraction, amusement . . . love. On Endeki, only biology and genetics came into play, giving the men a lifetime supply of sexual pleasure and the women an eternity of slavery to their own bodies—and ultimately, to the men with whom they bonded.

Alara glanced at the wall, where she'd hung a holopic of her mother, taken shortly before the Terran terrorists' bombing of her city—Terrans who had been aided by Rystani intel. She'd watched her mother die in agony and then, she'd gone on . . . alone.

She had raged, mourned, and buried both parents before she'd repressed her grief with work. As the sole survivor in her family, she'd studied harder and become more determined than ever to unravel the secrets of Endekian physiology. She wanted women to be free of the curse of *Boktai*.

She could never have foreseen that the government would choose her survival as the symbol to rally the masses against the Terrans and the Rystani. Alara had used her newfound celebrity to prevent the government from closing her lab. However, as the anger against the Terran-Rystani plot that had killed so many abated, she'd become less useful to the government and had fallen out of favor. With the current unpopularity of her work, she wouldn't be surprised if the visitor were here to close her lab.

"Alara." Maki's voice dropped to a whisper. "He's bristling with attitude."

"I told you to tell him I'm *busy*."

"I tried." Maki's tone conveyed vexation. "He refuses to make an appointment."

"Use your imagination. Get rid of him."

"I'd be perfectly willing to take him home for the night."

"Then do it."

Maki breathed out a delicate sigh. "I tried. But he wants *you*. He said he's willing to wait as long as it takes."

"Oh, for the holy structure of atoms." Alara shoved

back from the table. "He can wait out front all through the dark hours. I'm leaving through my personal entrance."

Alara picked up the disk to start her flitter and headed out the back of the facility. She intended to go home, soak in a hot bath, and take care of her growing arousal. Self-gratification was only a temporary solution for her cravings, one that would work for a short time and only if no males were present. Experience told her she couldn't hold out much longer and that within a day, two at most, she would lose control of her psi and her will, forcing her to seek out a male.

With a quick retina scan, Alara unlocked her back door and stepped outside into the balmy dusk. Automatically, almost unconsciously, she used her psi on her suit, to shield her from the cloying humidity. Anxious to be on her way, she didn't pause to take in the city lights beyond her building but headed straight for her flitter, climbed in, inserted the disk, and revved the engine.

"You were leaving without speaking to me."

A deep male voice, filled with vitality and a hint of humor, arrowed from the back seat and struck her full blown, causing her to jerk in surprise.

She used her psi filters on her suit, and just in case her control had weakened, she also held her breath, refusing to allow his scent into her lungs, but just the sound of his husky male tone kindled inevitable biological reactions. Her nostrils flared, automatically seeking his provocative aroma. Her heart's alpha rhythm escalated. Her pulse between her thighs quickened and blood rushed to her sensitive breasts. The suit cupping her skin seemed inadequate when her flesh suddenly yearned for male hands to caress her, seduce her, satisfy her.

However, she was not yet so far into *Boktai* that her brain had abdicated completely to the demands of her body. She still maintained enough psi control to remain clothed, but thinking was becoming more difficult. But she must . . . think. The man had anticipated her escape out the back of the facility and had followed her. He had some nerve. "This is *my* flitter. Get out."

"Not until we have a conversation," he countered, his don't-think-about-avoiding-me-again tone deep, determined, yet almost teasing.

Conversation? Ah, the combination of her needy cells plus the rumble of his voice must be clouding her thoughts. He was not here to mate. He was probably here to speak to her about the laboratory and her work. Aware that her long-ignored bodily needs would react to the sight of him, she refused to turn around. The moment the receptors in her eyes detected his male shape, her enzymes would elevate her hormones to the next level. In her worsening condition, he could be as ugly as a slime-covered Osarian, yet if she stayed in his presence long enough, her will to resist wouldn't matter—lust would ignite her synaptic reflexes.

She spoke through gritted teeth. "Make an appointment with my secretary."

"I don't have time to delay. Neither do you."

"Exactly. We agree. I don't have time," she practically growled. "Go away."

"Are you always so friendly?" His voice revealed more curiosity than sarcasm.

"Are you always so pushy?" she countered and took in a breath. Clean, musky male scent wafted to her nostrils, downshifted into her lungs, and revved her olfactory nerves into third gear. *By the mother lode.* Why did her psi have to fail now and let in his aroma, which reminded her of sweet grasses and summer rain? Surely no other Endekian male had ever smelled so incredibly delicious and she fought the primitive urge to look at him.

She tried not to savor his wondrous scent and distracted herself with analysis. There was something unusual about him. Something she couldn't quite pinpoint. Her mind tumbled and then settled. He didn't smell like an Endekian because . . . he *wasn't* Endekian.

Last year, or next year, she might have been more wary. This year, she was dealing with *Boktai* and wasn't herself. Her psi was already failing. Intoxicated by his seductive scent, she barely held back a sigh of infatuation, fought off the fantasy of his breath fanning her ear, his hands roaming over her body, his mouth skimming a trail of heat down her neck. And all the while her hunger to see him was building.

"Who are you?" Unable to remain cautious, she turned around. And he smiled at her—a charming, you-can't-resist-me smile that would have taken her breath away—if sheer surprise hadn't already done so. He was one giant of a man, one fantastic male specimen who was so damn appealing, he'd haunt her dreams—even if they never spoke again. As if the cooling in her suit had failed, sweat dotted her brow and her muscles tensed.

At the sight of bronze *male* skin molded over a powerful physique, her respiration increased. She salivated as every zymogen granule flooded with enzymes. With his black hair clipped short to reveal a very *male* neck that was supported by cords of muscle, her gaze skimmed from his bold nose to his lush mouth to his dazzling cheekbones. But it was his compelling violet eyes, the color of precious nebula flame gemstones, that sought her out with male interest and which almost did in her rioting nerves.

Only his focused expression stopped her inclination to move closer. He wasn't gloating with the usual male I-know-you-can't-resist-me arrogance. He actually appeared to be trying not to alarm her. Although he held still, he dominated the air around her, saturating her oxygen with his masculinity. "I am Xander from Mystique."

Despite the *Boktai,* her blood ran cold.

"You're a Rystani warrior," she accused him. His people had given the Terrans the intel that had led to the death of her parents. And she had forgotten none of the pain of losing her mother. The war between Rystan and Endeki hadn't been over for very long. Though many Rystani had emigrated to the newly discovered planet Mystique, her people still ruled his homeworld. Peace between the Endekians and Rystani remained uneasy, simmering with decades of distrust and hatred. Xander shouldn't be here. Rystani warriors, or any of their citizens, faced mortal danger on Endeki and visited only in official, well-guarded situations.

She stared at him, unable to move away. His presence injected the situation with danger, heightening her reactions in ways she could not control. Her stomach fluttered with excitement and her hands began to shake. Images of this bronze-fleshed Rystani warrior making love consumed her. Xander's hands in her hair, on her breasts. His body pressed against her aching flesh. Alara took little satisfaction that she'd managed not to reach out to touch him. How could she when she was so quickly losing control?

He spoke as if he had no inkling of what his presence was doing to her. "My purpose here is urgent. We need to talk."

His tone was calm, his eyes direct. Despite the

clamoring-for-attention thrill that she couldn't subdue, she shivered under his intense expression.

She couldn't imagine this Rystani warrior had any use for Endekians. Her people had appropriated his world fourteen Federation years ago and the rightness of their actions, the political reasons for war, had no bearing on the suffering they'd caused. Many Rystani had died in the invasion, as had countless Endekian males. Her own brother had not come back, a casualty of her government's need to invade and destroy. Rystani were the enemy. And here she was, confined with a Rystani warrior, a man her brother had set off to annihilate. A man whose people were responsible for her parents' deaths. Just his presence reminded her of the pain. The agony. She wanted him to go, but perhaps the best way to rid herself of his presence was to hear him out.

She turned off the flitter, opened the door, and exited her vehicle, hoping the fresh air would blow away his scent and allow her a few moments of peaceful conversation. But of course the wind currents didn't cooperate. When Xander unfolded his big frame from the vehicle, he was much larger than she'd imagined, more appealing than her most secret dreams. Inside the flitter, she'd only viewed his upper half, but his wonderfully flat stomach, sexy narrow hips, and long legs made him more intimidating, more domineering, more deliciously male. If the battle for his world had come down to hand-to-hand fighting, if all the Rystani men were this large, his people would never have lost.

But they had, thanks to the superior technology of her world. Too bad there was nothing superior about her situation right now. She wanted to listen, so he would quickly depart, but the effects of the *Boktai* nearly drove her mad.

Barely restraining a curse of frustration, she trembled.

"So why are you here?" she asked, deepening her voice to compensate for the breathy teasing tone that her physiology urged her to emit.

"I need your help." He spoke simply, appealing to her curiosity.

Yet her mind was losing the battle for control and the only way she wanted to help was to find a private place where she could entice him to ease her suffering.

She shifted her stance. "What kind of help?"

He shot her another one of his charming grins. "Could we go somewhere more—"

"I'm not going anywhere with you." No matter how perfect his smile, no matter how strong her hormones, no matter how badly her cells wept for satiation, she could not have sex with an offworlder. She was already at odds with her government. Taking a Rystani into her bed might be seen as a traitorous act.

He chuckled, his tone so warm and inviting that she barely restrained a gasp of delight. As her imagination conjured up sexual fantasies, she forced herself to listen while she tried not to stare at his full mouth, tried not to wonder how his lips, skimming past her earlobe, over her nape and shoulder, would feel.

He leaned forward onto the balls of his feet, his eyes locking on hers. "Is it true that you need merely look at a person to read his DNA?"

She shrugged and folded her arms beneath her aching breasts, hoping the light was too dim for him to see her hardening nipples. Why was he interested in her peculiar ability, one she found useful, although her skill mattered little to the nonscientific community? "My ability's common knowledge on my world. How do you know about it?"

He ignored her question. "It is said you can spot a flaw in the double helix chain at thirty paces."

She'd be willing to bet her last batch of test samples that Xander had never seen the inside of a lab, never mind looked through a microscope. He appeared to have spent his entire life outdoors, exercising and eating and growing muscles over his well-shaped bones.

"Why are you curious about my work?" she asked.

"I have no interest in your work," he replied, a keen intelligence in his eyes, a glimmer of humor in their depths, even as his voice carried overtones of intensity and power. "My interest is . . . in you."

Bloody stars. Endekian men didn't speak with such directness. Then again, they didn't have to. They simply waited for a woman to choose and took their pleasure. Conversation was rarely part of the arrangement, so Alara found his bold declaration of interest in her odd, yet exhilarating.

Reminding herself that her brain couldn't possibly be functioning on all neurons, she eyed the big warrior with renewed caution. "What do you want?"

"You must accompany me on a mission." Despite his demand, he softened his tone to a tempting and compelling coaxing that increased her interest.

She was not about to give up her work, or leave her friends and her home, but she'd satisfy her curiosity before she sent him on his way. "What mission?"

He shot her an engaging, come-with-me glance that promised excitement. "I am seeking the Perceptive Ones."

Despite his charisma, she snorted. "The Perceptive Ones haven't inhabited this galaxy in eons, if ever. They are a myth."

"Perhaps not." His lips curled into an adventurous grin that revealed he didn't take insult at her words.

"No one is certain they *ever* existed, never mind that they still live. You have no more hopes of finding the Perceptive Ones than bacteria have of understanding its origins."

"Have you no faith, Doctor?" He gestured to her body, causing a ripple of gooseflesh her suit barely contained. "You wear a suit that was manufactured by machines the Perceptive Ones left behind." His voice turned earnest and eager, and she suspected he was younger than she'd first thought. "The Perceptive Ones existed, of that I'm sure. And according to ancient records recently discovered on our starship's journey across the galaxy, out near the rim is a system named Lapau, colonized by a humanoid race called the Lapautee."

"I've never heard of them."

"Not much is known about the Lapautee." Xander's eyes danced with the call of adventure—a sparkle she'd seen once in the eyes of her brother before he'd gone off to war. "However, legend suggests their planet may be an outpost for a protector, a Perceptive One. I'm hoping that since their machines lasted through the millennia, perhaps they did, as well."

She didn't know if he was insane or on a grand quest. Either way, she couldn't help him. "I'm sorry. I must decline. I have my own work."

"This mission is of grave importance."

"And my work is not?" She arched a brow, daring him to insult her research because she was female and her purpose inconsequential to him. That is, if he'd cared to learn anything about her research at all.

But he didn't insult her. He paused. Thought. Considered. Her respect for him escalated. Clearly he believed in his mission, and she admired anyone who had that kind of dedication to their work. So she wasn't surprised when he didn't accept her refusal without argument.

"My mission to find the Perceptive Ones is necessary to saving the lives of billions." His every word vibrated with fervor.

She narrowed her brows, unswayed by his earnestness since she felt the same passion for her own research. "Then I wish good fortune to be on your side." She turned away to dismiss him.

He clamped a hand on her shoulder and electricity shot straight to her core. She restrained a gasp at the unexpected pleasure rippling through her. The Rystani warrior's hand was gentle, strong, and warm—warm enough to fire her flesh. Ruthlessly, she clenched her jaw and tamped down on her need.

His voice hardened. "You will at least do me the courtesy of hearing me out."

As if she had a choice with his big hand on her? She forced herself to shrug it off, and no doubt sensing she would listen, he allowed her to free herself. He couldn't know that his touch had set off a storm of need so great that her ears roared. He was speaking, but at first she couldn't think beyond the rushing sensation that threatened her composure. But finally she regrouped.

"The Perceptive Ones are believed to have been responsible for seeding life in our galaxy with DNA."

"That legend likely has no more substance than the propaganda offered by our esteemed leader, Drik." She took deep breaths, and as her chest rose and fell, she gave him credit—his gaze didn't once drop below her neck.

"I know little of your leader or your politics. I know

only that my mission is to go to Lapau in search of the Perceptive Ones and a pure strain of DNA."

"A pure strain? Why not use the alien time machine to go back and retrieve—"

"The Federation Council won't permit time travel unless we can prove with absolute certainty that we won't contaminate Earth's entire time line."

"Earth?"

The blood drained from her face, leaving her light-headed. She'd thought he was trying to help his *own* people, not the despicable race that had killed her father, and ultimately, her beloved mother.

He continued, obviously unaware of her past or he would never have sought her help. "Terrans have polluted Earth and their DNA is irreparably damaged. Soon they will be dying by the millions. To save them, I'm looking for a pure strain of Terran DNA; without it . . . they will all die."

He sounded just like a good soldier, all earnest and optimistic—like her brother had been before he'd gone off to war. Groaning, she leaned against the flitter, raised her hands to her pounding temples, trying to think past the sorrow, past the river of passion bubbling through her veins. Just the mention of Terrans had likely activated her fervor. Anger could trigger lust, the strong sentiment setting off signals, one emotion feeding the other.

"I'm not helping you save cursed Terrans. I hope they all die, and if they do, I'll dance a celebration to the Goddess."

"Why do you hate Terrans?" He actually sounded puzzled.

She had no problem setting him straight. "Fourteen years ago, the Terrans, bloodthirsty with their new power as Federation members and with intel from Rystan, launched the bomb that hit this very city. I lost my parents, my friends and coworkers. Terrans destroyed my life. They are savages, primitive and cruel. I won't so much as examine a bacterium to save a single one of them."

"Not all Rystani and Terrans are warlike—"

"You don't need me," she argued. "Any scientist with a microscope can do what I do."

He shook his head. "We may not have the opportunity to examine each species in a laboratory. You can walk on their worlds and merely look—"

"That is where you are wrong. Even if I wanted to help, and make no mistake, I don't, Endekian females are not permitted to leave our homeworld. Ever."

As if the law had been made to prevent him from carrying out his mission, a muscle jumped in his neck, a grimace tightened his lips. "Why not?"

She would not reveal her shame. She refused to tell him that their men didn't want their women to approach offworlders for life-giving sex. Selfish to the core, their men kept that pleasure for themselves. Still, she didn't lie, either. "It's the law."

Anger flickered in his eyes, whether it was for her inability to leave her homeworld or frustration that she couldn't accompany him, she couldn't discern. But all that male heat spiked her hormones another notch, flaying her with endorphins.

Krek. Forget the scientific explanations. She was ready to pounce. On him.

She had to get away before she did something really stupid, like leaning into his chest, wrapping her hands around his neck, pulling his lips down to meet hers, and finding out if the Rystani tasted as good as he looked. Or like rubbing her skin against his. Like grinding her pelvis against his sexy hips.

Reminding herself he was a stranger, a Rystani warrior and forbidden to her, reminding herself that contact with him would ruin everything she'd dedicated her life to, would only keep her restrained for so long. Starving cells demanded regeneration. She needed sex so badly she shook.

And damn him, she needed him to be out of sight so her gaze couldn't dwell on what he concealed beneath his plain black suit, which was molded to his frame with a precision that seared the image into her brain, branding her with flaming heat. Moisture beaded on her upper lip and seeped between her thighs.

But she would not yield to her need.

She couldn't have an offworlder—especially one who was a friend to Terrans.

She wouldn't succumb.

She'd remain strong.

Opening the flitter door, she eased inside, sensing he would not break the law to pursue her. Yet, even as she escaped his presence, his last words rang in her ears like a whispered promise. "Laws can be changed. We are not done, you and I."

2

Xander headed back to the shuttle he'd set down at the city landing center, a barren area of pavement, landing lights, and gray boxy structures that made him appreciate the greenery at home on Mystique. No one stopped him. Although he was deep in thought, his warrior instincts noted that the citizens kept their distance, often crossing to the other side of the rolling pavement to avoid coming near him.

If the Endekians had known their race was responsible for the death of Xander's mother, they might have not just crossed the street to feel safe—but have fled across the city. He'd buried his resentment and pain deep in his heart. Not only had Endekians invaded his world, captured and tortured him, they'd killed his mother. And for what? He'd still didn't understand why the Endekians had invaded a frozen world where survival was already so hard.

Food had always been scarce on Rystan. And Xander and Mogul had returned from the hunt to find his mother's lifeless body lying across the threshold, an Endekian knife in her throat. The other women in the village had fared no better. All had been slaughtered and it was a sight he'd never forgotten. His father's tears. Xander's pain at losing his mother at the age of seven still sliced deep. He could no longer recall her face, but he remembered the love in his household. Even when she had to go without, his mother had always saved food for him and a smile of welcome for his father. But it was her stories Xander missed most, and his favorite recollections were memories of sitting on her lap in front of a hot glow stone while she'd read to him about other beings and faraway worlds. He could thank her for his interest in exploration, one he'd never lost even after the tragedy or his subsequent relocation to Mystique.

The Endekians should fear him but Alara hadn't seemed the least bit frightened. His size hadn't appeared to faze her, either. In fact, her stare had been so direct he'd had to avoid shifting from foot to foot to reveal his attraction. No Rystani female would have been so bold. However, Xander had lived on Mystique with many races and understood that her behavior likely had been acceptable for an Endekian. Though he now realized that what she'd said was true—in all his travels, he'd never met an Endekian woman. As captain of a diverse crew, he tried to keep an open mind about etiquette and to respect different cultures, but even his fair-minded nature was taxed by this race. They'd killed and maimed and raped. They'd destroyed the life his family had loved so deeply—and might have murdered him too if not for Tessa, the Terran who had saved his life.

She'd freed him from torture. She'd purchased Mystique so that his people had a place to go and did not have to submit to surrender or slavery at the hands of their conquerors. He wasn't about to let some ridiculous Endekian law prevent him from taking Alara with him on his mission to save Tessa's race.

In the past, he'd worked his way up the ranks of Mystique's space fleet by using a combination of discipline and persistence. And the hunting instincts he'd learned from his father on his childhood planet of Rystan, a harsh world where the success of the hunt meant bringing home enough food to keep their starving people alive for one more day, had never left him.

Xander had learned that doing a task to his best ability could mean the difference between success and failure. Yet he also understood that determination wasn't always enough to succeed. Sometimes a warrior had to bide his time, choose the moment to strike to his best advantage. Sometimes, he needed luck. And sometimes a warrior had to make his own luck.

He'd considered using force to take Alara with him. But kidnapping an Endekian would cause an interplanetary incident and complicate his mission, especially if they sent a fleet of warships after him. While he was perfectly willing to negotiate for Alara through political channels, the need for a speedy departure remained his primary concern. If he asked the Federation to intervene, it might be months before anyone important even considered his request.

So as he entered his shuttle where Kirek, his newest crew member, awaited him, Xander decided to keep his options open.

Kirek greeted him with an easy, respectful smile. Although the boy was young for a mission like this one, merely eighteen years of age, he'd been born in hyper-space. He looked like a normal Rystani teen, with curious blue eyes, dark hair, and thin arms and legs that had yet to fill out with the full muscles of a warrior. But Kirek had special psi powers that few understood—powers that made him undetectable to machines. The last time Kirek had insisted on joining a space mission, he'd been only four years old, and his help had been invaluable on Kwadii, a planet on the rim where the citizens still believed him to be an Oracle.

"Did Dr. Calladar agree to accompany us?" Kirek turned off his computer console and gave Xander his full attention, his expression intense, almost as if he expected difficulties.

"Endekian law prevents women from leaving their homeworld." A good commander didn't let a mere setback heat his temper, so Xander's emotions were fully in lock-down mode.

Alara had gotten to him. Whether it was her combination of intelligence and hostility or the alluring tilt of her chin, her clearly restrained temper, or the flash of rebellious attitude mixed with sorrow in her beautiful eyes, he couldn't say. But from the first moment she'd spoken in her crisp voice, he'd reacted in a way he didn't wish to think about. Instead of recalling how her voice had choked when she'd mentioned the deaths of her parents, he turned to the computer console.

"Why didn't we know Endekian laws prevented her from coming with us?" Xander asked.

"There is much we do not know about the Endekians, Captain," answered Ranth, their sentient computer, who monitored billions of conversations simultaneously, both here on the shuttle as well as on Xander's beloved mother ship, the *Verazen*. Almost a decade and a half old, Ranth was still forming a personality, but he never shirked his duties. "While they are full-fledged Federation members, they tend to keep their affairs private."

"So not only are they warlike, they're secretive."

Xander used a psi thought on the materializer and helped himself to a cool drink of water, downing the packet in one long gulp. His conversation with Alara had taxed him. Not only had she been argumentative and uncooperative, but she'd seemed as uncomfortable around him as he'd been when he'd learned his mission required him to land on a world he considered enemy territory.

Never had Xander expected to set foot on Endeki, a planet that was home to a people who'd invaded his boyhood village on Rystan. Too often he relived the tragedy in his nightmares. He'd awaken in a sweat, his suit mopping up his perspiration, his heart pounding, his limbs as taut as when he'd still been a child and the Endekians had captured him and shot megavolts of agonizing electricity through his body. If the Terran, Tessa Camen, had not rescued him, he would have died. He owed her a great debt. Not only had she saved many of his people from the invasion, she'd personally risked her life to preserve his. And that's why he'd volunteered for this mission—Tessa and her kind were dying, and he sought to repay a debt of honor.

However, once he'd begun conversing with the alluring Dr. Calladar, he'd noticed much more than her attractive face and body. He'd liked the calm intelligence in her eyes. The way her mind had focused, assessed and countered his arguments. He suspected she kept a feisty temper in check behind her scientific demeanor. And he suspected that she could be almost as determined as he—she wouldn't change her mind.

He couldn't blame her for her animosity toward the

Terrans if what she claimed was true, but the actions of a few terrorists should not color her opinion of an entire race. He did not blame Alara for the invasion of Rystan. In fact, he found her incredibly alluring.

Since arriving he'd learned that Endekian women were incredibly beautiful—and she was prettier than most. With her spiky pink hair that surrounded her head like a halo, deep green eyes, and golden skin, she was exotic, yet sensual. He'd have to work hard to remember that her lovely curves encased a brilliant doctor and a hostile woman.

"Ranth, what's our best option?" Xander asked.

"Define 'best,'" the computer requested.

Xander thought for a moment. "We need Dr. Calladar with us on the *Verazen* for this mission, but I don't wish to start a war. Give me options that fit those parameters." Then he turned to Kirek. "You earned your berth on this mission by claiming that your presence was necessary."

"Yes." Kirek held his gaze but didn't volunteer more information. He might be a boy, but he'd always had an old soul, a wise soul, and he must have sensed that while Xander liked him, he'd have preferred to bring along an experienced warrior or another scientist instead of a lad who remained dear to so many people at home. While Xander would do his best to bring everyone back safely, he'd already decided that he would give Kirek the most innocuous tasks.

Putting his concern for Kirek's safety to the back of his mind, Xander gazed at the young man. Xander's father had taught him to trust his instincts during the hunt. Right now instinct told him that Kirek knew more about this mission than he was letting on. "Why is your presence necessary?"

"I'm not certain, yet."

Sometimes, like now, the young man vexed him. He often sat too still, just thinking. Yet, other times he seemed lighthearted. But he was never carefree. And he always appeared to carry too much responsibility on his youthful frame.

Before Xander could question him further, Ranth turned on a holovid and a three-dimensional map of their current location floated before them. "The Endekian political headquarters are located in the middle of their largest city. Their leader, Drik, possesses the title *Kalmata*. There's no direct translation of the Endekian word, but *Kalmata* means 'he who is in charge in this life and the next.' My calculations suggest that the best way to change the law that keeps Dr. Calladar from accompanying us is through this man. Drik's all-powerful. He's also guarded by a half-dozen of his most loyal men as well as an up-to-date security system, so we must proceed with caution."

"Kirek, get me Tessa on the hyperlink," Xander ordered.

Tessa's face appeared on the vidscreen, the circles under her eyes darker than when Xander had left the week before. Despite the suits that fought off illness and added longevity to normal life spans, Tessa looked unhealthy and her husband, Kahn, who stood beside her, appeared to be putting up a businesslike front, until Xander stared into the other man's eyes and saw the pain-wracked shadows.

Yet Kahn hadn't lost his steely determination, and Xander squared his own shoulders under his scrutiny. Although the Terrans were searching for answers to cure their sickness on many fronts, biological, medical, and even spiritual, Xander knew Kahn and Tessa were counting on him to save her and her people.

"What's up?" she asked, her Terran slang automatically translated by his suit into Rystani.

"No one's fired on us yet."

"We do have a peace treaty." Her voice had cracked. Slightly, but he'd noticed. How much time did Tessa have left before she succumbed to the breakdown of her DNA, caused by exposure to pollution during her many trips back to Earth? Her people, who lived there full-time, were much worse off. Thousands had already died and the numbers were expected to escalate into the billions if a cure wasn't found. Doctors were doing their best. However, medical scientists, geneticists, and biologists agreed that they required a pure form of Terran DNA to replicate, a DNA that had not been damaged by pollution. While finding the Perceptive Ones and the original DNA strands was a long shot, it might possibly be the Terrans' best chance of a cure.

"We can't rely on Endekians to honor their word, but I'm forced to deal with them. I need to see Drik, the Endekian leader, and convince him to change a law that will allow Dr. Calladar to accompany us," Xander explained, then followed up with more details.

Kahn leaned over Tessa's shoulder. "We don't have time for politics, and I'm not too concerned about violating their laws. With the new defensive armaments we've purchased, we won't be defeated so easily this time."

From Kahn's tone, Xander could tell the warrior was spoiling for a good fight. No doubt his frustration and helplessness over his ailing wife's condition exacerbated his ire.

Tessa squeezed Kahn's hand. "I appreciate that you're willing to go to war for us, but that should be our last option."

Before her husband could insert another word into the conversation, she smoothly continued, her eyes sparkling. "Do you think Drik might be open to a bribe?"

"Possibly." Xander frowned. "But are we still going through diplomatic channels?"

Tessa shook her head. "The Osarians have some dirt on one of the locals. Let me see what I can do."

Five minutes later, Tessa used the hyperlink to call back. "Be at the *Kalmata*'s villa in exactly six Federation hours, right after the shift change. The new men will be sleepy." Tessa grinned. "Apparently Endekian guards customarily accept free food from local eateries. The food will be drugged. You shouldn't have to kill anyone to slip by."

"Good." Xander nodded, yet he would miss the opportunity to do battle. Last time he'd dealt with Endekians, he'd been a child. As a man, he'd enjoy taking on several of them. He had not forgotten the torture he'd endured during their invasion.

Despite his attempt to appear stoic, he must have revealed his inclination to bust open a few heads. Either that or Tessa knew Rystani men too well.

She laughed. "Don't look so disappointed, Xander. I suspect on this mission you'll find other enemies to fight." Her gaze moved past him to Kirek and her eyes brightened. "Keep a close watch on that boy."

"He's no longer a boy," Xander contradicted, unwilling to admit that he would do just that, especially since Kirek could hear every word.

These past few years, Tessa's illness had kept her close to home and Mystique, but her words revealed that she'd lost none of her protective instincts. Xander had heard rumors that she didn't want to bear children until she was certain she'd live long enough to raise them.

"He's not yet a man, either. He's only a few years older than you were when the Endekians captured you," Tessa reminded him, as if he could forget.

But Tessa didn't usually waste expensive hyperlink time on small talk or on telling people how to do their jobs. He suspected she had an ulterior motive for the chat.

As mission leader and captain of the *Verazen,* his starship orbiting above Endeki, Xander was responsible for the safety of every member of his crew. Although the scars on his mind had lasted far longer than the ones on his body, he would put aside his hatred—for her sake and the sake of this mission.

"Don't worry, Tessa. When I go to Drik, I will do so with a cool head."

"And a ready weapon," Kahn added.

Always the warrior, Kahn remained protective of every Rystani. But the warning in Kahn's tone was clear. Endekians couldn't be trusted.

In the Milky Way Galaxy

They all need to die.

   The Endekians? The Terrans? The Rystani?

   I said—all of them.

   Let us not be hasty. I have no wish to—

   You don't want to admit that your plan has flaws. That you're behind schedule. That the grand experiment has failed because they are not worthy of our time.

   Can you not see their potential?

   Potential? Bah. Potential is not quantifiable.

   But that is exactly why we must continue. We must determine if they are meritorious. See if we can determine precisely if they have it within themselves to elevate to the next level.

They prefer to think short term and stay as they are.

Not all of them. And a few will evolve and lead the others.

You have proof?

Not yet.

You have a test in mind?

Let me consider it.

Do not consider for too long. The entire situation grows tiresome and unwieldy. Unless we see progress soon, it would be kinder to let them die.

Kinder? Bah. Don't pretend to a compassion you no longer feel.

We must make a decision. Move on.

Not . . . just . . . yet. I shall prove you wrong.

Alara turned on the flitter's autopilot and headed home. With every nerve on fire, she longed to use her psi on her suit. A few adjustments and she'd have the release her body so desperately sought . . . but a quick orgasm would only make the next buildup arrive more quickly and it would be more intense. Science and experience told her that the best way to handle her escalating lust was to find a male, spend several hours with him until she was in the deepest trance of *Boktai,* and allow her cells to completely regenerate.

However, since her lungs had cleared of the Rystani male's scent, since her eyes no longer looked upon his wonderfully built body, her senses had calmed enough for her to regain a bit of control over her need. She had won herself time to find a mate. Although the last man she'd joined for *Boktai* was away at a scientific conference, she had no wish to seek him out again—the morning after their last encounter had been most unpleasant. If her body hadn't driven her into *Boktai,* she would never have considered him as a partner at all.

And no matter how many times her friends told her that worthiness had nothing to do with *Boktai,* Alara couldn't forget the lopsidedness of her parents' marriage. Her mother had adored her father endlessly, but he only reciprocated during *Boktai.* The rest of the time, he'd treated her with indifference, coldness. Her mother had told her all marriages were like hers and it was the price women paid for being women. And Alara had believed her. Until she'd spoken to other women from other worlds, read their literature, immersed herself in other cultures. Until she'd learned that the Endeki way was the exception—not the norm.

For the moment, frustration and sadness over Endekian women's fates filled her and perhaps helped keep *Boktai* at bay. No other intelligent humanoid race in the Federation had to submit to biology like theirs, and Alara's determination to find out why Endekians were different filled her life with purpose.

She landed the flitter on her rooftop and entered her oversized suite. Many professional women shared quarters, but she liked the privacy of her own space and appreciated that she could easily afford it, thanks to her talent for finding and selling rare artifacts.

Her apartment was laden with treasures she'd collected over the years from small shops and bazaars. The shelves displayed her assortment of robots in various shapes and sizes as well as delicately carved reptiles sculpted from the finest *marbellite,* a doll collection made of *bendar,* rows of miniature *avabirds, Tatari* rugs woven of the finest silk in Nacene, toy flitters and rare pink pearl pebbles from Daran Beach. Her most exotic and dearest possession was a perfect bowl of ancient Lassa art, from her home village that had been destroyed in the bombing. She probably had the best Lassa pottery on Endeki and was proud that she'd lent some to a museum to share with the public—the rest she'd sold to fund her laboratory and research.

Surrounded by her lovely collection, with interesting friends in her life and busy with her research, she was happy despite the tragedy in her past. She lived as she wished, often staying up late at night to work. Since she lived alone, her suite taking up one entire floor of the building, she didn't have to worry about disturbing neighbors. With her own private rooftop entrance, she also didn't have to notice their personal activities. She needed no reminders of the way women needed men to survive, especially since she was no different.

Her suite usually soothed her. Never neat, the rooms were cluttered with her latest finds. On one recent buying trip, she'd brought home a multitude of unusual plants she intended to study. One that held particular promise was a lichen that adhered to rock. Right now, she headed to her favorite spot to relax. She'd turned an extra sleeping chamber into a giant bathing facility. Although the suit kept her perfectly clean, Alara liked to soak in water. With scented candles, the lights dimmed, and soft music soothing her flustered nerves, she had all the accoutrements to accompany her fantasy.

After her recent encounter with the Rystani, she anticipated she'd have no difficulty recalling his scent, or the shape of his muscles. With his image branded into her brain, she anticipated a lovely evening.

Alara ran hot water and added a scent of *rolilly,* a wildflower she'd collected last spring during a trip to the forest east of Nacene. She always took the opportunity to search for rare DNA combinations, so between experiments, she arranged to spend time outside the laboratory. Her numerous expeditions kept her gallery supplied with art and had led her to the discovery of many exotic plants and animals. She examined them, studied the DNA combinations, carefully mapping their genome sequences before returning them unharmed to the wild.

Using her psi to turn off the shield that prevented the water from reaching her skin, she sank slowly to her knees, hips, and waist until only her head remained above the surface. She could have submerged totally and adjusted the suit so she could continue to breathe underwater, but then she wouldn't have been able to smell her flowers, listen to her music, or let the candles bathe her in their flickering golden light.

Her thoughts wandered back to the most interesting part of her day. Xander. Ah, how ironic that the big Rystani warrior, an enemy, had been the first man to present her with an opportunity to go off world where she could examine alien DNA. She'd often wondered if the cure that she sought to alleviate the *Boktai* and the bonding might not be on Endeki at all, but elsewhere. If only Endeki law permitted her to leave, she might find the exact DNA sequence she required on another Federation world.

With her wealth, Alara could have broken the law, bought a small spaceship, bribed a port official to look the other way to allow her to depart. But she could never have returned. Despite her falling-out with her government, this was home. She had friends, her work, a successful business, and absolutely no wish to leave her world forever.

But that wouldn't stop her from fantasizing over possibilities. She reached for the special oil and dabbed a bit into her palm. She'd seen holovids of Rystani warriors, but Xander was the first one she'd ever met in person. And no holovid could convey his charm, or his sheer size or the blatant masculinity that had seeped from every pore like a potent drug. She recalled his features as easily as if he were still before her. Xander's startling purple eyes had seemed to stare straight into her soul. His massive muscles had shouted he was all male and his fabulous cheekbones and chiseled jaw had defined his face with broad appeal. Now that she was alone, she could allow herself to dwell on how attractive he was. With his hefty muscles, a body like his would make a wonderful *Boktai* partner.

Endekian men tended to be short and rounded. In contrast, the Rystani's long limbs allowed him to move with a graceful elegance that suggested he'd spent years training as a warrior. She hadn't missed that despite his size, he'd exhibited a balance and agility that reminded her of a *cheetark,* a wild feline, on the prowl.

If he'd been a sculpture, she would have purchased him. The idea made her grin in delight. Especially when her image of him contrasted with how he'd react in real life. His temper would undoubtedly flare at even the concept of his posing for her pleasure.

But the idea of him standing naked before her pleased her so very much. He was a beautiful man. No wonder her senses had gone into overdrive. Alara smoothed the oil over her neck, let the water soak into her tense muscles, and slowly, she relaxed. Another kind of tension began to rekindle. At the memories of the big warrior, her breasts swelled, so did her *labella,* the slick folds between her legs thrumming.

And her *yonia* yearned for sweet fulfillment. Ever so slowly, she spread the oil down her collarbone. In anticipation of touching her breasts, she arched her spine until she raised her chest from the water. Cool air wafted across her nipples and they tightened, the tips darkening.

She didn't understand why none of her partners ever grasped that she liked a slow, gentle touch. Perhaps it was her fault. She always waited until *Boktai* drove her into a frenzy of lust before seeking a partner—and by then she hadn't the discipline to suggest slow and easy.

Like all Endekian women, Alara knew what pleased her. But unlike most women she never seemed to find a man who shared her tastes. Her friends often told her she didn't look hard enough, that she should spend more time hunting for a man instead of searching for art treasures or missing DNA links.

Alara didn't have the answer. She only knew that it seemed much more pleasant to fantasize about the huge Rystani warrior than to go out and settle for an Endekian. In her fantasy, the Rystani warrior was perfect. He knew exactly how to touch and tease and caress. And as her fingers softly cupped her breasts, her thumbs slowly circling her nipples, she imagined doing so with Xander watching her, encouraging her, patiently waiting while they both anticipated what would come next.

He would look at her hungrily and his interest would feed her own. It would be difficult for both of them to wait. She imagined Xander joining her in the tub, his big body sliding next to her, his entry causing the waves to lap against her burning flesh. He'd place his hands on her waist, easily lift her and set her down so she straddled his hips.

And then he would take time to lock gazes. He'd smile an arrogant but tender smile that would cause the air to whoosh from her lungs. Oh, yes. The Rystani warrior would read her mind and know exactly what she liked.

His mouth would find her lips, her breasts. He would do wonderful things with his tongue. Gentle things. Rough things. Wickedly delicious things.

Alara's hand dipped lazily between her thighs. Lost in her fantasy, she drew tighter, the tension causing her back to bow, her breath to come in great gasps. When the fire flashed through her, she moaned softly, knowing that she still wanted more.

3

Xander had intended to leave Kirek behind, send him back in the shuttle where he'd be safe aboard the *Verazen* in orbit above Endeki. Especially after Xander had listened in on Kirek's hyperlink conversation with his parents.

"Mom. Dad." Kirek had greeted his folks with a youthful grin and a serious gleam in his eyes. "Don't worry if I'm unable to contact you for a while."

Back on Mystique, Miri and Etru exchanged long significant glances, their concern traveling through the vidscreen as clearly as if they'd been aboard the shuttle. Having a son who apparently had been born for great things was hard on Kirek's parents, but they didn't protest.

Miri's eyes filled with tears and Etru roughly cleared his throat. "We love you."

"And I love you." With his hands not visible to his

parents, Kirek clenched his fists, evidently well aware how difficult it was for them to let him go into danger. "I'll be fine. Please, don't worry."

"We won't." Miri's voice choked. "We have faith in you, son."

Xander saw the resignation in Kirek's parents' faces and they had his sympathy. While he didn't yet understand the importance of Kirek's accompanying him, he sensed the young man had a crucial part to play. If Kirek knew better than they exactly what his role would be, he was keeping the details to himself.

And after he'd ended the conversation with his parents, he squared his shoulders and unclenched his hands. "You'll need my help to deal with Drik."

Xander didn't know whether the boy could see the future or not, but he had a reputation. His predictions had never been wrong. Still, it wasn't easy being in charge and responsible for a prodigy, a legend in his own time. As much as Xander didn't wish to put Kirek at risk, he had a mission to accomplish.

"Fine." Xander spoke in an even tone. "But you take orders from me."

"Of course." Kirek shrugged his shoulders, but with difficulty, as if a huge weight pressed him down.

"And if one of my experienced crew orders you—"

"No one else should go with us." Kirek bit his bottom lip, his eyes worried, but his voice was certain and confident.

Xander had planned to have the second shuttle bring down several of his crew. If Tessa's scheme failed, he had no wish to take on six highly trained and armed Endekians, the elite of Drik's personal guard, with only a half-grown man at his side. And yet, he sensed Kirek would not have spoken without good reason.

Not once during the journey from Mystique to Endeki had he so much as made a suggestion. So Xander was willing to hear him out.

"Why must you and I go alone?"

Kirek winced.

Xander waited, his arms crossed over his chest. Kirek held his gaze and after an extended silence, spoke gently, almost as if Xander were the youth and he the experienced captain. "Have you ever experienced something you couldn't explain?"

Xander didn't have to think twice. One moment in his life stood out like a beacon of shame—one he wished he could have forgotten. Even when he managed to put aside the cursed memory during his waking hours, dishonor haunted his nightmares. Too often he awakened in a sweat, his heart hammering as he tried to figure out exactly what had happened. During his youth, the invading Endekians had captured and tortured him in order to make him reveal the location of Rian, his village. The pain had been extraordinary. And his mind had run away to escape the agonies his body had endured. He'd simply gone ... elsewhere. Xander had never spoken to anyone about how he'd resisted the incredible pain with an act of cowardice. Friends and family considered him brave. But in truth, his mind had snapped, separated from his body. He'd been lucky not to have gone insane.

Xander eyed Kirek warily. "Yes. I have experienced the inexplicable."

Kirek nodded. "Then you understand how difficult it is to put certain knowledge into words."

Xander was accustomed to making command decisions on the basis of facts, or the lack of them. But Kirek was asking for trust, faith—and not giving him one blessed reason to support his request. If anyone but Kirek had suggested that only two Rystani meet with Drik, Xander would have dismissed him as stupid or arrogant, but Kirek possessed the strongest psi known on Mystique. His IQ was immeasurable.

"All right." Xander handed Kirek a sidearm. "We go together. Just the two of us."

"Thanks."

Kirek attached the stunner to his suit and helped himself to a knife from the armory, as well. He might have been a prodigy, but Kahn and Etru had taught him how to fight. He should be fine. But as they flew the shuttle toward Drik, Xander had the niggling suspicion that he'd forgotten a crucial detail, that he'd overlooked some factor that might affect the outcome of their meeting with the wily Endeki leader. Although he racked his brain, nothing consequential occurred to him during the short flight.

They landed on a shuttle pad next to a public park without incident. Before Xander opened the hatch, he adjusted his portable computer unit that allowed constant communication with Ranth and those back home who would likely be monitoring the mission.

"Ranth, what kind of data are you picking up about our flight?"

The computer had already tapped into the Endekian communication system and was undoubtedly monitoring thousands of conversations. At the moment, Xander's interest focused on military chatter about any Rystani as well as the locations of civilian patrols.

"No one seems particularly interested in your whereabouts," Ranth assured him.

"If that changes—"

"I'll inform you pronto."

"Pronto?" Xander recognized the slang as Terran, one of Tessa's phrases. While the suit automatically translated the many Federation languages, idioms often didn't come through with the exact shade of meaning the speaker intended.

"I'm attempting to incorporate slang into my systems. It's supposed to make our working relationship more comfortable."

At Ranth's explanation, Kirek grinned, rolled his eyes, and stepped through the hatch. Whether Ranth understood enough humor to lighten their mood and had deliberately done so, Xander didn't know. But after he sealed the hatch, his steps through the park were lighter, his breath easier.

Tessa's plan could go wrong. But his awareness sharpened. He loved his job. Meeting the unexpected made him feel alive. He'd always enjoyed a good hunt, a rousing adventure, and journeys to new places. And ever since he'd met Alara, he'd felt inordinately invigorated.

Xander would settle for no less than a full-out effort to achieve his goal. He knew how to push himself, knew how to lead his crew. Proud that Tessa and Kahn had entrusted him with such an important mission, he was determined to succeed and neither the Endekian doctor's past nor his would stop him.

Night on Endeki was a long one, eighteen Federation hours. In the darkness, the park was almost empty. A late-night jogger ran beside his soaring *keyton,* an amphibious bird with a white beak. Embedded shop advertisements glowed in the sidewalk, the volume that pitched products muted. Xander and Kirek ignored the ads and made their way toward Drik's three-story residence that sprawled over a city block. They strolled openly past scraggly trees and prickly grasses, as if unbothered by the lack of more solid cover should they have a sudden need to hide from a suspicious patrol.

Despite the heat, Xander's suit cooled him, and while he would have liked to use filters to keep out the unpleasant scents, he didn't. Scent could warn him of a surprise attack. While their suits could withhold scent, Endekian men in battle emitted an odor that they believed weakened their enemies' soul. Xander doubted the truth of that religious belief, instead knowing that if he could pick up the odor from a distance, he'd have advance warning of attack. His steady pace gave no indication that the Endeki scent often came back to him in his worst nightmares.

Although Endeki prisons were harsh and the sentences severe, computers did most of the policing. At Drik's residence's outer gate, Xander's fake passes were accepted by guards without cursory questions. Apparently, their leader often entertained offworlders and no one seemed unduly alarmed to see two Rystani men, no matter how much they towered over the Endekians. Once inside the barren complex, Xander and Kirek strode down several long, narrow halls into an area of tighter security monitored by robots and a complex alarm system.

The robot asked Xander to remove his weapons and frisked him, but ignored Kirek, who didn't register on the machines. Calmly, Kirek scooped up Xander's weapons, and after the robot passed them through the sensors, he handed them back to Xander.

"I wish you could teach me how to make the machines ignore me and everything I carry," Xander muttered, admitting the kid was useful after all. He was now glad Kirek had come along. Otherwise he might not have made it through the second level of security without alerting every guard in the residence. Briefly, he wondered if Kirek had anticipated the problem, then refocused his attention on his surroundings.

Drik's home was large, ugly, and uninviting. Most leaders tended to have elaborate carpets, sculptures, and holovids. But the walls and floors here were made of plain stone, barren of all ornamentation and art, the lighting stark and gray.

When they reached Drik's last level of security, it was almost anticlimactic. Tessa's plan had worked. Their food half eaten and a bottle of drink overturned, all six Endekian guards slept, one slumped against a wall, several remaining in their chairs with their heads on the table. One was laid out flat on the floor, snoring loudly. The reek of spilled drink and half-eaten foul food permeated the room and made his stomach clench.

Kirek strode past the sleeping men and opened the door to the inner sanctum. Xander tensed, but when no alarm sounded, they slipped through. The change in decor was like walking from a prison into the gaudiest palace. Silver and gold holovids lined the walls, their intricate designs revealing changing scenes from Endeki life, battles, feats of engineering, colonies on their moons. However, the images were jarring. There was no pattern, no balance to the sequence of visuals, almost as if a computer randomly displayed them and gave no consideration to what came before or after.

Beneath their feet was a plush carpet that changed from silver to crimson to magenta as they strode over it. From frescoed ceilings hung crystal chandeliers that lit up the foyer with the brightness of day. And a fountain with two gracefully kneeling nude women laser-carved from smokey jadeite dominated the space, the water bubbling under a cloud of swirling smoke that appeared to be part of the sculpture.

It's too easy.

Xander looked right, left, over his shoulder and above their heads. Surely, the Endekian leader wasn't so lax that no security men stood guard inside this private area, that no computer system could detect their presence? However, the Endekian political system was filled with bribery and corruption. Where computers could go, so could hackers. But obviously the Endekian leader believed he was safe in the heart of his residence and that no one would dare to penetrate his personal quarters. His overconfidence might be the only reason they reached him without a fight.

Through their portable units, Ranth displayed a tiny holovid map of the residence's layout, so they knew exactly which path to take. And when they finally reached Drik's sleeping quarters, sounds of feminine laughter filtered under an ornately carved metal door.

Without hesitation, Xander shoved open the door and the two Rystani men moved inside, their weapons ready, their feet poised to send them into diving rolls if they encountered armed resistance. A naked Endekian male, Drik, sprang to his feet and reached for his weapon on a stand beside the bed. Before he could arm himself, Xander kicked over the table and the weapon skidded across the floor.

"Don't move and no one will be hurt." Xander aimed his stunner at Drik. Supposedly large for an Endekian, the leader of this world didn't reach the height of Xander's shoulders. While his yellow skin and rounded musculature magnified his potbelly, his eyes revealed a wily intelligence. Xander braced for trouble and didn't let down his guard.

At Xander's command and at the sight of the stunner aimed his way, Drik froze. At the same moment a lithe female walked into the room from behind them and her gaze settled on Kirek. "Finally, you've found a warrior pleasing to the eyes and much to my liking."

Drik used his psi to engage his suit, dressing in an ornate ensemble of pants in dusty blue and a matching jacket with gold braids that crossed his chest and dangled at the hem. He spoke with annoyance. "Lataka. How many times have I told you not to come to my private quarters?"

"Father. I wanted to meet your visitors." Lataka ignored her father, and her rounded hips and full breasts swayed as she walked straight to Kirek. Grinning, she stared at him as if he were a treat as sweet as *jarballa* sauce. Ignoring Kirek's weapon and the jaw-dropping surprise on his face, she flung her arms around his neck. To prevent them from toppling, Kirek steadied her with one arm, his eyes wide with astonishment.

"Yes. He's perfect for me. I want him, Father."

She shamelessly rubbed against Kirek in the most provocative manner. The woman wasn't attacking him as Xander had first assumed, and apparently Kirek had quickly figured this out as well, holding his fire. How odd. He'd been holding a stunner aimed at her father, but she ignored the weapon and appeared bent on seduction. She must be drugged or brainwashed. Something surely wasn't right with her. Unless she was using her body as a trick to distract them.

"Steady," Xander ordered.

Xander hadn't let the woman divert his attention. He kept his gun aimed on Drik.

Ignoring the weapon pointed at him, Drik spoke

with a voice that dripped with arrogance. "Why are you here?"

"Kiss me," demanded the golden-haired, golden-eyed Endekian woman. While the other females in Drik's sleeping chamber had clothed themselves, the woman in Kirek's arms kept rubbing against him, and every time he removed her grasping hands from one part of his body, she grabbed him elsewhere.

The scene might have been amusing, but the danger was real. If a guard found them now, they could be shot on the spot, and Xander had no illusion that the Endekian weapons would not be stunners, but lethal.

Leaving Kirek to deal with the seductive female, Xander lowered his weapon but kept it ready. "Drik, I'm sorry for barging in, but I couldn't wait to go through diplomatic channels. Our business is urgent."

"And your business is?" Skepticism turned Drik's face a nasty shade of green.

"I would like your authorization to take a woman—"

"Take anyone you'd like." Drik gestured to the females huddled on his bed.

Xander couldn't believe the leader was offering him a woman so casually but kept his astonishment in check. What man would hide behind a woman to save himself? Or did the Endekian simply not mind sharing? Xander didn't understand him, but clearly Drik didn't comprehend his request, either.

"I want to take an Endekian female on a mission in my starship."

The women all gasped. One collapsed in a faint.

Drik frowned and ignored them. "Our females are not allowed to leave Endeki."

"Perhaps an exception could be made." His comment elicited more gasps and wide-eyed stares.

"We don't make exceptions, especially with Rystani." Drik spat out the last word like a vulgarity and his expression suggested the mere idea was as distasteful as swallowing poison. A woman hid behind him, cowering as if in fear Xander would take her.

Ranth spoke in privacy mode, so only Xander could hear the communication through the portable unit. "According to my research, Drik's government doesn't approve of Dr. Calladar's research. If he knew *which* woman you needed for our mission, he might be more amenable to coming to an agreement."

Xander used Ranth's information. If that didn't work, he was prepared to try bribery. "Endeki doesn't need the services of Dr. Alara Calladar as much as we do."

Drik's facial muscles didn't change, yet his eyes gleamed with interest. "Why do you need Dr. Calladar's services?"

The frightened woman behind him looked at another, a strange expression in her eyes. Almost as if she knew Alara. More likely it was simply relief that she was safe. Either way, Xander focused his attention on Drik, who seemed to be considering the idea of Alara leaving Endeki.

"We are on a mission to find the Perceptive Ones in the hopes they can provide pure DNA to save the Terrans."

Drik shuddered as if he found the subject distasteful. "Terrans, Dregan hell. A red-blooded Terran female almost ruined our empire, disrupting our trading routes by doing business with the Osarians." Mentioning Earth had been an error, one Xander couldn't rectify, but he refused to give up, even as Drik continued his rant. "We care nothing about the welfare of Terrans. Or Rystani. So I won't permit Dr. Calladar to leave Endeki. No matter how useless and stupid her work. She belongs here."

The Endekian leader might be unaware he'd just insulted one of his own people. But Xander felt insulted for her. Compared to this slimeworm, Alara was a model Federation citizen.

"Since we seem to value her more than you do, perhaps you'd let us pay you for her services?"

Drik shook his head. "She's a heroine of the war. A symbol of Endekian strength and resilience. My people wouldn't understand if I permitted her to leave with you."

Despite Drik's insistence, Xander sensed that the Endekian would have liked nothing better than to send Alara with them, but that he couldn't, not without jeopardizing his political reputation. However, if Xander could find a way for Drik to save face, then perhaps they could both have what they wanted. Drik would rid himself of a woman he obviously had no respect for and disliked. Xander would gain a valuable crew member.

"Dad, I've never had a Rystani warrior to satisfy my needs. I want him."

Xander tried not to let Lataka's bold words or the distracting sight of Kirek holding the woman prevent him from focusing on the negotiations. The lad had clamped one of her arms behind her back and held her pressed against him to prevent her from groping him. He had her under firm control, enabling Xander to concentrate his attention on Drik.

Xander tried another tactic. "Your people might applaud your decision if you explained it to them in a way they understood."

"What do you have in mind?" Drik's tone sounded almost reasonable again. Could his rant against Terrans and Rystani have all been for show? Or to drive a harder bargain?

Xander kept his tone even. "If you told your people that Endeki was now at peace and that this gesture would serve to increase trade between our worlds, perhaps they might view Dr. Calladar's departure in a positive manner."

Drik shook his head. "Endekians would never believe I would allow one of our women to leave—not even one such as she. If she were to go, you must appear to use force."

"That can be arranged." Xander didn't like it but would do whatever was necessary.

"To guarantee her safety and to make it appear as if we weren't duped, we need to *capture* a hostage in exchange." Drik's smarmy gaze snagged on Kirek.

"Oh, Father." Lataka squealed. "You are brilliant."

At the Endekian's outrageous suggestion to leave Kirek behind, Xander checked his temper. Since he'd never abandon Kirek, he shouldn't be so furious. Nevertheless, if Xander had replied right away, he would have had difficulty restraining his tongue.

Drik's almost amused gaze rested on Kirek, who still held the struggling woman. "Lataka, if I let you keep him for a while would you agree to give up Barklon? You've been seeing way too much of him."

"Yeeees," she purred.

"No." Xander had to force himself not to raise the stunner and was pleased his voice remained calm, although he shook with indignation. Drik and Lataka had spoken of the boy as if they expected him to be this woman's plaything. "Kirek is essential to my crew. I will not leave him behind."

"Then Dr. Calladar will remain on Endeki," Drik

sneered. "My daughter will simply find another man to please her." As if the matter were settled, he turned back to his women and used the null grav in his suit to float among them. "You may leave now."

Lataka stamped her foot. "I don't want them to go."

Xander was not about to give up, even if he didn't understand Endekian customs. On Rystan and Mystique women and men took their relationships much more seriously than the casual ease he'd seen so far on Endeki. Still, despite their differences, he had to find a compromise. While he couldn't forsake Kirek on a hostile world, especially not with that woman, he still had options. "I would pay dearly for Dr. Calladar's services."

Drik didn't even look at him. "I'm not interested in your credits. I wouldn't mind Dr. Calladar's departure. During her absence I could dismantle her laboratory. Without her presence to defend her work, other Endekian women won't protest so much. However, I can always find another way to stop Dr. Calladar."

"I won't leave Kirek," Xander repeated.

"It's my destiny to stay." Kirek spoke with the quiet conviction of a warrior far beyond his years.

Lataka squealed in delight. "Oh, so you like me, too. We will have so much fun."

Drik grinned with fondness at his daughter. "Kirek pleases my daughter and I enjoy spoiling her. Either leave him as a hostage or we don't have a deal." Drik didn't appear to care one way or the other about Xander's answer or the stunner he held. He began to kiss one of his women.

"Why does your captain believe your spending time with me would be so terrible?" Lataka tipped back her head, her spine arching as she wriggled against Kirek. "I could teach you much about pleasing a woman."

"This is unacceptable." Xander turned to leave. "We will find another way. Let's go."

Kirek didn't move. "It's . . . all right. I'm willing . . . to be their hostage."

"Your staying *with her* is not under consideration." While Xander spoke in severe command mode, he wondered if Kirek was responding like any eighteen-year-old would with a willing woman in his arms, or if there could be more to his seeming acquiescence to place himself in jeopardy.

Kirek shrugged casually, but his stare was direct, piercing. "It's my fate to stay."

His words were simple but conveyed a world of meaning. And Xander finally realized Kirek had known all along that he wouldn't be going back to the *Verazen*. His journey ended here. Likely he hadn't told Xander earlier because if he had, Xander wouldn't have agreed to bring him.

Somehow, Kirek had known Drik intended to take him hostage. That's why he'd used the hyperlink to talk to his parents. And that's why he hadn't wanted anyone else to come with them. If not for Kirek's intuition, had more of the crew accompanied them they might have been taken as hostages, too.

Realizing he would have to consider leaving Kirek on Endeki made Xander feel as though he were being squeezed by the gravity of a black star, his heart racing out of sync. Many people on Mystique considered Kirek their most precious citizen. To leave him behind in the clutches of the shameless Lataka turned his stomach, but with Kirek's gaze calm and his poise self-assured, Xander didn't waste time wondering whether he'd ever had a real choice.

"You're certain?" Xander asked. "We have no idea how long we'll be gone."

"I understand. You have no choice." Kirek's tone was thoughtful, his eyes conveying those of an old soul more than a young lad's. His demeanor revealed a deep assurance that his fate was indeed to stay on Endeki, and the boy's attitude finally convinced Xander he should agree.

Xander exchanged a nod, conveying his admiration of Kirek's courage and willingness to be left behind, then he turned to Drik. "I accept your conditions. We have an agreement." He narrowed his eyes and hardened his tone, lacing it with a threat. "But if he comes to any harm—"

"Harm?" Lataka laughed, pleasure lighting up her face and a lingering smile showing off perfect white teeth. Kirek released her arm and she skimmed one seductive finger down his chest in a proprietary manner. "Why would we wish to harm such a marvelous man?"

We?

Two women separated themselves from Drik and joined Lataka. Their hands stroked, caressed, and they cooed with pleasure. And it suddenly struck Xander that Kirek wouldn't be only Lataka's plaything.

What in Dregan hell had he just committed Kirek to? And what kind of man would he become after his stint on Endeki?

Xander left the residence with his mood as bleak as a Rystani winter, his heart heavy as *bendar*. As captain, it was his duty to protect every member of his crew. Between Kirek's youth and status among their people, he was special, pure of heart and soul. Besides, Xander liked the young man. Leaving him behind seemed like a betrayal and a failure, but the mission must come first. Still, Endeki morals were not Rystani morals. The experience on Endeki would transform the young man, and Xander worried what he might become and how he might change. However, Xander couldn't stay and protect Kirek. Nor could he take back his words.

Xander didn't fail often but when he did, he had difficulty accepting it. Drik had held the upper hand, however, and short of kidnapping Alara for real and creating an interplanetary incident that might start another war his people could ill afford, he'd had no choice. But it had been the finality and acceptance in Kirek's tone that had convinced him. Knowing that didn't make him feel better. There should have been something else he could have done other than leave Kirek behind, but with so many people dying on Earth, Xander had to put the welfare of millions before any one person's safety.

For the moment, he must turn his thoughts to Dr. Alara Calladar. Thanks to Kirek's sacrifice and Ranth's spying, he had her home address. As the Endekian sun's first rays filtered over the black horizon, Xander left Drik's residence behind and stepped aboard his shuttle.

"Set a course for Alara's home."

"Compliance," the computer replied. "She's likely asleep. Do you want me to send a message to warn her of your arrival?"

Ranth's suggestion would be the polite thing to do. But since Xander was fairly certain his visit would be unwelcome and that she might even try to flee to avoid him, he shook his head. "Open communication with Mystique."

"Compliance."

Kahn's visage appeared almost immediately on the holovid. Xander filled him in on his decision to leave Kirek on Endeki and was relieved when Kahn offered to inform Miri and Etru that their son would be staying behind.

Kahn rubbed his brow wearily. "I'm afraid I have more bad news."

"What?" Xander's gaze sharpened. "Is Tessa—"

"She's the same. Maybe a little more tired. She tries to hide her naps from me. I pretend not to notice." Kahn loved his wife dearly, and he conveyed his worry over her health with his every breath.

Xander's concern turned to his own family. "My father—"

"Is well, as are your brothers. However, the Terrans have discovered that it's not only their DNA breaking down, but that of their plants and animals, as well."

"The plants and animals have been exposed to the pollution, but I wouldn't think they'd be susceptible in the same way." Xander frowned. He was not a scientist. "What do the experts say?"

"They're stumped. They've never seen anything like this. Panic is widespread. Earth now has a blockade in place. No one can land or leave orbit."

"But?" Xander sensed there was more.

"There are already reported outbreaks of the same problem on several Terran colonies."

"Did the Terrans get sick on Earth and bring the sickness with them to the new worlds?"

"That's what we believe, but Federation citizens are growing hysterical. Some are isolating themselves in fear. As the panic spreads, fear that the illness is caused by a virus and not pollution as we initially believed

will hurt the economy on thousands of worlds. Unless
we find a cure, the Federation could fall apart."

"The situation's that dire?"

Kahn nodded reluctantly. "If our best scientists can
prove the outbreaks on the Terran colonies originated
on Earth due to their pollution and not a virus, the fear
will die down. After thousands of years of trade, Federation citizens won't give up their luxuries without
good reason. But right now, panic abounds and the prevailing anxiety may make your journey more difficult.
Planets on your route may now be closed to outsiders.
You might want to assign the Terrans to ship duties
only."

"I understand."

Xander flipped off the shuttle's hyperlink with a
sigh of mounting frustration. Between losing Kirek
and the unrest throughout the Federation, before they'd
even departed Federation space, his mission was already at greater risk.

Now more than ever, he needed Alara's help. Still,
kidnapping a woman from her home and her world in
the hopes of coercing her to help them . . . stung his
honor. He'd prefer straightforward ship-to-ship battle
or hand-to-hand combat to sneaking into a woman's
home in the middle of the night with the intention of
abduction.

Did his purpose of saving billions of lives justify his
use of force against the innocent Dr. Calladar? He
shelved the ethical considerations for others to determine. He was the captain of the starship *Verazen* and
his mission was of the highest priority.

If his action left a sour taste in his mouth, he would
deal with his scruples later. But as he exited his shuttle
on the roof of Alara's apartment, he hoped this would

be the last argument he had with his conscience for the duration of the mission.

Although he didn't expect the scientist to give him much trouble since she was a tiny thing, he recalled that she'd been full of attitude. Quite likely she would shout. Perhaps cry. Or beg. But he would be immune.

After Kirek's sacrifice, she was coming with him— willing or not.

4

Satiated from the middle phase of *Boktai,* at least for a little while, Alara climbed out of her tub, blew out the candles and turned off the music, hoping she could sleep for a few hours before returning to the laboratory. She looked forward to checking on her latest batch of samples, a rare strain of DNA that appeared to have many chromosome patterns in common with Endekian women's reproductive systems.

Employing her psi to activate her null grav, she floated in a cocoon of air in her sleeping chamber. But when she closed her eyes, the same image that had fueled her fantasy kept her awake. A Rystani warrior in prime condition. Vivid violet irises in a determined face. She wondered how he'd heard of her ability to read DNA and decided it didn't matter. Surely she'd seen the last of Xander. For once, Endeki law was on her side and protected her from the likes of him.

While she'd have loved the freedom to explore new worlds in search of the DNA link that would free Endekian women, this was her world. Her home. She had a purpose that meant a great deal to her and she enjoyed her life here. For him to assume that his work was more important than hers and that she'd give up her research just because he asked was so malelike and arrogant that she should have easily dismissed him from her mind.

But she couldn't sleep. Despite her self-gratification, *Boktai* locked her in its grasp. Perhaps her encounter with the Rystani male had intensified her usual response. Or perhaps she simply had put off mating once too often.

At the creak of a loose shutter, Alara gave up all pretense of sleep. She might as well catch up on the latest research received via her hololink. She might not be able to visit other worlds in person, but that didn't stop the flow of data from coming into her computer. She could read DNA results laboriously compiled by other scientists on other worlds right from the comfort of Endeki.

As the shutter creaked again, she made a mental note to remind the building's caretaker to nail the boards flat to prevent the wind from ripping it from her building. Floating down from where she'd tried to sleep in the comfort of null grav, she regained her footing and glanced up at her doorway to see a black mass against a gray shadow.

The creaks she'd heard hadn't been a loose shutter. An intruder had sneaked into her quarters.

With a gasp, she flung up a psi shield, lunged for a weapon she kept hidden on a corner shelf. Despite the adrenaline pumping through her, she didn't move fast enough.

She bumped into something hard. Someone hard. Someone male. Experience told her to tighten her shield to prevent his male scent from reaching her lungs, or her rioting hormones would soon have her seducing the unknown intruder—even if he'd broken into her home to steal, even if he meant her harm.

At the alarming thought, she struggled, jerking wildly, her muscles burning with the effort.

But powerful arms and a strong psi closed around her like bands of *bendar*, encasing her, entrapping her, blocking her escape. Without hesitation, she slammed her head backward, hoping to deliver a knockout blow to his chin, but she wasn't tall enough. Instead of crunching bone, her head struck a muscular chest.

She knew only one man that tall. Xander. And as she was forced to take a breath to ease her burning lungs, his primal scent reminded her that he was mature male flesh and ripe for her choosing.

But while her hormones demanded she seduce him, her mind protested fiercely. Xander had broken into her home.

Every bone in her skeleton should have frozen to solid ice—except *Boktai* caused inaccurate and unacceptable reactions. Earlier he'd made his intentions and determination quite clear, but in the lab he'd seemed civilized compared to the primitive resolve he was flinging at her now. And damn *Boktai* and her needs, she wanted him with a ferocity that left her breathless.

"Let me go," she demanded, holding on to her will, wishing she didn't sound so sensual, wishing he couldn't feel her trembling with desire, wishing she had the raw strength to break his grasp as well as the grip her body held over her.

Ignoring her demand, he clamped her wrists behind

her back with one of his hands and placed *denar* cuffs around them, then lifted her and slung her over his shoulder.

"You must come with me, Dr. Calladar. Lives depend on your cooperation."

He'd trussed her up and had turned her upside down so quickly, she'd had no time to fight, no time to protest further. But she had plenty of time to realize that the fight between her mind and her body no longer mattered.

She was now his captive. He would do with her what he wished.

Anger made intense by a pure unadulterated thrill besieged her. With the blood rushing to her head as he toted her upside down like a feed sack, his shoulder jabbing her belly, her instinct and adrenaline took over. She kicked him hard. Her toes caught his thigh, doing little damage. He started carrying her toward the roof, not even bothering with null grav to manage her weight.

"You idiot," she panted, her breath hitching in her chest as he jarred her with every step down her hallway. "For the holy mother of atoms. Stop! If you abduct me, you'll start a war."

Her words had as little effect as her kick. Angry, frustrated, and more aroused than she'd ever been in her entire life, she bent her head and bit his back. And received a smack on her bottom for her efforts.

"Restrain yourself. There will be no war."

She stopped biting and squirmed at the marvelous sensations coursing through her. His smack had vibrated right through her bottom to her *labella* and her pleasure center. Even as she protested, she recognized that her complaint was an outright untruth. "That hurt."

Her head ached, her bottom stung, and he hadn't

slowed his steps one iota. But worse, the vibration from his smack combined with his scent and those powerful hands on her body had her pulse escalating. She'd heard that domineering men could intensify *Boktai,* but since she'd always sought to minimize the experience, she hadn't experimented.

She should be outraged. And yet never had she been so aroused. She had to grit her teeth to stop from biting him again and receiving another pleasurable smack.

Damn him to Dregan hell. She didn't want to know she could respond like this. No way was she leaving Endeki with him, when it would take him no time at all to discover exactly how much she was enjoying his rough treatment. Because once he did, he'd have the power to force her to do whatever he wished, and experience told her his knowledge would be to her detriment.

The moment he exited onto the roof, she screamed. "Help! Help!"

"Quiet," he demanded. "I do not wish to hurt you, but I cannot let you draw attention to our departure."

He thought he was hurting her? If her *yonia* could speak, it would be begging for more delicious slaps. She couldn't stop thinking about how good the big warrior would feel against her, over her, inside her. Her will broke and despite her determination to remain still, she kicked. She rolled from side to side. She screamed and tried to bite him again.

And all the while he carried her across the roof she anticipated another spank to her bottom, a swat that would incite her nerve endings to riot. A swat that would shoot an electric charge straight to her core. A swat that would incite, besiege, and provoke.

She held her breath. Waiting. Hoping. He didn't disappoint.

He smacked one big hand down hard on her bottom. And the erotic sensations, the vibrations, caused her body to tighten with wondrous tension and her *yonia* creamed with sweet moisture. She stung in all the right places with delicious heat.

And his big hand stayed where he'd slapped, as if to remind her he was in control. Why in *krek* hadn't she yet found a cure for *Boktai*? Her spinning thoughts had her grinding her teeth in frustration. With herself. With him. Was he so dense that he lacked all awareness of her arousal?

Under normal circumstances, she could use her psi to obtain release on her own. But the latter phases of *Boktai* prevented her psi from working properly. In fact, she'd already lost control of not only her arousal, but her suit.

She was naked in his arms, her suit transparent. Even worse, she no longer had shielding between her bare flesh and his hand. His hand that should be slipping between her thighs. His hand that should be skimming along her flesh. His hand that should be exploring her bare bottom.

Damn her Endekian biology. Even as he approached his spacecraft, she fought him with every muscle she could muster, but she yearned for him to find a way to keep her, to please her, to release his essence within her body. Strung tight, using her last reserves of logic, she gasped out words that sounded raw and breathless. "If you take me, they'll shoot you out of the sky."

"You have too much faith in your government. For the price of one boy, Drik sold you out."

Although she was outraged at his admission, her body ignored the meaning of his words and responded instead to his deep male tone. A zing of pleasure zipped to her core, even as her mind raged in helplessness. "That son of a sand buzzard. You and he will both rot in Dregan hell."

Oblivious to her curses and her nudity, he opened the hatch to his shuttle, slung her into a nook and webbed her in. As he adjusted the webbing over her bared flesh, she watched his eyes spark at the sight of her, the corners of his mouth soften into a delighted grin. Oh, he looked. And looked. And looked.

Her nipples tightened. Her throat drew tight. Her tummy fluttered and her *yonia* ached.

She didn't know whether to be furious at herself for losing control over her psi or angry with him for being so . . . male. He said nothing, but sweat beaded on his brow faster than his suit could remove it. Oh, he might try to remain unaffected, but a muscle at his jaw leaped and his pulse danced.

She'd always hated her descent into *Boktai,* into total vulnerability. But with the Rystani—the sensual slope was worse and occurring much too fast. Too soon she would lose all semblance of intelligence. She would become female lust personified. Already she tried to squirm, but with her hands trussed behind her back and the webbing tying her down, she couldn't budge.

But reality started to slip through her muddled mind. If she left Endeki, years of research would be ruined. She'd been working on a new mutation that showed such promise, and if she left her lab untended for even a few days, Maki would be unable to prevent her delicate experiments from being ruined.

She had to concentrate on more than rage and lust. "What are you saying? What do you mean Drik sold me out?"

"He's letting me borrow you."

"Borrow me?" she sputtered in fury, unable to hold back, even as her fierce need spiked into boiling passion. "That vile residue-sucking slug. I'm not for rent or lease."

But she was.

She was helpless, without her psi.

Naked.

Aroused.

"Apparently Drik doesn't think too much of you. He seemed eager to be rid of you." His tone sounded as if he thought Drik insane.

She let out another string of curses, mostly in frustration that she could do nothing to curb her need for the big Rystani's touch. She couldn't look at his fingers without thinking of him touching her breasts or dipping lower. But she was damned if she'd beg.

Oh, krek. *Please don't make me beg.*

Even as she prayed, she would happily have dropped Drik in a vat of acid for putting her in such a position. "Closing down my lab would have been too humane for that foul-breathed mudcrawler."

"Dr. Calladar, please calm yourself. I mean you no harm. And while you are at it, please cover your nudity."

Finally, he'd actually said something about her state of undress—but it wasn't the compliment her hormone-induced state made her long to hear. Clearly, he'd just asked her to clothe herself because he didn't like what he saw. Maybe she wasn't up to his high Rystani standards. Maybe he was celibate except during a rising moon. Maybe his race didn't have sex but once a year.

But whatever his problem, she had no control left for even the basic task of using her psi to cover her nudity. No matter how many times she told herself that she shouldn't let her natural state embarrass her, she couldn't stop the heat creeping up her face. She'd displayed her body, made herself vulnerable. His response had been to web her in so she couldn't reach him and to tell her to cover herself. Between her anger, her raw nerves, and her flayed hormones, she barely restrained a growl of frustration.

Her voice sounded strained to her own ears. "You have no idea what you're doing. You don't have one semblance of a clue why Endekian women aren't allowed to leave the homeworld, do you?"

"Ranth, fly us up to the *Verazen,* please."

"Compliance," a neutral male computer responded.

Then Xander turned his attention fully on her. Those brilliant violet eyes ignited with a spark of red fire, telling her again that he wasn't as immune to her bare flesh as he pretended. "If I release you, will you promise not to bite? Will you cover yourself properly?"

Gritting her teeth against *Boktai,* she ignored his questions, his handsome visage, his wondrous male scent, and demanded answers of her own. Perhaps her work could yet be saved if the journey was quick enough. "How long is our voyage to the Perceptive Ones going to last?"

"Until we find them."

"You aren't even certain which planet to search?"

"We'll begin in the Lapautee system, out on the rim."

On the rim? *Krek.* He intended to fly into unknown space. "Our journey might take . . . years."

Her situation was even worse than she'd thought. He didn't seem to have much of a plan, never mind a definite itinerary or a time of departure. Her work would be annihilated if the DNA wasn't kept at the proper temperature, combined with the correct nutrients. It wouldn't matter that Maki would run out of funds to keep open the lab. Her precious samples would be ruined long before.

"If the problem on Earth is solved, we'll return sooner. But while it exists, I will not turn back."

At the determination in his tone, she closed her eyes, wishing she could shut out his scent. Even though she couldn't see him, her psi was drowning in need. But she understood his kind of determination. He felt the same way about helping the Terrans as she did about finding a cure for *Boktai*. And while she didn't understand his love of Terrans, she still admired his dedication to his work. Her flesh strained against her bonds. Her stinging, hot bottom demanded more— so much more. "So in other words, you have no idea how long you're keeping me captive?"

To his credit he looked a bit sheepish, but his charming expression did nothing to alleviate her exasperation. She glared at him. Her work wasn't the only thing that would die. "Death from *Boktai* is most unpleasant, and if you insist on taking me with you, I'll be dead within the week."

He frowned, real concern in his eyes. "You are ill?"

"*Krek*. I am not ill, you idiot! You foul breath of a sick canine. You ill-bred son of a slug snail." She realized that he didn't understand Endekian biology, but it didn't mean his ignorance wouldn't kill her anyway. Or that she wouldn't die from the sweet wanting. "Unless I remain on the homeworld, my cells cannot regenerate."

"If your cells cannot regenerate . . ."

"I will die."

"Endekian women cannot regenerate in space?"

"Yes."

"I don't understand why." He appeared puzzled, willing to help, but she knew better than to rely on any man's expressions, even if his voice remained kind. "Is cell regeneration tied to Endekian food? Because we have materializers on board that can make anything you require."

"That's not the problem."

"Your gravity? The air? Your psi should—"

"Wrong again."

His brow creased in thought. "That leaves magnetic radiation that is unique to each planet."

"The scientific reason doesn't matter. You need to take me home. Immediately." She was telling him the truth. But only part of it. With the lust beating through her in a repetitive singsong demand that she *seduce him, seduce him, seduce him,* she wondered if she might yet escape her fate. But even at the thought, her body shuddered, demanding she reach satisfaction now.

"Ranth." He turned to the computer. "Are there other scientific factors I have not considered?"

"Unknown. I cannot confirm or negate her statements. Endekians are a most secretive people."

"So her claim could be a ruse to make us release her?" Xander asked, either her or the computer, she wasn't sure which, but she didn't deign to answer. What good was it to repeat herself when he wouldn't believe these words, either? Besides, she might slip up. She might reveal the very secret she most certainly didn't want him to know. But every second that crawled by, every second that *Boktai* took a firmer hold in her blood, was another second when she might crack.

When she remained stubbornly silent and tried to scowl at him, he leaned forward and, with a finger, tipped up her chin. His one gentle touch caused her lips to part, her heart to sing. For the moment she weakened and prayed he would kiss her. She longed for him to somehow comprehend without her saying more that she desperately needed to find out if he tasted as hot as he looked.

Such was the curse of *Boktai*. She loathed him for ruining years of work—and still she craved him.

She'd thought he'd tipped up her chin to look into her eyes, but instead, he bent to release the webbing. And her thoughts seesawed like a pendulum, swinging wildly in one direction then the other.

She didn't want him to release her. The webbing kept her nudity mostly covered.

Yet she wanted him to release her. So he could see her nudity and what she could offer.

She didn't want him to release her because the webbing kept her from throwing herself at him. The webbing kept her from falling to her hands and knees and begging him to take her.

Yet she wanted him to release her—so she could tackle him, run her hands over him, press her breasts against him. She was desperate to be free. She ached to learn the feel of the powerful muscles on his arms and neck and chest, thread her fingers into his thick black hair, tug his head down for a kiss.

Krek. Krek. Krek.

She must resist or he'd learn her secret. "You release me, and I'll kill you."

At her words, he paused and straightened. Her threat was an outright lie. Unless the man could die of an overdose of sex, he was safe from her.

Still tied, but with him no longer touching her and the delicious vibrations from his smacks slowing ebbing, she regained a measure of control, albeit not quite enough to cover her nudity. But he wasn't even trying to look at her body through the webbing and she still didn't know whether to be glad . . . or frustrated.

"Drik hates me. He'd be glad to see me dead." Or totally humiliated. No doubt he was laughing through his ugly yellow teeth at her current predicament.

"I don't doubt Drik hates you, but what he wants doesn't matter. I don't want you dead. We'll find a way to keep you alive. We left a hostage behind and I plan to return you to Endeki and bring Kirek home. So I won't let you die on me."

Ak, if he refused her, she would die all right. But first she would suffer the longings of the tempted. Nothing was worse than knowing that she'd already spent too much time with him for self-gratification to satisfy her. Nothing was worse than recalling that her father had once tied her mother to a chair and then left her to suffer for hours for an imagined slight, and that although Alara had sworn never to be in the same circumstances, despite all her education and research, she was in exactly the same position as her mother had been. Frustration entered her tone but she raised her chin a notch to meet his confused stare.

"Believe what you wish."

"You will tell me now why you made your suit transparent." He crossed his arms over his chest, his tone calm, his expression curious. "Did you think if you gave me your body that I would send you home?"

"Are you open to such a bargain?"

"No." His eyes burned as if *he* were insulted. But it was she who had taken the insult. He'd just turned her down.

Stars. Was he going to refuse her, humiliate her, and make her lie—that he had no option but to take her home or she would die—come true within the week? Angry at the suffering she would endure, hurt by Drik's betrayal, furious that her research would never help the women on her planet, knowing she faced a terrible death if Xander refused her, she wondered if she had the courage to take her own life—but she could not even do that webbed in and with her hands bound behind her.

The gentle nudge of the deck beneath her feet told her the shuttle had connected with the mother ship. But Xander made no move to leave.

"Alara, you will explain why you made your suit transparent." He glared at her as if determined to wait her out.

Her mouth went dry—even as a part of her applauded his male arrogance. She swallowed hard, hating that she was caught in such a circumstance. All her work, all her hopes, all her dreams had died when he'd abducted her. And now if she wanted to live, he was going to force her to tell him the truth.

Xander tried to keep his gaze above her neck. But he was male. And he couldn't simply ignore her lush curves, her silky smooth golden skin that would tantalize any man—except him. Xander didn't care if she had the curves of a goddess, or the green eyes of a nymphet or the face of a temptress. She was Endekian.

Her people had invaded his world, killed his neighbors, his friends, his mother.

Alara was an alien wrapped in an enticing package of silken gold flesh and tantalizing attitude. And she was hiding something from him. He didn't have to be an empath to feel her squirming or to note her discomfort. Perhaps he'd tied the webbing too tight, although she hadn't complained.

He had to admit he was disappointed that the brilliant Dr. Alara Calladar had resorted to offering her body to him in exchange for her freedom. A Rystani woman would put more value on her worth. A Terran had better morals. Even the ladies from the matriarchal society of Scartar chose lovers with more discrimination.

Disappointed in her behavior, he took no pleasure in her lack of clothing. He didn't want to be reminded that she was female. He didn't want to think of her as a person with a life. He didn't want reminders that he'd taken her away from her work and her friends and her home. He didn't want to have this conversation. As far as he was concerned, the sooner he could take her onto the *Verazen* and leave her alone in her quarters to come to terms with her predicament the better. Surely a rational being would come around to thinking that saving billions of lives was a good thing, a worthwhile endeavor?

But as a respected captain, he didn't want his crew to see him carrying aboard a biting, kicking, and screaming naked woman. While her kind of behavior wouldn't necessarily be frowned upon on his former homeworld of Rystan, he was now a citizen of Mystique, where the blending of cultures had opened his eyes. While his new world hadn't done that much to change his morality, he was certainly aware that his crew members from other cultures would consider manhandling a guest as offensive behavior. So if he and the Endekian were going to come to an understanding, he figured it would be better to have their argument here in the privacy of the shuttle. Besides, he didn't wish for the crew to lose as much respect for her as he had or their future working relationship might suffer.

Her actions were inexplicable. She hadn't simply changed the opacity of the suit. She'd changed the shielding. When his hand had come down on her bottom, he hadn't expected to meet warm flesh. It was almost as if she'd welcomed his not-so-gentle touch, but that made absolutely no sense since she'd been kicking and swearing at him at the time. Quite simply, he didn't understand anything about her except her commitment to her research. And he must. For his crew to work together as a team, he had to have some idea what had turned one of the most respected scientists in the Federation into a naked, irrational, and stubborn adversary. From the narrowing of her pink arched brows, the tense grimace of her pouting lips, he could discern quite clearly she didn't want to talk.

They were at a standoff, the silence building with a tension he didn't understand. Whatever her ploy, he couldn't allow her to win.

He tried to make his tone compassionate. "Disrupting your life and taking you from your homeworld was unavoidable. In time, you will understand."

Her eyes met his with resolve, but the irises dilated. "I will not. I demand you take me back."

Had she been a Rystani or a Terran woman, he

would have read her expression as fear. Yet, though she quivered, she didn't appear afraid but . . . on edge. And for the first time he wished he knew more about Endekians. He could be reading her all wrong. At the times when their eyes locked, he'd thought he'd seen a flicker of her awareness of him as a man that shouldn't be there. Perhaps Endekian female eyes dilated whenever they went into space. Or before they shouted at their abductors. He had no way of knowing unless she told him.

Once again he tried to persuade with logic. "My mission is too urgent to consider your preferences. Taking you back to Endeki could mean failure. Without you and your talent, our chance of success lowers significantly. I know you care not for my people and the Terrans, but I have made a pledge I intend to keep."

"Taking me with you will also cause failure," she insisted. "I will die if you keep me with you."

So much for logic. She obviously didn't believe he could keep her alive. But they had many resources aboard the ship—if she would tell him exactly what she required, he'd try to supply it. He forced his tone to sound kind. "Why will you die?"

"Every other year, female Endekians of childbearing age go through a biological cycle where our cells need regeneration. This year, I am in that phase we call *Boktai*." She swallowed hard and couldn't quite meet his gaze. She appeared to be looking past his right ear, as if the plain gray bulkhead behind him was the most interesting feature on the shuttle.

"I still don't understand."

"Your understanding isn't necessary. I know little about Rystan, but are you familiar with the concept of privacy?"

"Explain." Recalling what he'd seen of Endekian behavior with Drik and Lataka, he suspected their concept of privacy was very different from his. When she remained silent, he added gently, "Please." Every muscle in her body tensed. Her breasts heaved and as one coral-tipped nipple poked through the webbing, his mouth went dust-storm dry.

One thing was certain. She was no new Federation member who couldn't control her psi; likely she'd been introduced to her suit at an early age. She'd revealed her well-developed psi the first time they'd met when she'd had no difficulty controlling her clothing. So she remained naked of her own accord.

She bit her bottom lip. "During this year, I must regenerate my cells on a periodic basis or I'll die."

He had never heard of such a thing, but since he'd left Rystan he'd learned the universe seemed to take pleasure in propagating unique kinds of beings. The Zenonites were giant brains that required psi power to move due to the limited power of their bodies. Osarians were telepathic, but had no sight. Even aboard his ship, his crew was composed of different humanoid varieties. But because of her vague replies, he still didn't understand the problem. How could he help if she didn't tell him more?

"Why can you not regenerate on my ship?"

"Are there Endekian males aboard?" she ground out with so much frustration that if she hadn't been webbed in, she might have emphasized her words with a right punch to his jaw.

"My crew is loyal to me. None are Endekian. None will set you free on Endeki. The sooner you understand, the—"

"You aren't listening. Regeneration requires a male."

He couldn't think of one reason she'd need a male except for sex. But surely he'd misunderstood. He narrowed his brows. "Why?"

If her eyes had been a storm, it would have been a total *green out*, slashing rain, stormy seas, lightning balls of emerald fire. So great was her fury, he had to stop himself from taking a step back.

She fired words at him like blaster shots, fast, hard, and deadly. "Endekian biology is unique within the Federation. I could explain the process, but since you are neither a biologist nor a geneticist, you wouldn't understand."

"Explain in laymen's terms."

She didn't hesitate this time, as if she perceived he would not give up until she made her position clear. "I require periodic mating to stay alive. Without male essence to mix with mine, my cells break down."

Sex. He hadn't misunderstood. She required sex to stay alive. And male essence? Sweet Dregan hell.

He heard the ring of truth in her words and his heart thumped. "Is that why you're naked? You require sex?"

Her words dropped to a whisper but her gaze remained fierce. "During *Boktai*, I lose control of my mind and my psi."

"You require sex . . . now?"

"Very soon."

"How much time do you have?"

"You abducted me at the wrong time. Once the *Boktai* is over, I might be able to . . ."

He could only stare as her words registered. But he refused to accept defeat. There had to be a way to keep her alive short of taking her back. "Suppose I return to Endeki and find a male to—"

She shook her head. "Drik would never allow your ship to return. At least, not in time. You underestimated him. Thanks to you, he's found a way to get rid of me and my work. And I am no use to you. Already my mind is foggy. I can't even maintain proper psi. And once I'm dead, Drik will have no reason to keep his hostage alive."

Well, that explained why she sat before him naked. Xander cursed beneath his breath. He wouldn't fall so easily into the Endekian's trap—and he sure as *krek* wasn't about to give Drik a reason to harm Kirek.

"Tell me more about Endekian cell regeneration."

She stared at him. "The process is uncomfortable."

"You are in pain?"

Her lips turned into a rueful scowl. "I will be. For now, I am aroused."

Stars. Her eyes hadn't been dilated with fear. She'd wanted a man. And he didn't have an Endekian male on board his ship.

"There is no other way to keep you alive?"

"I already explained."

"You said you required male essence to combine with yours. This male must be Endekian?"

"I don't know. No Endekian woman has ever been off my world."

He recalled how she'd seemed on edge. "Are you reacting any differently to me than an Endekian male?"

She closed her eyes. Bowed her head in defeat.

And he knew.

He suddenly yearned for a stiff drink to numb his concern at the trap he'd placed her in. Her body had reacted to him because he was humanoid. Male.

If he wanted Dr. Alara Calladar's help on his mission,

he would have to attempt to regenerate her cells and hope that his Rystani essence would keep her alive. He'd have to have sex with her—even if mating with her went against every Rystani custom, even if his every warrior instinct warned of danger.

5

So much for Alara keeping her secret. Now Xander knew that mating with her would keep her alive. To negotiate her release, she'd tried to insinuate that only male Endekians had the chemistry she required. But with her blood boiling through her veins, and the heat rushing through her system, her need was too great to carry the ruse through. Desperation and the sizzling arousal from Xander's touch, plus his wondrous male scent, had forced her to explain what she must do to stay alive. If the sight of his big male body weren't flooding her with hormones that charged her senses into a frenzy, she might have controlled her psi, at least enough to keep her suit opaque.

Heat pooled between her thighs and her breasts ached for stimulation. Her nipples were tight, budding, and when she'd glanced down, she'd seen the tip protruding through the webbing. And swallowed hard.

She'd tried to shift position, but the webbing trapped her and her protruding breast. And when she caught Xander glancing at her nipple, she'd hoped he'd be intrigued enough to release her. She no longer wanted anything but . . . him. Holding back had been futile. But he'd forced his gaze to her eyes and the heat combined with his attitude that seemed to say "I'm in charge and having no trouble resisting" stung her pride all over again.

Under normal circumstances, she wouldn't have liked him any more than he liked her, but when it came to *Boktai*, the finer emotions didn't count. It mattered not if they had nothing in common. It mattered not if they came from different worlds. Her Endekian body read him as male, male, male. And demanded sex, craved sex, coveted his body inside hers with a hunger that made thinking of anything but him almost impossible. Even though she reminded herself that her brother had died in a war against Rystan, even when she reminded herself that this man had taken her from her home, her work, and her friends, she still wanted him on a level so savage and primal that concrete thinking didn't count.

But not even the rational part of her thanked him for tying her down. Because if he hadn't webbed her in, she'd no doubt be rubbing her bare flesh against him by now, satisfying her raging heat and emptiness.

Instead, her nerves were so on edge and her breath so ragged, she had to bite her lower lip to keep from moaning. Soon she would lose every shred of higher thinking. She would succumb to the cravings of her body both in mind and spirit.

As if he had no idea of her yearnings, his tone was flat, his expression seemingly disinterested. "Endekians invaded my home. Killed my mother. Because of your people's encroachment of Rystan, I can't even visit her grave." He stared at her, his eyes full of sorrow and menace, as if he'd rather strangle her than have sexual intercourse.

She bit down harder on her lip to keep the words from leaving her mouth . . . and failed. His scent was causing reactions she couldn't suppress, and if he wouldn't satisfy her, then she needed another solution. "If you find me so unappealing, perhaps one of your crew—"

"You are *my* responsibility." He folded his massive arms across his chest and glared at her as if she'd suggested he should shirk his duties. "And whatever job I take on, I do to the best of my ability."

She fought to keep her voice from breaking, raised her chin high and locked gazes with him, refusing to let him see that she was slowly losing every scrap of scruples and rational judgment. "If you wish to keep me alive, you must assuage my needs."

He cocked his head to one side, a lock of dark hair falling at a jaunty angle over his eye. His nostrils flared. "And what do I get in return?"

An Endekian male wouldn't ask such a question. The pleasure he took from her body would have been payment enough. But obviously, the Rystani considered taking care of her needs a chore. Distasteful. He acted as if he wouldn't be enjoying her body at all. He acted as if he were lowering himself to be with her. He acted as if he'd rather be with any other woman in the universe. Didn't she tempt him? Did he see her as unattractive and needy?

Rejection stung. She couldn't stop her feelings any more than she could put an end to *Boktai*. The universe had made her this way and she knew from experience that raging against her fate would do no good.

Even as Xander glared at her, even after he'd hurt her, she wanted him so badly she shook. Desperation and survival called for harsh measures. If he didn't find her body attractive perhaps she could bribe him. "On Endeki, I am not without assets. I could . . . pay you."

The muscles in his chest tightened. His lower jaw dropped. And if his anger could have heated her, she'd have been on broil. He stiffened and widened his proud stance. "If I took credits in exchange for sex that would make me no better than a *rintha*."

"What do you want?" she countered, so annoyed that he hadn't touched her again she could spit. He should be untying her. Caressing her flesh. Releasing her so that he could plunge into her body and take what she offered so freely.

Being webbed in was maddening. With every breath, the straps rubbed her flesh—just a little, never enough. Moisture trickled between her legs, but she couldn't so much as squirm. The sensation of enforced stillness combined with his enticing presence had her almost ready to beg.

He hadn't had to do one thing except be male and she was right on the edge of release. But release alone wouldn't be enough to satisfy her. She'd gone beyond the yen for an orgasm. She now needed him pumping and thrusting inside her, mixing their essences, feeding her lusty cells.

"If you want sex, then you'll have to give me your full cooperation." He spoke slowly, as if he feared her unable to comprehend his ultimatum, as if he didn't know that she would have agreed to any demand—if only he would touch her again. "Join my crew. Place all your energy, passion, and intellect into helping us find the Perceptive Ones and a pure DNA to save the Terrans."

Despite her pounding pulse, she kept herself from releasing a soft moan. "If I agree, then you'll service me?"

He nodded as if he couldn't bear to let a word of accord pass across his lips.

"Regularly?"

He nodded again.

As they reached a consensus, pure pleasure flooded through her. Her body looked forward to the news like a desert flower opening its petals to the morning dew. Her voice was hoarse, her words eager. "Then untie me. You can start now."

"Now is not convenient."

"But you said—"

"I will not go back on my word. I do have responsibilities. My crew needs me on the bridge for the jump into hyperspace." He eyed her with a mix of regret and concern. "Are you capable of covering yourself?"

"You don't understand." She ground her teeth in frustration. "If you untie me, I'm going to tackle you."

He laughed, no doubt thinking that just because she was half his mass that she couldn't budge him. But he'd never dealt with a woman in *Boktai*. He couldn't comprehend that the same potent hormones that incited her tremendous need for sex also strengthened her muscles. She saw no reason to inform him of his ignorance. But then he choked off his laughter, his eyes narrowing. "Are you aware that hyperspace intensifies sensation?"

"What?" She was already so on edge she was trying to break the webbing, but every twitch, every shimmy served only to increase the straps' friction and torment her further. And now he was telling her she'd have to endure more sensations in hyperspace? "I cannot wait. Delay the hyperspace maneuver."

"My crew has already set navigation to time our

jump with the gravitational waves being emitted from the Osarian black holes. We're scheduled to dip into the deep gravity well and fling ourselves into hyperspace at incredible speeds. A delay right now will add additional weeks to our journey."

"So?"

"The Terrans need—"

"I need—"

"Can you not wait one Federation hour?"

An hour. *Krek*. She didn't want to wait another moment. Every second seemed like minutes. Every minute an hour. An hour was . . . forever. "An hour can be a lifetime in *Boktai*."

"But you won't die?"

She wanted to lie. But honor would not allow it—at least not yet. If she slipped deeper into *Boktai,* she'd be capable of almost anything, but she wasn't quite . . . there yet. So she shook her head.

"Regulations require me to be on the bridge during a jump. If you cannot cover yourself, it would be best for you to stay here."

"Untie me." Her voice came out a croak. She refused to think of her tone as begging.

He shook his head, but his eyes looked thoughtful, if a bit amused. "Everyone webs in for the jump."

"Status?" Xander strode onto the bridge, already missing Kirek. Kirek's parents and his crew were now aware that he'd agreed to remain behind, but the bridge seemed emptier without him. While the lad hadn't been an officer, he'd lent an air of home and normalcy to the starship.

And after Xander's confrontation with Alara, he

craved normalcy the way a fish craved water. He was going to have to have sex with an Endekian. *Stars*.

"All scientists and crew are webbed in, Captain." Vax, a Rystani warrior and second in command, stood at the con, but upon seeing the captain, he changed position to the forward viewscreen where two black holes dominated the starscape.

Xander webbed himself in, thinking he'd been fortunate to inherit Zical's crew. The starship's previous captain was presently at home, ready to assist his wife Dora through the birth of their fourth child. Xander sometimes wondered if he'd ever be so fortunate as to love a woman enough to willingly give up a grand adventure like this one to stay at her side.

As he thought of the female waiting for him in the shuttle, a jolt of sadness mixed with his exhilaration. He'd successfully accomplished the first part of his mission, but in the process, he'd put her life at risk. And while Alara might be Endekian and the enemy, she hadn't personally attacked Rystan. He didn't hate all Endekians—just the ones who'd invaded his homeworld and who'd been responsible for his mother's death.

Under normal circumstances, he would never have forced her to come with them, so, as much as he looked forward to piloting the *Verazen* into the unknown, he had enough of a conscience to squirm over the position he'd placed her in. She was beautiful, intelligent, and clever, but only under these circumstances would he consider mating with her. Not because of her race, but because on Rystan, mating with a woman was an act of love, of intimacy.

Clearly, the Endeki had other ideas.

At times like this, he had to love his work. During

the past years since he'd left Rystan and made Mystique his home, he'd transported people and cargo from one planet to another, then served in Mystique's new starfleet, ready to defend his new home. But he'd been eager to explore more of the galaxy as well as to help Earth. He relished new challenges. Several years ago Xander had had an interesting relationship with Scartar's ambassador to Mystique, but she'd since returned to her world. And he'd experienced a Terran fling with an anthropologist during a vacation on Mars. But never in his most vivid imagination would he have thought that he'd be required to have sexual intercourse with an Endekian in order to keep her alive.

Stars zinging by on the viewscreen brought him back to his duties. "Engineering, report?"

"We're good to jump." Cyn, an exotic green-skinned woman from the matriarchal planet of Scartar, served as the *Verazen*'s chief engineer. Rumor had it that she crooned to her engines, coaxing extra speed out of the drives with the purity of her voice. Xander didn't care how she accomplished her job, as long as his engines remained in top working order.

"Navigation?"

Shannon Walker, a Terran grandmother who'd taken to space at the ripe old age of eighty, surveyed her vidscreen. "We're in the groove."

Thanks to the Perceptive Ones' suits, the Terran lifespan had increased tenfold and Shannon, who had been away from Earth long enough to be clear of the disease that ravaged her people, could expect to live for several more centuries. Almost two decades ago, Earth had sent Tessa Camen to take the Challenge and she'd passed the Perceptive Ones' test, proving Terrans were fit to join the Federation. Since then, they'd colonized dozens of worlds, including Mystique where Terrans, Rystani, and even Osarians lived together in peace.

Shannon was typical of the Terrans Xander had met. Adaptable, brave, and inquisitive, she often mothered those under her command. Like his officers, Xander could count on her in a crunch.

Despite the intricacy of the hyperjump maneuver, with Ranth monitoring all systems their flight appeared to be going smoothly. Under Zical's command, this crew and Kirek had taken a similar route fourteen years earlier, but this time, hopefully, no strange race like the Kwadii would stop the ship in hyperspace and interfere with the mission.

"Call coming through on the hyperlink," Shannon announced.

Xander checked his chronometer. The conversation would have to be a quick one. Once they jumped into hyperspace, communication with Mystique would be impossible until they returned to normal space—but by then the distances would be so vast that conversation would be onerous since messages each way could take years.

"Open a channel."

No sooner had the words left his lips, than Kahn's image filled the vidscreen, his expression bleak. Clearly aware the *Verazen* was about to jump into hyperspace, Kahn made his point quickly. "We've confirmed that the breakdown of DNA is caused by a virus—not pollution. And it has spread to other worlds."

"Only Terran worlds or other humanoids, too?" Xander asked, realizing his mission had just become more critical.

"Terran, humanoid, and other species—even the Osarians, the Zenonites, and the Jarn are infected."

All life in the Federation was now at risk.

Millions of worlds.

Billions of beings.

All about to die.

Xander was glad he was webbed in so that he couldn't stagger under the weight of the critical news. The Jarn lived underwater. The Zenonites were mostly huge, disembodied brains. The Osarians were telepathic beings with eight tentacles. No plague in the history of the Federation had ever been so widespread and infected so many worlds.

"Where did the virus come from?" Xander asked, ignoring the shocked faces of his chief officers.

Cyn's deep green skin had paled to a sickly hue. Shannon's wizened wrinkles seemed to deepen. And Vax went rigid. All had friends and loved ones back home. All three likely had one nagging question on their minds—if they jumped into hyperspace on a journey across the galaxy, would anyone be left to return to?

"The cause of the plague is not known, but we can discount pollution, as we first thought. The virus breaks down DNA at the molecular level. The science is unlike anything we have seen before. The virus attacks animal and plant life of every species, and is spreading fast. So far, it's one hundred percent fatal. Due to the contagious nature of the virus, the council has forbidden time travel. Many Federation worlds have imposed blockades to protect themselves, but these measures only seem to slow the sickness, not stop it."

Xander rubbed his brow, his head pounding at the enormity of the problem, the billions of lives at stake. "How is the virus spreading through the fabric of space?"

"We don't know."

The implications were staggering. From the first, the Federation's top scientists and physicians had assumed the disintegration of Terran DNA had been caused by exposure to the pollution on one planet. To learn the epidemic had not started that way and could be spread to other beings, even nonsentient life-forms, boggled the mind.

Xander had only seconds until the jump into hyperspace. "Should we abort?" Members of his crew could already be infected. They could be spreading disease to worlds on the rim. "Should we return home?"

"Reaching your objective is more critical now than ever before. Complete your mission."

"Understood."

"Twenty seconds to hyperspace." Ranth began the countdown.

Purple lights flashed on the bridge as the starship approached critical speeds. The antigravity shields hummed at full strength.

"Ten seconds."

The *Verazen*'s engines hummed. The vibrations of the deck below Xander's feet remained steady under the incredible forces, as did his crew, who had heard the terrible news yet remained steadfast. No one had asked to go home and his heart swelled with pride at their courage.

"Five seconds."

If one engine so much as hiccupped, the hull would collapse and disintegrate into dust fragments so tiny, it would be as if they'd never existed. Xander kept his finger on the abort button, just in case of a last-minute difficulty. But Cyn's engines remained smooth, the ship, as Shannon said, in the groove.

"On my order." Xander's voice was calm, his rush

of excitement at venturing into the unknown damp-
ened by the enormity of his task. "Now."

Real space disappeared. Hyperspace engulfed them.
Their mission had begun.

*And you said potential is not quantifiable. Look at
them now.*

*You sound like the proud papa of this unruly brood.
I am more impartial and see no progress, nothing except desperation, fear, and panic.*

*Not all are giving up and retreating. Some have the
courage to seek out a solution. They are determined,
these leaders.*

*Are you implying that their determination is what
makes them meritorious of life? Because if so, that can
only be part of the final equation.*

*I'm predicting innovative thinking, a coming to-
gether, an awakening, a growth. But can you not see
the proper configurations forming?*

I see chaos.

*Out of chaos will come order. Out of the order will
come a solution.*

Perhaps out of chaos comes more chaos.

*Give them time and they will convince you. Are you
satisfied with the parameters I've set?*

*Not yet. I will not be persuaded until I've fully as-
sessed the demarcations and maximum absolutes of
your foolish theory.*

The baseline's in place. However, I'm still tweaking.
With a mental snap, a star system disappeared and another replaced it.

*Ah, I've always liked creating. Do you prefer the
ocean as celadon blue or aquamarine?*

Details don't concern me.

But they should. Considering the details may mean the difference between admirable success or abject failure.

My friend, you are taking the demonstration process too seriously. No doubt they will falter again, and you will remain in a funk for eons. And this time, I will not coddle you. If they fail—

They won't.

But if they do, you'll agree to let them all expire?

I suppose.

And you won't complain?

Of course I'll complain. I don't like to fail.

Then you should stop putting your radical ideas on the line.

Never. They will succeed.

Kirek opened his eyes and smiled as he stretched. Despite his intellect, his parents, Miri and Etru, had done their best to keep him sheltered within a loving family unit. He'd been brought up in their home with Rystani morals. However, he also had an honorary Aunt Dora, who'd once been a sentient computer and who spoke quite freely about sex. But even Dora might have been shocked by the Endekian women with whom he'd spent the last hours. These women offered their bodies freely during *Boktai,* and didn't ask for or expect any emotional ties or commitment. Kirek didn't understand them, and though he'd always expected to one day form a stable and loving union like the one his parents enjoyed, he could accept that different peoples had different customs. While he was having a good time exploring his sexuality, he'd been taught that mating would be so much better with loving feelings to go with the pleasure.

Careful not to disturb any of the women who dozed in the sleeping chamber, Kirek padded to the food materializer and used his psi to order *jicken* and *karirice*. Hungry after his pleasant exertions, he ate, chewing slowly. The food wasn't home cooked or as tasty as Miri's, but as his gaze skimmed over the nude, entwined bodies in his chamber, he realized there were other delightful aspects to his predicament.

He would have been content to do no more than enjoy his stay on Endeki, but his powerful curiosity refused to allow him to lapse into a haze of pleasurable activity. He had the perfect cover. As a hostage, he had access to the entire residence. In fact he wasn't allowed to leave the building, but the computerized bracelet on his wrist that was supposed to monitor his location only showed up on the computer logs when he wanted it to. And since few guards were allowed inside the residence, Kirek could explore and perhaps satisfy his itching curiosity.

He'd never understood why the Endekians had invaded his parents' homeworld of Rystan. While over twenty-five thousand years ago the planet might have been a pleasant place to live, his ancestors had turned the world into a giant ice ball after setting off atomic weapons. Only the poles remained habitable—and survival there had been hard in the extreme cold weather. So the question burned in his mind—why had Endekians invaded Rystan?

His parents believed Tessa of Earth had formed a business with the Osarians that had altered the balance of trade in the Federation, hurting Endeki business. When Tessa had first settled on Rystan with her husband, most people believed the Endekians had attacked with the aim of killing Tessa.

However, Kirek had learned that the Endekians had coveted Rystan long before Tessa's arrival. And after his people had departed for Mystique, the Endekians had spent considerable credits to hold what most Federation people considered a barren world. Kirek wanted to solve the mystery.

So after he finished his meal, he awoke Lataka with a soft kiss. She stirred, opened her eyes, and reached for him, but after getting to know her so well over the last few hours, he read her mood as "cuddle me" rather than "ravish me." He would be happy to please her once again after she fulfilled her promise to show him around the residence.

He placed a finger to his lips, hoping she wouldn't awaken the other women. She stretched, grinned playfully, and ran a finger down his bare chest, then followed the same path with her tongue, shooting a lazy tug of desire to his groin.

Kirek gathered her to him and used his psi to propel them into the next chamber. As she cuddled against his chest, her unique scent wafted to him, sharp mint with a hint of rain.

Unwilling to disturb the others, he kept his voice low. "Didn't I satisfy you last night?"

She giggled and ran her hands over his bare buttocks. As a hostage, he wasn't allowed to cover his nudity, signaling to the Endeki females that he was available to serve at all times. And the females here had a refined and distinctive taste in pleasure. Kirek grinned at the memory of one of them explaining to him the phases of *Boktai* and how Drik spoiled his daughter, giving her whatever she desired. He could have been left in worse places.

Still, he knew his parents would disapprove of Endekian morals. While on an intellectual level Kirek understood their customs stemmed from their peculiar biology, on an emotional level these people shocked him. However, there was more to life than sensual pleasure. Although with Lataka's hands on his *tavis,* he was having difficulty remembering exactly what those other things were. Yet, a half hour later, after he'd enjoyed her once more, he insisted on taking that tour.

"What's so interesting about the residence?" she asked, taking his hand and leading him down a hallway with high ceilings and many connecting rooms.

"I want to see all my choices."

"Choices?"

"So I'll know where we can best . . . enjoy ourselves," he told her, knowing that while his words weren't a total lie, the prospect of her having him again would distract her.

Kirek saw no cameras. No locks. After gaining entrance to the residence, he'd found the security inside lax. Either Drik had nothing here worth hiding, or Lataka hadn't yet taken him to the area he most wanted to be.

"There are three hundred and twenty-five rooms in the residence." Her tone was light, her smile impish. "Perhaps we should experiment in each one."

He slung an arm over her shoulder and fondled her breast through her suit. She immediately lowered her shield so he could feel her bare flesh. But she kept her suit a deep gold to match her skin and to preserve her modesty from passing workers. His Rystani nudity, on the other hand, drew lots of stares, giggles, and an occasional fondle from a passing female. He was fair game. To be used for play by whoever wanted him.

He supposed he should have minded, should have found his status demeaning. But even a mental protest was rather difficult when he was enjoying himself so much. Kirek had spent much of his life studying, but there was only so much knowledge he could learn from computer programs. And here he was learning by hands-on experience.

And although he couldn't help but enjoy sexual pleasure, he wanted more. His parents adored one another. So did his aunt Dora and uncle Zical. And although Tessa and Kahn's fights were infamous, they'd each risked their lives so many times for each other there could be no doubting their connection. All lower animals could reproduce. Intelligent beings should elevate the pleasure to include the mind.

However, Kirek was a young healthy male and feeding his physical appetites pleased him. Eventually, he supposed he'd tire of his hostage situation. But for the moment, he was far from bored. In fact, he was in absolutely no rush at all for Xander to return.

6

After Xander left the shuttle, Alara fought her bonds. But the webbing had been designed to protect a body during high g-forces and not even the extra strength she'd gained from *Boktai* was enough to shift her position—not even a little. With her hands cuffed behind her, she couldn't release the ties—she could hardly twitch a thigh muscle.

At least with Xander's departure, her need eased. Without his male scent in her nostrils, without his handsome face and attractive body to taunt her, her automatic physical responses waned. Her thoughts cleared, and she realized that although the big Rystani had appeared shocked by her revelations, he hadn't said no, either.

Perhaps he was intelligent enough to comprehend that she'd had nothing to do with the war between their people. Or perhaps he simply looked forward to enjoying her body. He'd certainly had difficulty taking his gaze off her rebellious nipple that, no matter how much she tried to change positions, seemed determined to poke through the webbing.

With his departure, she renewed her hope of regaining her psi enough to cover her nudity. Alara was about to use meditation to calm her body further when the ship jumped into hyperspace. Xander had warned her that her senses would heighten, but neither of them had known that in her current state, the intensity would rock her as if she'd soared into orbit. Her every breath, each rise and fall of her chest, sent shock waves of electricity through her system. Blood rushed through her veins and raised her temperature. Her skin flushed. Desire flared.

When Xander returned, his presence slammed her again. Hyperspace seemed to make him larger than life, adding texture to his gorgeous bronze skin, magnifying his scent, intensifying his maleness. She would have been writhing—if she'd been free to move. At the sight of his rock-hard muscles over powerful shoulders and his virile chest, her heart pounded hard enough to rush the blood to her most sensitive places.

When his dynamic violet eyes caught hers and lit with a heat that could have fused *bendar*, she understood that her need was inciting his lust. She couldn't have been more pleased. For a while she'd feared he might not respond to her like an Endekian male.

Despite the fact that he clearly wanted her, his tone was full of concern. "Are you all right?"

An Endekian male would have had no interest in her welfare, but she couldn't focus on his compassionate qualities when he was keeping her bound.

She gasped, her tone low and husky. "Free me."

He took one searching look at her and reached for the webbing. As he leaned down she breathed in more of his male aroma, a spicy and evocative mix of a woodland scent that transported her into the next stage of *Boktai*. A stage where pride had no place. A stage where feeling and need dominated her mind. A stage that reduced her to her most elemental nature.

At his hungry gaze, need speared her. Every atom, every cell, every inch of flesh hungered for his touch, causing her breasts to ache, her *yonia* to yearn for sweet fulfillment. Again her nipples hardened, poking through the webbing. She had to give him credit. He began to do as she'd requested, but her protruding flesh distracted him.

"Would you like me to touch you?" he asked, his tone as polite as if he were asking to open a door.

"Yes." Why did he ask? Why did he reveal his manners now when she wanted him to ravish her?

Holy structure of atoms! He'd kidnapped her from her home, separated her from her work, forced her from her world, driven her mindless with need—and now he stopped for permission to touch her?

"Or would you rather I kissed you, first?"

She barely bit back a groan, realizing that he was teasing her. But she was in no mood for soft and gentle. Not when she longed for hard and fast. Anticipation had her lips parting. Her breasts heaving.

"Do everything. Please. Now."

But he held back, his gaze impudent and mysterious. "Are you certain?"

"Yes. I want you. I need you. I must have you."

He threaded his hands in her hair. His fingertips were gentle, his palms firm, as he tipped back her head with a commanding tenderness that oddly seemed to go quite well with his I'm-in-charge attitude.

"Does it make any difference to your cell regeneration if I go slowly or at maximum speed?"

She needed him so badly. Right now. She didn't want to wait one more moment. But like a storm swelling with every gust of wind, the longer the tempestuous forces built, the greater the fury, the more torrential the downpour.

So she admitted the truth. "If you take me slowly, my cells will regenerate more completely."

He grinned happily, revealing straight white teeth. "Ah, so you want me to take my time."

"Yes. No. I don't know."

He responded as if she hadn't just answered him in complete confusion. "My plan is to satisfy you so completely that we won't have to do this again for a while. Understood?"

"Yes."

"And since that means we need to proceed slowly to regenerate you fully, I plan to take my time with you." His tone was soft, teasing, charming.

As she realized he had yet to release the webbing, her stomach churned. Already she regretted her honesty. She'd made a mistake to tell him anything at all.

But then his mouth slanted down over hers, his hands behind her head, his fingertips pressing and holding her steady. At the same time, he used his psi. Lips sucked her nipples and seared her. His maneuvers were creating a delightful sensation across her breasts. Sensations she wished wouldn't stop.

"What are you doing?"

He grinned. "I just felt your psi shield weaken, so I took control."

Ah, holy goddess. She hadn't expected Xander to

figure out so quickly that while she remained unable to use her psi, he could manipulate her suit.

And so as his lips parted hers, as he nibbled and nipped and her tongue met his, he duplicated the sensations on her breasts, shooting arcs of pleasure straight to her *labella*. Sweet Stars. The man knew how to kiss. He had skills as honeyed as *tanii* pastries, more patience than a *Catallian* owl. And her breasts trembled with pleasure as she sighed into his mouth.

His kiss conveyed a demanding thoroughness that told her he would gift her with healthy cell regeneration—if she survived the wait. Being webbed in, she was at a healthy disadvantage. She couldn't rush him with her hands or her hips. He would set the pace. She couldn't press against his hard muscles. She could only wait. She couldn't even tell him what she wanted since he was keeping her mouth busy. She had no control. None. Null. Zero.

Waiting, wondering what he would do, she ached with the need for him to fill her and her *yonia* creamed with moisture. But he seemed quite content to focus on her mouth and her breasts that had never been so cherished or so exquisitely tender.

But he wasn't satisfied to excite only her breasts. The man kissed like a legend and soon her lungs burned for air. Her lips tingled. And he never let up his psi licks and nips of her breasts. Ah, she ached with nerve endings she hadn't known she possessed.

Still he took his time, until she was certain that she would go insane with the craving lust. His patience was driving her wild, but she kept thinking about where she was headed, as if she were rushing down an endless white-water river and waiting to shoot over the falls.

Finally, she tore her mouth aside, gasped for air, no longer caring if she begged. "Enough."

Immediately he pulled back. "You want me to stop?"

"I want you to hurry."

"And I already told you once, when I take on a task, any task, I do it to the best of my ability." A glimmer in his eyes revealed his intensity. "Before, you wanted me to go slowly, so you would have complete regeneration."

"That was before." Frustration fueled her desire. If only she could move, press her body against all that bronze Rystani flesh.

"What has changed?" He leaned back on his heels and crossed his arms, eyeing her as if she were an experiment gone wrong.

"You've pushed too far."

He raised an eyebrow. "And this is bad because . . . ?"

"No, it's good. Too good."

"There's no such thing as too good." His frown changed into a grin. Oh, the big male was very pleased with himself and she found him even more attractive. More compelling. He actually still seemed concerned that she get what she needed—even when that meant delaying his own gratification.

However, he couldn't possibly understand the blaze in her loins. If she'd been free, she would have shown him her ardor with her lips, her hands, her *yonia*. She tried to growl but even to her own ears the words came off as a sexual purr and nowhere near a genuine protest. "I'm not aroused by bondage or domination."

At her words, he laughed with a confidence that told her he wasn't buying her denial. "You enjoyed those smacks on your bottom."

"I didn't," she lied, and shook her head wildly from

side to side to prevent him from seeing the truth in her eyes.

With no warning, he used his psi to roughly flick the tips of her nipples.

"Uh . . . oh . . . ah."

His eyes brightened with amusement, and he spoke in jest. "I suppose you wouldn't like more, either." He squeezed her nipples again and she couldn't stop her soft moan from telling him exactly how much she liked his kind of attention.

"I assure you my cells will . . . ah . . . oh. Oh." His psi on her nipples made talking almost impossible. "I'll fully regenerate if we . . . finish now."

"Since I'm unfamiliar with Endekian biology, I intend to be very thorough."

She wanted to slap him. No, she wanted to throw him onto his back, take him into her yearning *yonia*, and grind her pelvis against his.

He began to unstrap the webbing by her shoulders, then stopped. "It occurs to me that when I release the webbing, you may try to touch me."

She raised her eyes to his. "Of course I will."

He shook his head, his demeanor serious yet taunting. "But that is against Rystani custom."

She groaned. "I'm not Rystani."

"I can see that." He parted the webbing with his fingers and cupped her breasts. "Our women have bronze skin. Yours is so pretty and golden."

She quivered in his hands, feeling wanton and wicked and willing to do whatever he asked. No man had ever taken this amount of time with her. She suspected that whatever task he took on, he'd accomplish to the best of his abilities. And that he had kept his word shot happy feelings her way. He might be toying with her emotional state as skillfully as he was caressing her flesh, but for now, she could only enjoy it.

"So we are agreed, then?" he asked.

"Huh?" She raised her eyes to his.

"We will make love like Rystani."

"And if I say no, you'll fail to regenerate my cells and let me die?"

"Of course not." He twirled her nipples between thumb and forefinger. "We'll simply continue our discussion and I'll be content to keep caressing your beautiful breasts until you change your mind."

The longer he took, the longer she could wait before she'd need him again. However, she hadn't expected him to be this *kreking* thorough. She hadn't expected this much attention. She hadn't expected him to listen to what she needed. And now the big Rystani was overdoing it. Overtouching. Overstimulating. And she'd wished she hadn't spoken so freely.

She licked her upper lip, hoping to speed up the process. "I'm surprised you have so much time to spare on me."

"I have a very competent crew."

Apparently, his threat wasn't idle. And it appeared as if he would be content to stroke her for hours before going back to his work.

"Fine," she agreed.

But she figured her word didn't count since she'd given it under duress. After he released her from the webbing, she had no intention of following his customs. Whatever they were. She'd agreed only out of desperation. And once she placed her hands on his beautiful body, he would not complain. He'd accept her caresses as she had his, and her hands would urge him on to satisfaction and completion.

However, he was not like Endekian men. After he released the webbing and her cuffs, she still could not move. He used his psi to hold her. She wanted to curse him, plead with him, but at the determined look in his eyes, her stomach clenched and she barely bit back her irritation. When he finally nudged her knees apart, she figured her wait was over. Surely he must be about to give her what she so desperately needed.

But he didn't touch her. Instead he floated her into the air by employing her null grav, stopping her knees at his eye level. Then he parted her legs wider, holding her gaze with his. The intimacy of the moment almost made her feel vulnerable, but excited yet uneasy.

She told herself she was an experienced woman and he wasn't looking at anything that was so different from any other woman's *yonia*. Blaming her unusual nervousness on the uncertainty of what he would do next, she longed for him to act, to move, to caress and to enter her. She didn't want to stop and feel or think. She didn't want to assess and analyze. She wanted to get on with it. To be done. To complete the regeneration cycle, so she could forget about her biological requirements until next time.

When she'd given him permission to set the pace, or do whatever he pleased, she'd never dreamed he would make such a production out of every teasingly slow caress. Or how very good he could make her feel. And when he'd very deliberately stared between her thighs, she could have sworn her *labella* swelled even more.

While she would have been pleased if he'd turned his suit transparent, apparently he had other ideas. He spread her thighs wider. With fingers as gentle as gossamer wings, he parted her sensitive *labella,* carefully stroking her delicate folds until she pearled with moisture. As gently as if she were a petal that he didn't wish to damage, he spread her inner lips. His hot breath fanned her most intimate core. With tiny puffs of air, he warmed her, teased her, taunted her, and she barely held back groans of delight.

"You smell delicious." With curiosity and skill, he finally fondled the triangle of curls at her mons, shooting a delicious shiver of anticipation through her as she imagined him dipping his fingers into her. "Our women fashion their hair differently."

Did he find her unattractive? She'd simply collapse in frustration if he dared stop now. "Am I unappealing to you?"

"Just unfamiliar." He grinned mischievously. "But I can fix that." He snapped his fingers, and with his psi, he changed the parameters of her suit. Her suit began to groom her, tickling her mons as it removed the hair in the Rystani pattern that pleased him. And when she glanced down to see that her formerly full triangle now resembled but a small sliver, she felt bare, and more vulnerable than ever.

But she held her breath, wondering how good it would feel if he ever got around to touching her newly bared skin. At the thought of him grazing his fingers over her, she quivered. Deep inside her, muscles clenched and tightened, drawing together in expectation of extreme bliss.

He surveyed his handiwork with obvious enjoyment, but still didn't touch her. Why did he delay?

"Surely I am ready for you now?"

"Not yet."

He stepped back and she gnashed her teeth in frustration. When he left her in the air and walked around her, she feared for a moment he would simply leave her again. But he stepped to a wall compartment and the materializer hummed. He returned with three bottles in his hand and a glint in his gaze that was beginning to warn her that she'd have to wait even longer to obtain what she wanted.

He held up the largest silver jar, removed the stopper, and a spicy aroma filled the air. "This is Panzi Dust from Interferia Three."

His materializer must be better equipped than the basic ones on Endeki. No machine on her world could make such an expensive potion. Although she'd heard the concoction was the ultimate aphrodisiac, she had no idea how it worked or exactly what it did or why the second scarlet bottle and the third tiny bottle were necessary, either.

He upended the silver bottle and poured the clear oil into his palm. After setting the bottles aside, he dipped his fingers into his palm and oil droplets adhered to the pads of his fingertips. With careful precision he skimmed his oiled fingertip over her newly shaved mons.

"That tickles." She would have squirmed, but of course his psi and the suit held her as immobile as the webbing had done. At first, she assumed the oil was a lubricant, with a fantastic scent that reminded her of *cinbar* and *sugarelle*. But as her flesh absorbed the oil, tiny arcs of electric energy danced along her nerve endings. She tingled, and he was by no means done. "Oh . . . Stars."

He dribbled the oil over the pink flesh of her *labella,* carefully coating the outside perimeter, then the inside. Not once did he touch her *yonia* or her nerve center. Slowly he tipped her backward and gave the same attention to the skin between the cheeks of her bottom.

Just when she thought the tingling sensation might soon become too much—it stopped. And he tilted her upright once more to apply the concoction to her areolae and nipples. She glistened under the lights in the shuttle, gritting her teeth at the tiny electric jolts on her breasts that followed the same pattern as before. If that was all the aphrodisiac did, she didn't understand why he'd gone to such trouble. It had been pleasant, but certainly nothing spectacular.

But then he blew on her flesh, sparking reaction that connected the tiny sizzles into one arcing current. At the sensation—like molten fire sparked with ice—she gasped and moaned. "What . . . have . . . you done?"

"What I wanted."

"But—"

"Rystani warriors take what they want. Right now, I like having you at my fingertips." Once again he took her nipples between his thumbs and index fingers. And then he tweaked her nipples.

"Ahhh . . . Stars."

It was as if he'd turned on a switch. The oil magnified sensation. Hyperspace magnified it again. She was certain she would orgasm without his ever touching her sweetest spot or giving her his essence.

"I don't think—"

"Thinking isn't required. You're enjoying my attentions. Admit it." He tweaked her nipples again.

"Ah, please." With the fiery and icy sensations, speaking was almost impossible. "You . . . don't . . . understand. I need your semen . . . inside me . . . when I orgasm to, ah, ah, properly regenerate."

"But delayed lust will help, yes?"

"I cannot—"

"You can."

His fingers played lightly over her *labella,* and she had to remember to breathe. What he was doing felt so good. But not quite good enough. Every cell strained and tightened, yearning for release, but he gave her none.

"You will wait for your pleasure until I place my *tavis* inside you." His tone was a command. Hard. Edgy.

His reminder almost made her flinch. Regeneration required his essence and her orgasm to combine at the same time. But how could she delay gratification with his finger finally finding and focusing on her sweet spot?

He tapped her with each word he spoke, shooting hot and cold sparks into her core. "You will wait."

"You must come to me now." She was losing control and it was all his fault. "I can't—"

"Time for me to help you out." He held up the tiny scarlet bottle, unstoppered it, tipped up her *yonia* to catch the droplets and shook them over her.

She was in the midst of fighting the budding orgasm, a battle that she surely would lose, and then the liquid splashed onto her. And snuffed out her yearning. One moment her body had been oh, so ready to orgasm— and the next, it was if he'd pulled the plug.

"What did you do?" She didn't know whether to be furious that he'd deprived her of satiating her lust or happy that he'd stopped her from release before he was inside her.

He ignored her question, but his knowing expression told her that while she was confused, he was aware of exactly what was going on. And he remained silent, apparently having no intention of clueing her in. When he went back to the silver bottle, again used the slick oil on her skin, she marveled at the time he was putting into their coming together.

"You're starting all over again?" Her tone rose in amazement. She'd been so close, so right on the edge—and then pffttt. Zero.

"Mmm."

Proving exactly how creative he could be, this time he ignored her breasts and the area between her legs. He spread the oil on her face, careful to keep it from her eyes. He smoothed it over her lips, and as she waited for the tingling sensation to begin anew, she recalled it had been much too long since their last kiss.

Leaving no part of her flesh untouched, he worked in the oil behind her ears, into her scalp, down her neck, and over her collarbone. She expected the same tingling icy/hot combination as before, but instead, her cells seem to stand up and shimmy. Her gaze flew to his hand. He was using the same bottle, but nevertheless the sensation was different.

Stronger.

Whatever had come out of that scarlet bottle must have changed her skin's reaction to the oil. And Blessed Stars, if before she'd been fire and ice, now she was sizzling.

Never in her life had she longed so badly for a man to touch her breasts or her mons. But the maddening Rystani ignored her, and when he flipped her facedown and applied the oil to her bottom, she almost cried in frustration. She wanted to lift her buttocks higher, spread her legs wider, guide his hand to where she was weeping with need.

Lust.

It's only lust.

You can't die from lust.

When he moved on to the backs of her thighs, she let out a sob. "Xander. Pleasssssse . . . I'm not used to waiting."

"When the need becomes too much for you, I will ease your discomfort with the scarlet bottle."

Oh . . . by . . . the goddess. He meant to build up her tension, incite her lust . . . and make it disappear. How many times would he repeat the cycle? She wanted to cry, hit him, but passion held her in its lusty grip. She wanted to scream at him, but the only sounds coming out of her mouth were tiny coos of encouragement.

Deep into *Boktai,* she was losing herself in the storm of need he'd created. No man had ever done such a thing to her. She hadn't ever imagined spending this amount of time taking care of a biological need.

He flipped her back so they faced each another. She licked her lips and tried to make him realize that what he was doing had no bearing at all on regeneration. "I can't stand another cycle of waiting. Delay is pointless."

"You don't understand." Again he took the scarlet bottle and used the unguent to cool her down. "Better?"

Again the tension eased from her, allowing her to think. He could do whatever he wished, whenever he wished. Knowing he intended to do a good job—if only so he didn't have to mate with her again soon— was causing conflicted feelings. Xander's skill and tenderness were changing her normal mating rhythm and lessening her irritation with the entire process of *Boktai.*

Perhaps it was because his lovemaking was all about her. Endekian men satisfied their own needs, and if the woman's cells regenerated, that was simply a byprod- uct of the process. But Xander was attempting to give her pleasure, and his attitude made a world of difference. Sure, he was commanding, demanding, dominating—but the choices he made were for her satisfaction and satiation.

After taking several calming breaths, she asked, "What don't I understand?

"Waiting increases your pleasure."

She shook her head. "You've taken away the tension." She wanted to wail, pound her fist, shake in rage. That he would take her right to the brink of the cliff but refused to allow her to plunge over was frustrating, infuriating, and had no sane rationale.

Xander grinned happily, rubbing his palms together. "The tension I took away . . ."

"Yes?" she prodded.

"It's *all* going to return at once, in one giant rush that's so powerful that you'll be thanking me for a week."

"What?" She'd never heard of such things. Her gaze shot to the bottles. Surely they had to be empty.

But then he held up a third golden bottle so tiny that she'd forgotten about it until now. "This is the nectar of heaven."

She thought he would place the newest liquid on her. But with a psi thought he made his suit transparent, revealing his beautiful body and bronzed skin. His shoulders were as broad as Sedan Mountain. His muscular chest tapered to a hard stomach and every part of him was equally gorgeous, masculine. Her nerve endings reacted to the stimulation of seeing him by dancing happily. His *tavis,* the Rystani word for "root of man," immediately stiffened. Without hesitation, he very carefully worked the oil over the part of him that would enter her.

She eyed him with curiosity. "The oil will give you pleasure?"

He shrugged. "Completing a task to my best ability gives me pleasure. Pleasing you will give me pleasure."

If she'd been a gambler, she would have bet he was finally going to enter her. But she was no longer needy. The wondrous tension was gone and she wanted to rage at him for stealing her pleasure.

But then his mouth angled over hers, and his fingers delved into her *yonia*. Fingers that were coated with the oil he'd just smoothed into his skin. And she moaned into his mouth as the tension came raging back, stronger than before. It was if he'd turned on her engines and flooded her with fuel. She revved with an intensity that would rocket her to the stars.

"Let me touch you," she growled into his mouth.

"No . . . Not yet.

7

Once Xander had coated his *tavis* with the last vial, her need linked with his on the most elemental of psionic, cellular levels. Since she couldn't control her psi, their connection wasn't mental. He'd had to rely on reading her body to know if he was arousing her. Between her dilated eyes, the hitches in her breathing, and her gasps, plus her hardened nipples, there could be no doubting her excitement. And once the chemical formula kicked in, it was if her body were calling to him and he no longer had to guess; he could know what she felt and what she wanted on a biological level.

Before he lost himself in the heat of mating, he adjusted his suit's filters to prevent him from impregnating her. Done with his preparations, he turned his attention back to Alara. He wasn't surprised that his body reacted to her. After all, what male could resist such beautiful golden curves and molten passion?

Before he'd understood that her biology triggered her need for sex, he'd been shocked by her behavior. No Rystani woman would act so immodestly. However, Alara had had no choice. A man could become accustomed to such a mating ritual with very little effort. Yet, as much as he enjoyed her lush body, he couldn't let her distract him from his mission. Hopefully, if he did a good job, if he took enough time with her and her cells fully regenerated, she wouldn't soon need him again.

Their voyage could be a long one and having Alara for his companion would be very sweet. He relished the way she'd accepted his taking control. Oh, she might have fought the idea at first, but she didn't deny her enjoyment. Her body had trembled under his hands.

He marveled at the texture of her skin, so golden, so soft, he could have spent hours stroking her, but he could read the impatience in her eyes. Since he didn't know her well enough to gauge how much waiting she required to fully regenerate, he'd wanted to make certain he upheld his part of their bargain. Between the increased sensations in hyperspace, her own biological drive, and the exotic oils, he'd hoped she was right where she needed to be. And now he knew. She was ready. Excited. On edge.

Xander had always loved adventure, and exploring this woman's body was fascinating. Kissing her pleased him. Her scent pleased him. Her marvelous golden breasts with luscious pink nipples that responded to his touch pleased him.

Now that he could literally feel her nerve cells calling

to him, it took all his willpower to hold back from plunging inside to heat her up one more time. Breaking their kiss, and immediately missing the exotic taste of her lips, he traced a path to her breasts. Taking the tiny bud between his teeth, he nipped and circled his tongue, enjoying her coos of pleasure. At the same time, he loosened his psi hold of her suit. Immediately, she writhed, and when she realized she was free, she reached for his *tavis*, grabbed him, wrapped her legs around his hips, and drew him inside her heat with a strength that surprised him.

Slick, hot, her tight muscles clenched him. Astonished at their strong connection, with her blazing touch stimulating his own heat, he wouldn't last long. With a psi thrust, he tried to regain control of her suit. But he'd become lost in her primal mating urge. Her hands grasped him, her legs locked around his hips, and he could not slow his excitement.

He held her shoulders and thrust into her, determined to hold back for as long as possible. He would take her higher, longer, harder. He would make certain she regenerated every cell.

Sweat beaded on his chest, his back, his brow, and his suit could barely keep up. She was riding him, urging him on with hands and lips and her legs wound around his waist with an enthusiasm that he easily matched.

Then his mouth found hers and the sweetness and spice of their coming together exploded. His own release was powerful, but with their nerve cells connected, he felt her shifting, shimmering, breaking, and shattering into a billion points of light.

He held on to her. Barely. Breath ragged, senses spinning, heart slamming his chest, he couldn't think.

He could only marvel at the exotic woman in his arms. As his pulse finally slowed and he relaxed, he drew her against him.

She tensed, then snuggled her head against his chest. Entwined, they slept.

With Xander rested and his mind once again in functioning order, he opened his eyes to find Alara staring at him. But he had no idea what she was thinking.

"How are you?" he asked, uncertain what type of conversation she expected. He for one, certainly hadn't anticipated enjoying her so much, or finding her skin so soft, her hair so silken.

She licked her lips, which seemed raw and parched. "I'm fine."

Her voice was raspy. With a quick psi order to the materializer, he called up a drink and pressed it into her quivering hands.

She sipped slowly at first, then finished the drink in long, graceful swallows. For a long moment, she kept her eyes downcast. After fortifying herself with a deep breath, she captured his gaze in hers.

"Thank you."

He quirked a grin and sat beside her on the shuttle's couch. "I suppose I should say the same."

The way she shrugged, the way she turned to the side, told him her pride had been wounded by her need to mate, by what her genetics forced upon her. He had the inexplicable urge to caress her chin, turn her face toward his and kiss away the shame, but he resisted. They'd had sex, not intimacy. He wouldn't overstep his bounds.

"Dr. Calladar, the interaction was pleasurable for

both of us. But you are on the road to recovery, and now more than ever, I require your full cooperation on this mission."

Before introducing her to his crew, they dined in the shuttle, giving him an opportunity to tell her about the spreading virus. As a scientist, she was clearly interested in the spread of the plague across the galaxy, and any lingering effects of their wild mating were washed away. When she spoke with concern for all their people, she sounded warm and compassionate, giving him hope for success.

But she finished her meal in silence, apparently deep in thought. He liked that she didn't need to fill the quiet with extraneous chatting. When the meal was done, she spoke simply. "I will do my best to help find a cure for us all. And again, I thank you for the regeneration. For keeping your word."

Xander kept his annoyance in check. Of course he'd kept his word. But perhaps the men on her world did not.

Their mating had been unhampered and adventurous, and yet Xander couldn't help his amazement at how much he'd enjoyed touching her and holding her. He'd never expected their encounter to give him so much pleasure—especially because she was an Endekian. And yet he was far from suffused with joy over the situation. She had done nothing wrong, of course. In fact, after she'd stated her needs, he'd given her little choice about how things progressed. So the problem didn't reside in her, but in him.

Coming to her, filling her needs, gave him satisfaction on a level he didn't understand. They'd shared pleasure, but they remained strangers. Perhaps that was what threw him off.

He'd taken other women, but none had been Endekian, of course. While he found dealing with different peoples and cultures fascinating, it could also be confusing.

With Alara, the experience had been different. While he could not place the blame on her for his discontent when she'd been quite clear that she'd accepted his attention for regeneration and regeneration only, he'd instinctively expected her to react afterward like a Rystani or a Terran—but she hadn't. Obviously he brought expectations into this sexual encounter that he hadn't anticipated—hadn't even known were implanted in his psyche. But she'd been so hot in his arms just a few hours ago, he hadn't figured that she'd return to acting like a stranger so quickly, as if they hadn't shared their bodies.

He tried to keep the discontent from his voice. "How do you live this way?"

"What do you mean?"

"Sharing sex for purely genetic reasons. With no feeling. No connection to the person in your bed."

"We didn't exactly use a bed," she quipped.

He frowned. "You know what I mean."

She glanced down briefly, then leveled her gaze at him, striking him with her clear emerald eyes. "It's the only way we know."

Her matter-of-fact answer speared him.

The thought of repeating the experience no longer seemed like a lark, and he wondered if he would come to think of mating with her as a duty. "How long until . . ."

"I need your services again?" She raised her brows, finishing his question. She sounded cold, composed and careful, almost brittle. Yet when he searched her eyes and looked deeper, he saw regret, perhaps hurt, and a flash of irritation—with him or herself, he couldn't be certain. "During our childbearing years, every other year female Endekians repeatedly go through *Boktai,* that's our predictable biological cycle. But it makes sense to theorize that since the object of sex is procreation, if the species are different, hence making impregnation more difficult, then mating might be required more often. I believe the more alien the male, the more often regeneration may be necessary."

And he'd thought that the more he satisfied her, the longer he'd made her wait, the more fully she'd regenerate. And the more time he'd have until she required his services again, the less she'd distract him from his mission. Apparently, he hadn't taken all factors into consideration and had been very wrong. He glared at her. "Define 'alien.'"

"I can't." Frustration entered her tone and irritation flashed in her eyes. "We have never been able to quantify the elements of *Boktai.* Certain pheromones play a role. As well as personal preferences. And perhaps there are issues at the cellular level that we have yet to discern. I don't know enough about Rystani physiology to make a prediction."

"You've fully regenerated?"

"Yes."

"Your psi is now back under your control?"

She nodded, her eyes full of secrets. He gestured to her body. "Why haven't you covered your nudity?"

"You wish me to do so?" It was if she'd dropped a shield over her face and emotions, and he had no idea what she was thinking from her businesslike tone.

He nodded. With a psi thought and no explanation for why she hadn't done so sooner, she changed her suit to a pink blouse and dark gray slacks. He was about to ask another question when his com beeped and he answered the summons. "Go ahead."

"Captain, we need you on the bridge."

After Xander had expressly asked not to be disturbed, Vax wouldn't have used the com unless there was an emergency.

Xander gestured Alara toward the shuttle's hatch. "We're on the way. Is there trouble with the Kwadii, again?"

The last time the *Verazen* had been in this quadrant of hyperspace, the Kwadii had towed the ship to their homeworld with a powerful clutch beam. However, with Zical at the helm, the *Verazen*'s crew had prevailed, and since then, the Federation had established an uneasy truce with the Kwadii.

"Captain," Vax said through the com system. "We have an unidentified ship heading toward us off the starboard bow."

Alara followed Xander to the bridge, eager for a distraction. After he had seen her at her most vulnerable during *Boktai*, she knew Xander would never think of her the same way again. Reduced to mindless raw passion, she hadn't been able to think or express how degrading she found her situation. Her blood pressure rose every time she considered that Xander was bound to remember her as brainless and perverse. It was bad enough with an Endekian male who understood the process, but a Rystani warrior likely couldn't comprehend that her brain was back to working intelligently. Xander would always wonder if she was about to lose herself in *Boktai*, if she could be thinking clearly the rest of the time. No doubt, he'd never take anything she said seriously again.

Recognizing the captain's eagerness to put the experience behind him and join his fellow crew members, she tried not to blame him for not understanding. She ignored the hurt of rejection that came afterward. By the stars, she was used to feeling more alone when she was with a man than when she was by herself. Xander was not so different from Endekian men in all respects. She didn't need him to spell out his feelings. What else could he feel but pure disgust?

After forcing her nerves to settle, she used the opportunity on the bridge to take in the starship, very likely her new home for some time to come. The circular bridge rested atop the rest of the ship. Viewscreens set in the *bendar* hull and around the perimeter showed off the beauty of hyperspace in a 360-degree circle. Toward the bow, stars streaked toward them, seemed to split around the sides of the ship, then disappeared behind them in a spectacular display of what appeared to be bursting lights of ribbon streamers that lit the blackness of space. She saw no planets in the starscape. Perhaps they were too small or passed by too quickly, and the lack of anything familiar aroused her scientific curiosity.

She'd seen holovids of space but now she was here. And it was awesome. The engines hummed and the air seemed crisper. Space seemed so vast compared to their tiny group on the ship. Yet while the spectacular view was daunting, it also excited her. Out here, anything seemed possible.

Once she looked into the forward right viewscreen, she understood why the second in command, Vax, had summoned Xander. Sharing their hyperstream, but coming at them from the opposite direction, a tubular ship tumbled toward them, spinning erratically side-ways, as if totally out of control or piloted by a mad-man.

Surely they weren't about to crash? The odds of a collision in hyperspace had to be infinitesimal, with as little chance of occurrence as her having a real rela-tionship with a man, Endekian or otherwise.

Vax, another brawny Rystani warrior, with dark hair and amber eyes and an intense look on his handsome face, commanded his portion of the console with a competent air. Yet the moment the captain stepped onto the bridge, he changed position from the com-mand console to another station.

"Status, Vax?" Xander asked.

"All ship's systems are functional. Vidscreen is at maximum magnitude."

"Will we pass close enough to determine the ship's planet of origin?"

"It's too soon to calculate. I'm monitoring."

"Captain?" A Terran woman at the communication console placed a headset over her ears.

Alara had never met a Terran but she looked harm-less. The oldest member of the bridge crew, she hunched her gangly limbs over the console and frowned, the wrinkles around her eyes deepening. Alara found it difficult to hate the stranger on sight—even though she'd told Xander otherwise. She wasn't so narrow-minded and prejudiced as to hate an individual for the actions of terrorists.

"Yes, Shannon?" Xander said.

"I'm picking up a message."

"Must be background noise." Vax went over to her station. "We're in hyperspace. Ship-to-ship communi-cation isn't possible."

"Just because it's not possible for us," the communications officer disagreed, "doesn't mean other beings aren't capable of hyperspace communication."

The computer broke in. "Captain, ship-to-ship communication is theoretically possible. It requires a powerful transmitter, one small enough to carry onboard."

Alara didn't understand the science behind the discussion, but every schoolkid knew that hyperspace communications required a major power source. To communicate with their ships, Endekians had built a huge com base on their homeworld that drew power from their sun. Along popular trade routes, they'd built substations on asteroids and comets to boost additional power to their ships. Whatever technology was aboard that tumbling vessel had to be vastly superior to their own—and, therefore, should be considered dangerous.

"Captain, it's definitely a distress call." Shannon boosted the signal and cut in the audio until a tinny voice, muffled by crackles, hisses, pops, and whistles could be heard by all.

"Help. Assistance necessary. Help." The message kept repeating.

"Opinions?" Xander asked his crew, surprising Alara. An Endekian captain would consult only with his superiors. He would request orders to avoid making a decision where he could be held accountable for an error in judgment. Xander had done the opposite, asking his crew, a move an Endekian captain would consider weak.

"Captain, the message could be a trap," Vax suggested. "Last time we ran into another race in hyperspace our mission was delayed. We almost died on their world. I suggest after we jump into real space, we report the ship to Mystique and let the Federation deal with the distress call. Our mission is too important to stop."

"I disagree." The Terran shook her head.

"Shannon, please explain," Xander requested.

"It's a law of space to give aid in emergencies," Shannon replied. The Terran's attitude startled Alara. She'd hated Terrans for so long that hearing compassion come out of Shannon's mouth shocked her into wondering if the race might have some good traits, after all.

"You're referring to the Federation's *unwritten* law," Vax clarified. "Ranth, any chance the ship belongs to the Federation?"

"The technology is unfamiliar."

To Alara's surprise, Shannon kept arguing. "Their message is clearly asking for assistance. Even if the Federation sends a rescue team immediately, by the time it arrives, they'll likely be dead."

And what startled Alara even more than the Terran's compassion was that Vax seemed to take no offense that a subordinate disagreed with him in front of the captain. Was he so certain of his position that he had no fear that Shannon sought to usurp him in the captain's eyes? Or did he not care? Or was this simply standard procedure? Alara didn't know enough to judge but watched the interplay carefully, learning what she could.

"Cyn." Xander faced a green-skinned woman from the planet Scartar. "Is a hyperspace rescue possible?"

"I'm not certain, Captain. We've never attempted one before. If I rig a Kwadii clutch beam, we might tug the vessel aboard. It's small enough to fit."

"Do we have the specs and materials?" Vax asked.

"The problem's a lack of power." Cyn was likely the engineer. "A rescue will drain our systems."

"Scan the alien vessel," Xander ordered. "Does it have a power source we can modify and use?"

Cyn concentrated on her vidscreen. "Our scanners can't penetrate the hull. I've never seen material like that."

Ranth sounded impressed. "I'm detecting an incredibly efficient power source radiating outward from the hull."

"So why do they require help?" Xander asked.

"They could have a malfunction in navigation or steering or in their jump drive," Cyn suggested.

"We could bring the ship aboard only to have it blow up," Vax warned. "And we could drain our power source in a rescue attempt only to discover that we can't adapt the other ship's power for our own use."

As Alara watched the crew work together, her admiration for Xander increased. She liked how he sanctioned independent thought, encouraged his people to analyze, and belittled no one. His connection with his crew reminded her more of her working relationship with her friend Maki than a structured hierarchy where everyone covered their back and tried to look good in front of their superior in the hopes of winning a promotion. Although she found the give-and-take odd, she also liked the freedom.

She'd never suspected a crew could interact in such a manner, and couldn't understand why discipline didn't break down with such chaos—yet each of them performed their jobs. And the lack of animosity over the divergent viewpoints impressed her and attested to Xander's leadership skills. That he actually possessed the self-confidence to allow free discussion upped her opinion of him as much as the care he'd taken during their mating. She should have been unsurprised that his crew responded as she had—with respect.

So many times during her life, she'd had to hold her tongue to avoid calling attention to her nonconformist ideas. A female physiologist, one who specialized in genetics, was rare on Endeki and her search for a "cure" to control or put an end to *Boktai* had been considered absurd. Her research had often been mocked by her peers, who likened her quest to searching for a reason to stop eating. The prevailing attitudes might have isolated her if she hadn't built a good business and made many female friends. Her status and wealth had protected her, but aboard this vessel, she was very much alone and had unconsciously feared that the others would look down on her for her strange attitudes. But perhaps not. These people seemed more open-minded than Endekians.

It was clear that Xander would make the final decision on whether to attempt a rescue of the alien vessel and she wondered how he would choose. Unsure what she would do if the command decision were hers, she was glad she was a scientist and not a starship captain with the weight of saving the Federation from a plague on her shoulders.

Yet he seemed to handle his responsibility and the burden of his mission with impressive ease. He was clearly determined to do his best, and she couldn't help but see a certain nobility in him—even if he'd had to kidnap an enemy and work with her to succeed.

Xander seemed to have no difficulty issuing orders. "Shannon, send out a signal and monitor to see if there's a response. Vax, assign a security team to the shuttle bay in case we bring the alien ship aboard. Cyn, estimate how long it will take to assemble the clutch beam."

"Captain," Shannon said, "I've hailed the alien ship, but there's no response."

"Keep trying. Check all channels and frequencies."

Cyn stood and exited the bridge. "I'm heading down to engineering. When I have an estimated time of completion, I'll let you know." The green-skinned woman walked with a confident sway of her hips that emphasized her femininity. Under her breath she appeared to be singing and no one else seemed to find that odd. When Alara caught her eye, she nodded a friendly greeting but didn't miss a note.

It seemed peculiar to Alara to be in the middle of all the decision-making and have nothing to do. While the others worked, she allowed her inner eye to focus on Xander and his crew. Alara's special skill didn't work like hearing or sight—she had to consciously turn on her vision and then, instead of faces, she saw DNA coding.

She expected to see normal activity, healthy membranes, mitochondria organelles involved in cellular respiration. But around the cell nuclei of every crew member, she saw a haze that indicated DNA infection and breakdown, all in various stages of the disease. Xander's sickness was the least advanced, the woman officer in charge of communications, Shannon, seemed the worst.

Alara suspected the Terran had been the first to pick up the plague and had spread it to the crew. No doubt she already had it, too.

Alara must have had an odd look on her face as she surveyed the damaged DNA, a breakdown unlike anything she'd seen before, because Xander joined her and spoke quietly so as not to disturb the others.

"Are you all right?"

That he had made time to ask about her in the middle of a crisis astounded her, and that he could hone in so keenly on her mood made her wonder if they'd become more attached to each other during *Boktai* than she'd realized. Usually it took many sexual encounters to tune in to a specific partner. The genetics of Endekian females required that eventually, the tuning between male and female become so complete that only a chosen mate's essence could regenerate his spouse. That's why after the Terran terrorists had killed her father, her mother had died. That's why Alara was careful not to regenerate too often with one mate.

But if Xander was already reading her so well, that might mean his essence was particularly compatible with hers. Or that she was paranoid about dying the same painful way her mother had. Or perhaps Xander just needed a distraction—or he'd simply read her expression.

"I'm fine."

"Then what's wrong?"

During an emergency, she had no intention of revealing that his crew was infected. Nothing could be done, since they didn't possess a cure. Turning back wasn't an option, either. Not when it was quite likely that every crew member would be similarly infected.

She shook her head. "Nothing that can't wait. However, when you have a chance, we need to speak privately."

"Captain." Cyn's voice over the com interrupted their conversation. "I can modify our clutch beam within twenty minutes, but employing the Kwadii device will leave us with only enough power to maintain life support. There won't be enough *magtites* left to jump out of hyperspace."

"Understood. Rig the beam and wait for my order."

"Acknowledged."

Xander searched Alara's face as if seeking clues to what had previously disturbed her. "If you'd like to settle into your quarters, Ranth will guide you."

And miss all the excitement? She might not have a task but she was enjoying watching the action, even if she had been abducted. "If I'm not in the way, I'd prefer to stay here."

"Sure."

Relief that he wouldn't press her about the DNA problem right now eased the tension from her shoulders.

"Captain." Shannon's voice remained steady, but Alara could hear the thread of excitement in the Terran's tone. "I've established communication. Correction, *he's* established communication."

"Put him through," Xander ordered.

The alien's weak voice came over the com. "Clarie requires help. Clarie's ship broken. You fix Clarie?"

"Clarie, can you tell us about your power source?" Xander asked.

"Clarie explorer. Clarie not engineer. Clarie die if you not fix ship."

"Clarie, we would like to help. But if we save you, we will not have enough power to jump back into normal space."

"Rescue Clarie. Ship broken. Clarie need help."

Xander drew his hand across his throat. Cyn silenced the intership com and signaled they had privacy.

Xander fiddled with his vidscreen. "Ranth, are the translators working?"

"Suit and ship translators are fully functional. The

being known as Clarie may be injured. Out of his head.
Or he may normally communicate by means other than
speech."

As the onboard computer made suggestions to explain the alien's muddled message, Vax paced. "Cyn?
How long until the clutch beam's operational?"

"Two minutes."

"Shannon," Xander ordered. "Try to get more information from Clarie about his ship's power source."

"Aye, sir."

Alara liked the calm manner in which Xander approached the problem. Although the tense situation on
the bridge required multitasking skills, he stayed professional and projected confidence.

"Captain." Shannon held one hand to her headset
but her gaze searched for and found Xander's. "Clarie
says if we don't rescue him very soon, he will die."

"Understood."

A muscle in Xander's jaw clenched, the only indication of his stress. He had to make a command decision
and he had to do it soon. The logical choice would be to
continue their mission, a mission whose success or failure would determine if billions of Federation beings
lived or died. And yet, Xander had surprised her too
many times today for her to predict what he'd decide.

So, like everyone else, she waited for his order.

8

"Let's play a game called hide-and-find."

Kirek believed the Terran game would suit his purpose of exploring the residence, especially if modified to jibe with Lataka's sexual interest. "I'll hide, and when you find me you get a reward."

"What kind of reward?" She eyed him with budding enthusiasm.

He winked at her and employed his most charming grin, knowing exactly what she wanted—more sex. In the short time he'd been on Endeki, he'd adjusted to the concept of *Boktai*, and planned to use her hormone-induced interest in him to gain an advantage.

Kirek's recent behavior would have been unacceptable to his strict Rystani parents. Although he had no choice in the matter, even if he hadn't been a hostage, he wasn't certain he could have resisted the learning experience Lataka offered so freely.

At home, Kirek obeyed his parents and followed their customs. But now that he was on Endeki, he would follow Endeki rituals and etiquette. His tone sounded coaxing, as if he were flirting with a Rystani life mate, not one of his captors. "After you find me, you can claim whatever reward you like."

"If we didn't play your game, I could have my reward now." She bit her bottom lip, displaying indecision. Meanwhile, she ran a possessive hand over his chest.

"True." He grabbed her wrist, stopping her from going lower to fondle his *tavis*. However much he enjoyed her caresses, he also had set himself a task that required exploration of Drik's home. "But wherever you find me is where you'll have me. And I promise you won't be disappointed."

"All right." She grinned and rubbed her hands together in a childish gesture. He reminded himself there was nothing childish about her appetites. When it came to sexuality, Lataka was greedy and insatiable, but he'd found himself enjoying her eagerness. Reminding himself her patience wouldn't last long, he'd have to remember to let her find him relatively quickly, especially if he wanted to play this game again.

"Cover your eyes with your hands and count to fifty," he instructed.

"Now what?" She did as he asked and peered at him through parted fingers.

"Don't peek. When you reach fifty, you come looking for me."

He hoped she would wait that long. The spoiled daughter of Drik, Lataka was accustomed to her whims being fulfilled in an instant.

Her lips curved into smile. "My favorite place for fun is the courtyard garden."

"I'm picking my hiding place—not you." He swatted her bottom with affection. "Think creatively and no peeking."

Kirek used his psi to move away from her at the speed of thought. The places he wanted to search would not be romantic. But he had only so much freedom, so he expended a considerable amount of mental energy to search quickly.

"One. Two," she counted and giggled. "Three. Four."

He sped down a hallway and used his psi to fool the door's locking mechanism and to deactivate the alarm. Once inside the chamber, he observed towering urns of Endeki flowers that ranged in color from burned maroon to garish crimson. Colorful blue and purple leaves and deep green vines crawled over a monstrous dining table that looked so old he wondered if the residence had been built around it. As if waiting for Drik's presence, gigantic gourds, overflowing with fruits and pastries, flanked silver plates and a bottle of rare Denubion wine rested on ice in a platinum bucket on the matching sideboard.

Doubting he'd find sensitive data in here, Kirek departed the room. Back in the hall, he heard Lataka counting. "Twenty. Twenty-one. Twenty-two."

He zipped down a different hallway and randomly unlocked another door. This room appeared to be a stage for seduction. Soft music, a string and Zenon concerto, poured from the speakers and blended with the pounding of the surf on the holographic 3-D vidscreen. A Rystani glow stone sat in the fireplace grate, causing Kirek to stop and examine it. He'd been taught that glow stones were unique to Rystan. So what was a glow stone doing in Drik's residence on Endeki?

His curiosity rocketed. Glow stones emitted heat

and light and possessed a natural nuclear energy formation. When lobbed from cannons, the glow stones exploded like man-made weapons. Ten thousand years before, his people had destroyed ninety percent of Rystan and almost all their population in a war that employed glow stones as the primary weapon.

But glow stones never worked when taken from Rystan—they always exploded with atomic force. The scientific explanation had to do with planetary magnetic kinetics keeping the atomic ionization stabilized. Crouching in front of the glow stone, Kirek placed his hand on the smooth surface that reminded him of his childhood and home, a planet now under Endeki occupation.

Sure enough, the warmth flooded into Kirek's palm, exactly as he remembered. He didn't understand how it was possible for the glow stone to exist here and wished he had access to Ranth.

But he couldn't waste more time thinking. According to the time clock in his head, he had only a few more moments before Lataka left her position to search for him.

Kirek headed for the courtyard Lataka had mentioned and immediately understood why she'd suggested this location for seduction. When he'd stepped from the residence, elaborately shaped hedges greeted him. Paralleling the moss-covered walk, a bubbling creek filled with jillyfish misted the air on a light breeze. The moss soon gave way to an open expanse of *marbellite* tiles that surrounded a quadruple-tiered fountain. Tropical plantings and enormous cages filled with exotic singing birds made the large area private. Covered with flowering vinelike greenery, an arched bower welcomed him with scented burning tapers and deeply padded *bendar* loungers. He grinned and settled into a lounger, content he'd found the perfect place to wait for Lataka—and perhaps, create a new game that would help him discover why the glow stones were on Endeki, and how the aliens had found a way to keep them stable.

"Prepare to initiate clutch beam." Xander saw the doubt in Vax's eyes. Sometimes a captain didn't have time to explain an action that would place the crew in danger. Sometimes his orders demanded secrecy. His crew would have obeyed without knowing his reasoning, but Xander also considered the crew his friends. If they were going to die because of his decision, they had the right to know why.

"Whatever disabled that ship could be waiting out there for us. In addition, if he has a superior form of power, we might adapt it to our systems and shorten our journey to the rim."

"Clutch beam ready for deployment." Cyn's voice came over the com from engineering.

"Activate," Xander ordered, watching the vidscreen and praying it would work. Leaving their ship bereft of power and also failing to rescue Clarie would be a disaster.

The clutch beam, made up of magnetized particles of energy, streamed through hyperspace in a spiral of swirling silver light. Snaking toward the spinning ship, the beam actually narrowed as it extended, due to the peculiarities of hyperspace. Without Ranth's guidance and superior calculating abilities, the procedure wouldn't have been possible. In hyperspace, the laws of normal physics simply didn't apply—there was a whole science of higher mathematics to explain the other-worldly phenomena.

"Power status?" Xander leaned forward over his console as the beam reached the three-quarter point to the alien ship.

"Fifty percent and draining," Ranth said.

"Do we have enough power to pull the ship into our shuttle bay?"

"It's going to be close, Captain. The two ships are moving toward each other and that should help."

Xander considered cutting off the beam while they still had enough power to jump from hyperspace. So many lives rested on his decision. His mission on La-pau remained critical. He was risking much for a stranger. Then again, Clarie was coming from the direction they sought to go. And knowing the mishap the alien had faced might help them survive.

"Power down to twenty-five percent," Ranth informed him.

The clutch beam spiraled around the alien ship. And like an insectoid caught on glued paper, the ship was caught by the beam.

"Retract." Xander held his breath.

"Power fifteen percent."

"Ranth, power estimates?"

"Still uncertain."

Xander didn't usually second-guess his decisions. But he was a hairbreadth away from cutting the alien ship loose. If they couldn't save him, there was no point in wasting the very last of their power.

Sweat beaded on his brow and his suit could barely keep up. He glared at the vidscreen, heart pounding. Was he making the biggest mistake of his entire career?

Was he jeopardizing his mission and the faith the people at home had in him for a stranger?

Stress poured through Xander. And suddenly, his mind snapped. He floated above the bridge, and looked down at his crew. They were all going about their jobs as if nothing unusual had occurred. Vax monitored engineering from his vidscreen. Shannon continued her communication with Clarie, informing him of their progress. And Alara stared at him. Him, standing by the others and clutching the console. But his mind was no longer in his body.

Stars!

Following the tractor beam, he flew straight toward the alien ship. He should go back. His crew needed him. The Federation needed him.

Coward.

With a sudden snap, his mind returned to his body. Under the abrupt return of weight to muscle and mass, he staggered. Blinked. What in the seven rings of Rangor had just happened? Was he going insane from the pressure? Was he unfit to command? Once before he'd experienced the dichotomy of his body staying behind while his mind escaped. The last time he'd been a half-grown boy. The Endekians had been torturing him to make him reveal the location of his village. The pain had been incredible. So he'd fled.

But this time, he had no excuse. He was a grown man. The only pain he suffered was that of command. Still, against his will, he'd run away like a child, floated from his responsibilities as he soared right through the hull.

Now was not the time for analysis. The alien ship was almost aboard.

"Power at two percent," Ranth said.

"You all right?" Alara asked, and Xander realized she must have seen him stagger.

He nodded but didn't look her way. No one else appeared to have noted his lapse and for that he was thankful.

Cyn controlled the delicate rescue operation from engineering. "Opening shuttle bay doors."

"Purple alert. Power less than one percent." Ranth's tone didn't change.

Purple warning lights flashed. Alarms blared.

Xander shut off the distracting lights and noise. They couldn't afford the power loss. "Have we got a lock on the ship?"

"Life support on emergency generators." Vax leaned over his vidscreen and shut down several duplicate systems to save energy.

"Got him," Cyn told him as the shuttle bay doors closed.

Xander let out the air he'd been holding in a quiet rush. "I'm heading to the shuttle bay. Vax, the bridge is yours."

Did you see that?

What?

A third-level transformation.

That lasted less than two seconds? I'm not impressed.

You should be. They are capable of evolving.

Only under stress. It means nothing.

Don't deny you witnessed adaptation to a higher mental plane.

The fish on Fantos Prime turn color when they are

frightened. It doesn't mean they've evolved or are capable of doing it of their own volition.

Such impatience. I'm telling you, they have the wherewithal to save themselves. To save us.

Bah. One creature among billions goes to a higher level for two seconds and you celebrate. It's not enough to combat the gathering forces. It would be kinder to put an end to the suffering now.

I'm not interested in kindness. I'm interested in survival. You will follow my thoughts. All they need is a giant shove in the right direction.

We're all running out of time.

So I'll push harder.

Alara followed Xander from the bridge, half expecting him to send her to her quarters. Curious to see the alien ship and the being aboard, she hoped she might be of some help on this journey beyond her ability to read DNA. Alara had always worked hard. Not having a position and a task made her feel useless. She might not have come aboard of her own accord, but now that she was here, she'd promised to join the crew in return for his essence. And keeping her word meant she could be worthwhile and have something to do.

Xander finally spoke as they walked down a brightly lit hallway. "You wanted to tell me something?"

So he hadn't forgotten their discussion on the bridge. She sighed, knowing she couldn't keep the bad news to herself any longer.

"Everyone aboard your ship has the virus. Shannon's DNA has deteriorated the most and may start affecting her soon."

"Affecting her how?" Xander stopped, turned to her, his stare hard and focused. It was unfortunate it had taken such bad news to make him look at her.

"She'll get sick." She held his gaze, suspecting he was asking her something she didn't understand.

"Will she hallucinate?"

"I'm no expert on Terran physiology, but I doubt it—at least not until the end stages." She cocked her head, puzzled. "Why?"

Xander shrugged. "I'll need to know when she's no longer able to perform her duties."

Alara had the distinct impression that Xander was hiding something. She wondered if he had cause to believe Shannon was hallucinating, but the Terran had seemed fine to her when she'd been on the bridge. Xander started walking again as if to cut off further questions, and his long legs ate up the distance so quickly, she almost had to run to catch up. "Do you have a healer aboard?"

"Why? Are you hurt? We have an automated—"

"Perhaps I could assume that task. While I'm not a trained healer, your computer can help with the diagnosis and perhaps I could study the DNA breakdown?"

"You will help us?"

Hadn't she given her word to do so? Or perhaps all he could remember was her begging for his touch. She could barely recall what she'd said. Perhaps she had deliberately blocked out the memory of her words, but she recalled how gentle his hands could be, how he'd created a blaze in her that had suffused her with bliss. Too bad he now judged her by that mindless reaction.

When he'd told her during their meal that the virus had spread throughout the Federation and would kill her own people, she'd become affected on a personal level. For him to think she wouldn't help her own dying people showed how little he thought of her. Pain sliced her, and it shocked her how deep the cut went. Perhaps he wasn't so different from other men after all.

His tone turned harsh, accusatory. "How do I know you won't hurt Shannon? You've already told me that you'd celebrate if every Terran died."

"I may have spoken . . . hastily. Shannon's concern for a being she doesn't know has altered my thinking."

"Really?"

Ignoring her hurt, accustomed to fighting for what she wanted, she held out her hand and grimaced to see the deteriorating DNA. "Besides, I've already caught the disease. It's spreading faster and wider than a radiation storm." She scowled at Xander. "Maybe I should relax for as long as I have left and die along with the rest of you."

"Was that sarcasm?"

"Does an atom have a nucleus?"

"You really want to help?"

"I really want to live."

He eyed her with renewed interest, his expression curious. "You seem . . . different."

How dare he be so rude. She might need him during *Boktai,* but her cells had regenerated and her brain had returned to normal. "Don't be insulting."

"Hey, that was a compliment."

She perused his face and saw genuine bewilderment. "This is only the second conversation we've had where my hormones weren't overloaded." And the first time, after mating, she hadn't yet fully recovered from the experience.

"Oh." He stared at her, his bronzed face turning a shade of burned red.

She refrained from thinking about or asking which way he liked her better. Some things she didn't need to know. "Even if you doubt the sincerity of my desire to help others, self-preservation means that my helping your crew will help me and my people."

Xander nodded and gestured for her to walk beside him down the hallway. "Let's go meet our new guest."

Xander met his security team in the shuttle bay. The alien vessel rested beside their own planetary transport vehicle, but took up only a quarter of the space. Would such a small ship have a strong enough power source that they could adapt it to their needs? Had stopping to rescue a stranger when it might cost them the mission been the right thing to do?

Xander might never know. Whoever was inside might step out and shoot him. Or eat him. Without Ranth's sensors being able to penetrate the alien hull, he could only go by what he saw, and the shiny silver ball that reflected their own images back at them looked like no space vessel that he recognized. However, the ship he'd seen tumbling in space appeared to have had a tubular shape, while this object in his bay appeared perfectly spherical.

"Ranth, did the ship change shape after it arrived?"

"It's possible. My sensors are unable to determine the metal's composition. But hyperspace is infamous for distorting sensory data, especially in dust clouds. However, the power source radiating from the hull that I detected earlier disappeared when the clutch beam grabbed the ship. He probably shut down the engines."

"Are we going in?" Alara asked, her tone impatient, her eyes bright with curiosity.

"Do you see a hatch?" Xander countered.

Alara had yet to show fear of death, but when she stepped toward the ship, her courage astounded him.

Surprise didn't stop him from grasping her upper arm, tugging her back and noting once again how soft her golden skin was. Touching her caused sensual memories to flow, memories he couldn't dwell on at the moment, but ones he'd never forget. "Let's wait."

"For what?" Her mouth drew up in one corner, showing aggravation. "Or have you forgotten we're dying and running out of time to save the universe?"

He ignored her quip and motioned for the security team to split in half, each to circle the ship from opposite directions, before turning his attention back to her. "If I'd known you had such a great sense of humor, I would have snatched you sooner."

"If I'd known you were so careful, I'd have brought along a herding prod to zap you into action."

"If it is action you want, I can show you to my quarters."

"I'm certain I'll be quite sick of them before this **voyage is over.** And I haven't agreed to spend all my time with you." Her banter had turned serious.

He recalled earlier when he'd mentioned she'd seemed different, and wondered if she'd been insulted. He reminded himself to keep a wary eye on her—as an Endekian, she had yet to overcome his distrust of her people. He still had too many mental scars from Endekians.

So she might share her beautiful body with him, but he would never forget her race. Yet she was full of surprises. Alara had an interesting sense of humor— except when it came to *Boktai* and sex. When those topics were broached, she turned stiff as *bendar*.

The previously seamless metal of the alien ship hissed and a rounded hatch opened outward. His men raised their stunners and held their ground. A light, so bright Xander had to adjust the psi filter in his suit to protect his eyes, shone from the interior and prevented him from seeing inside.

"*Krek*," Alara swore. "If the alien's trying to impress me by giving me a headache, it's not working."

Xander restrained his grin. Alara could go from prickly to sarcastic to courageous and back so fast he couldn't predict what she'd do next. Sometimes humor, especially sarcasm, didn't translate well, but he was having no difficulty following her words. He hoped he had as little trouble with the alien.

Musical horns trumpeted, as if to make them aware of the being's importance. At least Xander hoped the noise wasn't language because he found the clangs irritating.

"I wonder if they built that noisemaker with an off button?" Alara scowled, obviously finding the sound as unpleasant as he did.

The music's jarring beat quickened. At the buildup, Xander steeled himself, expecting someone to exit; he hoped the creature was humanoid. Although the Federation's members were comprised of a variety of intelligent species, birds, rare reptiles, and even fish, or beings like the Zenonites and the Osarians that were difficult to classify, the vast majority of races resembled Terrans, Endekians, and Rystani, taking humanoid form.

"Maybe that's an invitation." Alara tried to advance toward the ship.

Again, he held her back. "Maybe not."

Floating out of the ship in sets of three, clouds of

multihued lights shimmered, the color changing from aquamarine to *cinbar* to deep jadeite green.

"Ranth? Are those clouds . . . or our aliens?" Xander asked.

Alara shook her head. "I see no DNA in the mist. That's merely part of the show."

Xander bristled. "This is a rescue operation, not a musical holovid production."

Alara laughed, her tone warm and alive and very much amused. "Then I suggest you tell that to your guest."

9

Fascinated by the unknown, Alara yearned to approach the alien craft. Freed of Endeki's gravity, she also seemed free of her normal caution. Without the restraints placed on her by her culture and her world, she wondered what kind of woman she could be out here in space.

The future suddenly seemed wide open. Interesting. Liberating.

With her cells regenerated, she couldn't account for her impulsive curiosity, but she hadn't left only her cautious nature back on Endeki; she seemed more confident, more curious and open, more free to think about herself. And alien DNA interested her. Excited her.

Alara tried to shake Xander's hand from her arm. "You risked all our lives to save Clarie and now you don't want to go say hello?"

Shrugging off his strong hand worked as well as trying to put off regeneration. His grasp remained firm, keeping her right by his side. "Federation first contact requires that we follow certain protocols."

"There's not going to be a Federation if—"

A short humanoid, with a prominent head that rotated in 360-degree circles, shuffled out of the hatch and down a ramp. With his overly large head capped by two antennae, lack of a discernible neck, coal-black eyes, and a rounded body with very short limbs and pearl-white arms sticking out of his bright blue robe, he reminded her of a snowman that she and her mother had built during a rare trip to Endeki's south pole.

"Clarie lost. Clarie lonely. Clarie need friends." His tone blared from his diminutive body, and Xander motioned his security team to remain in place. With dignity, he strode forward to greet the alien.

Alara advanced alongside him, relieved and pleasantly surprised when Xander didn't insist she stay put. When Xander didn't answer the alien, she spoke softly. "Hi, Clarie. I'm Alara. This is the captain, Xander."

Beside her Xander bristled and she wondered if she'd violated protocol. But surely saying hello and introducing oneself couldn't be a bad thing.

Clarie dropped to his angular knees and bowed his head until his forehead touched the floor, his antennae flopping forward. He modulated his volume to match hers. "Clarie grateful. Clarie happy—happy for rescue. Clarie want new friends."

The creature seemed harmless enough. When he straightened she noted that he carried a tiny four-legged fur-covered animal with big brown eyes and a long tail on his shoulder. The creature remained still, not even blinking, its tail lightly flicking over Clarie's head, neck, and back, occasionally winding around his delicate antennae.

With her inner eye, she focused on Clarie's DNA. She looked below the skin to the skeleton, deeper past a host of internal organs she couldn't identify to focus on his cellular structure. And barely restrained a gasp. She'd never seen any creature like Clarie. His DNA made no sense. He had double and triple and quadruple helixes, chromosomes in combinations so complex her brain reeled. And he possessed anatomical structures on the subatomic level she'd never seen and so could only guess at their functions. Who was he? What was he?

"Clarie happy to meet Xander and Alara."

Xander gestured to his craft. "Can you tell us what damaged your ship?"

Clarie's head swiveled. The creature on his shoulder continued to stare at them, but loosened its tail hold of Clarie's antennae or the fragile-appearing organs might have broken.

"Clarie not captain. Clarie only passenger. Clarie asleep."

Obviously Xander couldn't be pleased with Clarie's vague answer, but by his demeanor, she wouldn't have known of his displeasure. He remained motionless, his voice calm, his expression pleasant and neutral. "Can your ship's systems tell us what happened?"

"Systems? I do not understand."

"Can we go inside your ship?"

"Yes. Yes. Follow Clarie." The being zipped back up the ramp on his short legs that churned with amazing speed, and he disappeared into the spherical ship.

They followed him into the alien ship at a more sedate pace. Alara had no idea what they'd find inside—more creatures like Clarie, or other beings that might attack, or a welcoming band. As she ducked to cross over the threshold, she thought that the hatch might snap shut behind them and trap them inside. It didn't, and she tried to settle her nerves and braced for the sight of strange objects. But the alien machines, monitors, and controls she'd expected were not there.

The entire ship was empty—like a hollow eggshell with shiny metal walls.

She stared at the shimmering hull, ignoring their distorted reflections and focusing deep below the surface to the elemental structure. She'd expected metal, circuitry, engineering systems. Not living cells. Cells that resembled Clarie. "Captain, this ship has the same DNA as Clarie."

"What?" Xander stopped and stared at her as if she'd lost her mind.

"It's almost as if the ship's part of him. Or he is part of the ship. We're inside a living creature."

Clarie ignored her comments. The animal on his shoulder scampered down his arm and dropped to the floor. It stood on its hind legs and chirped, almost as if begging.

"Yes. Clarie feed Delo." Clarie reached for his pet and the creature jumped into his palm. He stroked Delo and the little guy's fur turned from brown to orange. Alara had heard of such animals. On Terra certain lizards changed color in different kinds of light. On Bomar, marsupials altered their fur color with their feeding cycles. And she'd heard of a Federation race whose skin changed color as their emotions altered. But she'd never seen such an animal up close on Endeki.

Curious about the biochemical change on the DNA level of his pet, she focused her inner eye on Delo, but she couldn't read him at all. She saw nothing. No cells. No chromosomes. No mitochondria. It was if Delo were wisps of smoke, or a holosim, created from light and complex computer software.

Men on Federation planets and luxury starships often used holosims to satisfy their sexual urges. So bringing a holopet into space to avoid loneliness wasn't inconceivable. But why would a holosim require food?

More importantly, why was Clarie's cell structure exactly the same genetic material as the hull of his ship?

An outrageous theory began to build in her mind, but she kept silent, wanting to mull over the ramifications. If Clarie and the ship were one being, and if the ship were damaged, could Clarie's mind be damaged? Was that why his simple speech pattern resembled a child's? Or maybe he was a child. She wanted to ask Ranth, and made a mental note to consult him later.

"Where are your engines?" Xander asked.

"No engines." Clarie continued stroking Delo and his orange-furred pet emitted a hum, the sound low and pleasant.

Xander frowned. "Where's the power?"

"Power?" Clarie shook his head. "Delo is hungry. Clarie must feed Delo." Clarie shuffled over to the wall, pushed his finger into the shimmering metal. His pet immediately glowed a luminescent blue-green.

If Clarie was feeding Delo, the food seemed to come out of the ship, through Clarie's body and flow into Delo. Perhaps there was power here after all.

She had to give Xander credit. Although Clarie wasn't answering his questions, Xander kept his demeanor steady—even in the face of the glowing pet.

"Our ship uses power to travel through hyperspace. When we rescued you, we used our spare power, but our scanners noted you had plenty. I was hoping we could modify your energy source to replace what we lost."

The alien's expression remained unfazed. He pulled his finger from the wall and Delo's glow slowly faded. "Clarie only passenger. Not engineer."

"Where were you going?" Alara asked.

"Everywhere. Nowhere. Clarie on a learning voyage."

"Where are you from?" Xander asked.

"Clarie from ship." His answer made Alara wonder if her theory could be correct—that Clarie and his ship were one being and that if the ship was damaged so were Clarie's thought processes.

"Ranth, is the translator working properly?" Xander asked.

"All my components are fully functional. However, I have shut down unnecessary functions to save power. In addition, your suits and Clarie's are in working order."

"Clarie has a suit?" Alara didn't think the being had come from Federation space. Ranth had neither recognized his technology nor known what planet he was from, or the computer would have informed them. But she'd never heard of anyone from outside the Federation who wore a suit. Yet it was not inconceivable that the Perceptive Ones had left suit-manufacturing equipment on other worlds far from Federation space.

"Clarie now needs rest." The alien backed against a wall in his ship. He sagged. The antennae on his head went from upright to slumped. He turned his head toward his pet and shut his black eyes.

Xander knelt beside Clarie, his face full of concern. Even on his knees, he towered over the alien. "Are you injured?"

When Clarie didn't answer, she did. "I think he's asleep."

Delo sat quietly on Clarie's shoulder. His color had lost its luminescent sparkle and had turned back to brown. Grooming himself with a long pink tongue, Delo ignored them.

Xander lowered his voice as if he didn't wish to disturb the sleeping Clarie. "Want to take a guess how long he'll sleep?"

"I have no idea. But I'd like to do some research." She stepped out of the alien craft, excited about the biological puzzle. Sure, she missed her laboratory and her work, but she couldn't restrain her excitement and finally admitted to herself that if not for her fear of forming a permanent bond with Xander through *Boktai,* she would have been glad to be here.

"I know just the place." Xander followed her out of the ship. The head of security approached and the captain gave orders quietly. "Stand guard. Don't approach Clarie and notify me the moment he awakens."

"Understood."

Xander slipped his arm through hers. "I have a surprise for you."

Alara stiffened. Whenever her father had had a surprise for her mother, it was usually followed by tears and angry words. Her mother had loved her job as a teacher. But her father had wanted her to stay home, tend the house, cook, clean, and take care of him when he was there. One time her father's "surprise" had been to arrange for her mother's employer to fire her. Her father had been so satisfied with his surprise, wearing a look very similar to Xander's right now. Alara recalled her mother had been furious, but resigned to giving up the career she'd loved. At the memory, Alara steeled herself for an unpleasant experience or a confrontation.

As Xander led her through the ship, she saw new areas, but her nerves tensed with anxiety. The *Verazen* was larger than she'd originally thought. She saw game rooms, exercise bots, crew quarters that included common areas where people socialized. With the power shut down to the bare minimum, providing only life support, people entertained themselves by playing board games, throwing tiny balls at a spinning bull's-eye and even training for combat. Despite their dire circumstances, the crew's attitude remained positive and upbeat.

As they passed by, people said hello, nodded and waved, but continued with whatever they'd been doing. On an Endekian ship the captain's presence would have required salutes and bows. However, the less strict Federation regulations didn't seem to hurt morale or keep the crew from their duties. Each station was manned, the crew alert.

She suspected Xander was taking her to his quarters, where she needed to explain in private that her body would not be available to him at all times—only during *Boktai*. She thought she'd explained adequately, but apparently he either hadn't believed her or had misunderstood.

However, when Xander flung open a hatch, all previous thoughts fled. *Stars*. What had he done?

Inside the hatch was a laboratory that rivaled her own. No, it was her Endeki lab—moved in total to this ship. Every scientific instrument from her lab, her test equipment, her computers, all her precious experiments were on the *Verazen*.

She hurried between two counters and randomly yanked out a test sample. The control DNA she'd altered last week had failed to replicate without the *Boktai* chromosomes, the result exactly the same as the week before. She'd expected that he'd provide her a space in which to do her work—after all, he'd brought her on the mission for her expertise. But she was amazed that he'd saved her work on *Boktai* when he hadn't even known what it was.

She spun around on the balls of her feet to face him. "Why did you . . . ?"

He shrugged as if unaware how oddly he'd acted. "You said your work was important to you."

"I never imagined . . ."

He'd saved her work. Precious years of research. DNA mutations that showed promise. It was all here. Every cell. Every line. Every chain. Some of her experiments had taken years to grow and couldn't be duplicated without very specific genes she'd culled from rare mutations and had spliced into the DNA strands. She'd been especially hopeful of a few recent variations in the genetic coding on an aging chromosome. Being forced to leave them all behind had been almost as bad as when she'd lost her home during the terrorist attack. But he'd saved them—for no reason that would do *him* any good that she could discern. Her DNA research on *Boktai* had absolutely nothing to do with accomplishing his mission to find a cure for the virus. While her laboratory equipment would help his mission, he'd made room for her experiments, which was for her sake alone. If an Endekian male had acted with such kindness, she would have been suspicious that he wanted something in return.

But Xander's eyes twinkled and a corner of his mouth

turned into a smile, as if he'd enjoyed making her happy. "Maki helped move everything. She assured us that your samples would live."

"Oh . . . my . . . stars." She bit her tongue to make sure she wasn't dreaming and had the oddest impulse to hug the big Rystani. She couldn't go that far off kilter. "I don't know what to say. No one has ever done anything like this on my behalf."

He grinned wider, clearly pleased that his surprise had delighted her. When his demeanor was stern, his stubborn jaw and sharp cheekbones reminded her he was a warrior. But when he grinned, he seemed less combative, more approachable, more likable.

Even his tone mellowed. "It seemed a common courtesy to take your work with us."

"Even though you have no need for my research?"

He nodded. "I would never have forced you from your home against your will if the need hadn't been so urgent."

"Hmm. I think you enjoyed manhandling me," she teased, and appreciated how his pupils darkened with violet and deep scarlet sparks.

"I can't deny you are a pleasant handful."

She thought he might reach for her, draw her into his arms, and she wouldn't have objected. The big man had gentle hands and an easy touch. He'd stroked her skin with care, as if she'd been made of delicate cloth. But he didn't touch her. Instead, he gestured to her lab equipment. "This is my way of making up for some of your inconvenience."

"Words alone cannot express my thanks." She swallowed the lump in her throat. He'd saved her work. A stranger had thought more of her research than her own people.

Without stopping to think, she flung herself into his arms, embraced him. She was pleased when his arms closed around her. Tilting back her head, she raised her lips to his and tugged his mouth down to hers.

His eyes widened with surprise, sparked hotter with passion. She might have made the first move, but he didn't hesitate to angle his mouth over hers, taking all she offered. And oh, stars, could the Rystani kiss. Her head swam, her breath raced, and her heart leaped.

When his powerful arms gathered her closer, when her chest pressed against his heat, when her hips cradled his pelvis, when his powerful thighs met with hers, she wondered why the big Rystani made her feel so free as he took care of her wants and needs.

When she finally pulled back for air, her lips tingled and her blood smoldered. As if knowing exactly how much he appealed to her, he teased her, his words soft and goading. "If you would like to thank me in another way, I would not object."

From the heat in his gaze, he could mean only one thing. He wanted sex. Or did he? After that kiss, she supposed he had every right to think she would give him more. Heart pounding, breath hitching in her chest, she wondered why she'd felt compelled to kiss him and why she'd enjoyed herself so much. Her cells were not in need of regeneration. Yet her pulse had escalated and her blood still hummed.

Careful to keep her voice on an even keel, she cocked her head to the side. "How else can I thank you?"

His eyes burned with a violet-red glow. He obviously had known exactly what she'd been thinking—that she wasn't ready to mate again. The arrogant man seemed to enjoy keeping her off balance. "Share dinner with me."

"Of course. Where?"

"In my cabin, if that is acceptable to you."

His cabin. She had so little understanding of Rystani culture, since they'd been an enemy for so long. What she had heard about Rystan was likely government propaganda, since what she'd learned so far was that as fierce and stubborn as Xander could be, he was also kind and open-minded.

"Where will I sleep?" she asked, curious about how she'd fit in with the *Verazen*'s crew. They were all so different from her. She'd met few offworlders in her time, but after encountering Clarie and Xander's bridge crew, she couldn't wait to explore the other cultures on board.

Xander pointed to an area near the back of her lab. "I've had quarters set up for you behind that panel. There isn't a lot of space . . ."

Alara walked to the nearest countertop and lovingly ran her hands on the slick surface, wondering what new experiments she could devise in space—what new discoveries she might make if she explored the many different strains of DNA on the ship.

"I do not need more space to sleep. When the *Boktai* comes again, I will simply go to the cabin of a crewman."

"Crewman?"

His eyes blazed and Alara instantly recognized the proprietary flash. "I cannot mate with you again, Xander. The act could reset my cell regeneration process. I will adapt to you."

"Good." The tension didn't leave him, but his eyes softened a tad.

He didn't understand. She'd taken *Boktai* for granted for so long—assuming that all males understood the urges and the consequences—that she had trouble explaining what to her people was simply the way things were. Fear iced down her spine. The Rystani were so different. Would he ever accept her ways?

"After my cells adapt specifically to yours, if I go to anyone else for regeneration, I will die."

"Stars." He swore under his breath, staring at her as if she were a monster from one of the five seas of Jarn.

"You haven't even heard the worst part." She figured she might as well reveal the rest, before he again judged her wrongly. Before her mouth turned so dry she couldn't speak, she forced out the words. She drilled home her meaning. "If by chance you should expire, I would die within two weeks of your death."

At the implication, he paled in shock. As if she might actually lie about something so terrible, he wore a suspicious look, his skin tone changing from his normal healthy bronze to a sickly shade of grayish white. "Are you certain?"

"As certain as death itself. My father died in a Terran terrorist attack. My mother and I survived the bombing, protected from the explosion in an underground lab. But since my parents had been married for thirty years, my mother's biology had adapted to her husband's. Over time her body changed until only my father's essence could regenerate her cells. I delivered her to the Goddess one week after my father's death."

He remained silent a moment as if digesting her terrible news. Finally, a bit of bronze returned to his face. "How long does it take for your cells to adapt?"

"I don't know. Everyone is different."

"How many times can we . . ."

She shrugged, ignoring the tingle of her kiss-swollen lips. "You aren't listening. Sometimes adaptation can take several months, other times years."

"You should be fine. Hopefully our voyage won't take—"

"Since I am the first Endeki woman to leave our world, I cannot give you an exact timetable. But your essence is strong." She raised her hand to her lips—never had a kiss left her trembling inside. His love-making had impacted her deeply on the most basic cellular level. "Just a few more 'encounters' with you might cause my cells to adapt."

At her uncertainty, she expected to see obvious disgust cross his features and steeled herself against his reaction. No doubt he considered her unsuitable for permanent mating—for marriage. Not that she'd ever consider the option, but she knew enough about the Rystani to expect he could never comprehend the ways of her people. Yes, she hated the *Boktai* and had devoted her life to reversing thousands of years of evolution, but she also accepted that she could not escape the way she was raised. If he'd given her a chance to explain before he'd taken her from Endeki, perhaps he would have chosen differently. But now she was stuck on the *Verazen*—without power, they couldn't even turn back—with only alien men to choose from when she entered *Boktai* again.

He held out his hand to her, almost like a peace offering, his eyes determined. "Stars. I have never heard of such things. But somehow, we will work out your problem. Perhaps one of our scientists—"

"Please." His gentle compassion was almost worse than when he'd been glaring at her. He couldn't understand how much she detested her own biology. How much she hated when she turned into a woman who would do anything for a man in exchange for regeneration. "I don't want everyone to know about my biology.

I don't want them to look at me with loathing . . . or pity."

"Or lust?"

She winced. No, not with lust. Not when she knew the wanting spawned simply from knowing she would comply—not because of who she was as a person, as a woman.

She raised her chin and pulled back her shoulders. "Now you understand why my work is so important. Women should not have to live like Endekian women do. Our men need not treat their wives well and frequently don't. Why should they? Once our cells adapt, we cannot leave our mates or divorce, or we die. And we cannot withhold pleasure. We are slaves to our biology."

He cocked his head to one side and kept his tone even, almost light. "Rystani also wed for life. We have this in common. But we do treat our women with more value. So perhaps we are not so different after all."

He kept his hand out, his offer of companionship still open. She finally placed her hand in his. When his fingers closed around hers in a gentle grip, she squeezed back, the gesture almost natural.

She couldn't recall ever holding a man's hand before, at least of her own inclination. But then she'd most certainly never kissed a man without *Boktai* driving her hormones. She looked at him and could see he was pleased and wondered if they might yet become friends. She'd never had a male friend. She'd never considered the idea until this moment, and though the ship's power situation seemed dire, she couldn't suppress a burgeoning hope for her future.

They shared a pleasant meal in his quarters, and that night when he didn't even try to press his attentions on her, she wasn't sure if she was disappointed or relieved. After that sizzling kiss in her laboratory, she wouldn't have minded another. Or cuddling. Touching Xander's body was always a pleasure. She adored the heat of his skin, his toned muscles, his exotic male scent. But most of all, she liked watching his eyes spark as he heated up right with her.

During their kiss, she couldn't miss his carefully checked desire. He might have had her just last night, but clearly, physically, he'd been ready again. Yet he'd held back. Perhaps her words had given him pause. He might not like the idea of her body adapting to his. Why would he? He'd been given no choice but to mate with her—and as he explained, Rystanis mated for life. This warrior took his responsibilities seriously, and she thought it likely he wouldn't want to hold her life and her future in his hands. She was, after all, Endekian. And in the end, she wanted to go home.

The next morning, they were sharing a light breakfast in her lab when Vax's voice came over the com. "Captain."

"Yes?"

"The security chief says that Clarie's awake."

He tossed his plate into the refresher. "I'm on the way to the shuttle bay. I want you, Shannon, and Cyn to meet us there."

"We're leaving the bridge right now."

As he and Alara hurried to the shuttle bay, Xander queried the computer, his tone professional. "Ranth, what have you got for me? Have you learned anything new about our guest or his ship's power?"

"Captain, I have nothing. Either no one in the Federation has ever come across his species or his type of ship or they haven't lived to report it."

"Are you saying Clarie's dangerous?" Xander's tone didn't change. He sounded more curious than alarmed.

"I'm saying he's an . . . unknown."

"Ranth," Alara asked, "have you ever come across biology like Clarie's or his ship's before?"

"My brain is a combination of living cells and matter, but Clarie and his ship are totally organic. Scans of his anatomy have registered a peculiar arrangement of biological and physiological structures whose functions require more study before I can even hazard—"

"Ranth, save the science." Xander opened a hatch for her. "We require helpful information. I want answers. Where did that ship come from? What powers it? Are we in danger from the same thing that required us to rescue it?"

"We don't have enough data for me to answer those questions."

"Keep on it," Xander instructed.

Alara and Xander met with Shannon, Cyn, and Vax at the shuttle bay hatch. "I've asked everyone to join me because communicating with Clarie is difficult. Since we're all from different worlds, I'm hoping one of us will be able to get through to him."

Vax's hand went to his stunner. "If he's refusing to cooperate—"

"He's not." Xander shook his head and Vax released his grip on the stunner. "At least, I don't believe so."

"Talking to Clarie's like speaking to a child," Alara explained. "He doesn't appear aware of the ramifications or implications of his statements, and he only replies at a very basic level."

"But his ship is constructed of a sophisticated material unlike anything in Federation space." Xander turned to Cyn. "Ranth said power radiated from the hull. It came from somewhere. We need to find the source and adapt it to our needs." Xander stepped onto the ramp leading into the alien ship. "It seems odd that his technology is so advanced we can't even determine the nature of his systems, yet his mind is so simple, he can't communicate fully. Something doesn't feel right."

10

Xander's grand gesture to save Alara's work, followed by his inclusion of her in the discussion with his supervising officers, made Alara feel valued and part of the team. Too often, she'd kept her ideas to herself when in the presence of male colleagues, all too certain whatever she offered would be frowned upon—if anyone listened at all. With Cyn and Shannon both well-respected female crew members, Alara believed that if her suggestions weren't taken seriously, it wouldn't be due to her sex.

Looking forward to their next encounter with Clarie, Alara approached the alien ship with Xander, Vax, Cyn, and Shannon. Security covered them from a distance and the shiny spherical ship appeared exactly the same as they'd left it, with the hatch open, the ramp rolled out.

As if sensing their presence, Clarie shuffled down

the ramp, stroking Delo, its fur still a soft shade of brown. Xander made the introductions between Clarie and his crew, who comported themselves like the professionals they were.

"Captain, you require power?" Clarie surprised Alara by bringing up the subject they wanted to talk about most. While they spoke, she again checked out his DNA, fascinated by the complexity of his makeup and the absence of any DNA in Delo.

"Yes, we need power." Xander nodded and Alara's hopes rose. Surely Clarie wouldn't have mentioned the power problem if he didn't understand their needs and didn't plan to help.

Clarie lifted Delo onto his rounded shoulder. The animal clung to his robe with tight prehensile fingers, his bushy tail winding up the back of Clarie's head and stroking a fragile antenna. "Why do you need power?"

Cyn jerked her thumb back toward the *Verazen*'s engines. "Come with us to engineering and I'll show you."

Clarie ignored Cyn and spoke to Xander. "What is interesting in engineering?"

"It's the ship section that houses our engines, which powers us through hyperspace and that we will use to brake us at the journey's end. Without power to jump from hyperspace, we cannot go to Lapau."

Alara liked the way Xander didn't talk down to Clarie, but used simple words. He seemed to also believe that they had a communication problem and that Clarie must be more intelligent than he seemed.

"Why go across the galaxy to Lapau?" Clarie asked.

Across the galaxy? His statement implied he knew of the system. Alara exchanged a glance with Xander, and from his expression, she realized he'd caught the implications, too.

"You know of Lapau?" Alara asked, but Clarie didn't answer her, either.

Except—Clarie's DNA glowed. Glowed bright as the sun.

No sooner had she thought to use her psi to filter the light from her suit than she stumbled. One moment they'd been walking from the shuttle bay toward engineering, the next, Vax, Xander, Clarie, Cyn, and Shannon were finishing their steps in the middle of a busy market.

They were no longer on the ship, but outside—in a strange place. The sensual sensitivity of hyperspace had been replaced by gravity, scorching sunshine, and tantalizing aromas.

They stood on another world.

Son of a slimeworm. In mid-stride, she'd left the ship and stepped under an azure sky and a burnt orange sun. The pitter-patter of humanoids passing by them in a market seemed so ordinary. And the people around them paid little attention to the strangers among them. Wearing flowing clothing in soft pastels and sandals on their feet, people chatted and went about their business like in any other city on thousands of cosmopolitan worlds.

Alara counted several species of humanoids, a predominant one composed of men and women with blue-tinged skin, others with larger, shell-shaped ears, and still another race of white-haired, pink-eyed people who possessed tails that they decorated with ribbons and sparkly gewgaws.

Around them vendors sold trinkets, fine art, and a variety of household goods, lighting, appliances, foodstuffs, and carpets. From the deliciously scented aromas, a wide assortment of sweetmeats, pastries, and snacks were available. A man tapped a beat on a box with his foot while playing a flutelike instrument. Admirers stopped and placed shiny golden metal pellets in a sack by his feet. Surrounding the busy square, elegant, pale turquoise buildings with steep gable roofs and tiered balconies supported by majestic columns revealed more eateries, where people dined at leisure with a view of the busy market below.

Where was this place? How had they arrived here? Despite the smooth polished tile under her feet, Alara couldn't seem to find her balance and stumbled, again.

With a lightning reflex, Xander reached out and steadied her. "What in the seven continents of Icorn just happened?"

Vax's hand dropped to his stunner that was no longer attached to his suit. "Either we're hallucinating or we are no longer on the ship."

Until they figured out where they were and what had occurred, blending in to avoid calling attention to themselves would be the safest course. Although she could do nothing about her golden skin, Alara modified her suit to match the current styles and placed a hood over her pink hair; she noted the captain and his crew reclothing themselves, as well. Clarie didn't bother, continuing to wear his bright blue robe that stood out like an embryo among a colony of amoeba.

"Does anyone recognize this world?" Xander asked. His robe left one shoulder and one powerful bronzed arm bare and the image of pillowing her head on his shoulder popped into her head. The timing was incredibly unfortunate. She should be working, using her abilities to find out what was going on. She didn't even have the excuse of *Boktai*.

To distract herself from inappropriate thoughts of

Xander, she used her inner eye on the closest humanoid stranger. Alara noted only subtle differences among the different races. The blue-skinned woman's DNA was very similar to her own, right down to carrying the virus. She moved on to examine other beings that seemed related in DNA type. All were infected.

Alara kept her voice low. "Captain, wherever we are, they already have the virus."

"With their own lives at stake, they should be more likely to cooperate," Shannon suggested.

"Let's not make assumptions," Xander cautioned, keeping his stance casual, his demeanor wary. As the others looked to him, he maintained his normal role of leadership with an ease that was so much a part of him that she speculated whether he'd been born to command or if he had learned to maintain his authoritative presence through years of serving his people.

Cyn frowned. "We need to figure out where we are. I don't even want to think about how we zapped out of hyperspace. Or how we'll zing back. It's giving me a headache."

Clarie's head swiveled around until he met Xander's gaze. "You wanted to go to Lapau. Yes?"

Xander's eyes widened. "This is Lapau?"

"You say go. We go."

"Where's my ship and the rest of my crew?" Xander eyed Clarie with suspicion.

"No worry. Ship where you left it."

Delo suddenly leaped from Clarie's shoulder. Using all four limbs, the animal scampered toward the vendors, his pace so fast, his limbs blurred with the churning motion. Clarie shuffled after his pet, moving with a swift confidence that made her wonder if he'd been here before.

"We should stay together." Xander spoke loudly enough for Clarie to hear, but the alien ignored him.

"You want me to bring him back?" Vax's tone implied he'd use force if necessary.

"Let him go," Xander ordered, and within moments Clarie had disappeared from view. "If this is Lapau, we need to find a library, a computer system, somewhere to get information. Let's split up. Cyn, Shannon, Vax, see what you can learn without alerting the locals to our presence. Alara and I will try and find out who's in charge. Remember, we're looking for anything—stories, artifacts, machinery—about the Perceptive Ones. Keep in mind that the Lapautee may call them by other names."

"Without our ship in orbit, we cannot stay in contact with each other," Shannon reminded them. The Terran's lips compressed into a thin line, as if she hadn't taken the transfer as well as the others—possibly due to the more advanced nature of her DNA illness. To her credit, she said nothing about her sickness.

Vax checked his timepiece. "I suggest we meet back here in three hours."

"Good idea." Xander nodded, but his gaze veered to the crowd and stopped on a woman who passed a golden pellet to a vendor and received a sweetmeat in return. "Keep a look out for Clarie and your thoughts tuned for a way to earn credit. We'll need food, water, and shelter by nightfall."

"That's assuming this place has nightfall." Shannon shaded her eyes with her hand and peered at the peculiar sky. "The clouds haven't moved since we've arrived. And there's a sharp demarcation line between bright and unfaded paint on every building, indicating shade and sunlight positions are constant."

Planets where one side remained in daylight and the other in perpetual darkness were rare. Alara wished she'd asked Ranth more about Lapau when she'd had the opportunity. After she and Xander split from the others, she noted that many couples walked hand in hand, and she took Xander's, telling herself her gesture was to blend in, but liking the idea of touching him. "Are we certain this planet is Lapau?"

"I'm certain of nothing." Xander guided her between a row of vendors. "Ranth collected parts and pieces of data the last time the *Verazen* came this way. Apparently, after examining the data from libraries and museums from many worlds, he theorized that the Perceptive Ones might still be alive in this system. But we've always known most of what he'd gathered might be inaccurate."

She pulled the hood closer around her face, wishing she and Xander didn't stick out so much. Hair here came in hues that ranged from brown to gold, and if her pink locks showed, it might startle these people more than Xander's size, which seemed to go unnoticed. "I assume you don't want to stop someone and ask for information?"

"We don't know the laws or customs of this world. They may arrest strangers who don't have a permit or who don't have political agreements with them. We can't afford to end up in the local equivalent of a jail."

She stopped in front of a sign with moving images that projected an art show and a map that displayed their current location and how to locate the building's exhibit. While they couldn't read the language, the images were simple enough. "Perhaps we can find access to a computer there."

Her assumption could be incorrect. But art galleries were often in upscale areas near museums and libraries that might contain the information they sought.

"All right." He glanced at the sun that still hadn't moved since their arrival. "Shannon may be right. They may always have daylight here."

"Yes, but why aren't the clouds changing shape or scudding across the sky?"

As they strode past vendors, Alara noted certain sections carried similar products. Once they reached the market's edge, she slowed her pace to gawk at semiwoody tropical vines, evergreen shrubs, plants with weakly winged stems, and unlobed crimson flowers for sale under a canopy that provided shade from the sweltering sun.

She would have liked to examine a sampling of the local flora in her lab, but had to make do with her special sight. "Plants have the virus, too."

"Keep your eyes peeled for anyone official or in charge, like civilian peacekeepers and military. Most worlds designate them by a difference in dress."

She didn't know if Xander didn't want to hear about her plant observations, or if he simply had a lot on his mind. Clearly, he was focusing on the mission. But after years of no one listening to her ideas, she'd learned to keep her opinions to herself. Knowing that she tended to be overly sensitive, she didn't say more about the plants, but when one of the vendors stood before a booth of budding perennials that had yet to flower, she led Xander toward it.

"Buy my glory glades very cheap. Lovely flowers will bloom in a few days." A sinewy woman with sultry eyes spoke in a singsong tone, and Alara could tell from her despondent gaze that she expected them to move on like the others who were drawn to the brightly flowering plants at other booths.

"Why not make them bloom now?" Alara asked, jutting her chin at a jaunty angle.

"Why not make the sun set?" the vendor countered, grim-faced and antagonistic. Clearly she either didn't believe the buds could be coaxed to bloom now or was unaware of the technique to help them do so.

Xander tugged at Alara's hand, trying to pull her away, but she planted her feet firmly. Keeping her tone friendly, she spoke to the vendor with confidence. "Do you have a light and some *blane*?

"*Blane*?" The woman's suspicious gaze fell on Alara, almost making her wish she'd walked on without stopping.

"*Blane*'s an element in fertilizer," Alara explained.

The woman bent behind her counter, pulled out a flexible pot, and dipped her hand into tiny balls the color of sandbark berries. "Will these work?"

Alara sniffed the familiar tart scent and smiled in approval. "Now, for a light." The vendor handed her a tube that flashed a pure white light. It wasn't the best source for what Alara had in mind, but it would do. She poured water from a nearby ceramic jug into a bowl, stirred in the *blane,* sprinkled the mixture onto the bud and applied light for a catalyst. Within moments the bud expanded and the petals unfolded, revealing a lovely celadon flower with a periwinkle center.

The vendor oohed and aahed as several potential buyers stopped to watch. "Do it again, please."

Alara sprinkled more of the mixture onto the plant and the buds opened in all their ethereal radiance. "*Blane,* water, and light accelerate blooming."

"That's a neat trick." A sharp-eyed customer held out a few pellets. "I'll take two plants and that mixture to show my husband."

"Me, too." A young man made a purchase and handed the plant to his girl.

"Thank you." The vendor quickly took care of her customers and grinned at Alara who repeated the process on another plant. While Xander stood protectively close, she worked to coax more flowers to bloom and the bright petals added a light fragrance to the air.

With bright-eyed happiness, the vendor handed the plant Alara had just worked on back to her along with a handful of *blane* balls. "For your help."

Xander shook his head. "That's not—"

"Thank you." Alara placed the *blane* in her pocket and accepted the plant in one arm, waved goodbye and with her free hand tugged him past the growing group of customers, around a corner. "Shh. Don't be impolite."

Exasperation at the delay and the notion of carrying the heavy plant edged his tone. "We can't carry—"

"You said to watch for economic opportunities. Do you have anything on your person you can sell?"

"Are you suggesting we attempt to sell . . . a plant?"

"Gentlemen at art shows might pay a goodly sum for a blossom for their lady." Although she half-expected him to reject her idea, she nevertheless made the suggestion in the hopes he wouldn't.

They strode through the busy market in silence, winding their way past a juggler, a cart pulled by a six-legged equine bot, and a stone fountain spouting frothy green bubbles. A woman hawked finely wrought anklets from her booth and Alara shook her head and caught Xander's eye.

He gave her a sidelong glance that she couldn't read. "You're just full of surprises."

She arched her brow. "How do you think I fund my laboratory?"

"I assumed the government—"

"Drik hates me." They wound their way through the dwindling crowd into a side alley. "The government was never in favor of my research. I buy and sell rare and luxurious items to pay the bills." She didn't say more.

In the narrow alley, the taller buildings blocked the sun. She appreciated the shade and the relative privacy. And she enjoyed the opportunity to speak frankly with Xander. Her father had belittled her mother's every effort to work outside the home. If he'd lived, he would have disapproved—just like every Endekian male—of not only Alara's research, but her entrepreneurial success. But Xander came from Rystan and she didn't know their customs. Would her commercial acumen make him question his self-worth as it would most Endekian men?

"You must be a very successful businesswoman to fund your research facility."

"I do all right."

Conversation ceased as Alara handed the plant to Xander, then broke off flowers and stems until she had a bouquet. While she had yet to ascertain his opinion, she supposed she'd have to be satisfied that he hadn't belittled or mocked her. Come to think of it, Xander had only done that once—when he'd mistakenly believed she'd trade her body for freedom. The rest of the time, he'd treated her almost as an equal.

Except during mating—then he'd demanded, commanded, taken total charge. Due to the big Rystani's mating skills and his attitude, for once the memory of *Boktai* wasn't horrible. Memories of their joining heated her flesh and lightened her heart as well as her step as they found the gallery.

She stuck one flower under her hood and behind her ear, arranging it to poke out at a jaunty angle, pasted a smile on her face, and stepped into the gallery. The inside sported monochromatic gray walls, ceiling, and floors to set off the colorful art display. Patrons drank bubbly drinks in long fluted glasses and helped themselves to bite-sized pastries passed out by bots with trays.

Alara went to work. She picked out a distinguished-looking gold-haired gentleman with a flirty young woman by his side. Jewelry dripped from her ears, neck, and wrists, jingling and calling attention to her wealth.

Alara placed the flower near the lady's nose so she could take in the aromatic scent, but spoke to her escort. "Buy a flower for your lady?"

The young woman sniffed in delight. "Yes, please."

"How much?" With a warm glance of approval at his lady, her escort reached into his pocket and withdrew several pellets.

"That will be fine." Alara plucked the credits from his hand and kept working the crowded room. Since she had no idea of the monetary system on Lapau, she had no notion what she was earning. But something was better than nothing.

When she was down to her last two flowers, she took a break. With admiration in his eyes, Xander handed her a well-deserved drink of caramel-colored liquid and a plate of flaky pastries with delicate pink, sienna, and ocher icing. Sipping from her glass, allowing the fruity alcohol to soothe her parched throat, she leaned against a wall, pleased with her efforts, gratified that Xander appreciated her creativity.

She didn't know exactly when earning his approval had become important to her—but it had. And along the way, they'd become a team. While she'd sold flowers, Xander had moved among the crowd, listening to conversations and picking up knowledge—hopefully useful information. A man as big as Xander could never be unobtrusive and the ladies had swarmed around him like bees to nectar. However, he'd kept a protective eye on Alara, and when he'd spotted her resting, he'd broken free of the flirting ladies to join her.

He leaned his head close to hers and kept his voice low, his tone husky. "I overheard a woman talking about obtaining a procreation license. Maybe the authorities issue licenses here."

Although shocked, she also kept her voice low. "They require a license to have children?"

"Apparently."

He shook his head, obviously thinking the idea as peculiar as she did. "You want Arc Six."

"Arc?" She raised an eyebrow. It seemed as if every bit of new information brought surprises. "Not a block or a street but an Arc?"

A slender, dark-haired woman in a stiff pastel dress with annoyed green eyes approached and gripped Alara's arm. "You have no right to sell flowers in my establishment. Leave immediately."

Xander stepped between the gallery's owner and Alara, breaking the other woman's hold on her arm. "We are leaving right now."

Alara understood that Xander wanted to depart immediately but she feared the woman might call the authorities after them. While they needed to speak with someone in charge, they also had to stay out of trouble. If Alara could make things right with the store's owner, she would.

She handed a flower to the angry woman. "I'm sorry. Please accept this as my apology. We are new here and didn't know we'd . . . trespassed. It won't happen again."

Slightly mollified by the apology and the flower, the woman lost her scowl but jerked her chin to the door. "Out."

Xander took a step toward the exit, but stopped to speak over his shoulder, raising his voice so the other patrons could overhear. "We're trying to find Arc Six. If you could point us in the right direction . . ."

Xander had neatly placed the gallery owner in an awkward position. If she didn't answer, she'd appear rude to her clients. And clearly she didn't wish to cause a disturbance and call attention away from the art hanging from the ceiling. However, Alara guessed from her dark expression that she spoke grudgingly. "Make a right and then your first left. You'll run straight into Arc Five."

Five? They needed to find Six. But perhaps the Arcs were in order. Or the woman had misunderstood. Landing in a strange place could certainly be confusing, and Alara now understood why the Federation left first contact to the experts. Who would have guessed that anyone would object to her selling flowers to patrons inside an art gallery?

When they left the building, Xander turned left, not right as the woman had directed. Alara stayed beside him. "Where are we going?"

"Back to meet the others." But Xander suddenly stopped, stared across a wide boulevard and took her hand. Dodging pedal-propelled vehicles, strolling cou-

ples, and several children in motorized cubicles on
tracks and a skimmer or two, he rushed her across the
open street.

"What is it?"

"I just saw Clarie."

"And?"

"He exited a skimmer and entered that building with
the pink fountain out front."

She hurried to stay with him as they crossed the busy
boulevard. "What about meeting with your crew?"

"If we're a little late, Vax will wait."

*I see no further signs of higher brain function. No
signs of evolution. No sign of progress.*

Go start a universe or something. I'm working.

*The virus is spreading and they have done nothing to
counter it. They don't even know where it came from.*

And you were born knowing everything?

*I can remember my birth quite clearly, even if it was
several million eons ago. And I had more intelligence
in the tip of my brain stem than—*

*You didn't have a brain. You've never taken corpo-
real form. But you should try it. There are advantages.*

Like?

Eating.

We digress. My point—

*I'm not interested in your points, your theories, or
your tests. My work is only beginning.*

*It's taking too long. They will expire from the virus
before they evolve.*

You have no faith in good winning out over evil?

Not since I was in training mode.

With your lack of patience, I'm surprised you survived to the next level.

Clearly, I'm a superior being. I do not fail.

You do not try. You pick apart my work and do none of your own. If you have nothing positive to contribute, you should leave.

Very well. But I shall be back, and if they have not shown any improvement, we shall simply allow the virus to win. Agreed?

I agree to nothing.

You have no choice.

There is always choice.

And the right choice would be to let them all die.

11

Xander and Alara never caught up with Clarie, but Xander's curiosity was more than piqued. If the alien had brought them to Lapau, had it really been because of their request? And were he and his ship one being—as Alara suspected? But if so—where was his ship?

The rendezvous back at the market with Cyn, Vax, and Shannon had gone according to plan. However, Shannon didn't look her sprightly self and he wondered how bad she felt. Given a choice, he wouldn't have selected her for a ground mission that would tax her strength. Vowing to keep a close watch on her, he planned to assign her the easiest of tasks.

His crew confirmed that Arc Six was indeed the right place to connect with the Lapautee leaders. And Xander hoped those leaders could help point him in the direction of the Perceptive Ones. But first, they purchased food and drink in the market with the credit Alara had earned before heading straight to the government offices, where they proceeded to wait for an appointment.

Unfortunately, from the wretched furnishings in the shabby office they finally entered, Xander suspected that the overweight man before them was a minor bureaucrat, without much clout. With his pale gray skin and shaking hands, his health was obviously on the decline.

After watching the previous applicant come out of this office sobbing, Xander's hopes of gaining access from this official to a higher authority who could put him in touch with the Perceptive Ones weren't too high. While Vax, Shannon, and Cyn waited outside, he and Alara had gone in together. Xander had chosen her to accompany him because she'd proven resourceful. Vax tended to think like a Rystani warrior, his first instinct to protect his captain. Cyn's specialty was engineering, and while Shannon was good with people and was open-minded for someone her age, she tended to think within the rules. Alara didn't even know the rules existed and he found her company helpful and refreshing.

And the more time they spent together the less he thought of her as alien, as Endekian. He watched her go to work again as she had in the art gallery, this time charming the Lapautee official, Lithdar, in a manner that eased the tension from the man's shoulders. He'd even thanked her after she'd given him the plant as a gift to soften him up.

But now they were down to the reason for their visit and the bureaucrat's pink eyes narrowed with suspicion. "You aren't here for a procreation permit? Because I cannot—"

"We have come to Lapau from another world and are in search of beings we call the Perceptive Ones," Xander explained. "We know of these ancient ones because we wear suits built by machines they manufactured and left behind over a millennium ago."

Lithdar rubbed the bridge of his nose. "I have never heard of—"

"But you wear their suits?" Xander pressed.

"They come from Saj, the dirt eaters below." Lithdar spat the name like a curse.

"Where is Saj?" Xander asked.

The Lapautee official pressed a button and spoke several words that didn't translate but caused a three-dimensional holovid to appear over his desk. A spinning planet with aqua oceans and three continents, one mountainous, one apparently covered by ice, and one dotted with rivers and lakes floated between orbital rings.

Lithdar pointed to a spot on the ring above the planet's northern ocean. "Lapau is here."

No wonder the sun didn't set—they weren't on a planet, but a ring in orbit. The sky was artificial. The city of Lapau was built on the planet's widest band, hundreds of miles above the world below.

"And where is Saj?" Alara asked.

Again, Lithdar pointed, this time to the planet's southern continent. "This is where our suits come from."

"How do we get there?" Xander asked.

Horror caused Lithdar's mouth to form a wide grimace. "No one goes to Saj."

"Why not?" Alara asked.

"Because of the war."

Xander recalled the atomic wars of Rystan and wondered if these people had ruined their world with radiation. Or had they polluted the planet beyond redemption as Earth had almost done, making the air unfit to breathe? Was that why they lived on the ring? But if the Lapautee still wore suits, someone must be down there to operate the equipment. "Do radiation or pollution problems prevent access to the planet?"

"You aren't listening. We're at war."

"Now?" Xander had lived through war on Rystan. There had been hunger, not the prosperity he'd seen here. There had been fear. His people had hidden in underground caves to avoid the Endekian invaders. But the Lapautee they'd seen had gone about their business as if there were no threat.

"We're always at war. Yesterday. Now. Tomorrow. There is no difference."

Lithdar spoke about war as if the Lapautee were in a perpetual state of conflict with the Saj. But Xander had no arguments or hatred for the people on the world below. "*We* are not at war with the Saj."

"They allow no one from Lapau to set foot on dirt."

"But if you trade with them to obtain your suits, there must be some communication. You could inform—"

"No communication. We send the ova from our women, they send suits."

"You're giving the Saj your ova?" Alara asked.

Lithdar popped a pill into his mouth and washed it down with water. "Sending the Saj our ova is part of the treaty. If we don't send the ova, we don't get suits. We tried refusing them once and they attacked. Since the Saj control the machines that manufacture the suits, we have no choice and are at their mercy."

Alara's expression was alive with curiosity. "What do they do with your ova?"

"You don't understand. They demand the ova of our women to prevent our population from growing. Saj are despicable and bring much sadness."

"If you send genetic material to them, then the Saj have the virus, too." Alara sounded as if she were thinking aloud, but Xander suspected she was testing Lithdar to see his reaction.

"Virus?" Lithdar's eyes opened in a pretense of horror and he shoved back from the desk, as if fearing he could catch something from his visitors. But he was not a good actor. Even Xander could see the man had already heard about the virus.

Xander explained anyway. He saw no point in calling Lithdar a liar. "Every plant and animal on Lapau, as well as throughout our Federation, seems to have this virus. Our genetic material is breaking down. We hope to find the Perceptive Ones and a pure form of DNA to cure us all."

Lithdar shuddered. "You must not speak of the plague. People will panic."

"We have come in search of a cure—not to frighten your people." Alara sought to reassure him, but Xander could read the growing concern in her eyes.

"However, we need to go to Saj," Xander insisted.

"Even if I wished to help you, and I would very much like to do so since both my daughters are ill, we have no way to communicate with the dirt eaters."

"How do you trade the ova for suits?" Xander asked.

"It's automatic. The arrangement was made five thousand years ago."

Alara's eyes widened. "You've had this arrangement for five thousand years? Why don't you make peace?"

"The Saj don't want peace. If we change the agreement, the dirt eaters will attack."

"But if you don't help us contact the Saj, everyone on Lapau will die of the plague," Xander countered. "You really have no choice."

Lithdar trembled and tugged at the collar of his robe as if it choked him. "I don't have the authority to make such an important decision. I will arrange for quarters and refreshments for your group and send your request to the ruling council."

"That's kind of you," Xander said. The less time they spent on survival, the more time they could devote to their search for the Perceptive Ones.

"Meanwhile, you must enjoy our hospitality as if you were *Sumaik*."

"*Sumaik?*"

"Women who lose their ova are treated with the utmost respect. For their sacrifice, the government compensates them." Lithdar stood, ending the audience. "I'll contact you as soon as I hear from the council. In the meantime, enjoy our hospitality. If you go to Saj, these days are likely to be your last."

Kirek didn't have much time. Lataka expected him to find·her by the waterfall, but in the meantime, he would search this corridor of Drik's residence. Luckily, Drik mostly posted guards to keep people from entering and leaving, so with his guards congregated on the perimeter, once one was inside the building, moving about was relatively easy—as long as Kirek avoided the Endekian women in *Boktai*.

Ever since he'd found the Rystani glow stone, he'd intended to search the only corridor where Drik always posted guards. If Dora, his computer teacher, had been there, she could have entered and changed the system in seconds, but it had taken Kirek two days to find a back door and then an override code in the residence's program. Hopefully, no one had noticed he'd reassigned the guards from their station in the corridor to other duties during the time he planned to search. Hence, the corridor he sought was temporarily empty and the computer modifications couldn't be traced back to Kirek—or so he believed.

Taking care that no one followed, Kirek slipped down the hall, wary and watchful. Although the guards followed their routine, one order from Drik could change everything. Although so far his captive status had been mostly pleasant, Kirek was all too aware that Endekians had a long and violent history that included torture.

While Xander had never mentioned his boyhood capture by the Endekians who invaded Rystan, Etru had spoken of Xander's extraordinary bravery. The Endekians had repeatedly shot painful volts of electricity through him in an attempt to force him to reveal the whereabouts of his hiding people. Xander had not talked. After the Terran, Tessa, had rescued him, Xander had killed one of his torturers, taking a full-grown Endekian warrior's life before he'd grown to full manhood.

Although the *Verazen*'s captain never spoke of the incident, Kirek had once gone to Xander's quarters to awaken him with a message from the bridge. When Xander hadn't answered, Kirek had entered and found his captain thrashing in a nightmare. Kirek had never forgotten Xander's inhuman grunts of pain or the wild look in his eyes when he'd awakened and the miserable seconds it had taken for him to regain control.

The Endekians had treated Xander with brutal

savagery and Kirek reminded himself the incident had taken place merely a decade ago. He doubted the Endekian way of dealing with their enemies had changed in such a short time. And as he padded naked down the corridor, he remained fully alert, lest the same thing happen to him.

If Drik's men caught him—there would be no rescue. Kirek was the only Rystani on Endeki. As he ducked into the critical corridor, he hoped whatever he found outweighed the risk he was taking. But he had to know more about the glow stone.

After a thorough search of Drik's private computer in his office, Kirek had found nothing useful. There had been no mention of the glow stone. No mention of the real reason Endeki had invaded Rystan. And the official reason, that Rystan had violated trade agreements, wasn't enough to justify the massive effort they'd put into the invasion. The fact that the data had been purged or had never been imputed in the first place led Kirek to believe he was onto something significant.

His hand closed over a door and pressed on the latch, but it wouldn't budge.

Kneeling, Kirek quickly used his psi to pick the computer lock and slipped into a dark room. After shutting the door behind him, he waited for his eyes to adjust to the darkness and listened. Machinery hummed, but he didn't hear the sound of footsteps, talking, or breathing.

Wishing he'd thought to bring a tiny laser light, he edged forward cautiously, his feet sinking into a luxurious carpet. A soft glow from a computer vidscreen helped him make out details of what appeared to be an office. Careful not to make any noise, he searched the room's four walls. There were no windows and he'd entered through the only door.

Believing it was safe to turn on a light, he flipped a switch, blinked, and discovered the heaviest concentration of computer equipment he'd seen since entering the residence. A yellow light flashed as did the vidscreen that requested his retina scan to proceed.

Kirek swore under his breath, cloaked his body from the machines, and flipped off the light. Tensed, he waited for the sound of pounding feet of guards coming to find out who was here. If the scanner had caught sight of his eyeball and recognized that he didn't belong here before he'd cloaked, the system would likely have set off an alarm.

His ragged nerves insisted he retreat—before Drik or his guards discovered him. But convinced he'd penetrated Drik's command center, Kirek hated to lose this opportunity. He had no idea when he'd have another chance to return.

With every second of delay he risked capture. And yet if he'd succeeded in shielding himself before the computer had registered his presence, he might still be able to bypass the retina scan and find out what Drik was hiding.

Keeping his body concealed from so many different types of machines required a huge mental effort. If he could have plugged his brain directly into the computer like Dora, he could have been into the system within seconds. Or if Ranth had been there, Kirek wouldn't have had to remove the control pad and rearrange the wiring. The simple manual manipulation wouldn't have been difficult since the wiring relied on the mechanical sensors to warn Drik of an intruder— except it was dark, except he feared capture, except it required more concentration than he'd expected.

Holding back his fear, he kept up his shield to hide from the sensors and forced his shaking fingers to switch the wiring. With his heart pumping like a galloping *masdon* and sweat pouring from his skin from his mental exertion, he fought to keep his hands steady.

Despite his fierce concentration, he almost dropped the casing.

Come on. Come on. Come on.

Ignoring his physical and mental fatigue, Kirek finally snapped the altered control pad into place. He'd rigged the setup to allow him access.

Finally, he was in.

At the sound of pounding feet, he jumped. There were no exits but the way he'd come in. And if he fled into the corridor, he would be seen for sure.

What the hell. He was as good as caught. He might as well learn what Drik was hiding.

Estimating from the sound of the running and yelling, he had another three or four seconds. Kirek opened the vidscreen, found a file for glow stones, and opened it.

The Lapautee government assigned the *Verazen*'s crew to two rooms, albeit in different high-rise buildings. Although the women's quarters would be crowded, Alara was grateful for a place to rest, food to eat, and the prospect of the authorities working with them to contact the Saj.

Oddly, during the walk to their new quarters, Clarie had showed up with Delo. He now shared a room with Xander and Vax. The alien claimed he'd been exploring, and while Alara hoped the men could squeeze more information from him, she had her doubts. Some intelligent species had so little in common that they had no starting place to communicate. The universal translators in their suits usually did an impressive job—but she'd heard that the telepathic Osarians required touch to communicate their emotions. Speaking with one of them tended to be flat and awkward and left much to interpretation unless one held their slimy tentacles.

Alara, Cyn, and Shannon settled into their room that reminded her of a cheap overnight chamber for rent. Compact, their quarters didn't have many amenities. The blue carpet appeared worn, the lighting dim, and the walls dingy. If this place indicated how much the Lapautee government thought of their most treasured women—the *Sumaik*—then this world was a mass of contradictions.

When she recalled the research she'd left behind on the *Verazen*, sadness weighed on her. However, Alara tried not to think about her untended DNA experiments, tried to keep her emotions level—a habit that prevented *Boktai* from occurring as often. Trying to focus on the hopeful side, she looked forward to getting to know the women better.

Alara missed her female friends from back home. Since arriving on the *Verazen*, she seemed to have spent all her time with Xander. A break would be a good thing. She liked people. She liked having friends, and without her normal relationships to fill her need for sociability, she'd relied on Xander too often.

On the *Verazen*, Shannon had impressed Alara with her concern for the alien, and Cyn's love of her engines combined with her acceptance of being a woman fascinated Alara. In her experience, women who competed with men in their careers tended to take on male characteristics—but anyone who watched Cyn take three steps, her hips sensually swaying, could recognize she exuded femininity.

Shannon opened a cabinet and cool air escaped into the room. "They stocked us with enough food for six days."

Cyn floated into the room's center, locked her fingers behind her head and crossed her ankles. "I wonder if six days is how long it'll take for them to contact the Saj."

"If they haven't sent a message back and forth for over five thousand years, predicting when we'll get a reply's impossible." Ignoring the slight tremor in her hands due to her illness, Shannon took out a bowl and began adding ingredients as if she recognized them. "I say we eat while we can." She lifted a creamy dark substance to her nose and sniffed. "Umm. This almost smells like chocolate."

Cyn cocked open one eye, her expression eager. "Save a piece for me."

"You want some, then get off your lazy ass and help me make dinner."

Alara expected Cyn to do as Shannon asked. Instead, she closed her eye again. "And spoil all your fun? Alara, don't let Shannon fool you. She loves to cook."

"Do not."

"When you feed us, you can pretend we're family."

"You are family." Shannon sliced a long, yellow rootlike vegetable. "I've spent more time with you than my own daughters."

"That's because you don't stay in one place long enough for them to visit," Cyn countered.

"I'll help," Alara offered, feeling almost as if she

were interfering in a private conversation. But Cyn probably didn't know that Shannon's health was failing, and Alara wished the Terran would rest. But if Shannon didn't want to reveal private details about her health to Cyn, it wasn't Alara's place to do so. While the women had included Alara, as the newcomer among them, she couldn't begin to comprehend the complexities of their relationship.

When a rap on the door interrupted the discussion, Alara changed direction from Shannon and the eating area to the entrance. "I'll get it." She opened the door, expecting to see Xander or Vax with Clarie in tow.

At the sight of six burly, official-looking Lapautee men, she braced for trouble. She'd dealt with enough Endekian officials to recognize the Lapautee ones and she sensed trouble in their rigid demeanor. Hoping her past experience with officials wasn't coloring her judgment, she stepped outside and left the door slightly ajar, so the men couldn't see inside, but so Shannon and Cyn could overhear the conversation. "Yes?"

A blue-skinned thin man with a severe nose and tight lips read a document displayed on his portable vidscreen. "I'm here to collect Shannon Walker, Cyn from Scartar, and Dr. Alara Calladar."

Alara warily eyed him. Lithdar had indicated it would take some time to make the arrangements and they'd just left his office. But if the agreement between the Saj and the Lapautee had been quickly made, why weren't the men being "collected" also?

Alara spoke loudly so Shannon and Cyn wouldn't miss a word. "Have you already contacted the Saj?"

The Lapautee shook his head. "Our job is to collect the donors."

"Donors?"

The man frowned at his vidscreen where he perused details, then looked at her with sorrow. "Ah, I see that you are unfamiliar with our ways. Your lottery numbers came up."

She frowned at him. "All females in this sector are scheduled as donors," he explained.

"Donors?"

"Everyone female on Lapautee must comply with the Saj demands. The dirt eaters require us to keep our population under strict control for fear if we multiply we'll invade their territory. Many women are in this very same predicament. I'm sorry to inform you that all humanoid females must donate their ova to the Saj."

Alara braced one hand on the doorway, her stomach dropping in a sickening swoop and her knees going weak. The idea of these Lapautee harvesting and then destroying her ova sickened her. While she didn't know if she ever intended to have children, and certainly not for the duration of this mission, it wasn't right or natural for these people to invade her body, to take part of her away, especially without her consent.

She forced words through dry lips. "How many ova?"

"All of them."

Stars! She thought they meant to take the ova moving through her fallopian tubes during this cycle. But he sounded as if he wanted her ovaries. "You want to sterilize us?"

She'd shouted the question to warn Cyn and Shannon, but also to cover the snick of the lock. Staggering, she'd clutched the doorknob, hoping it appeared she'd shut the door accidentally as she tried to hold herself upright. While the men broke through the lock—and she was certain they would by the determination in their eyes—at least Cyn and Shannon could escape out the

back since these people built front and rear entrances
on their high-rise buildings.

In the meantime, even as panic gripped her, she had to
stall. The longer she delayed, the better Cyn's and Shannon's chances of escape, of finding Xander and Vax and
of informing them that these men had taken her. Oh, she
would fight, but she was going to lose.

The man swore under his breath. "Do you know
nothing? Only one in a hundred women can have
children."

"That's barbaric." She glanced around for a way to
escape in the crowd as other guards gathered the
women from their side of the hallway into a group; but
then the guards herded the group away, leaving her on
her own.

"With the extended lifetimes the suits allow us," the
Lapautee said, trying to feed her the official line of
slug crap, "if we didn't limit our population, we would
overrun our resources."

"So why don't you expand your resources instead
of sacrificing future generations?" she countered, her
anger so great she barely knew what the *krek* she was
saying.

"I don't set policy." He offered her a circlet of flowers. "Put this on your head and all will know of your
sacrifice and treat you with respect."

She knocked aside his hand and the ringlet fell to
the ground. "I'm not from Lapau, and I have no intention of making this sacrifice. I intend to be gone in a
week."

"While you're here, you must obey our laws."

"No." If he expected her to cry or cringe or beg, he
would learn differently. She remembered much of the
self-defense classes she'd taken in school. And with

her adrenaline surging, she figured she'd have extra strength.

Surprise was an advantage. She lunged straight at him, jabbing with a fist. Shocked, he moved slowly, and she struck his mouth with her knuckles. His lips split and bluish blood streamed out. Then the two of them slammed into each other, stumbled to the hallway floor, and rolled. Fear surging, she came to her feet first and caught a second opponent with a straight-edged hammer blow to the neck, and jammed a foot at another's knee. He howled with pain and hopped awkwardly on one foot, clutching his injury. But she had no time to finish him as a pair of strong hands grabbed her arms from behind. Still, she kneed a third man's crotch and almost broke free.

The door behind her opened, and Shannon threw her gangly body into the fray. What was she doing? Shannon was sick. She was supposed to have run away with Cyn. While Alara appreciated the help, the fight was by no means even. Six strong men against two women— one of them elderly and ill.

"You want my ovaries, you sick bastards," Shannon spat, catching one man with an elbow strike to his nose, "you'll have to beat it out of my unconscious body."

12

"Six officials took Alara and Shannon," Cyn informed Xander between gasps. Sweat pouring off her skin, her chest heaving as she sucked in air, she stumbled into their already crowded room, looking as if she'd sprinted to their building and then raced up seven flights of stairs. "Alara single-handedly attempted to fight—"

"Alara was fighting?" Xander's jaw dropped open. He recalled her supple golden skin, her unmarred perfect flesh, and couldn't envision her in a fight. Xander had known women warriors. Tessa was first-rate and had defeated him on several occasions; even Cyn could throw a mean fist under duress. But the idea of Alara fighting with anything but her brilliant mind rocked him.

"Alara delayed them long enough for me to escape. When the officials began to win, Shannon joined the fray and I escaped out the back."

Xander had always admired the Terran's spirit, but he wished she hadn't sacrificed herself. With her failing health, she should have saved her strength. There was no certainty her weakened body could recover from injuries she might suffer in a fight.

"Why did they want them?" Xander asked, furious that the Lapautee had interfered with his mission and, worse, taken the women. He prayed they weren't hurt, or if they were, that the Lapautee would see they received medical care.

"The Lapautee collect the ova from any female who sets foot on their world to send to the Saj—it's part of their stupid treaty for the suits."

Vax swore. Cyn drew in more air and spoke quickly. "If we don't find them soon, they'll never have children."

Shannon already had all the children she wanted. She had kids and grandkids and great-grandkids. Xander doubted she could have more children at her age— but he still worried about her surviving the alien procedure in her frail state. His concern for Alara was just as great. She was young, healthy, in perfect physical health—if he discounted the beginnings of the plague. Besides, he'd forced Alara to accompany them. That she was in danger because of his actions made him more determined to save her.

"Contact Lithdar," Xander ordered Cyn. "See if he'll help us."

"I'm on it." Cyn turned to the room's com, then spun on her heel to face him.

"Vax, you're with me." Xander headed for the door.

"Wait." Cyn hurried across the room to hand him a few pellets that Alara had left behind. "Use these to contact me. If Lithdar will help, I need a way to tell you. Put them in the public machines to pay for access and we can communicate through their system."

Until this moment the alien had been silent. Xander wasn't sure if he could follow the conversation. "Clarie go. Clarie help."

"Thanks, but you'll slow us down." Xander hurried out the door.

Every moment was critical. If they could reach the women before the officials locked them up inside a building, the rescue would likely be easier. Six men had taken the women, and although he and Vax were outnumbered three to one, a Rystani warrior in full fighting mode could surely take out these weak-bellied blue-skinned Lapautee.

Running at full speed, Xander counted on Vax to keep up. Their suits, which allowed them to move and fight at the quickness of thought, were good for only short bursts. Saving the speed for later when it might be necessary for a fight might be a mistake—but he'd made the call and Vax didn't question his tactic.

Feet slapping the pavement, they raced past startled Lapautee. Clearly the people here were unaccustomed to strangers running through their streets. Most gave them a wide berth and no one tried to stop them.

Still breathing easily, Xander and Vax reached the building where the women had been housed. The high-rise covered a city block and had several exits and entrances but he saw no sign of them at the front. Not good. Apparently they'd already left and could have disappeared in a street vehicle or by air in a skimmer. But they might still be here, and he and Vax would check out their quarters. Leaping onto a lift, they rode it to the tenth floor.

The moment the lift's doors opened, Xander knew

the women were gone. The door to their quarters tilted, one hinge busted. Spatters of red blood against one pale beige wall told him that either Shannon or Alara was injured.

Vax stepped into the room. "They're gone."

"Get Cyn on the com." Xander's heart pounded—more from despair than the run. He feared he might never find the women. "See if she's contacted Lithdar."

They'd been speaking loudly and several doors opened. People stared through the cracks, but after noting the offworlders' scowls, they slammed them shut. Like people everywhere, when trouble came they didn't want to become involved.

Xander waited, and when the next curious Lapautee opened a door, he used his psi to move fast, wedged his foot in the crack and shoved his way inside. Two young women with tears in their eyes trembled as if he were about to strike them.

Keeping his voice gentle was an effort, but he tried. "Where did they take them?"

"The PPC."

"What's that?"

"The Procreation Prevention Center."

"Tell me how to get there."

"It won't do you any good." The younger woman trembled and pointed. "The facility is as big as Arc Six."

"Show me. Please."

Either they'd decided to help due to the desperation in his tone or they figured he wouldn't leave until they did as he requested. They pulled up a map on a vid-screen. He stared at the huge facility and realized they'd have no difficulty finding it—however, entering the city-block complex and then locating the women was another matter.

"Thanks." He was about to return to Vax, when he skidded to a stop and asked the two girls, "When they take their ovaries, do they kill them?"

"Only if they fight. Why did they fight?" The girl's tone was accusatory and she sniffled, wiping her tears on the back of her wrist.

Xander didn't answer her question. He met Vax back in the damaged hallway and one look at his face told him the news from Lithdar was bad. "He wouldn't take Cyn's call."

The lift opened. Vax and Xander moved to either side, ready to attack in case the officials had returned. But Clarie, with Delo holding on to his antennae, shuffled out. "We go rescue."

Xander had no idea how Clarie had found them. Or how he'd followed so quickly. But he agreed with his sentiment. "Yes, we go rescue the women."

"We need to figure a way out of here because the captain is never going to find us," Shannon muttered.

Alara had to agree. The complex was huge, and even if Xander learned where they were, pinpointing them inside this building would be impossible. As the officials had dragged them inside, she'd seen few guards and no cameras. But the facility had mazelike corridors that twisted and turned back on themselves for no apparent reason. They'd passed lots of weeping women and others who stared straight ahead with hollow eyes, their hands cradling their stomachs as if they ached inside for what had been taken from them.

Eventually, the officials had thrown Alara and Shannon into a holding area. With a locked door and bars across the front where the guard could watch them, they had no privacy.

"How's your head?" Shannon asked.

"Hurts like Dregan hell," Alara admitted, hoping that if she complained, the Terran might feel enough at ease to talk about her own failing health. "But I think the bleeding's stopped."

"Sorry I didn't get there sooner."

"You shouldn't have come at all. You're sick."

"And let you have all the fun?" Shannon muttered, saying nothing about her illness—but she didn't deny it, either. She stuck out her tongue at the guard, who paid no attention, but had to be listening.

"If I can get us out of this cell, can you recall the way back?" Alara asked, invoking privacy mode on her suit so the guard couldn't hear their conversation.

"The body may be failing, but my mind's still sharp." Shannon kept her back to the guard so he couldn't see her lips move. "How are you going to get us out?"

Alara didn't miss the fact that Shannon hadn't directly answered her question—but it was the first time she'd actually admitted to the disease. Unless the woman had a photographic memory, no way would she recall their route. But Alara said no more about it. When Alara had been hurt, her head slamming into the wall, Shannon had thrown herself into the fight. Instead of escaping with Cyn, she'd won Alara's gratitude, but unfortunately now she was caught, as well.

Alara no longer thought of Shannon as a Terran, but as a friend—a good thing because there was no estimating how long they might be stuck in this cell together. While Xander would try to rescue them, he faced almost impossible odds. To search every room in this building might take years, but she couldn't resist *Boktai* that long.

"I have an idea." Alara reached into her pocket and touched the balls of *blane* she'd procured from the plant vendor. Looking through the bars, she eyed the guard as he ate his meal. The Lapautee was large, devoid of expression, yet his eyes remained alert. "Can you distract him long enough for me to drop some plant fertilizer into his food?"

"Then what?" Shannon asked. "He's going to turn green and leafy on us?"

"Green and sick would be more likely. Maybe green and dead. I can't predict the effects the *blane* will have on his biology with any real certainty."

"Okay, I divert him, then what?"

"He'll unlock the door to check you out. I'll drop the *blane* in his food."

"Sounds like a plan."

Alara appreciated that Shannon didn't pick apart her idea. So many things could go wrong. The guard might not fall for the diversion. She could put the *blane* in his drink but he might not swallow it. Or he might drink it and feel no effects.

And Shannon hadn't asked what they would do after he got sick, and Alara couldn't have answered— because it depended on what happened next. But any escape attempt was better than waiting in the cell for the creation prevention butcher to slice them up.

Alara sat on the floor, positioning herself against the bars but far enough from the door so he wouldn't see her as a threat. When she'd been there a while and the guard was halfway through his meal, she nodded to Shannon.

The Terran let out an ear-piercing scream, then

gagged. Clutching her throat, she moaned, gyrated, and twisted as she slumped to the floor. Shannon's lips twisted and she drew her limbs to her chest. Her legs twitched and she curved her wrists until her hands looked like claws.

The guard set his tray of food down. But it wasn't close enough for her to reach. *Krek.*

"Do something," Alara demanded, scooting back as if to show she wouldn't get up if he entered the cell, but in truth, she shifted closer to the food.

He didn't unlock the cell, but advanced one step closer. Shannon obligingly moaned and thrashed, drawing the guard's eyes. But he didn't unlock the door, warily keeping back.

Instead, he spoke into his wrist, but she couldn't hear what he said over Shannon's groans. Alara still couldn't reach the food, but this might be her only opportunity. Taking a chance, Alara tossed *blane* balls into his food and drink. Then she held her breath, hoping the fertilizer didn't turn his water to purple or green—but the drink remained clear.

But several balls had landed on his food and they weren't disintegrating. If he found them, he might not eat or drink. But there was nothing else she could do.

"If you're not going to help her, I will." Alara shoved to her feet, hurried to Shannon and placed her hand on her forehead. Placing her body between the guard and the Terran, Alara pretended to manipulate her neck. "There. Is that better?"

"Ah . . . yes. Thanks."

The guard peered at her. "What did you do?"

"Her neck needed an adjustment. Don't Lapautee's bones ever require manipulation?"

The guard shook his head, picked up his food and

began to eat. Good. But she didn't want him paying close attention to his food while he ate.

What was the best way to capture a man's attention? That was an easy question to answer. She frowned at him. "But surely you know the secret way to manipulate the neck and back to give your wife the greatest sexual pleasure?"

He forked food into his mouth but his gaze stayed on her. "What are you talking about?"

"Well, everyone knows that certain body positions create the best alignment for mutual pleasure. Why, I once was with a man whose orgasm lasted for five Federation minutes."

"That's possible?" He guzzled water as if the topic she'd picked had made him hot.

"Of course."

"Tell me how it's done," he demanded, setting down his water and his food.

Not good. He'd become so interested in her story that he'd stopped eating. Inspired, she pointed to his tray, hoping he'd do the exact opposite of what she suggested. "The first requirement is ignoring your food, going hungry."

Shannon almost choked as she bit back a snort. Then she covered her lapse by holding up her hand. "I'm okay."

"Are you saying if I ignore my dinner, you'll *show* me?" The guard now looked as suspicious as an Endekian trader being offered water during rainy season in exchange for priceless gems.

Obviously he was wary of placing one foot inside their cell. She hardened her tone, hoping to confuse him. "You think I want you in this cell? Try to enter and I'll scream."

"That's what I thought. You're all talk." He turned his back on her, picked up his food and continued to eat.

Alara pretended annoyance while she helped Shannon over to the wall nearest the guard. She remained silent, hoping the *blane* that had landed on top of his food was in his belly and dissolving in his digestive tract.

When he grunted oddly, she glanced over to see him stagger. He dropped the tray. The remainder of his food and drink spilled, the plate, bowl, and tankard crashing and rolling by his feet. With a thump, he hit the floor hard, landing on his back, his limbs sprawled wide. His eyes closed and he didn't wriggle so much as a finger.

"Is he dead?" Shannon stood to peer at him. "No—not dead. His chest's still rising and falling."

Alara had no idea how long he'd be zonked, or how long until someone walked by and discovered what they'd done. She didn't hesitate to extend her hand and arm through the bars. "*Krek.* I can't reach him."

"Let me try," Shannon insisted. Although she was a bit shorter than Alara, she was extremely thin. She shoved her shoulder through right up to her neck, extended her arm and her fingertips until she just barely touched the edge of his sleeve. "Push me."

"You're already wedged in so tight, it'll take a lever to pry you—"

"Push me," Shannon insisted in a tone that snapped like an order.

Alara placed her hands on the Terran's shoulder and applied pressure. She feared the older woman's bones were so fragile they might snap. But while Shannon might not have much mass, she possessed a wiry strength.

Still, Alara didn't use all her force. "Am I hurting you?"

"Another quarter inch," Shannon gasped.

Alara had no idea what an inch was but threw more weight into her effort. Glimpsing their progress over Shannon's head, she saw her fingertips touch the guard's sleeve, then clutch the material. "You've got him."

Shannon groaned. Her body trembled with effort. "He's too heavy for me to pull."

"Hang on to him and I'll drag you both in." Alara braced her feet against the bars, clamped both hands around Shannon's upper arm, and yanked. Shannon popped out from between the bars and the guard slid toward their cell.

"Oops." Her strength gave out; Shannon let go.

Alara toppled hard and Shannon flattened her, knocking the wind from her lungs. For a moment Alara's chest froze. She couldn't draw in air. And pain rolled through her in waves as if she'd broken ribs.

"Sorry." Shannon scrambled off her. "You okay?"

"Ur-ek." She sounded like a wounded animal.

Shannon moved toward the guard. "Sorry, I don't speak Endeki and the translat—" She caught sight of Alara's twisted lips. "Oh, God. You're hurt."

Shannon knelt, smoothed back her hair. "I hope I didn't break any bones. Don't move."

Alara would like to see Shannon follow her own instructions and remain perfectly still when she couldn't breathe. But Alara couldn't talk. She clutched her throat as her chest spasmed and locked up tight.

Shannon leaned over Alara, her eyes full of concern, her voice reassuring and calm. "Sweetie, I know you can't breathe. My son used to race skim carts and the g-force sometimes knocked the wind out of him. You feel like you're dying—"

Alara nodded vigorously.

"But if you relax your chest muscles, you'll be back to normal in moments."

Alara nodded that she understood and closed her eyes. Shannon smoothed her hair back from her face in a loving gesture that reminded Alara of her mother. When she'd been a little girl and her father's shouts had scared her, her mother would often come to her, pull her into her lap and rock her, smoothing back her hair with gentle and tender strokes.

"Sweetie, you're going to be fine. Your plan worked. The big oaf is out like a light, and as soon as you're able, we're going to frisk him, find a key and bounce."

Alara envisioned her muscles relaxing and finally they obeyed. She drew in air and it had never tasted so sweet. She didn't try to test her hurting ribs yet, simply looked into Shannon's eyes. "Bounce?"

"Leave."

"Oh." Alara sat up slowly, hoping the dizziness was due to lack of air. Or her aching ribs. At least she didn't think any had broken.

But Shannon gasped. "Your head."

Alara gingerly placed a hand to her former injury and when it came away bloody she realized she'd re-opened the wound. "I don't think it's—"

"Use your suit to apply pressure," Shannon instructed. "It'll stop the bleeding."

Alara had never before employed her suit in quite that way. But it made sense. Using her psi, she applied force and the suit acted as a pressure bandage. Unfortunately, it couldn't also stop the throbbing ache. But she could live with the pain if they could escape. "I'm better now. Get the key."

Shannon stretched through the bars again and frisked the guard. She found holovids of a woman, more pellets which she appropriated, and a key to the cell which she held up in triumph. "You did it."

"*We* did it." Alara could never have reached the guard through the bars if Shannon hadn't been there. And between the exhilaration of success and the adrenaline flooding her system, her breasts began to tingle, signaling the early stirrings of *Boktai*. And her sexual need for regeneration would keep cycling repeatedly for this entire year.

By the four rings of Darica—why now?

Alara didn't need the distraction of her body signaling that it needed regeneration. Sex was the last thing she wanted to deal with now. But *Boktai* was never convenient, and she prayed they truly could escape. The alternative was simply unthinkable. If they were caught . . . and her body needed . . .

Breathe.

She could buy some time by staying calm.

Shannon inserted the key into the lock and an electronic buzzer hummed. The cell door opened, and it took all of Alara's presence of mind not to sprint down the corridor. "Let's lock him in the cell."

"Good idea." Shannon took one arm and she took the other. Unwilling to touch male flesh, Alara grabbed him by the sleeve and refused to look at him, knowing the sight of a male would advance her biological state. With her weakened psi, her suit's filters weren't working well and her nostrils drew in his male scent, making her even more eager to put distance between them.

In tandem, they dragged the unconscious guard into the cell. The effort cost Shannon. Her lips turned almost white but she didn't complain, so Alara didn't mention her bruised ribs.

Alara wished they'd had cuffs and a gag but they

had no material to work with. And in truth, she didn't like the excitement thrumming through her and realized the danger might be speeding up *Boktai*.

They locked the cell door behind them. Shannon glanced at the key as if she were considering leaving it. Alara spoke quietly, ignoring the male and her physical reaction to him. "Keep it. Maybe it'll unlock more than this cell door."

"Good thinking."

Shannon slipped the key into her suit. "Where do we go now?"

"To the nearest exit."

Shannon frowned. "I don't think I saw any—not even one—after we entered the complex."

"Can you cry on demand?" Alara asked.

"Sure." Shannon gave her a strange look. "Why?"

"So here's the plan. We walk slowly. We keep our hands over our wombs as if they've already taken our ova. If anyone stops us, we cry storm-sized tears. Keep your head down, shoulders hunched, take shuffling steps, and hopefully no one will even question us."

"Nice. You have a good head for tactics and remind me of my third granddaughter." Shannon smiled fondly, and Alara could tell from the softening in her eyes she loved her family. "That one could plan a military campaign if she wasn't so busy raising her brood."

They walked through corridor after corridor, past what seemed like hundreds of rooms. They passed many groups of women and when one traveled in the direction they were going, they attached themselves to them, believing there was safety in blending in. Shannon, bless her courageous heart, didn't once ask for a rest. Instead, her lips tightened and her breath turned raspy with the effort of remaining so long on her feet.

Luckily, the guards didn't question them. Alara tried to hold her breath every time they passed. She didn't look at their male forms, either. But just knowing they were close by sent signals to her brain that released hormones.

Ignore them.

Ignore the need.

She gritted her teeth, reminded herself that in the past she'd resisted *Boktai* for a day, even two. But she'd had her work to distract her. No males in her laboratory. And adrenaline hadn't been a catalyst.

They'd walked for a long time, women joining them as others departed, and she'd seen no sign of an exit. While the building didn't seem to have a day or night, Shannon simply wasn't able to keep up with Alara's overcharged body. Alara had to slow her pace, then slow it again.

However badly she needed to escape and seek regeneration, the exhaustion of their capture, her rumbling stomach, and her parched throat, never mind her aching ribs and head, had Alara searching for a place to rest. Shannon couldn't keep wandering the corridors without sleep and they both needed food and drink, so when she spied two food trays on a cart, Alara swiped the cart.

Although Shannon had yet to complain, at the sight of food, she perked up, picking up the pace slightly. She also plucked the key from her pocket and tried several doors. The first three didn't open, but the third one buzzed and led into a supply room.

The two women slipped inside and shared the stolen food. The Lapautee nourishment had an odd but not unpleasant taste. Between bites of meat and vegetables and sips of drink, Alara considered their options. While she could have kept going, Shannon required rest and no way was she leaving the Terran behind. "We need sleep."

"Should we take turns?"

Alara shrugged. "The night janitor is the likeliest person to find us. If he does open the door, we'll just say we're lost."

"Too bad it's the truth." Indicating her true exhaustion, Shannon didn't argue over whether anyone would believe the flimsy argument that they could get lost in a closet. She floated by the ceiling with her null grav and flipped off the light.

"We aren't lost," Alara said quietly, hoping she could sleep as the need for regeneration coursed through her.

"We aren't?"

"We're in Arc Six on Lapau," Alara teased her, pleased with the give-and-take and her developing friendship with the Terran. She needed distraction and doubted she'd sleep at all, but she didn't want Shannon to know.

"Oh, Arc Six. Right. I feel so much better now," Shannon mumbled. "Even Xander can't find us in here. He must be frantic with worry by now, but he won't show it—reminds me of Todd."

"Todd?"

"My fourth son."

"How many kids do you have?"

"Ten biological children and then there's the three I adopted."

"Ten wasn't enough?" Alara asked. She'd never known anyone who'd had that many children. But then Endeki men didn't like their wives so busy with the kids that they couldn't take care of their needs.

Shannon was a feisty old lady. She'd left her family

behind to explore the stars. In many ways, Alara admired her spirit.

"If I could have afforded more children, I would have had twenty. Children are God's blessing, especially after they move out and have kids of their own. Grandchildren are God's miracles—you get to enjoy them and then hand them back for the hard stuff."

"So why did you leave them?"

"A girl's got to live. And the truth is that the kids don't need me anymore. Neither do the grandkids, and I have so many great-grandkids, I can't even recall all their names." Shannon's voice turned husky. "They keep in touch. One of the great-grandkids wrote a paper about me for a class in school. She called me a legend. I told her legends were for dead people and I still have a lot of living to do."

Alara prayed that statement was true. Because even as Shannon made the claim, her voice weakened.

Alara also could hear the pride in her tone, despite her denial of legendary status. Earth must be very different from Endeki. If an Endekian woman had lived Shannon's adventurous life, her relatives would revile her for leaving her family. But then Terran women had a freedom from *Boktai* that allowed them to accomplish more than her people could.

And as need poured through Alara, she mourned the loss of her work. By now, her untended DNA samples would be dead, the mutations she'd wanted to study would have died and decomposed. Starting over might be impossible.

Might be. But probably wasn't. She'd persevere. She'd find a way to achieve her goals. With Shannon as an example, Alara hoped she could be as brave, as adaptable and resourceful and strong. Perhaps she too could make a home among the stars. Perhaps she even belonged here.

Sex with Xander had made her realize she could deal with *Boktai* without Endekian men—they weren't the only males in the universe. Who would have thought that she'd come to admire a Rystani? While her need for regeneration might be influencing her thought patterns, she couldn't deny that when she thought about mating with Xander again, her heart skipped and her tummy tightened.

Although her body had reacted to the male guard, it was Xander she wanted to kiss. Xander she wanted to touch. Xander she wanted as she'd wanted no other man before.

13

Xander, Vax, and Clarie found Arc Six and the Procreation Prevention Center without difficulty. Arc
Six *was* the PPC. The structure was larger than
some cities. While they'd spotted many women arriving and departing through one main entrance, after
several hours of surveillance, they'd seen no men entering the complex, only women. Either the officials
who'd taken his crew had used a side entrance or a
back door Xander had yet to find, or not many males
had access, creating a tactical and strategical problem.

Even if Xander and Vax could alter their skin color
from bronze to blue-tinged, it was impossible for them
to disguise themselves as Lapautee. They were too
large, too broad. And without knowing the women's
exact location within the complex, they would be foolhardy to attempt to enter the building.

Yet Xander refused to abandon Shannon and Alara.

"Options?" he asked Vax as they reconnoitered on a park bench opposite the complex. Around them couples strolled, vendors sold drinks, and the tangy aroma of hot meat pies made him recall *octar* meat and *jarballa* sauce, Kahn's favorite meal. Thoughts of Kahn quickly turned to Tessa and her failing health as well as the failing health of everyone back home—and here. How was Shannon holding up after the fight?

Pressure built on Xander's shoulders at this delay in his mission. Were his loyalty to Shannon and his personal connection to Alara risking the entire mission? He had no idea how much time he had, or if he could trust Lithdar. It bothered him that the official wasn't taking their calls, but his reason could be anything from a full-blown betrayal to simply that he had another meeting or had gone home for the day. Cyn was trying to find him. But until Xander had more choices and Lithdar finalized their arrangements to go down to the Saj planet, Xander would use every moment to find Alara and Shannon.

Vax might appear relaxed on the bench, but the warrior in him never ceased perusing his surroundings. His gaze constantly assessed the danger from the passing street traffic, the approaching vehicles, and even above for skimmer activity. "We will tap into their computer system."

"What good would that do when we can't read the language? Our systems are voice-activated, but theirs aren't," Xander reminded him.

"We question the departing women," Vax suggested.

Clarie remained silent. He petted Delo and paced, almost as if he were nervous.

"If we question them, they could report us to their authorities and stop us from entering the building,"

Xander thought aloud. If he had to shoot down Vax's suggestion, he owed him a reason. "And with the size of that complex, the likelihood of any female having seen Shannon and Alara and remembering where they saw them is slim."

"We could try forcing Lithdar to help us." Vax gave him a third option, but Xander knew he hadn't mentioned the Lapautee official until now because there was no guarantee they could find him, and even if they did, he might not be able to help—even if coerced.

"Must rescue them." Clarie stopped pacing in front of them. Although his facial expression didn't change, Xander thought he glimpsed impatience flashing in his black eyes.

Xander wished he'd stop telling him what he already knew and zap him into the building. But Clarie never did the expected. The being appeared to have no physical strength, poor communication skills, and contributed no ideas. He and his pet wandered off exploring as if this place were a tourist attraction.

And yet, he shouldn't be quick to judge. Clarie may have brought them halfway across the galaxy by means he couldn't explain. Although the alien seemed childish to him, perhaps he was so sophisticated that he was talking down to them.

Still, Xander didn't need another puzzle or responsibility right now. "But how do we find them?"

"Get them out," Clarie responded.

Xander tried to explain. "If we go in there without knowing where—"

"No." Clarie swiveled his head from side to side. "Don't look outward. Look inward."

Clarie's words stabbed Xander like a hunting knife to the heart.

Surely he couldn't be suggesting . . .

He couldn't possibly know . . .

Xander stared at Clarie in shock, the hair on his neck tingling. "Look inward? What do you mean?"

"Can't find what you seek by looking out, so look inside."

"But if we go inside," Vax protested, "we won't know where to—"

"I know what he means." Xander stared at Clarie, his stomach churning. How had the alien known about the incident that he'd never shared with anyone—not even with his father? How did the alien know of his shame? His act of cowardice under torture and then again on the bridge when he'd hesitated to rescue Clarie?

And for him to suggest that he . . . no. He'd sworn to himself that he would never again think about his lapse, that he'd been hallucinating due to his pain and upset. But that was an excuse—to comfort him from the nightmares that made him awaken in a sweat, a scream lodged in his throat.

Vax stared at Xander, his gaze curious. "What?"

Even saying the words made acid churn in his gut. But better to admit to cowardice than to allow the women to come to harm. "There might be a way for me to explore that building without physically going inside."

"I don't understand." Vax held his gaze, but withheld judgment. "But whatever must be done, you can count on my help. And my discretion."

Throat tight, Xander nodded. "Let's find somewhere more private."

"There's a closed retail establishment a block to the left," Vax suggested.

Xander shook his head, honored to have such a steady friend. "I require a location as close to the complex as possible."

With quiet curiosity, Vax jerked his thumb to a building painted the same color as the larger complex behind it. "There's what appears to be a shed of some kind right up against the main building."

"That might work." Mouth dry, Xander didn't waste time, and began to explain. "I'll need you to restrain and beat me."

Vax gave him an "I don't like that idea" scowl. "Why?"

Xander's tone was tight, hard, but the words must be said. "When the pain turns extreme, I lose courage."

"Captain, you withstood Endekian torture when you were no more than a boy. No one doubts your courage."

"You don't understand. I cracked under the torture."

"You did not. You did not reveal the information they sought."

"I ran like a coward."

Confusion clouded Vax's eyes. "How could you run? They tied you down. I don't understand."

"My experience is going to sound . . . odd."

"I'm listening."

"The pain did something to me. And—"

"And?"

"My mind . . . snapped."

Vax frowned. "What do you mean, you snapped? You lost consciousness? You went crazy?"

"My being, my consciousness, levitated out of my body. I didn't have eyes, but I could see the Endekian flipping the switch that shocked my physical body while my mind floated by the ceiling above us. I saw my body twitch. My mouth scream. But I no longer felt pain and my mind was no longer inside my bones and flesh. I could move through the building's walls, and during that time, I scouted the enemy camp. I saw Tessa sneak past the Endekian scouts. Only when she was about to rescue me did I force my mind to return to my body."

Vax blinked, taking in what Xander had said. Xander expected disbelief and shock, but saw only empathy in his expression. Clearly deeply affected, Vax spoke thoughtfully. "Captain, what happened to you was no loss of courage. Your experience sounds similar to what we do in a healing circle. Only you took the out-of-body experience one step further."

Xander shook his head. "A warrior would not have fled."

"A warrior finds a way to survive and to win," Vax countered. "And now you're asking me to cause you great pain to save Shannon and Alara. There is nothing shameful in your past—only great courage. You still think upon your torture with the eyes of a boy instead of the maturity of a man."

Stunned by Vax's words, Xander stopped walking. One reason he appreciated his first officer's opinions was that he never lied. Xander also respected Vax's judgment—even when they disagreed. Could Vax be right? Could the pain and the fear of breaking under torture when he'd been young have so confused him that even now he couldn't think clearly about the incident?

He'd been frightened that the pain would be too much to bear—that he'd reveal where his people were hiding, and that he'd stain his soul with the responsibility of their deaths. He'd been determined to remain silent, and his screams had shamed him. In his mind, he should have been able to withstand whatever they'd done—so when he'd snapped, when he'd left his body behind, he'd assumed he'd acted with cowardice.

Perhaps he *had* been looking at the incident through the eyes of a half-grown kid. He'd been too ashamed to tell anyone. For years he'd tried to forget. And then he'd snapped once again on the bridge—but then, no pain had been involved. No fear—only the stress of attempting to make a grave decision. But perhaps leaving his body had been a way to seek out Clarie before the clutch beam had drawn the alien in.

There was nothing wrong with exploration, using his senses—especially if he could find Alara and Shannon.

Vax had seen what he could not and a huge heaviness lifted from his heart. "Thank you, my friend." Xander slapped Vax on the shoulder. "Your words will make repeating the experience less painful—at least in my mind."

"I have been thinking about that, also. Perhaps pain isn't necessary to repeat what happened."

Xander considered the suggestion, but with no other trigger, how could he do what he must? "Pain is necessary, even in the healing circle when we take on the ills of the sick one, and also during the birth of a child when we take on the mother's pain."

"But we don't physically injure our bodies. We accept their mental pain."

"You want me to induce mental pain without experiencing the physical pain?" Xander turned the idea over in his mind, wondering if Vax was right. During his lifetime, the out-of-body experience had occurred twice. His mental anxiety on the bridge had caused the same reaction as the physical torture. But he could see no way to invoke such mental pain once again. It seemed unlikely they could figure out another way to induce the mental state required without a strong, agonizing electric current passing through his body.

"What about inducing a trance with hypnosis?" Vax suggested as they proceeded to the shed's door.

"If Ranth were here, he might know how, but since neither of us is an expert—"

"Clarie expert."

Xander had almost forgotten the alien was still with them, but Clarie had trailed after them, silent as a shadow. The little guy didn't speak much, but Xander was beginning to realize that Clarie understood more than he let on and was more advanced than he appeared.

"You can help me achieve the mental state required?" Xander let Vax pick the lock on the shed while he focused on Clarie.

"Yes. Clarie help."

Interference is unacceptable.

Back off.

Mutation and adaptation must proceed from a natural cause of progression. To allow them to live we must see meritorious improvement and adaptation.

We will.

Instigating action will nullify all the results.

Why?

You cannot break the rules.

What is the difference between stirring a little stardust to create a universe and helping a species survive by forcing evolution to the next stage?

Even if you succeed, you will have failed.

Only if we employ your narrow-minded definition of success.

Did you just resort to insulting me?

I merely pointed out the fact of your unwillingness to see beyond what has always been.

You're going too far.

I will not accept less than success. That is the difference here.

Exactly. You will go to any lengths to prove your point.

Now you've finally got it.

Unacceptable. Unsatisfactory. Unsuitable.

Go away. I'm busy.

You're cheating.

That's absurd. There is more than one way to accomplish a task.

We should let them all die, now. It would be kinder. They simply are not up to the mission before them.

We don't know that yet. Let the forces set in motion do their job. Let me work.

Your machinations will come to naught because your methods are faulty.

So you've already said. Go away.

I am here to observe. As much as I would prefer to be elsewhere, my task is to monitor.

Then monitor in silence.

Kirek scanned the secret file and read quickly. Any moment the guards would burst into the room and discover him. His heart pounded, sweat wept from his pores, and his muscles twitched with the need to flee and save himself. But he read with fascination. For over three decades, the Endekians had meticulously planned their invasion of his childhood homeworld of Rystan because they wanted the glow stones.

The Endekians had spent a fortune to discover how

to replicate an artificial geomagnetic field that balanced the glow stones' atomic activity when they removed them from Rystan. Since the invasion, they'd harvested the stones, mining deep into Rystan to obtain and transport them to Endeki.

But why?

Sure, the glow stones could be used as atomic weapons of massive destruction. However, the Endekians had access to much more sophisticated weapons. While the glow stones were unique in nature, they were also primitive compared to what the Endekians could manufacture for less cost and a lot less effort.

As the soldiers burst into the room, weapons aimed at him, Kirek still didn't have the entire picture. He'd needed more time to access other files—time he didn't have.

"Don't move," a soldier ordered.

With a nonthreatening tap of his finger, Kirek erased the vidscreen image and placed a frightened look on his face. "Don't tell Lataka you found me. Please. I needed a rest. The woman's insatiable."

The soldiers took him to a bleak interrogation room. All around Kirek machines hummed and sensors measured his physical reactions. He knew the next hours wouldn't be pleasant. Although he didn't believe they would kill him, he couldn't be certain. The coming interrogation would be tricky. These men didn't know he could manipulate the machines that monitored him, and he appeared to be a boy, not a full-grown man. Yet they'd caught him someplace he shouldn't have been, someplace with information he wasn't supposed to have seen.

However, when Drik strode into the room with four guards, Kirek recognized that he'd discovered something extremely important. But what?

With no warning, the guard smacked him across the face. "How did you unlock that office door?"

Kirek shrugged, let his eyes tear from the sting, hoping his immature reaction would remind them of his youth. He wanted them to see fright through an attempt to appear courageous—not so difficult to feign in light of his circumstances. "I tried every door in the corridor. That one was unlocked."

The guard raised his hand for another blow. Kirek pretended he had no fighting skills, that he didn't know how to avoid the coming blow. The guard shouted in his face. "So it was an accident that you picked that room?"

Kirek pulled back and let them see him tremble. "The doors all looked the same. How could I know you'd have a computer in there until I went inside?"

The guard slapped his other cheek and his head slammed to one side. "What were you doing?"

"Hiding from Lataka." Kirek let tears rain down his cheeks, pleased with his performance. The weaker they thought him, the easier it would be to convince them he told the truth. "The woman is insatiable. I required . . . a rest."

"Sir," said one of the guards to Drik. "According to our truth detectors, he does not lie."

Kirek could make his body invisible to the machines. Although he'd never fine-tuned his skill before, he made a slight adjustment, altering his elevated heart rate and higher body temperature and breathing rates to appear steady.

"What were you doing behind the desk?" the inquisitor demanded.

Kirek had to be careful. He suspected they could go into the computer system and discover he'd logged on.

And if they caught him in a lie, they'd realize he could fool their truth detector. While he couldn't hide his log-on, he hoped they'd never learn which file he'd read.

Admitting the part of the truth they could check, he hoped his computer skills had covered the rest. "I logged on to the computer."

"Why?" The guard smacked him again and his ears rang.

He cowered, hoping to appear sheepish and contrite. "I missed the vidgames on Mystique."

"You wanted to play games?"

"Playing with Lataka is . . . tiresome. I thought to amuse myself while I hid."

The guard raised his hand to strike again. Kirek's cheeks burned but he was determined not to reveal any of his fighting skills.

"Stop." Drik regarded Kirek with amusement.

"Sir, his story's ridiculous."

"How long was he inside my office?" Drik asked.

"Less than a Federation minute."

"You think he could have gotten past our encryption and found anything in a minute?"

"No, sir. Our security is too good for that."

"But you don't believe his story?"

"A few jolts of electricity through his body would—"

Kirek put a quiver in his voice and hoped he wasn't going too far. "Please, no. Don't hurt me. I meant no harm. I just wanted to play some games."

Drik shook his head. "If we torture the hostage, we cannot give him back to his people without causing an interplanetary incident."

"What do you want me to do with him, sir?"

"Lataka obviously can't control him. Take him to Vansek. She knows how to punish bad boys."

"Yes, sir." As the chief guard roughly grabbed him, the other guards broke into loud guffaws.

Punish? At hearing that Drik was turning over his punishment to a woman, Kirek figured he'd gotten off lightly—but then, he had yet to meet Vansek.

14

"Clarie, what do I do first?" Xander asked. At least if he failed to astrally extend his mind from their hidden position inside the shed, no one could witness their odd behavior.

"Close eyes," Clarie instructed, petting Delo on his shoulder, the animal's bushy tail waving back and forth.

Once Clarie had entered the shed, Delo had changed color from his usual brown to a glowing orange that gave off enough light for Xander to see that Clarie's antennae seemed to have grown longer.

"Close eyes and concentrate," Clarie insisted.

Knowing Vax had his back, Xander did as the tiny alien instructed. "Now what?"

"Relax all muscles. Begin with face. Let tension flow from body. Picture stream of energy leaving mouth, cheeks, and forehead. Head is light on shoulders. Body is like water flowing in gentle river."

Xander used his psi to float his body, then concentrated on Clarie's words. He relaxed his jaw, his mouth, and his eyes by imagining Alara running her fingers over his skin and smoothing out frown lines. He envisioned her lips skimming along his neck. Ever so slowly, he allowed the tension to drain from him as he visualized Alara next to him, her hands finding every knot and soothing his taut muscles.

"Good. Keep head and neck relaxed. Focus on chest and breathing. Breathe in. Breathe out."

Xander felt light, comfortable. He imagined the tension as purple, the color of alarm. Stress streamed out of him, leaving him suffused with a golden glow that matched Alara's soft skin. He took her golden color and wrapped it around him, like a soothing blanket made of her true spirit.

"Hips and buttocks—relax them. Float in river. Allow river to carry you to warm, welcoming sea where all life thrives." Clarie's tone droned in a tranquilizing monotone that helped Xander loosen his muscles and calm his soul. "Relax down body to calves, ankles, toes. Body is now one with river."

In a cocoon of warm water, Xander floated. He could no longer tell where his body ended and the water began. So peaceful.

"Body is safe. Water will protect it. Let mind lift and go free."

At Clarie's words, Xander soared out of his flesh. As he'd done once before, he could see his body beneath him with Vax and Clarie in the shed. But the shed was too tiny to contain his elation.

He'd done it. He'd left his body. He was free to search for Alara. And without his body, he could travel at the speed of thought. His energy seemed limitless and he rocketed into the building, his hopes rising.

I'm coming, Alara.

Hold tight, Shannon.

Xander flew right through the exterior walls, into a huge reception area. Dozens of women with apprehensive expressions milled around listlessly. But he saw no Terran and no Endekian woman with golden skin, so in a flash of thought, he moved on. Although he could travel at unbelievable speed, he couldn't process information as quickly as he visualized his surroundings. After entering each room, he had to slow to search before moving on.

And there were hundreds, perhaps thousands of rooms. Tiny cubicles where women gave up their ova to the Saj. The sight depressed him but he determinedly kept on, all locked rooms accessible to his mind. He explored offices, a cafeteria, a place where the ova were stored at critical temperatures for a reason he couldn't determine. He flew past barred cells—all empty except one where a guard was locked inside. Pausing, he wondered if Alara and Shannon could have been there and escaped, locking the guard in their place.

And finally, in almost the center of the complex, he found them in a janitorial closet. Relief and elation filled him. They'd obviously escaped and now were hiding out.

Neither woman appeared harmed.

Light filtered in under the door, allowing him to make out their shapes. Shannon slept soundly, her back to him. As always, Alara looked beautiful, perhaps more beautiful than he remembered. Her hair floated around her head, framing her high cheekbones and lush mouth. He'd been so frightened of losing her that he'd spoken to Vax about the shame that had

haunted him, a shame that was now gone. He had yet
to deal with his growing feelings for the Endekian—
but now was not the time.

Seeing them, being unable to speak to them, was
both comforting and infuriating. Shannon's deep
snores indicated exhaustion, and he wondered how
much this adventure had taxed her remaining strength
and shortened her life. And Alara—by the stars! He
could tell from her irregular breathing pattern that she
was far from asleep. In fact, he was almost certain
from her tension that she was entering *Boktai*.

Of all the bad timing . . . she had enough to deal
with as she hid from the Lapautee without fighting her
hormones, too.

Recalling how strong her need would grow, knowing
that she would require sex to regenerate, the urges so
strong that lust would overcome her need to hide, elevated his frustration. They didn't have much time before
she would be forced to approach a man—and as much
as he hated the idea, he understood she would hate it
more. The only men inside were guards. Approaching
one meant recapture. And stars, with them hiding almost dead center in the middle of the complex, they
couldn't have been in a worse position for extraction.

While he shouldn't stay long, he nevertheless tar-
ried, wishing for a way to communicate. He couldn't
shake Shannon awake without hands or speak without
a mouth, couldn't so much as whisper a sound. Desperate to do something, he prayed.

Hold on.

We're coming to get you out.

Now that he was with them in spirit, he didn't want
to leave, but he had to find the best way to come back
and physically reach them. He flew through air ducts

and heating systems to the roof. If they could borrow a skimmer and land on the roof, an extraction might be doable.

Once he mapped the likeliest place to land a skimmer and branded it into his mind, he visited the women one more time. Without knowing if they could receive his message, he focused hard on one thought.

Climb to the roof.

Up.

Go up.

Up to the roof.

Xander had no idea if his thoughts could reach them; he wasn't telepathic. But perhaps in his astral state he might have abilities he didn't normally have. And there was no harm in trying.

Even if the women stayed put, and he and Vax landed the skimmer on the roof, he would know where to find them—unless in the meantime, they left the closet and tried to walk in another direction. The urge to stay and watch over them was almost overwhelming, but he couldn't help them from here. Thoughts heavy, he forced himself to leave.

His mission done, he snapped through space in a flash, reconnected with his body, the physical merging smooth, the mental adjustment jarring. It took all his strength to open his eyes. Delo no longer glowed bright orange but emitted a dull blush—barely enough to see by.

The shock of reentering surprised him—especially since leaving had been so easy. Xander couldn't move his arms or legs or even turn his head. His psi was so weak, he couldn't maintain his null grav. He fell from where he'd been floating, but Vax cushioned the blow, breaking his fall.

"I found them." Xander ignored the pain of landing

on the shed's floor. Speaking took almost more energy than he had. But he forced his mouth to work, his tongue to wrap around the words. "Find us a skimmer."

"Slow down." Vax peered at him, worry in his eyes. "Are you all right?"

"Okay. Weak." The out-of-body flying had given him awesome energy during that time, but apparently the strength he'd used tapped his physical body to the max. If he hadn't returned when he had, he might not have been conscious right now. "You may have to . . . carry me. Can't . . . wait. I know where the women are *now*. If they leave . . . then everything we did—"

"Rest. I understand."

"Go. Hurry."

Vax squeezed Xander's arm. "I'll find us a skimmer. Clarie, stay with him."

"Clarie stay. Delo stay."

Knowing the Terran desperately required rest, Alara allowed Shannon to sleep for four hours, as long as she could bear to remain confined in the dark closet. Alara's physical reaction to danger seemed to have instigated a need for cell regeneration. Feeling as though fingertips trailed over her flesh and incited her nerve endings, Alara required a distraction from her budding lust. She needed Xander.

Oddly, she could have sworn his presence touched her, reassured her that he was coming to get her. Alara wasn't given to flights of fancy and wondered if the combination of stress and biological need had caused her to dream for a few minutes, yet she hadn't shut her eyes or fallen asleep.

"Shannon, wake up."

"What's wrong?" Shannon stretched.

The Terran appeared to have awakened fully and had obviously picked up the concern in Alara's tone. Alara tried to make light of her unease. "What could possibly be wrong? You're sick and we're sleeping in the middle of the Lapautee, who want to steal our ova."

"You haven't slept, have you?" Shannon guessed.

Alara ignored the question because if she answered it, she might have to lie about why she couldn't sleep, and talking about *Boktai* would only make her problem worse. Yet if they ran into a male, Alara needed to strengthen her psi shields and avoid his scent and his touch, and realizing she might not have time to fill Shannon in later, she changed her mind about confiding.

"At certain times, Endekian women lose control over their psi and our suits' shielding fails. We become very susceptible to male touch and scent. Even seeing a man right now could cause my thinking to muddy."

"So we avoid the guards." Shannon accepted her statement and didn't ask questions, treating Alara's condition much like she did her own illness—with quiet dignity.

Alara had the strongest urge to hug her. She didn't. Instead, she cracked open the door. "No one's there. Let's move."

Shannon followed Alara into the hallway and stepped beside her. "You have a preference which way we should go?"

"Not really. Why?" Alara glanced at her. She'd gotten to know Shannon fairly well during the last day and she'd never seen her so hesitant.

"I have the strongest urge to go . . . up."

"Up?"

"To the roof. Maybe if we go outside, we'll see the best way out of this complex."

"Okay. Let's do it."

Alara and Shannon had strolled through the corridor for no more than four minutes when several guards headed straight for them. Turning around would have made them conspicuous, so instead, they kept their eyes downcast, held their tummies, and feigned sadness.

Instead of walking by, two guards halted in front of them, causing Alara's pulse to jump into hyperdrive. Their musky male scent taunted her and she barely controlled her trembling. Allowing her eyes to take in their male shapes added a new sensory stimulation to the mix, but Alara also sensed their watchfulness.

When they'd escaped from the cell they'd attached themselves to groups of other women and no one had bothered to notice that they didn't have the bluish skin tone of the Lapautee women. But these guards were staring at them with suspicion. Alara tensed. Either these men were more alert than the others, or word of their escape had gone out.

"Halt," a guard ordered.

Looking frail and helpless, Shannon stumbled forward, hooked her leg behind one guard's knee. As they went down, she grabbed his weapon. Alara didn't wait to see more. When the second guard reached for his own weapon, Alara ducked her head and rammed it right into his gut. All four of them went down in a jumble of knees and elbows.

Male scents inundated her. Alara raised her psi shields against the male flesh touching hers, but she required her sight to fight. Even as she damned her biology, her lust escalated and she feared that soon she might lose control of her psi and her suit might again go transparent. However, that didn't stop her from jamming an elbow into the guard's neck and kicking his weapon across the hall.

He rolled on top of her, placed his hands around her neck and began to squeeze. She couldn't draw a breath, but didn't panic. Alara grabbed his pinky finger and pulled it back until the bone snapped. With a howl, he released his grip on her throat and precious air filled her lungs. Air filled with male scent. Even as she battled for life, she realized the irony that her body would rather mate with her killer than fight him. But she had yet to lose the battle for control.

Still, lucid, she knew she couldn't take much more stimulation. Lust wasn't creeping over her, but barreling down.

Shannon, bless her fighting soul, came up with a weapon and blasted both men twice. They twitched but didn't stir. Shaky, Alara rose to her feet, gasping for air and fighting the lust and adrenaline coursing through her.

Shannon didn't ask questions. She grabbed Alara's arm and yanked her from the men. "Come on."

Alara couldn't move. She needed regeneration so badly her brain couldn't make her legs take a step. Her need for regeneration seemed to have speeded up her normal timetable and she had no doubt it was her constant proximity to the virile captain over the last few days that had accelerated this phase of *Boktai*. "Go without me."

Shannon pointed the blaster at her. "Either I shoot you and carry you, or you walk away."

Alara bit her lip. The image of the tiny, sick woman carrying her would have brought a smile to her face at any other time. "Does that blaster have a pain setting?"

"Yeah."

"Use it."

"On you?" Shannon's eyes filled with questions but she pointed the weapon at Alara.

"Pain will make the lust go away for a little longer." Alara nodded her readiness and closed her eyes. Nothing could be more demeaning than mating with a man who'd just tried to kill her. Not even agonizing pain.

"Shannon. Hold your fire," Xander shouted, skidding to a halt at the end of the corridor. He'd never seen anyone so brave as Alara. She was willing to endure tremendous pain in order to prevent her hormones from taking over. With her eyes closed, her entire body trembling, her chin high—she looked like a star princess out of a fairy tale.

Relief on her wizened face, Shannon lowered her weapon. "About damn time you showed up."

As Xander and Vax hurried to the women, Xander didn't know which of them was in worse shape: Alara in *Boktai*, Shannon who looked very ill, or him—still in recovery from his out-of-body exploration that had left his psi almost tapped out, his body weak as a boy's.

But there was no possibility of him allowing Vax to carry an aroused Alara. She wouldn't be able to stop her response to his first officer, embarrassing Vax and humiliating herself. That she'd been willing to go to such an extreme as to ask Shannon to stun her to maintain control had made him realize her immense inner fortitude.

Alara might look as soft and sensuous as a monarch's mistress, but her core was pure *bendar*. If he hadn't found a way inside the complex, they might have made it out by themselves. But he'd promised to protect her. He'd given his word. So he used what was left of his psi to gather her into his arms, unsurprised to feel her trembling as she wound her arms around his head and buried her neck in his shoulder.

"I'm almost gone."

"Hang on," Shannon muttered.

He never knew where he found the strength to carry Alara to the roof where they'd left Clarie and the skimmer. The ride back to the building Lithdar had assigned to the men passed in a blur as Shannon filled him in on what had happened. Although returning where the authorities might find them might not be a good idea, they had to remain where Lithdar could contact them. With the last of his reserves, Xander carried Alara to their quarters while his crew rejoined Cyn and returned the "borrowed" skimmer.

And when he sank with Alara to the floor, she planted kisses over his brow, his nose, his mouth, and slowly he revived, but she was having such a good time taking charge, he pretended otherwise.

"I don't know how you found us, but thank you."

"I'm totally spent," he exaggerated, wondering if any man had ever given her control, wondering if he could feign exhaustion when he wanted her so badly. "I'm afraid I don't have enough psi left to—"

"You rescued me. Now I'll take care of you." Her voice was soft, seductive, sexy as spun *siltie* thread as she floated them both into the center of room.

Among the Rystani, the female was supposed to accept the male's caresses during lovemaking, but Xander wanted her spirit to heal. He wanted to give her back her self-respect. "I'm—"

"Exhausted." She grinned, her eyes bright with happy amusement. "But one part of you still has energy to spare."

His *tavis* didn't seem to comprehend that he was tired. While custom demanded that he remain in charge of their mating . . . he saw no harm in breaking tradition this one time. He'd also promised to regenerate her cells. Caught between an ancient convention and a current promise, he might have taken time to consider his options, but when Alara brazenly kissed his lips and inserted her tongue into his mouth, his thoughts spun lazily out of control.

Thinking seemed too much trouble when he could put all his focus into kissing her back, although holding still wasn't easy when he longed to do more. Her lips tasted sweet, familiar, and best of all, the burgeoning emotional connection between them added spice to the mix. He'd come to admire Alara's intelligence and her bravery along with her delectable breasts and her ever-soft skin. He also admired her open-mindedness in accepting a Terran as a friend, her adaptive nature and determined spirit.

The first time they'd simply mated. This time, with their growing appreciation of each other, they'd be making love. And the difference shocked him.

Every nuance of her expression now meant something precious. Each caress seemed special.

"Mmm." She whispered into his mouth. "How long do we have . . . alone?"

He grinned up into her beautiful eyes, enjoying her heat. "Not long enough to do you justice."

"In my state, regeneration won't take long." She nipped his earlobe and then leaned back and caught his gaze.

"Tell me I mean more to you than regeneration." He watched the wildness in her eyes brighten.

She bent forward and nibbled along his neck. "I'll say whatever I must to have what I need."

"Liar."

"When *Boktai* takes over, I cannot be held responsible for my words or actions." She spoke as if by rote, but he wanted her to admit to him and to herself that they had a connection.

He shook his head and repeated, "Liar."

He'd never forget the self-loathing on her face as she'd tried to walk away from the Lapautee guard. But when Xander had scooped her into his arms, she'd appeared to stop fighting herself. She'd held on to him with relief, as well as passion, and her eyes had lost their tortured glaze.

"Must we talk . . . right now?" She trailed her hand lazily around his nipples, fondled his chest, then slowly dipped over his ribs to his stomach.

"You're trying to distract me with sex."

"Is it working?" She outlined his hips with her fingers, creating a tightening in his gut.

He grabbed her wrist, and she looked up and held his gaze, her eyes wide and puzzled. "What?"

"Why are you waiting to take your pleasure?"

She drew her brows together. "Regeneration will be better if we wait."

"You'd never have caressed that guard," he told her. "Or you'd have held back until the last moment possible."

"What does it matter?" She yanked her hand free and closed her fingers around his *tavis*.

And all the blood in his body surged there. He'd never felt so tight, so large, so hard. His *tavis* seemed to draw every drop of tension from the rest of him, and he responded to her caress like a charging fuel cell. He groaned but again reached for her wrist.

But her mischievous expression held him immobile, reminding him that she was in charge. With a frown, he hissed at her through gritted teeth. "Just what in the five Seas of Jarn do you think you're doing?"

"Whatever I want?" She tossed back a lock of hair from her eyes, her grin naughty as she turned the words he'd once used on her back on him.

In truth, he hadn't expected her to take things so far, but that didn't mean she could . . . ah . . . by the stars. She'd taken his *tavis* between her lips.

While her reaction to him mattered, as her tongue circled the ridge at the head of his *tavis,* as her hands stroked and tugged on his balls, he gave himself up to the wondrous sensations. Her wicked fingers. Her clever tongue.

Sensations rolled through him that he'd never experienced. Being the recipient of her affection spiked the kindling need in him to burn hotter. Although she was using him for her pleasure, she was giving him incredible bliss.

Any more and he would spill too soon.

15

"**S**top." The hoarse insistence in Xander's tone put a hitch in Alara's rhythm.

But having him at her mercy was too much fun to obey his demand, so she kept right on doing what she was doing, licking his proud flesh, stroking under the ridge where he seemed especially sensitive, and breathing in his erotic scent. Fondling him had her every nerve receptor clanging wildly, but although she must cope with *Boktai*, since she was in charge, delaying gratification was easier. Perhaps this was because she hadn't forced herself to wait as long, or perhaps because she'd made love recently.

"You . . . must . . . stop."

"Why?" She nibbled and nipped, enjoying how he responded to her, his entire body tense, all his beautiful muscles bulging.

"You . . . ah . . . need me inside you . . . to . . . regenerate."

"We'll simply have to wait."

His groan made her giggle, but her mouth and fingers sensed the tension in him growing. A moment before he would have spilled his precious essence, she clamped down hard at the base of his *tavis.*

When she stopped his release, he let out a roar of frustration, but his fingers threading through her hair remained gentle. "When I . . . regain my strength—"

"You mean," she teased, "if I let you regain—"

"Two can play this game." His fingers closed in her hair, but he either lacked the strength or the desire to pull her away.

"Today, I'm the one playing with you." Sensing he was on the raw edge of frustration, she nevertheless recalled their first encounter when he'd kept her webbed in, tied down. The idea of giving back some of what he'd given her gave her the courage to continue. "You pleased me . . . a great deal. Now it's my turn to . . . please you."

"But—"

She took his flesh between her teeth and bit him, then sucked away the sting. And all the while she enjoyed his male scent that she breathed deep into her lungs, his heated flesh that was so smooth and tender, yet hard and oh, so ready. Despite the urgency of *Boktai,* she liked his waiting for her. She enjoyed his wondering what she would do and where she would touch next.

Alara couldn't recall ever having had such power, and it made her bold and brazen and ultimately very feminine. Once again she stopped him from spilling and he gasped. "Enough . . . you go . . . too far."

"Then I shall go elsewhere." She straddled him, but didn't take him inside her *yonia*. Instead she leaned forward until her nipple teased his lips. Immediately, he drew her into his mouth and the swooping pull shot straight to her core.

His hands clasped her waist and his eyes sparkled with fiery purplish sparks. And then he expertly maneuvered her hips, sheathed himself inside her with a surprising strength that had her wondering if . . . No. He couldn't possibly have allowed her such freedom unless he had been unable to stop her.

As he filled her *yonia* completely, never letting go of her nipple with his mouth, he took command with such easy dominance that she suspected he'd been leading her on. If he'd been as exhausted as he'd appeared, he'd certainly recovered.

But he gave her no time to dwell on anything except what he was doing right now.

Sliding his hands around her hips to her bottom, he squeezed her flesh. Then he slapped her cheeks.

"Ow."

Shocked, she gasped. At the sting, she automatically tried to sit up. But he held her nipple firmly between his lips. "What are you . . ."

He chuckled, slapped her bottom again, then reached between her thighs, parted her slick *labella* and found her center. Moist with wanting him, she began to roll her hips, but again, his mouth held her still. With one hand he pleasured her, the other slapped her.

"Oh . . . oh . . . oh."

The stings created heat.

"Ah, stars."

The slaps caused vibrations that ignited a quiet blaze into a wildfire. Heat met heat.

And she burned.

Her hips, seemingly of their own accord, pumped upward, as if eager for his smacks. With his long arms, he had no trouble repeatedly slapping one cheek, then the other. He swatted her up high on her bottom, over the curve, and down low, until she could no longer feel anything but intriguing heat and delicious vibrations. His busy fingers between her legs added to the stinging of her backside and had her demanding more. More of him. More sensation.

"Yes. Yes. Yes." Deep in *Boktai,* her hormones cascaded, drowning her in wondrous sensuality, but the wonder of mating with him came straight from her soul.

Her muscles spasmed, tightening around him, drawing his precious essence into her. He'd given her exactly what she'd needed. And with a hoarse cry, he pumped into her and she accepted his gift with a bright happiness that suffused through her body and warmed her spirit.

As his arms closed around her and she snuggled against his chest, her tender nipple and hot bottom a reminder of what they'd shared, she couldn't deny her physical satisfaction or her joy. Never would she have thought she'd savor such treatment.

The big Rystani had spanked her.

Thinking how much she'd loved what he'd done made her blush.

But she couldn't lie to herself—she'd adored every hot slap. Even though such behavior was outside the boundaries of normal behavior, so was leaving Endeki. So was mating with a man from another world.

Yet, he'd spanked her.

And she'd liked it.

She couldn't decide which was worse, his action, or

her reaction. She supposed that eventually she would find a way to rationalize how much she'd enjoyed what they'd done so they could do it again.

Since leaving her world, she'd faced one new situation after another. And one by one, her Endeki values had fallen by the wayside. If Xander hadn't abducted her, she might have lived her entire life hiding her true nature—even from herself.

Because she hadn't really changed—she'd become free to be whatever she wanted to be. And she barely recognized her true self.

"You're very quiet." He smoothed her hair from her forehead.

"Why did you pretend to be helpless?"

He laughed. "Surely, that's not what you're thinking."

"So now you can read my mind?"

He caressed her very warm bottom. "You liked the heat?"

She squirmed and caught sight of herself in a mirror. Her hair had that just-regenerated, messy look. Her face glowed happily, but her bottom—was pink. Hot pink. Crimson pink. She didn't want to think how much she'd enjoyed herself and she really didn't want to talk about it.

When she remained silent, he didn't press her and she snuggled closer. Endekian men usually wanted a woman to leave after regeneration, or if they stayed, custom required her to remain naked. But she knew from her last experience with Xander, she had a choice. So cuddling with Xander was another new experience as was her willingness to remain bare. But though she liked the tender side of him, she warned herself not to become too attached. She couldn't afford to regenerate with him too many times or her cells would adapt, and

adapting would limit all her options—options she was
only now realizing she truly possessed.

Lithdar frowned at Xander, stopping Vax, Alara, Shannon, and Cyn just outside the conference area. "We
haven't spoken to the Saj in centuries. Only the sever-
ity of the plague has opened communications, and due
to the Saj response, the council will overlook the refusal of your crew women to give up their ova."

They had done a lot more than refuse, Alara thought
as she realized Lithdar, ever the politician, was already
spinning the official Lapautee version of what had really occurred.

"Use this opportunity wisely," Lithdar continued,
"and take care you don't escalate the war."

"Understood." Xander nodded, his expression
serene. "I appreciate your help in arranging these
negotiations."

Lithdar's pink eyelids blinked. "Remember the
Lapautee . . . when you find a cure."

Xander clapped the man on the shoulder and stepped
toward the meeting room where he would speak with
the Lapautee and Saj leadership. "We appreciate your
help and won't forget our friends."

Lithdar had told them that both his daughters had
caught the plague early, and Alara suspected that his
desperation to save his loved ones had overcome his re-
luctance to help strangers, and he had therefore sped
their request to the top of the Lapautee council's agenda.
Or perhaps they simply wanted to be rid of them after
their refusal to give up their ova—and Xander's rescue
mission.

The Lapautee Council convened inside a rotunda,

with tiers of seats for their citizens. The round center stage, currently empty, was raised so all in the audience had a good view. Around the edge of the stage, dignitaries sat behind desks, but it was the holovid equipment on one side that drew Alara's gaze. The image kept flickering, but she could just barely discern a man's silhouette and bright green leafy vegetation highlighted with brilliant yellow sunshine.

"Who is that?" Xander asked.

"The Saj leader." Lithdar led them to seats in the second row behind the dignitaries. "We couldn't simply send you to the planet with the ova. Doing so would surely have been seen as an act of war."

"Understood." Xander kept his tone reasonable and diplomatic, yet Alara sensed a tension in him she didn't understand. Was he concerned because Clarie had wandered off again? Or about the behind-the-scenes politics they couldn't control? These people had hated one another for thousands of years, and predicting a viable outcome from these negotiations would be foolhardy.

Finally, the holovid image's static cleared. She wished she could read the leader's DNA—but she could only do that in person. A holo image wasn't precise enough to allow her to see on the molecular level. Like everyone else, she had to rely only on her eyes.

The Saj and the Lapautee may have once shared common ancestors, but if so, it had been many thousands of years ago. While the Saj were humanoid, they had none of the delicate Lapautee features. Short, squat, and powerful, the bald Saj had a pronounced forehead with ridges, greenish-brown skin, and high, flat cheekbones that gave his triangular head set on a thick neck a hostile demeanor. His hand casually rested on what was most likely a ceremonial sword, yet from his warriorlike stance, Alara had little doubt the man was an expert swordsman.

"That dirt eater," Lithdar said quietly, "is Malk Drummon Daheeni, their Chosen One."

"What's the protocol?" Xander asked Lithdar.

"There is none. No one alive has ever addressed a Saj."

Xander nodded. "So when do I speak?"

"You take the stage and all will hear your words."

Xander climbed the steps two at a time, portraying a careful man, but one in a hurry. The humming voices of the audience abruptly ceased. He gave the crowd a moment to settle, to let all eyes focus on him, his natural timing skillful.

Xander turned to the holovid. "Malk Drummon Daheeni of the Saj, thank you." He turned to the Lapautee. "And I thank the Lapautee, also. It's time for all worlds and beings to come together or soon we shall all be dead of the plague."

Malk growled, his tone harsh and arrogant. "The Lapautee sent the virus along with the ova to kill us. Are you saying they are all infected, too?"

"Yes. And no one understands how the virus spreads, so the Lapautee are not at fault."

"So *you* say."

"So I say," Xander acknowledged with calm, as if the Saj's accusation didn't question his honor. "This plague of all plants and animals is galaxywide. Worlds light-years away from Lapau are experiencing the deadly sickness. Our Federation has sent us to find a cure."

Alara expected Malk to laugh at the notion and disappear. But some hostility seemed to vanish, and if she interpreted his expression correctly, while he still glared at Xander, from the ridges on his crinkling brow and the twist at his tightening mouth, he appeared almost thoughtful.

Malk's fingers curled on his sword handle. "We have no cure on Saj."

"Do you not have machines that build your suits?" Xander changed the subject slightly.

Malk didn't respond. He folded his arms across his chest and scowled. Xander outwaited him and finally Saj spoke. "The suits don't cure the virus."

Alara hadn't expected Malk to admit that they couldn't find a cure, but from his statement she assumed his people and healers had searched as hard as every stricken Federation world.

"We have our own suits. Our interest is in the beings that built the machines that create the suits. We call these beings the Perceptive Ones."

"Where are the beings who created the machines for *your* suits?" Malk countered.

"Gone. Our best thinkers believe they spread from the galaxy's center to the rim, leaving their seed as they progressed. Your world is very old, but not as old as others. We believe, we hope, the Perceptive Ones exist on Saj."

Malk opened his arms, his demeanor sincere. "I have lived all my life on Saj. I have never seen the beings, nor have any of my people. We believe they either died out or left Saj eons ago."

"But according to the Lapautee, your southernmost continent is uninhabited and unexplored. Perhaps they still exist there."

"And you know about Saj because the Lapautee spy on us, just as we have always suspected." His scowl lines deepened. "How do I know your request isn't a Lapautee deception and an advance scouting trip to invade Saj?"

Xander gestured to Alara, Vax, Shannon, and Cyn to join him on the circular stage. "This is my crew. My first officer, Vax, and I are from a planet called Mystique. Alara"—he gestured for her to step forward—"is from Endeki, the land of my greatest enemy. Cyn is from Scartar and Shannon from Earth, a planet hard hit by the plague. You can see we are different races from many worlds. Friends and enemies alike have come together on this quest. All our people are dying of the plague. We have homeworlds we love. We wish to find a cure, not take over your world."

The Saj leader scowled. "The Lapautee almost wiped out my people. How do I know you aren't in league with them?"

"You don't know." Xander spoke as warrior to warrior. He didn't back down, but stayed firm without deliberately antagonizing the Saj leader, a tactic Alara admired. "But what do you have to lose? Your people are dying. Your plants and animals are dying."

"Perhaps *we* will find your Perceptive Ones and a cure for only the Saj."

"If you could find them alone, I suspect you wouldn't be speaking to me right now."

"True." Malk laughed. "We had the same idea to find the Creators. We exhausted all of our resources to search our planet. Why do you think you will be any more successful at finding the Perceptive Ones than we have been?"

"There is strength in our differences. The reason my crew is made up of many races is that one of us may see or think of something that others cannot." Xander turned to the Lapautee leaders. "Will you let us leave Lapautee?"

While the Lapautee leaders remained silent, they must have given Lithdar permission to speak for his people—either that or Lithdar had never been the minor bureaucrat he'd claimed. "If the Saj accept you, we will most assuredly allow you to go."

"Will there be peace between your peoples while we search for the Perceptive Ones?" Xander asked. "No bombs, no raids, no killing, no deception?"

"We will agree if the Saj agree." Lithdar sneered at Malk. "And during this time we will not send more ova."

"Agreed." Malk didn't hesitate and Alara understood why. He needn't worry about an overpopulated Lapau looking to colonize Saj when all were dying of the plague.

"And if we find a cure—we will all share," Xander insisted. "And the Saj and Lapautee will negotiate their differences. If you would agree to impartial Federation mediation, I can arrange that for you."

Alara appreciated the way Xander didn't stop negotiating for what he wanted. His interest in finding a real peace between the two peoples impressed her. And she hoped they all had a future in need of negotiation.

Drik's guards yanked Kirek from the office. He supposed he'd gotten off lightly. At least they weren't going to kill him. However, they hemmed him in and one shoved him between the shoulder blades. He stumbled and the guards laughed and talked among themselves.

"Vansek will know just what to do with a Rystani."

Another guard jeered. "Yeah, she'll keep you where you belong."

"On your knees."

"Servicing her with your tongue."

"And you won't be escaping again." Another guard joined them and held up chains. "Vansek will teach him his place."

Kirek saved his strength. Although his adrenaline surged, he was no physical match for five Endekian guards. And if he used his psi, they would learn his true strength. There was no point in revealing his secret when Drik could simply send more men to overpower him.

The guard wound the chain around Kirek's neck, then crossed it over his chest. They forced his wrists into cuffs that attached to the chains at his side and allowed him almost no freedom. Drik's man kneeled and placed shackles on his ankles, the length of chain so short, he could walk only in quarter stride.

"You think this is bad?" a guard scoffed, his sour breath slapping Kirek's face. "Vansek has a taste for pain. Your pain."

He'd heard of such deviations though he'd never known anyone so twisted, but he refused to show apprehension. However, the chains would slow his exploration of Drik's residence, and after what he'd learned, he had to find a way to continue.

Something was very wrong. The Endekians hadn't used the glow stones against any Federation enemy or Kirek would have heard. And yet from the inventory list he'd seen, the total number of glow stones collected from Rystan was far greater than what the Endekians had in inventory. So where had the unaccounted-for glow stones gone?

Kirek speculated to keep his mind from his current circumstance. But he couldn't help but notice the women who passed by in the hallways looking at him with pity, and his gut clenched. Had they shipped the glow stones elsewhere? Were the Endekians amassing the stones for a future attack that wasn't near their homeworld? Trading them outside Federation space?

But why?

Nothing made sense. Although glow stones could cause atomic explosions, the Endekians had more advanced weapons. And yet, glow stones were cheap. The Endeki had suffered many financial setbacks in the last decade. Their trade routes were no longer as profitable. Their colonies drained the homeworld of precious resources.

The shackles rubbed the skin on his ankles, but the minor discomfort was nothing compared to his frustration at being caught before he'd solved the glow stone mystery. Perhaps he was kidding himself, trying to make his mission seem important because his hostage situation was demeaning.

However, as the guards prodded him into Vansek's quarters, he checked his illusions at the door. "Go. She's waiting for you."

"Salivating."

"She loves to break in anyone new."

He shuffled inside and the door slammed behind him. But he wasn't alone. The dark hallway was lined with men—all of them chained. All naked. No one met his gaze. And every single chained man had a light shining on his erection.

At the end of the hallway a woman lounged on a raised scarlet dais. A naked slave rubbed her shoulders with oil. Another knelt beside her, his role limited to holding a platter of sweets within her reach. Scars

across his broad back and a bleeding welt on his bare
buttocks caused Kirek to shudder. But despite the
man's obvious injuries, his *tavis* was jutting proudly.
What kind of hell had he entered?

16

Between one breath in and the next out, Xander's crew left behind the Lapautee chamber to find themselves on Saj. Reunited once again with Clarie and his pet, Delo, who glowed bright orange under the hot yellow Saj sunlight, Xander saw that Malk was no longer a holosim, but living flesh and bone. Xander immediately adjusted his suit to the increased gravity, the thinner air, and the higher temperature of another world.

An enormous marsupial with two strong hind legs and two short front ones with a giant pouch and wearing a strange harness towered over Malk. At their sudden appearance in the forest clearing, the warrior unsheathed his sword and the metal glinted in the sunlight, drawing Xander's attention.

Xander stepped in front of his crew. Vax joined him on the right, Cyn flanked his left. Together, they formed a united front, automatically placing themselves between the threat of Malk and the less experienced fighters of his crew.

"What happened?" Malk demanded, showing restraint. Although he held his sword ready, he didn't attack. "Where have you hidden your ship?"

As much as Xander longed to look around for other dangers, he kept his attention focused on Malk and relied on Vax to keep a careful watch for an attack from warriors who could hide easily in the thick foliage. While Malk seemed as surprised to see them as they were to be on Saj, the man could be acting. He could have brought them there to die.

But Xander answered Malk as if they were allies. "The Lapautee must have sent us. You did give us permission to come to your world." Xander wasn't certain his statement was true. They seemed to have traveled to Saj the same way they had from his ship to Lapautee. The journey had been effortless and almost instantaneous. While he suspected Clarie's pet might be a gigantic conductor of an alien energy source, he wasn't about to reveal that to Malk.

Malk lowered his sword but didn't resheathe it. "*How* did you get here?"

"We do not know." Xander didn't move. He wanted Malk's cooperation. For a world leader, he certainly seemed to be in an isolated spot. Where were his guards? His residence? Why were they in a jungle—in the middle of nowhere? "The Lapautee probably kept many secrets from us and their mode of travel is not our concern. While we didn't expect to arrive without warning, the Lapautee have saved us much time. Can you lead us to your machines where the suits are made?"

As he made his request, a plant sprouted and grew beside Malk. The rate of growth was extraordinary, but Malk paid no attention. Interesting.

Sensing Malk didn't intend to use his weapon, Xander allowed his gaze to wander. The jungle growth around them expanded, filling in the empty places at an extraordinary rate.

He saw no paths from the clearing. Thick plants with leafy stems surrounded them like a prison cell. When a plant grew between Malk and Xander, the warrior calmly slashed the stalk with his sword and Xander immediately understood the usefulness of such a weapon on the strange world. Meanwhile, the marsupial ate tall grasses behind it, barely keeping back the overflowing foliage.

"I have no idea how I got here," Malk admitted. "I was transmitting from my headquarters and the next moment I was here with you and my *darup*."

"*Darup*?" Xander asked, since his suit failed to translate.

"The animal behind me." Malk looked around. "I'm not even certain where we are. If I had to guess, I'd say we are somewhere near the center of our uninhabited southern continent."

"And where does that place us in relation to the machines that make your suits?" Xander asked.

Malk shrugged.

"Could you estimate?" Xander prodded.

Alara spoke up for the first time. "These plants are closing in on us. If we don't move soon, they may trap us here."

Xander glanced at the clearing they'd arrived in to find the perimeter much smaller. The rate of plant growth rivaled anything he'd ever seen or heard about.

In the space of a few Federation minutes, the plants had taken over most of the clearing. The formerly bare hillock now appeared to be overgrown as densely as the surrounding jungle.

"I can't even point you in the correct direction." Malk slashed down a plant that had grown too close to his elbow. "We have never seen any ancient machines on Saj."

"Then where do your suits come from?" Xander and Vax exchanged glances and he noted Alara examining a leaf in her palm.

"We are born in our suits."

Malk's information startled Xander. No other Federation race was born in the suits. They'd all had to adapt to them after birth. "Where do you obtain the suits that you send to the Lapautee?"

"We recycle by taking them off our dead. That's why we keep the population rates between the Saj and Lapautee equal."

"Sir," Vax interrupted as he grabbed a stalk and yanked a plant from the ground, "we can't stay here much longer."

"Agreed." Xander locked gazes with Malk. "This is your world. What do you suggest?"

"I could scout the area on my *darup* and figure out which way to go." He grabbed the animal's reins, tugged it closer, and offered Xander his sword—hilt first—in an unmistakable gesture of friendship. "And I'll leave you my sword to fight off the foliage."

"Won't you need it?" Xander hesitated to accept the generous offer that would leave Malk without a weapon.

"The *darup* is the perfect traveling animal. I wish we had more of them for us all." Malk handed the sword to Xander, grabbed the animal's furry leg and climbed up its haunch, hand over hand. The patient beast didn't seem to mind. It continued to munch the high grasses until Malk reached its pouch. He climbed inside and peered down at them. "If I'm not back before sundown, I'm either lost . . . or dead."

Xander nodded. "Don't get lost."

"Or dead," Shannon muttered, then stomped on a plant and ground her heel into the roots. But another two stalks simply sprouted to either side of the one she'd killed.

"Clarie like plants." The tiny alien's antennae waved in the breeze and he stepped toward the thick jungle.

Cyn tugged him back. "Dangerous animals might hide there. Or the plants could eat you."

"Delo hungry. Clarie feed Delo."

"Let Clarie go," Xander ordered, curious to see what the alien would do.

In the meantime, Malk slapped the reins and the animal, with him riding in the pouch, bunched its powerful rear haunches and leaped into the air. They couldn't see where it landed, only glimpsing it again when it leaped high once more. But after one more appearance, Malk vanished, leaving Xander alone with his crew.

As the plants encroached on the clearing, the fresh air ripened with the aroma of too-sweet grasses. A breeze stirred the fronds and the sun beat down on their heads.

Xander handed Vax the sword. "Don't use it until we must."

"Like that's going to be very long." Shannon stomped on another plant with vigor, but dark circles under her eyes and hollowed cheekbones revealed the progression of her illness. It wouldn't be long before it began to affect all of them.

Clarie sat down, folded his legs, and handed Delo a plant stalk. His pet ate, seemingly content with the alien fodder, then closed its eyes and slept as if it hadn't a care.

Alara had been extremely quiet and thoughtful since their arrival, and when Xander turned around, he found her examining the plant, her eyes puzzled. "I've never seen or heard of DNA that can replicate this fast."

"Can you find a way to stop or slow the growth?"

"Without a laboratory?" Eyes bright more with curiosity than alarm, Alara stared at first one plant with tiny needlelike leaves, then another with broad flat ones. "Normally such a wide variety doesn't grow within one climate zone. But then Malk's DNA was also strange."

"In what way?" Xander asked.

Vax slashed at the base of the plants that encircled them. He was clearly losing the battle. He'd cut two down and five would spring up in their place.

Alara's expression went into scientific-analysis mode—far off and distant. "The sequencing was . . . unusual."

So were the plants. No matter how hard Vax worked to annihilate them, they grew back—faster, bigger, denser.

"Vax, stop." Xander understood his first officer would keep cutting down the plants until he dropped of exhaustion, but Vax and the sword would only delay the inevitable for an hour at most. And he might even be accelerating the process. "Can we hike out of here by squeezing between the plants?"

Alara shook her head. "Plant density is too thick."

Although she was likely considering the scientific questions, she also was keeping up with the conversation. She had a practical head on her shoulders, one that might make the difference between completing this mission or failure.

"All right, let's form a circle and extend our shields until they touch each another," Xander ordered.

Standing between Alara and Shannon, he used his psi to extend his shield until it grazed theirs. The others did the same. While they couldn't travel through the plants with their shields connected, the psi protection held the plants back so they only grew around them . . . and over them—not between them.

"It won't be long before these plants entomb us." Shannon rubbed her forehead. From a big city, she was accustomed to congestion and tight quarters; of them all, she liked the wild outdoors the least. Yet Xander could count on her, too, and if he had to be stranded here on Saj, he couldn't think of a better crew.

"You think Malk will even try to return?" Cyn asked, staring toward the horizon as if he might reappear any moment.

Xander stepped into the center of the circle. "If you can keep the plants at bay, I'll search for a way out of the jungle."

"Look for Perceptive Ones, too," Clarie reminded him as if Xander could forget his mission. The only problem was, Xander didn't know what a Perceptive One looked like . . . so even if he saw one, he doubted he'd recognize it. To make that determination, he'd require Alara's expertise, but even she had never seen a Perceptive One. He hoped something in the DNA would clue her in—but first he had to extract them from the jungle and figure out where to head next.

Xander sat amid his crew, closed his eyes and focused. He recalled Clarie's words of relaxation and one by one he coaxed his muscles to release the pent-up tension. He imagined his stress streaming from his body in lazy cloudlike ribbons, and in a process that became easier each time, his mind followed.

He left his body and soared skyward. From above, his tiny group appeared fragile, but they would hold the shield until he returned. His belief in them remained firm as he tried to mark their precise position. He triangulated his location with the mountain range's irregular peak to his right, a forked tree on his left shoulder, and the highest tree within miles to his back.

He scanned in all directions but saw only a flat plain covered by the thick jungle in every direction except the mountainous one. If Malk was nearby, he must be resting amid the foliage. Xander soared higher, where the air thinned and he could see the planet from the atmosphere's thinnest vantage point. Far away, the jungle met the sea on three sides and mountains continued to the horizon.

He took his time, taking note of his bearings and searching. He spied no cities or sign of civilization or life. But then a uniform mountain formation caught his attention. The ridge line appeared unnaturally straight and smooth. Wind and rain oddly hadn't worn down the ridge in what should be a natural asymmetrical formation.

Nature didn't normally form straight lines.

On Mystique, the Perceptive Ones had carved out a mountain and placed their ancient machines inside—machines that even now guarded the galaxy from the Perceptive Ones' ancient enemy, the Zin. Perhaps the Perceptive Ones had built another complex here, hopefully much more recently than the machines they'd left behind at the galaxy's center.

Xander soared straight to the mountain, aware that the setting sun limited his time. He needed the sun to see and to find his crew, but before journeying over a difficult trail across the jungle, he wanted to make sure the mountains ahead were their best option.

When he arrived, he was certain of only one thing—the ridge line wasn't natural.

You cheated.

It's impossible to cheat when there are no rules.

You're actually helping them to evolve.

So? Did you think I'd let all my work end without guiding them in the appropriate direction?

You said they would evolve on their own.

I said they would evolve. They would have done so on their own given another few thousand years. But we don't have another few thousand years.

Isn't speeding up the process dangerous?

Yes. If they die, it may take too long to reintegrate the right combinations into my sequence.

So don't let them die.

That's the tricky part. To prematurely force evolution to the next stage, they must stay right on the edge of disaster.

So?

So, I'm juggling millions of details. Do you think creating an entire world is simple?

Yes.

Well, maybe one world, but I'm balancing a galaxy of millions. A little too much pressure here, a little less there, and they will all die.

If they don't die during evolution, they'll die of the virus. They simply can't go as far as you want so quickly.

Was that an admission that they have evolved?

Their minds aren't capable of such developed thinking.

The raw material is there. It just needs sculpting.

You can't forge bendar *from water.*

Sure I can. I heat the water and mix the steam with castrabonine, throw in stardust, let it sit under the pressure of a moving continent for two decades, then—

I get the idea. But you're running out of time. The next time the Zin open a wormhole—

I haven't forgotten.

The glow stones aren't even near the nexus.

I'll take care of it. I'll take care of everything, but it wouldn't hurt you to pitch in.

Me? Work? Not anytime in this millennium.

Why not?

Work is . . . so . . . pedestrian.

No. Work is fascinating. Watch.

Alara wished she had her laboratory equipment because she didn't trust her eyes or her judgment. How could she when the planet seemed to have kicked her into the beginnings of *Boktai*? Xander's ability to leave his body had surprised Alara, but although his ability was unusual, she had heard of such skills— although she hadn't believed they existed until now. She only wished that instead of staying behind, she could have joined him and explored this world. But she couldn't have been more pleased by his astrally extending. Shannon was in no condition for a strenuous hike. And the planet was affecting Alara, too.

She supposed it made sense in a weird kind of way.

The plants here grew at fantastic rates, so why shouldn't her metabolism also speed up? However, she wasn't a plant. And the foliage had evolved here, she hadn't. Wondering whether their growth would slow to more normal rates if she took the plants out of this environment didn't stop her from worrying about Xander. Not even her humming blood and her burning flesh could stem her tide of concern.

He should be back by now. It was almost dark. As the minutes passed slowly, anxiety fueled her hormones and stirred her passions. *Krek.* She had no idea when Xander would return to his body, and her biology was already making clear thinking difficult, drenching her with the demand to regenerate her cells. Even if Xander returned, there was no privacy.

And they were in danger.

And they had a mission to complete.

But with her cells shouting for regeneration with an urgency that left her suit hard-pressed to maintain the shield and cool her heated flesh, she prayed Xander would return quickly, for his sake as well as hers. Closing her eyes, she tried to meditate, attempted to impose calm on her rebellious biology.

Of all the planets in the universe for her to land on, why did it have to be Saj—one that speeded up *Boktai*? Or was she simply adapting more quickly to Xander than she'd thought possible? Perhaps it was merely worry over his absence that had started *Boktai*. Filled with frustration, worried for his safety, she waited for Xander to return. And recalled how her father had made her mother wait for him.

The spineless mudsucker.

Alara had only been five or six, but when she'd come home from school, she'd heard her mother on the holovid, her voice low and pleading. "Come home, Speaker."

Her father's cruel laugh had shocked Alara into silence. "Surely you don't think I'd leave my work in the middle of the day for you?"

Her mother trembled, but she'd held her chin high. "If you'd done your duty last night, I would not be in such need now."

Her father glared, his lips twisting into a mean grin, and then he punched the console, ending the holovid conversation. Confused by her father's abrupt refusal, Alara, the child, didn't understand what had caused her mother to beg. Or why her father had been so nasty and refused to come home. After all, he often took time off from work.

When her mother had collapsed into her chair, Alara had run to her, climbed into her lap and flung her arms around her neck. She'd never forgotten how her mother had tried to hide her tears, but several had fallen onto Alara's neck, branding her with the belief that her mother shouldn't have been crying. Alara had vowed to do whatever she could to make her better.

Although it was years before Alara had fully understood the significance of her parents' argument, when she had, she'd chosen to study science in the hope of finding a solution. She would fix the biological problem. However, her promising work had been cut short.

And now she found herself in the same biological nightmare as her mother.

Calm yourself.

There were differences. Her father had enjoyed tormenting her mother, but if Xander knew of her need, he would find a way to ease Alara's suffering. His kindness was only one of the reasons she worried about his safety. She liked the way he treated his crew. She liked the way he treated her. Unfortunately, her extreme anxiety was provoking her lust. If she knew he was safe, she could slow her descent into *Boktai*.

But she had no way to contact him. Although this was the first time she'd seen astral roaming, she understood the principle. His mind was gone. Tapping his shoulder would do nothing. Talking to his limp body would do nothing. He wasn't in his body. He'd left her behind and she longed to join him.

By the holy order of the universe. Maybe she *could* follow him. There were legends on Endeki of women whose need for their husbands and regeneration had been so great that they'd become comatose, and when their delayed husbands had returned, they'd inexplicably awakened. Could those women have left their bodies?

Dregan hell. For all she knew, they may have taken a sleeping potion.

Still, if Xander could leave his body behind, why couldn't she do so, too?

"Do you know how Xander leaves his body?" she asked his crew.

Although weak and swaying on her feet, Shannon gave her a sharp-eyed look. Of them all, only she knew Alara's secret; Alara nodded slightly, signaling, yes, she needed Xander now.

Vax's very male voice slammed her hormones. "Why?"

Alara refused to look at him. She dared not. He was male. Too male. But she wanted Xander.

The thought startled her right down to her toes. Vax was the safer choice for regeneration. Her cells might adapt to Xander if she absorbed his essence too many times. And while she knew Xander would be furious if she mated with Vax, it was not concern about Xander's customs that drove her.

She wanted Xander.

Only Xander.

The knowledge burned to her core and she stumbled. Shannon's and Cyn's hands tightened on hers, their strength holding her up. She wished she could blame *Boktai*. She wished she could blame her yearning for him on the fact that she disliked Vax—but she didn't. Vax was a fine officer. An honorable warrior.

But she wanted Xander, wanted him badly enough to try and find him. So although she refused to look at Vax and risk that the mere sight of him would enflame her hormones to burn even hotter, she spoke firmly and hoped he wouldn't see through her lie. "If I could also leave my body, we could scout twice the area."

Vax answered immediately, dismissing her idea. "Leaving your body is dangerous."

As plants looped over them and blocked out the sun, Alara tilted her head back. "Staying here is dangerous. Besides, Xander might need my help. He and Malk should have returned by now."

"We need you to help maintain the shield over Xander's body. Besides, when he returns, he may require care. Last time after he came back, his body needed time to recuperate."

Shannon, bless her Terran heart, defended Alara. "Vax, let her try. It's possible Xander is lost, and she may be able to point him back to his body."

Vax remained stubborn. "Xander is a hunter. He'll mark his path and follow it back."

Cyn squinted at the sky that could barely be seen between the canopy of overhead plants. "It's difficult to mark a path that is ever changing. Besides, the sun is setting. In the darkness, he may truly need Alara's help."

"If she goes, she may also become lost."

"That's a risk I'm willing to take."

Vax still sounded determined, yet she heard the thinnest thread of indecisiveness enter his tone. "Even if you succeed, he may not be able to see you."

"I don't even know if I can do what Xander does. But if I can, I'll go straight up and come back. I won't get lost, and perhaps I will be able to—"

"Alara rescue Xander," Clarie interrupted, inserting himself into the conversation with his childish yet insistent voice that oddly carried weight.

"Clarie," Vax asked. "Can you teach Alara what you taught Xander?"

"Clarie teach. Alara learn."

At finding this unexpected ally, Alara felt her heart speed. Between her real concern for Xander and the need for regeneration, she gritted her teeth and prayed she could focus on Clarie's instructions. "What should I do?"

"Use *Boktai*."

Alara's jaw dropped in shock and she jerked her gaze to Shannon, who shook her head. "I've said nothing."

"Nothing about what?" Vax demanded.

"Hush," Clarie ordered with a wisp of impatience. "Use the *Boktai*."

"*Boktai?*" Vax asked.

But Alara ignored him and honed in on Clarie. He

spoke in a singsong incantation that almost hypno-
tized. "Gather the energy in body. Pull energy to center. Let the energy froth and bubble. Collect the burn.
Hold it close. Embrace the blaze."

Collect the burn.

Hold it close.

Embrace the blaze.

Alara tried to do as he suggested. Never had she embraced *Boktai*. All her life she'd fought her physiology,
battled the spiraling out-of-control thoughts, resisted the
submersion into her senses. But if Xander needed her,
maybe even more than she needed him, she would
draw on the energy of *Boktai*.

Electric arcs raced through her body and she coaxed
and collected them, forced them to coil upon themselves. Her core felt like an explosive lightning ball.
Currents energized and sizzled. The sensation escalated and coalesced. If she'd been in space, her speed
would have been hyperdrive. If she'd been a storm, it
would have been a planetwide event. If she'd been a
star, it would have been a supernova.

"Now release the energy and ride it."

Ribbons of energy surged outward and she latched
onto a streamer. By the stars. At first she thought she'd
simply stood up straighter, but she wasn't tall enough
to elevate her head beyond the shielding and the
branches.

She'd done it.

She was floating. She had no weight. No body. Yet
she could see—even though she had no eyes. She
could hear the wind whistling through the branches, although she had no ears.

She glanced down and saw them move her body into

the protected circle. Clarie had taken her place to help
reinforce the shield. Free to worry about Xander without inciting her body's lust, she soared straight up.

But she saw no sign of him.

17

In her altered state, Alara didn't know what Xander would look like, but suddenly she discerned his presence. Without doubt, she knew he had joined her, and oddly, she identified him in a way similar to how she'd recognize rain on her face—even if her eyes were closed. Although they weren't touching in the physical sense, she could feel him on a level she couldn't name. It was almost as if she had developed another sense—a second vision. Xander glowed with a pure molten bronze aura that she instantly recognized.

Alara?

She heard him speak into her mind. Telepathy? In this altered state could they communicate mind to mind, or was she imagining things that couldn't possibly be?

Alara, is that you? The bronze aura approached.

Yes. Clarie helped me leave my body, so I could search

for you. When you stayed away for so long, I was worried you might be lost.

So you came after me? Nuances of emotion came through the mind link. Although she couldn't hear his voice or see his face, his words broadcast straight into her mind, with warmth and curiosity attached.

Floating serenely above the planet, holding a stationary position, she slowly adjusted to her altered state. On the horizon, the last rays of the setting set splashed golden-red streaks across the lush vegetation below, reminding her they had to return soon—but not just yet.

My body is going into Boktai. She wasn't ready to admit more to him than that her cells required regeneration.

Your timing could have been better. Amusement and irony sizzled through the link along with molten male heat.

Tell me something I don't already know.

He tamped down his potent interest, replaced it with . . . responsibility. *How long can you hold out?*

My biology seems to have adapted to this planet's abnormally rapid development. I've never experienced such a quick-paced change. So answering your question is impossible.

And my crew?

Are holding the protective shield around our bodies. There is no privacy. She admitted her lesser concern. She didn't mind that the others knew they were mating as much as she hated them knowing that she had no control over the timing—which was totally inappropriate. They were in danger. Cut off from their ship. Without supplies. And yet lovemaking could not be put off much longer.

Let me take care of the logistics. With all these plants, we need only be a few steps away to remain out of sight. And we have another problem.

Malk?

I haven't seen him but that's not—

What?

This out-of-body experience taxes physical strength. We need recovery time. So here's the plan. I'll report my findings and then we'll "nap."

As he sent the thoughts into her mind, he glowed brighter, as if he looked forward to their coming physical union as much as she did. With business taken care of for the moment, she loosened hold of her curiosity. *What do I look like?*

Huh?

To me, you look like a glowing bronze aura in a ball-shaped form.

Really? In the mind-to-mind connection, she noted his surprise. *You appear ghostlike, golden. I can see every feature.*

How odd that we see each other so differently.

Perhaps we see only what the other wishes to display. Or how we think of ourselves?

You would have made a good scientist.

At her comment, he laughed. He had no vocal cords, but nevertheless, his laughter rang in her head. *Considering the possibilities is one thing, having the patience to test them is another.*

And exactly how are we communicating? she asked. *Will the mental link continue once we reenter our bodies?*

There's one way to find out.

He dived toward his crew. And sliced right through their psi shield to reenter his body. The moment he linked his mind with his flesh and bones, their mental link severed.

Left behind and feeling all too alone, she hastened to follow. The reintegration process was smooth and natural, like pouring milk into a glass, but taking only fractions of a second. After the transition into her body, her first instinct—to reach for Xander's hand— revealed her exhaustion. Never in her entire life had she felt this deep, numbing exhaustion. Sapped, totally drained of all energy, she focused simply on taking her next breath, very aware that the mental link she and Xander had shared was gone. Too bad her hormones were raging.

Beside her, Xander exhibited more strength than she and shifted to a sitting position. Vax kneeled beside him. "Are you all right?"

"I found evidence of the Perceptive Ones on a mountain ridge."

"Evidence that they're still alive?" Shannon cut right to the major point of the mission. Her mind was still sharp, but she trembled all the time now.

"There's a niche in the mountainside with the same symbol the Perceptive Ones carved into the stone cornice that we found on Mystique. Without equipment, I couldn't tell how old the marking is."

Alara had read accounts of the ancient complex found on Mystique. Inside Mystique's highest mountain, the Perceptive Ones had built a control center that had lasted a millennium. Had they left behind another complex on Saj? Was it possible they might even find a Perceptive One who still lived here?

She thought the odds slim. But then again, before she'd left Endeki, she wouldn't have thought the chance of exploring with her mind and leaving her body behind were too great, either. Or that she'd crave a certain Rystani warrior to assuage her yearnings. Because although she couldn't summon the energy to wriggle one finger, desire crashed and washed over her, drenching her in pure, fierce tendrils of frothing need.

Xander's gaze met hers and he must have caught sight of the intensity ripping through her. "Vax, use your sword to make another clearing. Alara and I need some private time to rest."

Vax frowned. "I don't like leaving you until you've fully recovered."

"You'll be within shouting distance. Besides, there seems to be no danger—except from the plants."

"Sir, in your state," Cyn also argued, the first time Alara had ever heard her disagree with the captain, "your psi might not be strong enough to hold a shield."

"I don't believe that's necessary any longer." Xander raised his eyes to the plants that curved above them. Plant stems had bowed over the shield. Additional plants had layered over the initial growth to form a protective pocket so thick that the first plants might protect them. "Lower the shield."

They obeyed and Alara tensed, half expecting the plants to crumble under the weight of those above. A few sturdy stems creaked and groaned, but the structure held. But would more plants spread beneath their feet?

Nothing happened. Either the plants required sunlight to sprout or the germinating process had ceased for another reason. Vax followed Xander's orders and hacked through one wall. His arm strained and his effort required repeated slicing, but he persisted, working up a fine sheen of sweat that his suit did nothing to evaporate.

Apparently, Vax was so focused on the plant tunnel that he'd forgotten to alter his own suit's comfort with his psi. As soon as he moved forward, Cyn with an arm around Shannon to help her walk, stepped behind him, then Clarie and Delo followed.

Xander immediately rolled close to Alara and gathered her into his arms. While they could hear his crew settling close by, as long as she and Xander invoked privacy mode, they would have all the seclusion she craved.

Xander shot her a wicked smile. "You still can't move, can you?"

"Uh-uh."

"Luckily for us, my energy's not as depleted. I'm either getting stronger—or more accustomed to leaving my body behind."

The heat in his eyes caused her to recollect the last time he'd had her at such a disadvantage, when he'd first taken her aboard the shuttle and webbed her in. Back then her fury had been the catalyst to elevate *Boktai*. This time she wasn't angry, but eager. However, she might be just as frustrated. She could move no more now than she could then.

The difference was that this time not only were her hormones urging her to mate, she craved his touch. Not a man's touch—*Xander*'s touch. And it simply amazed her how much her realization upped her anticipation.

So when he leaned over her, angled his mouth over hers and ever-so-slowly nibbled and nipped, coaxing her lips apart, she wanted to fling her arms around his neck and draw him closer. She yearned to arch her back and raise her breasts to him. She had a yen to twine her feet with his.

But not only had the energy sapped her physical strength, *Boktai* depleted her psi. Luckily for her, her suit turned transparent.

Xander's eyes brightened, but he kept his tone low and sexy. "I'll take that as a yes."

As his warm breath fanned her cheek, she recovered enough energy to use her vocal cords. "I like a man who makes the correct assumptions."

"Oh, I intend to make a lot of them." Lazily, he drew one finger down her rib cage and her breasts ached in response, her nipples tightening. Still, keeping his voice to a very male whisper, he murmured, "I'll also assume that you'd like my mouth to close over your breast."

At his suggestion, her stomach clenched. Yet he didn't so much as touch her breasts with a fingertip, never mind with his lips. Instead, he swirled lower, drawing a line over her fluttering rib cage and coiled stomach. Watching her eyes, he slid his fingers into the curls at her mons. Very slowly, very gently, he tugged, first one curl, then another.

Hot sensation doused her in a storm of desire. If the storm had been hail, it would have been off the charts. If the storm had been rain, it would have caused a flash flood. If the storm had been lightning, it would have jolted the heavens.

But the storm took its own form, linking them as if they were once again in their astral state. Not only could she feel the touch of his fingertips on her mons, she could feel her delicate soft skin through *his* fingertip.

Oh my, she thought.

Oh, yes, he thought back. Their minds linked as if they were once again in the astral state. But this time she could feel her body and she could feel how he felt when he touched her body.

What's happening?

It's rare, but some Rystanis' minds link during love-making.

I never thought I could feel so good to you.

Mmm.

Beneath his clever fingers, her flesh shimmied. Her cells pleaded for rejuvenation and regeneration. But her thoughts swirled about Xander. How was this special link possible? Until now, she'd believed the planet was influencing and accelerating her need to mate . . . but that was because she hadn't wanted to admit the shocking truth.

She was adapting to Xander. His powerful male essence had trapped her in a web of desire that she didn't even wish to escape. By the stars.

Biology wasn't simply taking over. Her mind was leading the way, in a manner she'd never expected.

His pleasure intensified the storm until she was caught up in a vortex of sensuality. She'd never been so needy in her life. And had never been so scared of letting go, of doing exactly what she wanted—even if her actions were contrary to everything she'd ever believed.

To give herself to Xander again would mean tying her life to his—literally. Other women had explained she would always have a choice before taking this last, final step . . . but she hadn't understood what they'd meant until now.

She should have been happy that she'd developed feelings for a man . . . but she wasn't. As much as she craved him, as much as she longed to stay with him, she had no idea what he felt for her.

"What?" As if reading the confusion in her mind, he leaned forward and kissed her lips. "For a moment there, you went somewhere else."

She didn't stop to think, she blurted the truth. "If your essence regenerates my cells again, my body will adapt to yours. Permanently."

His eyes widened and his fingers stopped their delicious swirling. "But you've always said that you wouldn't know—"

"I was wrong. I can feel . . . changes coming on. It's like a gathering, a tightening, a final awakening." She scoured his face, searching for a clue to his thoughts. Although she could read his mental messages, she didn't know what he was thinking unless he sent the thought at her.

The moment stretched. When he remained silent and still, no longer grazing his fingers over her taut flesh, she couldn't stand the tension any longer. "Say something."

"What would you have me say? We have always known this might happen."

"And?" she prodded.

"And . . . what?"

"How do you feel about . . . us?"

His eyes darkened to a deep violet. His mental turbulence widened and broadened and deepened. "I wish we had more time. I wish you had more choices."

The sudden tightness in her chest and the lump in her throat made her leery of her highly emotional state. Trusting and judging a man was something she hadn't expected to do. Ever. Was he really thinking about *her* first? Or did he wish *he* had another choice, too?

Because Xander would do whatever he must to complete his mission. And if achieving success meant he had to keep her alive, he would do so. If success meant mating with her, he would do that, too, and pride would make him do it well. And if success meant tying himself to a woman he didn't want for the rest of his life, he would make that sacrifice, also. He would keep his word—she trusted him enough to know he wouldn't desert her once the mission ended.

And after he made a promise, he wouldn't complain. He wouldn't rage. He would stand by the bargain and would deal with fate on his own terms and go on.

But mere acceptance wasn't good enough for her. Mere physical lust wasn't good enough, either. Neither was a mental connection on a level she couldn't put into words. She'd always wanted more.

She wished she knew more about his culture. She wished she knew more about him. He'd never spoken of his background—not his family or his friends or his life before this mission. She didn't even know if he intended to spend his life in space or if he craved home and hearth on Mystique.

When he bent to take her mouth with his, her concerns no longer seemed so important—but she could no more resist him than a beach could stop the next tide from surging ashore. It was if he were a force of nature and she'd take whatever he flung her way.

Luckily for her, the man's mouth could have been classified as a secret weapon, his psi an unlikely arsenal of secret forays over her yearning flesh. Flesh that seemed more sensitive than ever before.

Returning to her body had made her very aware of Xander's male aroma, and she reveled in his heady scent that caused her breath to hitch, her senses to heighten with the promise of so much more to follow. When he used his psi to adjust her suit, she felt as though he possessed a dozen pairs of lips, all of them intent on arousing her arms and legs, her fingers and toes, her shoulder blades and her neck—but not once did he so much as skim her erotic zones.

His violet eyes kindled with scarlet sparkles. *Can I assume you like—*

I'd like it better if you'd touch my breasts.

Sure.

She tensed, waiting for him to follow through. Instead he raked her earlobe with his teeth, shooting fire down her neck. *What about—*

Such impatience. He practically growled. "If I can wait, so can you."

When he used his psi to float her into the air, she groaned. Now he had access to all of her and he took wicked advantage. And when he turned her facedown and spread her thighs, she gasped.

"What are you—"

"Are you nice and comfortable?"

"Yes." *No.*

He used his psi to tweak the tips of her breasts. Delightful sensations stole through her and she didn't even mind that if she'd been on the ground she would have been on her hands and knees. Instead all she could think about was that he was parting her thighs and sensuously teasing her bottom. And not only was she eager for him to touch her *yonia,* through the mind link she understood that he was just as eager to delve inside her. But he resisted. His big palms caressed her curves, following her hips and down her legs, yet never opening her *labella* where she wanted him most.

Alara loved the way he took his time, as if she were precious starfire. Knowing more pleasure was to come, a shiver of yearning coursed down her spine. Always, Xander was creative, but she'd never understood how much pleasure he took from taking absolute control.

He made lovemaking about her.

He made lovemaking special.

And all the time her nipples received the most outrageous tugs. Moisture seeped between her parted legs and she wished she could lean back into him. Never had she so ached to fill her *yonia*.

But he held her so firm, she might as well have been webbed in. While he ignored his cravings and her yearnings, he remained steadfast and controlled his urge to take her hard and deep.

"Do you feel how much I want you?" Amusement and a knowing awareness entered his tone.

She couldn't think when he kept tormenting her flesh. He felt so good. Why did he insist on talking? Trying to stem her impatience and her swirling thoughts, she ignored for one moment the demands of her cells. "What?"

"Remember when you were webbed in and had to wait?" If she lived a thousand years she wouldn't forget it. Even then, she'd wanted him—but not as much as she did right now.

"Ah . . . oh . . . So?"

"You liked it when you didn't know what would happen next."

At his words, her *yonia* clenched. His reminder made her all too aware that his roaming hands were ignoring her *labella*, and she suddenly felt . . . bare.

Vulnerable.

Excited.

"Are you asking my permission?" she gasped, unwilling to admit to herself what he was forcing her to think about.

"I'm telling you what you like. I've always wondered why you liked my taking control, and now I'm going to know." He chuckled wickedly. He intended to tease her again. It wasn't enough that her own body betrayed her. He'd understood what she liked better than she did herself and now he would experience both sides of the anticipation—just as she would.

And she would like more of the same and now he knew that in the deepest part of him. By the sweet stars. Without a doubt, he knew she wanted him to follow through. She had no idea what the *krek* was wrong with her.

Ah, you crave my focused attention.

Had she broadcast her thought at him? She had no idea. She only knew she was having trouble thinking. Too many sensations, his and hers, were gathering into a whirlwind.

Yet still, enough of the physiologist in her knew he was right. Merciless teasing would cause heat and the heat would make her . . . burn.

We'll both burn, he promised.

Every muscle in her tightened. Waiting would cause the most erotic kind of irresistible pleasure. And at the idea of sharing that with him, anticipation charged up her throat until she finally asked, "Why don't you start?"

"I'm trying to make up my mind."

"About?"

She ground her teeth and shut her eyes. She couldn't quite know for certain what part of her anatomy he was looking at, but with her bottom up in the air, she had a good idea. The nips and caresses of her suit never ceased and his palms rested for a moment on the insides of her parted thighs, deliciously teasing.

Through the mind link she gathered that to him, her skin was marvelously soft. And beneath his fingers, she quivered in expectation.

He placed a hand ever so sweetly on the curve of her bottom. Her flesh was smooth, curved, rounded beneath his touch, and through the link, he shot admiration. "Whether I want to start here." He parted her *labella* and blew warm air on her delicate flesh. The heat and the vibrations were so deliciously sweet that she didn't have time to bite back a moan of encouraging pleasure. "Or here." He nipped her cheek and licked away the sting and she envisioned his teeth marks on her pale flesh.

But she also felt her flesh quiver under his lips. His fingers slowly stroked between her legs.

"Or here. Here. Or here."

He slipped inside her *yonia* and spread moisture over her *labella,* and she sensed no hesitation in him about mating for life. With every stroke, genuine heat sizzled through her. And through him. Melting together, merging bright and hot.

He started slowly, the caresses from his fingers gentle and easy to take as he explored every exposed inch of her. And when he brushed her sensitive core, the firestorm almost swept her away.

She gasped and somehow she was arching her back, raising her *yonia* to welcome the heat of each stroke as he coaxed the fiery heat until she swelled to a blissful inferno. And when he stroked harder and faster, she lost her breath. Lost her last inhibitions. And his mind linked tight and he was right there with her, feeling everything: her wants, her hopes, her needs—and the burning.

She was so close to release. Just the tiniest increase in pressure would make her explode.

And when he suddenly stopped . . . she moaned a complaint straight into his mind.

"Easy." He ran his hands over her bottom, clutching her flesh, testing her patience, and then with no warning his mouth closed over her *labella*. Privacy mode prevented the crew from hearing her scream of pleasure, but she'd always wonder if they felt the air shudder from her desperate gasps.

And now she knew the pleasure he took from placing his mouth on her so intimately. She felt his pleasure as her own—and it was too much.

If she'd been free to move, her legs would have kicked out. Her hands would have clutched what was in reach. But she could do nothing except enjoy what he was so very good at. Do nothing but enjoy his expert mouth and tongue that swept her higher, tauter than she'd ever been.

And of course with her feelings wide open, his clever tongue knew exactly what she needed, but he never applied quite enough pressure in just the right spot for her to achieve satisfaction. Between his psi and his hands holding her firmly, he seemed determined to keep them both right on the edge. She couldn't so much as twitch. And she marveled that he could resist his own demanding needs.

He was keeping her exactly where she wanted to be. Burning. For him. Burning for more of Xander's lovemaking.

Although the big Rystani warrior might never give her his heart, she would take all he had to offer, and that would have to be enough. And she would love him enough to make a permanent pairing work.

As he buried his tongue in her *yonia,* she moaned with pleasure at the thought at his claiming her for his own. For life.

But she lost her thoughts to the wondrous sensations

he created. And finally when he filled her with his *tavis,* he rode her hard, swift, and deep. She felt his pleasure as he lost himself within her and it added to her own. With every thrust, his pelvis slapped her bottom, with every thrust, he kept up his psi attention to her breasts, and when his hands grasped her hips and rocked her to him, she'd never felt so appreciated.

But it was his mental claiming of her that she savored. For long moments she couldn't discern her thoughts from his. Swirling passion. Dominating lust. Captivating seduction. It was if they were one mind, one body, one soul.

When she spasmed and he released his essence— her cells adapted. And she was glad. Glad that he was the one. And yet she still had enough of the realist in her to hope that now that she'd made the biggest decision of her life, it wouldn't also turn out to be her worst mistake.

18

Kirek's primary mission hadn't changed, but as he sneaked out of Vansek's private chamber, using his psi to counteract her automated surveillance system, his muscles protested. Muscles ached that he hadn't known existed until the sick woman had abused his body with her peculiar tastes.

While he'd tried to check his ego when he'd accepted his hostage status, he couldn't quite control his rage at what she'd demanded of him. For once, he'd worn her out and she'd succumbed to sleep before placing him back into physical restraints, giving him his first opportunity to return to Drik's private command post.

Putting Vansek's deviant behavior aside was close to impossible, but for the sake of all those Kirek had left behind, he tried. With every step deeper into the residence, his heart beat a run-and-escape tattoo against his ribs. The last time Drik's men had caught him, the punishment had left physical scars that would heal— he wasn't so certain about the mental ones. Yet he'd endured.

However, most assuredly, if Drik caught him again, next time the consequences would be worse than Vansek's depravity—although Kirek couldn't imagine much worse than he'd already suffered. Yet, despite the risk to his body and spirit, he had to return to Drik's private office. He'd overheard a guard talking about extra security and hoped that meant more sophisticated computer systems—not additional brawn.

Physically, he would never have enough strength to take on mature Endekian guards, but in his weakened state, he feared he might resort to using his psi powers to defend himself—powers that, so far, he'd kept secret.

Naked, Kirek traipsed through the maze, his presence unquestioned. Anyone who saw the welts on his body hastily looked away. To encourage his deception that he was on a mission for his mistress, he kept his head bowed, his eyes downcast, his shoulders hunched. It was no problem to limp or to flinch as he passed other people as if fearing he'd be struck.

Despite his trembling, despite breaking into a panicked sweat, he forced himself back to Drik's command post. Two burly guards stood in front of the door. One spied Kirek, and neither his nudity, nor his scars, nor his demeanor made a difference. The Endekian's hand reached for his stunner. And Kirek attacked, at the same time putting all the strength of his psi into his shield. For beings born in real space, a psi shield wouldn't have sufficed as a good defense. But Kirek had been born in hyperspace.

When the stun struck Kirek's shield, the force

reflected back on the guards—like a mirror reflecting light. Luckily for them, his shield dispersed the effect, and they didn't receive the full force of the stun as he would have if his shield hadn't protected him.

Wide eyed, mouths open, the Endekian warriors dropped to the floor, struck from the ricochet of their own discharged weapons. Kirek kicked the weapons aside, used his psi once again to open the lock to the command post and nullify the alarms. Sweat pouring off his chest, lungs pumping, Kirek dragged first one heavy Endekian into the room and then the other. Scooping up their weapons, he placed them close by, hoping after the stun wore off and the guards awakened that they wouldn't remember what had happened. His other choice—killing them—not only went against his moral objection to taking life, except in self-defense, but his knowledge that his captors would not look kindly on such an act.

Knowing his time was limited before their superior noticed the guards' absence, Kirek booted the computer system, unsurprised to find more locks and encryption since the last time he'd been here. Quickly he bypassed the codes, aware that each passing second could be his last one of freedom.

Finally. He was in.

Ignoring the temptation to send a message home to his parents, a communiqué that might be detected and lead to his recapture, he sorted through the files in search of information pertaining to glow stones and Rystan and missing inventory. If the Endekians didn't have all the glow stones they'd stolen from Rystan, who did have them?

Kirek perused file upon file. The Endekians had first invaded his home world many years ago and the vast number of records staggered him. The resources the Endekians had committed to the project had almost bankrupted their world. But why? Why did they want the stones? What did they do with them? Where were they now?

One of the guards he'd dragged inside moaned. Kirek set the stunner's beam on the lowest setting, aimed and fired. The guard made no further noises. But the distraction had cost him precious seconds.

Again he dug into the files, his mind sorting, looking for connections, seeking a reason behind the invasion and subjugation of his world. The glow stones were the key.

And finally he found a clue in a treatise written by an Endekian university professor who'd speculated that the glow stones worked on the same subatomic frequencies as a wormhole. Wormholes were simply tunnels where space curved in upon itself.

Kirek's own teachers had suggested he think of space like a three-dimensional blanket. Where the folds touched, wormholes could provide a shortcut between two distant coordinates. Kirek thought of spatial dynamics in simpler terms. Instead of going over the mountain, a wormhole was the tunnel through it.

Before hyperspace travel, scientists had theorized that wormholes might be the best way to functional space travel. However, wormholes were submicroscopic. So people and glow stones would never fit into the hole—unless a way had been found to enlarge and stabilize them. And to accomplish such a task, the wormhole would have to be propped open by an exotic substance that had an outward pressure equal to a neutron star. And the ends of the wormhole would have to be located where one wanted to go to and fro. The idea had proved impractical and remained pure theory.

The Endekian professor had gone on to suggest that a glow stone's explosion might disrupt a wormhole— since they shared certain scientific parameters—by tearing the fabric of space-time apart on the subatomic level. He'd speculated such an explosion would cause space to implode and the wormhole to collapse onto itself.

Interesting.

Were the Endekians following up on the seemingly obscure theory? But why were they devoting enormous resources to the project? The Endekians were infamous for their warlike natures—not scientific study.

Obviously, Kirek had yet to find all the pieces, but the implications worried him. If the Endekians were trying to blow up a wormhole, they had to be concerned about what was coming through. Since no Federation world had the kind of advanced technology to create and maintain a wormhole, the threat had to come from outside the Federation—and if that were the case, why had the Endekians kept their endeavor to collapse the wormhole a secret?

Kirek copied the pertinent file and searched through the rest of the data, pulling out the most arcane references to glow stones. And then knowing that what he did next would undoubtedly cause his recapture, he sent all his information to Mystique, marking the data "most urgent."

As he suspected, moments after he employed the com systems, Drik and his elite guards barged into the command center. Although he'd expected them, he still couldn't stop his nerves from jumping.

His weapon aimed at Kirek's chest, the guard in charge shouted, "Move away from the con. Keep your hands up where I can see them."

Kirek lifted his arms over his head and stepped away from the con. Drik frowned at the unconscious guards then at the compromised computer system. "How did you avoid setting off the alarm?"

Kirek took a stab in the dark. "Did using glow stones to close the wormhole work?"

Drik shook his head in disgust. "Revealing that knowledge was stupid. Now I'll have to kill you."

Kirek's mouth went dry. Even knowing his actions might cause his death, he'd had no choice. Still, he'd rather live. "My death won't stop the truth from getting out. I've already sent the data to Mystique."

"That's where you're wrong." Drik approached him with a scowl. "Since our computer system couldn't stop you last time, I decided not to rely on it again."

"You're saying the data I found is false?"

"I'm saying your communication didn't go past our hyperlink system. We intercepted your message."

"Captain." Vax joined Xander and Alara the next morning in their pocket beneath the plants. Vax spoke quickly and kept his voice low to prevent Shannon from overhearing, since she remained only a few body lengths away with Cyn. "Shannon's too sick to go on. She can barely turn her head."

Xander had known the Terran was ill, but every jump in space had caused her to deteriorate more quickly. Without a trained healer, with no communications and no supplies, he could do nothing for her. Although he never forgot that millions of beings would die of the same disease if his mission failed, watching Shannon's decline increased his frustration and weighed heavily in his heart.

"We aren't leaving her behind." Alara spoke heat-edly, defending the woman who came from a race that had killed her parents. Xander couldn't have been more proud of her. "If we must, we'll carry her. She doesn't weigh—"

"Captain," Vax interrupted her. "There's something else."

"Yes?"

"Clarie's gone, again."

"What do you mean he's *gone*? He couldn't have wandered away through these plants. As little as he is, he's still too large to twist his way through."

"Maybe he transported away, just like he did when he brought us here," Alara suggested.

Vax looked from Alara to Xander as if he believed Alara had lost her mind, but Xander thought she might be onto something. "Alara may be right. Ever since we found Clarie—"

"Maybe he found us," Alara suggested, her ideas clearly skipping ahead.

"We've traveled in a manner I can't explain." Vax's brows narrowed. "And Clarie's always around during the process, first during the journey from the ship to Lapau, then from Lapau to Saj."

"And Clarie's pet, Delo, glows during the transport as if he's a power source," Alara added. "I wish I could read Delo's DNA, but he's blank to me. At first, I thought he was a holopet but now . . ."

"Now," Xander thought out loud, "we have to find a way to that mountain and search for the Perceptive Ones, and Shannon isn't up to such a strenuous trek."

Shannon limped into the tiny area, helped by Cyn. "We Terrans have a saying. If Mohammed can't go to the mountain, then the mountain should come to Mohammed."

"Who is Mohammed?" Vax asked.

"That's not the point," Shannon snapped as Cyn carefully helped her to sit with her back propped against the plants for support.

Xander shot her a look carefully devoid of pity, wishing he could offer her food or water. He didn't like the look of her pinched lips that indicated pain or her delicate skin that appeared too thin. "Do you mean the mountain should come to us?"

"You're taking her too literally." Alara nodded at Shannon as if she understood. "She means we should leave our bodies again and explore with our minds. Why waste time trekking when we can soar?"

"Good idea." Xander should have thought of the option himself. But after spending most of his adult lifetime thinking that leaving his body was cowardly, he had difficulty believing in the usefulness of his skill.

"I don't like you leaving without me," Vax argued.

Xander clapped Vax on the shoulder. "I need you to protect our bodies."

Vax snorted. "From what?"

Xander didn't answer. Instead he knelt by Shannon. "Can you hold on a little longer?"

"Find a cure, Captain." Shannon held his hand, her grip weak. "It may already be too late for me, but I'd like my grandkids to live."

At Shannon's words, Alara looked away, but Xander caught sight of her eyes brimming with tears. "We'll do our best."

"Count on it," Alara added.

Xander lay on the ground and motioned for Alara to

lie beside him. She'd been so exhausted after leaving her body last night that he hated to ask her to repeat the experience so soon, but she joined him without hesitation.

Still he had to ask, "Ready?"

"Yes." She interlocked her fingers with his, and he couldn't think of anyone he'd rather have at his side.

Since he had more experience in astral extension, he altered his mental state more quickly, but didn't have to wait long for her to join him. Today was another sun-filled day. With no clouds in the sky and no wind, the planet seemed devoid of life—except for the woman at his side who vibrated with energy and determination. Together they soared toward the mountain and the straight ridge he'd noted yesterday.

Out-of-body extension had distinctive advantages. When they reached the portal similar to the one on Mystique's Mount Shachauri, a stone door with the sign of the Perceptive One's symbol carved into it, they passed right through the physical barrier. They needn't fear falling off the mountain or a strange animal threatening them. Their bodies were safe.

Now what? Alara's thoughts entered his mind as she floated down a long stone hallway. Right angles delineated where walls met floor and ceiling, signifying this was no natural formation. Although no sunlight penetrated, their auras lit the way and they could "see."

Let's follow it into the mountain, he suggested.

Didn't the entrance on Mystique have machinery? And didn't bright lights come on when your people entered? Alara asked.

Yes. Perhaps it takes a physical body to trigger those mechanisms. Or perhaps the Perceptive Ones built this complex for other reasons. If Xander had had a neck, he would have sworn the hair on his nape would have been standing up. Something felt . . . wrong and he tried to figure out what his subconscious was picking up that his mind couldn't figure out—and he came up with a skinny, paltry zero.

Hey. Alara pinpointed the problem, seemingly with no trouble. *This is a dead end.*

The passageway simply stopped. It was if someone had ceased tunneling and abandoned the project—only they'd done so neatly. The wall he faced was as smooth as the other walls, floor and ceiling.

Alara turned to him. *Do we go through?*

Sure. Perhaps it's another blockage like the one that led in from outside.

Alara slipped through the rock and he followed. But they'd eased into solid stone. And despite the fact that he didn't require air, he felt as if he'd been buried alive. Still, he wouldn't back out without following through. *Let's proceed a little further.*

Do you suppose this journey is creepy because we aren't used to traveling through solid mass?

Even if I got used to astral extension, it'd still be creepy, he admitted.

Her laughter filled his mind and they soared right through rock, dirt, and even a tiny cavern. Judging the passage of time was impossible. So was estimating their progress. To him one part of the mountain looked just like another.

But when they suddenly exited into the air and sunshine of the other side of the mountain, disappointment washed through him. *I was so certain we'd find . . . something.*

Let's go back and try again. Maybe we missed a clue.

Her willingness to return inside the cloying mountain

impressed him. *If we soar around the outside, maybe we'll spot another entrance.*

But after an estimated hour of careful searching, they'd returned to where they'd begun by the first entrance without discovering anything of use. The idea of going back to Shannon with nothing to show for their efforts weighed on him. *Are you up for following this same passage again?*

Maybe we should go more slowly this time.

The urgency of their circumstances, the lack of food and water, in addition to Shannon's worsening condition, might have made them hurry. *You think we missed something?*

Nothing obvious. But maybe there's a secret entrance. We only flew in the direction the tunnel would have continued if they'd kept tunneling straight ahead.

He caught on to Alara's idea and followed it to a logical conclusion. *Suppose they went left or right and changed direction?*

Or up or down? Or diagonally?

Or suppose they went nowhere? The Perceptive Ones might have stopped on this world for just one day over a millennia ago and then moved on for reasons of their own. He kept the discouraging thought to himself.

Since the mission had begun, they'd run into one surprise after another—but all along he'd been aware that the information Ranth had collected from this part of the galaxy was pure theory. Xander and his crew might be on a useless mission—no, he would not think of failure. Not when they had once again entered the cavern. He would focus on the seamless black stone.

Alara floated by the ceiling. *I wish I had hands.*

Why?

To brush away the dirt and cobwebs.

Keep looking. He tried to sound encouraging, but in truth, her even-tempered spirit was keeping *his* hopes alive. Last night when she'd adapted to him, for a moment he'd felt as trapped as he did in this airless tunnel. But after she'd given herself to him fully, he admitted to himself that he liked knowing she would always be with him. Alara was intelligent, beautiful . . . and Endekian. But he no longer held that against her. And he knew that if there was one planet that would accept a union between them, it was Mystique—a planet where the laws allowed complete freedom, as long as one didn't harm another. Beings from many planets lived there side by side.

So what had held him back?

Taking Alara as a permanent partner would alter his future and his career. Risking his life on one adventure after another meant he would also be risking hers. But finding another occupation shouldn't have been on his mind right now, either. His thoughts rarely strayed so far from his mission, and he wondered if he was losing focus due to his altered state, the weakness of his body from lack of sustenance, or from the breakdown of his DNA.

When they hit the dead end for the third time, he suggested, *We should go back.*

One more time. I'll take the floor, you check out the ceiling.

Fine. They reversed positions. But it wasn't fine. He'd been the one who'd suggested leaving and she was the one with the determination to continue. It was almost as if every time he thought about really looking at the stone, his mind refused to concentrate.

Or maybe there was more here than met his astral eyes. Maybe other forces didn't want him to find what he sought? Or was he making excuses for coming up with nothing?

Alara's aura glowed below him. He should be examining the rock, but her silhouette seemed abnormally bright. *Are you all right?*

Come here. Look.

He floated down beside her. *I don't see anything.*

Look harder.

I still don't . . . is that an arrow?

Excitement made her words louder in his mind. *Which way do you think it's pointing?*

Down?

That's what I thought. Let's go see.

We've been gone a long time. We could come back tomorrow.

Shannon can't wait, she reminded him gently.

And he shouldn't have needed reminding. What was wrong with him? He wanted to slap his face. Step under a cold waterfall. *Alara, think carefully, do you feel . . . your usual self?*

Her aura nodded. *What's wrong?*

There's mental pressure. Distractions. I'm not making good decisions.

Well, I think we should take a quick look. If we don't find anything, it may not pay to return.

He didn't trust his own judgment but he trusted hers. *All right. Let's do it.*

They merged with the floor, eased into the rock.

And slammed into . . . blackness.

Ha. I told you they couldn't do it.

Stop gloating. Your trick didn't work. He trusted her judgment more than your false trails.

They've still failed. You've failed.

Nonsense. They simply need to make further adjustments.

Watching their progress is as slow as the erosion on Delta Jameda.

But you must admit, they have made progress.

Not enough. You simply can't accelerate evolution. They aren't meant to evolve further. We should let them die and be done.

They are much closer than you think.

Really?

Just a few more manipulations and they will be on the verge of another breakthrough.

And still they will fail. Their brains simply don't have the capacity to comprehend what you are so dutifully trying to accomplish.

Understanding all is unnecessary. However, the parts must come together. They must each do their task.

They're at the breaking point. They'll give up.

They will overcome the obstacles and be stronger for their endeavors.

Perhaps. But they are running out of time.

19

Alara groaned and opened her eyes to see Cyn peering over at her. "Are you all right?"

"What happened?" Vax asked, his tone gruff.

Alara blinked and shoved up on one elbow. Although she had no memory of returning, she was back in her body, lying next to Xander, who gazed at her, his eyebrows furrowed in puzzlement. "We were exploring a passageway. And something struck us."

"I think we struck . . . a wall . . . no, we didn't have bodies. It must have been a force field that could repel our astral extensions."

Vax scowled at her. "Do you realize how bizarre—"

"It happened." Xander rubbed his brow. "I have the headache to prove it." He sat up and peered at Shannon, who didn't appear to have moved since they'd left. Her eyes were closed. Her breathing was shallow, her skin pale. But it was her total lack of expression that scared Alara.

"What did you find besides the force field?" Cyn asked.

Xander spoke slowly, summarizing their failure as if he were as discouraged and drained as she was. "The Perceptive Ones' symbol on a stone led us to a passageway that ended, then Alara found an arrow pointing downward. When we tried to follow, we ran smack into the force field."

Cyn grinned, her green skin showing off her excitement by deepening to a darker hue. "That's wonderful."

Alara frowned. "Getting smacked in the head is wonderful?"

"You found a force field." Cyn's tone rose with excitement. "No one builds a force field without a reason. Something important is down there. The Perceptive Ones likely built the force field to protect . . . it."

"It?" Alara scooted closer to Shannon. "We have no idea what's there. And we have no way to penetrate the barrier."

Xander shuddered. "It was like running straight into *bendar*. Even my teeth ache."

"You reached the barrier before me." Alara closed her eyes, trying to envision every detail. "And the barrier lit up with an incandescent orange color, raining red-hot sparks. I edged forward, too, and for a second, the sparks dimmed." She opened her eyes and found Xander's."

"You think the dimming indicates that we weakened the force field?"

She shrugged, wondering what they had to lose by going back. Her stomach was making terrible growls of hunger. Worse, her throat was so parched, talking actually hurt. And Shannon . . . God . . . Shannon was dying. "Perhaps if we *all* hit the field together, we could go through."

"Clarie hasn't come back. We need him to teach us how to leave our bodies," Cyn objected.

Vax shook his head, his shoulders sagging in defeat. "I've already tried and failed to—"

"If Alara and I can astral-extend, then so can you," Xander disagreed firmly, taking control—even though he was flat on his back and clearly in pain.

Alara scooted over and tugged until he lifted his head into her lap. While they discussed a plan, she used her fingertips to massage his scalp in an attempt to soothe away the pain. Slamming into that barrier had taken a toll she didn't understand. How could their bodies hurt—when their bodies hadn't been with them?

Clearly, they had to solve the mystery by using their new skills . . . Or were they all going to perish on Saj? Like Malk? The Saj leader had said to assume he'd died if he didn't return.

This was his world and if he couldn't survive here, how could they? Perhaps they might last another day, maybe two without water. Every passing moment, their bodies weakened. The others felt it, too. The tension among them was as thick as the plants surrounding them.

"Alara and I need rest. We'll all try to go in a few hours." Xander glanced at Shannon, then Alara, his face drawn. "Make that one hour?"

She nodded agreement. Shannon's breathing was so shallow, she couldn't last much longer. All eyes rested on her and the group went silent. Shannon suddenly gasped and shuddered. Then went completely still.

"Shannon?" Cyn kneeled beside the Terran and placed two fingers on her neck in search of a pulse. When Cyn's hand dropped and she sagged, her head bowed, Alara's throat clogged with tears.

"She's gone?" Xander asked, his voice tight.

Alara couldn't bear to look at anyone. If Shannon hadn't thrown herself into the fray on Lapau to help her, she might have saved her strength to fight the virus. She might have lived . . . Stars. She couldn't be gone. The Terran may have been getting on in years, but she'd been so full of life. She should have had another century or two to gallivant around the galaxy. She shouldn't have died in some nameless spot of the rim without her family around her. Sure, she'd been among friends—and they'd done nothing to help her because there had been nothing to do.

The hopelessness tore at Alara, and knowing that billions more would die of the disease if they failed weighed upon her heart like lead. Her mind boggled at the thought of billions of deaths—Alara could barely take in the enormity of losing Shannon.

Alara's throat tightened with tears and she choked on the bitter sorrow. She'd been proud to call Shannon a friend and would miss her lively Terran attitude.

Vax hacked the thicker branches with the sword, taking his grief out on the plants. The men used the sticks Vax carved to dig a grave. Alara dug with her hands, scooping up the earth, letting it drizzle between her fingers, hoping the hard work would numb her sorrow. But the potent ache of knowing she would never again hear Shannon talk about her large family, never again see her smile or cook, made her angry.

Xander said a few words over the body, but Alara

couldn't listen, couldn't take comfort from them. She kissed Shannon on each cheek and then her forehead, saying her own goodbye. Tears fell unashamedly down the Rystani warriors' faces as well as her own. Only Cyn didn't cry, but sadness was evident in her weary eyes.

It would be so easy to lie down next to Shannon's grave and give up. Exhausted, head hurting, bone weary, Alara felt as if her brain were swathed in cotton. She couldn't even maintain her anger. Shannon was dead. Soon the rest of them would join her. And the entire Federation wasn't far behind.

They hadn't found a cure, and just like Shannon, even these plants would die—as would every last living creature.

Xander gave them until morning to rest. Alara didn't sleep well, her sorrow over losing Shannon invading her dreams. While she stretched out the kinks in her neck, Vax dug deep into the ground and found several roots that held moisture. Each of them swallowed a few reviving sips of water.

Afterward, Xander spoke with renewed determination. "Shannon wouldn't have wanted us to give up. So today we will teach Cyn and Vax to leave their bodies. Together we will soar to the force field and use our combined strength to break through."

But after repeated attempts, neither Cyn nor Vax could leave their bodies. And the harder they tried, the less they relaxed their muscles and failed to sink into a deep meditative state. Alara and Xander couldn't figure out what was wrong with their teaching method.

However, it had been Clarie who'd taught Alara and Xander, and the alien had disappeared when they needed him most.

As the sun rose in the sky, it took more psi energy to cool their suits. Tempers grew frayed and short. Finally, Xander called for another rest.

Vax dug deeper in search of more water but found none. Cyn sat beside Shannon's grave, her feet drawn to her chest, her chin resting on her knees. "Maybe my people can't leave their bodies."

"It's more likely we aren't teaching you right." Xander patted her shoulder. "We'll no doubt get it this afternoon."

Alara leaned against the plants. "Let's go over what Clarie said one more time."

"Found some." Vax yanked more roots from the ground.

Xander accepted the bulbs from Vax and handed one to each of them. "We've gone over and over Clarie's words. We're missing something . . . else."

They all sipped the precious water in silence. Finally, Cyn straightened her legs. "Clarie also spoke in a singsong rhythm. Maybe the tone and rhythm are as important as the words?"

Alara stared at her. "Perhaps those tones helped deepen the mental state. Like hypnosis." She looked at Xander. "I have no voice at all for music."

Vax chuckled, the first time anyone had laughed since Shannon's death. "Xander can sing like a holovid celebrity. He has perfect pitch."

Alara had had no idea he could sing. She'd only known that she'd been drawn to his voice from the first time he'd spoken to her. And Xander always seemed able to convey emotions through his deep voice. "Can you replicate Clarie's rhythm and notes?"

"I believe so." He gestured for everyone to lie down. And this time, when he repeated Clarie's words, both Vax and Cyn soared above their bodies.

We did it.

How like Xander to give everyone credit when it was his voice that had made the difference. Alara recognized Vax by his tight silver aura that was about the same size as Xander's, but not as bright. Cyn was still green, but she didn't project a silhouette of her body as Alara did. Instead, she resembled a formless but pretty cloud.

Xander led them straight back to the mountain and the passageway. With four of them inside, their auras lit up the airless tunnel as bright as daylight.

Before we try to pierce the force field, I'd like to try a theory. For the first time, Xander's thoughts sounded hesitant.

What? Alara encouraged him.

There's nothing to prevent us from combining our auras.

Alara marveled at the audacity of his idea. Would they be stronger as one unit than as four separate entities? Who could say? Until they tried, they wouldn't know what was possible. However, the notion tugged at her own desire to be close to Xander.

Vax, as usual, had questions. *Suppose we can't separate again? We could never return to our bodies.*

And if our bodies die, Cyn asked, *what will happen to our minds? Will we die, too? Or will we be stuck together for eternity? I'm not nixing the idea. I'd just like to know.*

Alara understood the implications and yet . . . merging with Xander appealed to her on so many levels she was having difficulty sorting her feelings from her thoughts. *Why don't Xander and I merge first?*

Good idea. Xander's warmth and approval seeped into her mind, but she wondered if that was due to her willingness to try to merge to defeat the force field or because he welcomed the idea of being close to her.

And if the joining worked, would their mental connection change? Would they be able to read each other's thoughts? She wasn't certain she wanted to know what he thought about her. After the last time they'd mated and her cells had adapted to him, he'd said little about how their lives would forever be joined and nothing about his feelings.

Suppose she merged and learned that he'd mated with her for reasons she didn't like?

Krek. Now was not the time for personal issues. Still, she wouldn't be a female if she didn't wonder . . . Suppose she lost her own identity?

The thought made her hesitate, but then before she changed her mind, she floated, holding perfectly still, allowing Xander to close the distance between them. If she'd had lungs, she would have been holding her breath. Instead, anticipation mixed with wariness as the bronze glow of his aura moved into the space of her silhouette.

You okay? His thought, bold and concerned and determined, seemed to come from inside her head.

Our minds aren't merging. She was very much still the individual.

I hope not.

But I can feel your . . . will—like tendrils wrapping around me, running through me.

And suddenly she couldn't determine where his will ended and hers began. Her thoughts remained her own—but somehow, he'd fused their determination. Strength poured through her. For the first time, she thought his crazy idea might actually work.

By the stars. Vax swore. *I can't tell where one of you begins and the other ends.*

Join us, Xander coaxed.

What if we can never separate? Vax asked.

It won't be a problem. It's like holding hands and letting go. Together we're stronger than each of us alone, Alara encouraged him, already understanding that the union would not be permanent and elated by the power that seemed to expand exponentially with their merged auras.

Alara fully expected Vax to join and strengthen them yet again. He edged close. Their auras touched his—but like a skittish feline, he backed away.

You have to hold still, Xander instructed.

Vax's frustration poured into her mind. *I'm trying, but it's as if your auras are deflecting me. Every time I approach, you shove me back.*

Cyn floated forward. *Let me try.* Vax moved aside to give her room. The nebulous green cloud that was Cyn scudded toward them, but like flesh that approached too close to fire, she jerked back. *You're blocking me out, or I can't find an entrance.*

Perhaps Vax and Cyn should try to link. Alara figured at least they'd multiply their strength as she and Xander had done.

Good idea. Xander's admiration was genuine. *Perhaps there are limits to how many can link. Or maybe*

we have to be compatible on a level we don't under-
stand.

Vax held still and Cyn approached. Tentatively, she dipped a fragment of her aura into his silver brightness. And the silver took on a green sheen. *It's working.* Their thoughts came through simultaneously.

Alara watched the merge, fascinated. The brightness gleamed and the hard edges that had portrayed Vax had softened as Cyn and he merged. She wondered what she and Xander looked like, but sensing Xander's eagerness to attack the barrier, she didn't ask frivolous questions. But she couldn't help thinking about whether the merging required one female and one male—or simply two beings. Her scientific curiosity was streaming at hyperdrive speed, but she had to force herself to focus on the moment.

All set? Xander asked.

Ready, Captain, Vax replied.

Alara held her mental breath as they eased downward toward the force field. Although they were certainly much stronger now and the attack through the barrier would be a two-pronged strike, she couldn't even begin to estimate if they would get through—or be knocked back into their bodies like last time.

She had no idea if their speed or shape or timing would make one bit of difference between success and failure. It was possible they should be spinning or flattening their auras, or sharpening them. The entire procedure violated every scientific premise. Instead of testing, instead of figuring out exactly what they needed to do, they were literally going to throw themselves at the barrier and pray it worked.

Talk about crazy notions—this one had to be the riskiest experiment she'd ever taken part in. Yet there was no time for careful research. No time to bring in experts—as if there were any. They simply had to go with what they thought best.

Stop fidgeting, Xander ordered.

Huh?

You're squirming.

How can I squirm when I don't have a body? she countered.

Ah . . . that's better.

But I didn't . . . Had he felt her doubts? She didn't know. But as they descended through rock, then flowing red-hot magma, toward the planet's core, she tensed. Striking that barrier hadn't been pleasant. This time they were traveling faster, hurtling at speeds that blurred her surroundings.

Vax and Cyn had no trouble keeping pace. Their dazzling silver/green brilliance rocketed beside them, the only constant in the ever-changing planetary core. As they closed in on the invisible barrier, Alara tried not to tense.

Almost there. Xander's excitement reverberated through her, and she realized he was enjoying himself.

A moment later . . . they crashed through.

The collision separated Alara from Xander and their tight bond ceased to be, as did Vax and Cyn's. Xander returned to his normal astrally extended self and spared no more than a passing thought about the split. Instead, he adjusted to the stunning sight within Saj's centermost core.

And it wasn't the streaming magma that drew his attention but the astral being awaiting him with a gratified expression.

Clarie?

The alien and his pet Delo, their auras so subtle, Xander had to search for a fuzzy edge to their silhouettes, floated calmly as if they'd been awaiting their arrival. So sharp was Clarie's image that Xander would have thought him real if it had been possible for a solid being to project to Saj's core.

But what was he doing here?

Clarie's head swiveled and his antennae bent back and forth with excitement. *Finally. You have progressed to the next level of evolution.*

The next level of evolution? *I don't understand.* Xander stared at the little alien, disappointment washing through him. He'd expected to find the Perceptive Ones, not Clarie.

You have succeeded. Clarie spoke as if reading Xander's mind. *You have found what you sought. Me.*

Alara gasped. *That's why your DNA is so complex and why I couldn't read Delo. You are both Perceptive Ones?*

Yes. Clarie grinned.

Delo glowed bright orange. *Even now they do not understand. They are not ready.*

Xander couldn't quite take in all the implications. Clarie and Delo were Perceptive Ones? *But why did you make us come—*

Here? Clarie finished his thought for him. *I already explained. I had to ensure you would evolve.*

You mean leave our bodies? Alara asked.

Exactly. Clarie beamed at her as if she were his brightest pupil.

Xander might not have been as quick, but he had a mission to accomplish. *Can you give us the DNA to—*

Cure the virus? Yes, of course. We seeded the galaxy

*with DNA. We left you suits to encourage the develop-
ment of your psi powers. We created the Challenge so
your worlds would unite, and we protected you with the
Sentinels to give you time to form a strong union based
upon the principles necessary to succeed at the coming
task.*

The coming task? Xander's mission was over. If
Clarie gave him the cure for the virus they could go
home.

Delo glowed a dark orange. *Time and again they
have proved unworthy.*

They got here, didn't they? Clarie countered.

Only because you manipulated the universe—

So?

*I have to admit I didn't expect them to make it this
far—but they simply are not up to the task before them.*

What task? Xander didn't like the situation. He
didn't understand why Clarie wanted him to evolve.
He didn't understand the antagonism between the two
Perceptive Ones. And he most certainly wasn't pleased
that the two beings seemed to be playing some kind of
ego game when the Federation's billions were dying.

Clarie's head swiveled back to meet him. *The Zin
have opened a wormhole into Federation space. It was
the Zin's creations, tiny nanomachines, that brought
the virus through the wormhole.*

Stars. The Zin were the Perceptive Ones' ancient enemy, and the Sentinels, giant machines built by the
Perceptive Ones, stood guard on the galaxy's edge,
preventing invasion. But obviously the Zin had found a
way to create a wormhole, another way to penetrate
the galaxy, and to kill every living thing inside the
Federation.

The virus was no accident. The Zin had attacked and

the Federation hadn't even known they were in a battle.

Since the Sentinels stood guard, the Zin had found another way to hurt them. At least that's what Xander thought Clarie had said.

The Zin sent the virus through a wormhole?

Yes.

But you have a cure?

Yes.

So why didn't you simply give it to us? Why let so many beings die?

You had to evolve.

So you orchestrated our journey to make us evolve?

Delo glowed hot orange. *Ah, really. You spell it out for it, and then when it finally understands, it's actually proud of itself. They are too stupid to exist. Let them die now. It would be kinder than to give them false hope.*

When a good parent teaches a child to walk, he must sometimes allow them to fall down. Only by failure and success does a child learn balance. Only through living can a being evolve.

This is futile. Delo's aggravation grew. *It's too late.*

It's too late to cure the virus? Xander asked, confused. Clarie had said he had a cure. Was he refusing to help? Or had the virus spread too far? *Is there a point where the cellular degeneration cannot be healed?*

Delo's sarcasm slapped him. *Curing the virus will do you no good. The Zin's machines will create another and another and send them through the wormhole until you are all dead.*

The wormhole must be closed, Xander said.

It's too late, Delo shouted, the words an accusation reverberating in Xander's head like a curse. *You have failed. Even as we speak, a multitude of new viruses are invading the galaxy.*

Is that true? Xander demanded, his thoughts burning with fury that they had come so far, but not far enough.

Clarie's astral shoulders shrugged. *I have a solution. Wormholes cause time distortions. So that you can close the wormhole, I will send you back in time.*

20

Alara's mind was spinning with Clarie's statements and the ramifications when she found herself back in her body—on the bridge of the *Verazen*. Cyn was at her engineering station and ship's power seemed fully restored. Vax was at the con.

Xander's jaw dropped and she followed his stare to the navigation officer. "Shannon?"

"What happened?" Shannon frowned at him. "The last thing I remember was . . . I must have been out of my head with a fever because . . . I thought . . . I . . . died."

"You were very sick." Xander spoke calmly, as if they hadn't just witnessed a marvel. "How do you feel now?"

"Well. But I'm . . . missing time." Shannon's brow furrowed and then she grinned. "I can't recall everything."

Stars! Shannon was alive. And she had some memories of her death. They'd buried her. But now she was floating at her station with a silly smile on her face as if she realized she'd been given a second chance.

By the stars. Had they all really gone to Lapau and Saj or had they had a joint hallucination?

Or had Clarie really brought them back in time and across half the Milky Way Galaxy to close a wormhole in one stunning display or power that had Alara so unbalanced she had to grab a console for support? She didn't know whether or not to believe her eyes.

Shannon was alive.

"Captain." Ranth the computer sounded almost as puzzled as Alara felt. "I've noted certain spatial irregularities. And I can't account for the course correction, but we are headed for Earth."

"Remain on course," said Xander. He had recovered much faster than Alara. She doubted she could yet speak.

Stunned, she couldn't wrap her mind around the puzzles. Had they ever left the ship or not? What in Dregan hell was the date? And if they'd gone back in time as Clarie had stated—why were all her memories intact? Why did she recall her cells adapting to Xander, but now knew that they were no longer connected in that way? Her physiology had gone backward, but her mind recalled every detail of the cell regeneration and the ensuing adaptation—which no longer existed. Nothing made sense.

But then when she considered that she'd left her body, astrally extended to the core of a planet, and met a Perceptive One who wanted them to close a wormhole to prevent the Zin from sending viruses into the Federation, even to herself, she sounded like a lunatic.

When she noted a young Rystani male, standing naked and bleeding on the bridge, she merely blinked. Her mind couldn't wrap around one more bizarre puzzle.

Xander approached the boy, his tone calm. "Kirek. Are you all right?"

"How did I get here?" Kirek demanded, clearly confused.

"You might want to cover your nudity," Xander suggested, as if a naked and bleeding Rystani appeared on the bridge every day and needed reminding of proper attire.

"I've been naked so long . . ." Kirek adjusted his suit. "How did I get here?" he repeated.

"The Perceptive Ones sent us back in time to close a wormhole," Xander explained, as if time travel were a common occurrence.

Maybe Xander's practical approach was the way to go. She didn't need to understand hyperspace to fly through it. She didn't need to comprehend how her flitter flew to drive it. If she stopped trying to figure out the impossible and simply accepted it maybe her world wouldn't feel so shaky.

"I know all about the wormhole," Kirek muttered. "That's why the Endekians invaded Rystan. They needed the glow stones to close the Zin's wormhole."

"Did the Endekians succeed?" Xander asked.

Leave it to Xander to hone in on the most important point. Alara had never been more proud of him than she was right then. They'd all been through a major upheaval. Kirek looked like he'd been to Dregan hell and back. Shannon had even returned from the dead. But Xander was carrying on his command, as if saving the galaxy were his sole mission—and maybe it was. The

Perceptive Ones had chosen him for their own reasons, but she believed he was the best man for the job.

Xander was holding his disturbed crew together by sheer determination. Clearly he intended to carry on his mission in the past, present or future, against any enemy, against any odds. He wasn't torn by doubts about what had just occurred. He accepted what was. And he forged onward.

Kirek faced his captain, apparently not the least embarrassed by his lapse in attire. If he'd been Drik's hostage, he wouldn't have been allowed to cover his nudity on Endeki and likely would have become accustomed to walking around naked—as well as being used by women. Alara wondered what the long-term side effects would do to him, and hoped he'd recover swiftly from his ordeal.

Kirek spoke quickly and clearly, stoic about his wounds. "Many years ago the Zin opened a wormhole from their galaxy to Endeki. The wormhole was tiny, not large enough to pass anything through. But Endekians were convinced their survival depended upon closing the connection between the two galaxies. After much experimentation, the Endekians learned that the explosion of Rystani glow stones would disrupt the wormhole and close it."

"But the Zin opened another wormhole," Xander guessed.

"Correct, Captain. Each wormhole was a bit larger. More stable. Desperate for glow stones, the Endekians invaded Rystan, keeping their need for the glow stones a secret."

"Why?" Xander asked.

"They feared the Zin would return and attack through the wormhole and they wanted to hoard all the glow stones for their own use. They kept them stored on many different ships in their fleet—so in case the Zin opened a wormhole, they'd have ammunition to close it."

Xander nodded. "So now we finally know why Endeki invaded Rystan."

Kirek held his gaze. "Since the Endekians kept closing the wormholes, the Zin moved the wormhole to Earth and sent through the virus—"

"Speaking of glow stones," Ranth interrupted, "the *Verazen*'s cargo hold is full of them and I can't find an inventory in my memory banks."

"Clarie's been busy," Alara muttered. "He also put the cure for the virus in my head. The reason our suits can't filter the virus is because the infection is inorganic. The Zin built the virus out of microscopic machines, of a size so miniscule our equipment couldn't find it."

"Can you send the cure to Mystique?" Xander asked.

"I believe so." She moved to a console and sent the vital data to Mystique where it would be shared with the entire Federation, including the Lapautee and the Saj. She also instructed Ranth to manufacture the cure for the crew.

"Who's Clarie?" Kirek asked.

"One of the Perceptive Ones." Vax frowned at the bleeding stripes across Kirek's neck. "How did you learn—"

"I did a little exploring."

"And got caught?"

"Twice." Kirek winced.

"Why didn't you use your suit's shields to protect you?"

"On Endeki, for a hostage to use his suit to protect

himself from a master is not allowed. Disobedience means death." Kirek bit his bottom lip. "Sore flesh is the least of my worries."

"What else is wrong?" Xander hovered protectively over Kirek.

Alara finished sending out the cure for the virus and turned her attention to Kirek. While she suspected a lot had gone wrong for him while he'd been a hostage, his tone indicated a more serious problem.

"Can we contact Clarie?" Kirek asked.

"Why?"

"When the Perceptive Ones placed the cure for the virus inside Alara's mind, they placed calculations in mine."

Xander looked at Kirek curiously. "What kind of calculations?"

"Formulas on wormhole theory. I should know how to find the wormhole on Earth and close it . . . but . . . the calculations are incomplete."

"Maybe my people," Alara said, "can help. If we closed one wormhole, we should—"

"The Endekian wormhole was tiny and stable. The Zin/Terran wormhole is moving. Opening and closing rapidly. I don't understand why I only have part of the necessary formula."

Xander spoke thoughtfully, as if choosing his words with care. "Clarie told us that the Perceptive Ones see us as children. They'll only help so much. The rest is up to us."

"He probably gave you enough to figure out the rest," Vax said encouragingly.

Kirek's eyes turned inward. "I have a lot to figure out before we reach Earth."

"Captain." Shannon's gaze flew over her console.

"The Endekian fleet commander is demanding we stop. He claims we have stolen cargo on board."

Xander caught up with Alara in her lab several harrowing hours later. He'd refused to stop the ship's progress and—thanks to several well-placed bribes, plus Tessa and Kahn's pull with the Federation political council after sharing the cure for the virus—the Endeki fleet had backed down in their demands. Kahn had just filled him in on details and Xander had come to share the good news with Alara.

He found her in her laboratory, fussing over her experiments. When he entered, she looked up, a pleased expression on her face. "I expected everything to be dead, but with the time travel, I can take up where I left off."

"Good."

Alara seemed a bit preoccupied and was avoiding his gaze. But perhaps she was simply so happy to be back in familiar surroundings that she wasn't paying him the special attention he had become accustomed to. During their time on Lapau and Saj, ever since her cells' adaptation to him, they'd seemed close and very aware of each other. He'd often caught her gaze following his as she'd watched for his reactions. They'd often communicated with a silent glance, a direct look, but now that they'd returned to the ship, she seemed more distant.

And he automatically reverted to formality to ease the tension between them that had arisen from someplace he couldn't pinpoint. "Federation scientists had no difficulty manufacturing the cure."

She held up a capsule that contained the cure and a

packet of water. "Everyone else on the *Verazen* has already taken theirs. This is for you."

He accepted the cure with a grateful nod, popped the capsule into his mouth and chased it with water. And all the time he wondered what was different about her. She looked the same as the first time he'd met her, but her beautiful golden skin had become more familiar. He now knew how he enjoyed snuggling with her and how he looked forward to her satisfied gaze after he pleasured her. But the open and friendly woman he'd known was gone, as if she'd drawn into herself. And it wasn't just her scientific demeanor. She'd handed him the capsule and water without touching him.

"What's wrong?" He crushed the packet in his fist.

She picked a nonexistent speck of dust off her immaculate counter and brushed it aside. "Remember when you said you wished we had more time?"

He had no idea what she meant. "More time . . . ?"

"For my cells to adapt to you."

"I remember." His stomach clenched as if to take a blow, but he still had no idea where the conversation was going.

"Well, now your wish has come true."

He folded his arms across his chest and braced his feet. "I don't understand."

"The time travel backward—it has nullified my cell adaptation. We are now . . . free."

Despite bracing himself, he rocked back on his heels. He finally understood. Biology no longer linked their lives together. She was free to go to any man, and she'd delivered the news in such dry scientific language, he couldn't guess her thoughts. He wished she'd look at him, give him a hint as to her emotions. But she'd shut down every female signal.

He weighed his words with care, sensing what he said next was critical but not sure why. "We may have gone back in time, but the situation on this ship is the same. You will come to me, and only me, when you have a need."

Her voice turned icy, chilling him with her frost. "We'll likely arrive on Earth before my biology requires more attention."

"I see."

Was her icy demeanor covering her relief? How dare she withdraw from him after all they'd been through. Stars. In her astral state she'd merged with him on a level he still didn't understand—yet it had been beautiful, as if they were meant to be together. And now, due to a backward twist in time, she would deny everything? She would deny him?

He tightened his arms against the urge to reach out and shake her. After all they'd shared, did she feel nothing? Had their mating been simply sex—and not one thing more?

Hurt that she could be so cold, furious that she didn't want him now that she no longer needed him, he churned with a rage he didn't understand. His hands seemed to move of their own accord and he reached out, grabbed her shoulders, pulled her into his arms. When she tilted up her head, he caught surprise in her eyes.

Before she said a word, he angled his mouth over hers. She tensed, then trembled against his chest. The heat that always kindled during their kisses sparked and ignited a possessiveness he'd thought he'd suppressed.

And when she kissed him back, he took immense satisfaction in eliciting a response. Oh, yes, she most definitely was responding. And not because of her damned *Boktai*. Her nostrils flared delicately and a pulse at her neck throbbed.

His voice was gruff, demanding. "So you don't need me anymore?"

"No."

He nibbled her ear. "And you don't need this?"

She shook her head, her eyes wide, her bottom lip quivering. Yet she sent mixed signals, planting her palms on his chest and trying to edge away.

He didn't budge.

Instead, he clutched her back and bottom and kept them chest to chest, thigh to thigh, and whispered into her delicious mouth. "So if you don't need me, then tell me no."

"No." Her word came out a breathy whisper, her tone shaky, and yearning and sexy.

"If you want me to back off, you'll have to sound more convincing." He enjoyed the sight of her eyes dilating, the slight rasp of her breath, the feel of her trembling as he aroused her. "This time, you can't blame biology for what you are feeling."

"And what about you?"

"Me?" He lightly pressed his *tavis* against her loins. "Here's proof of my desire." With a groan, he tipped back her head, plundered her mouth. And Alara responded with just as much fervor as when her cells required regeneration, giving him more than he'd thought possible.

Alara knew he enjoyed it when she arched her back and her breasts caressed his chest. She knew that he adored the way she threaded her fingers through his hair. She knew he liked making love by the fervent way he responded. With her flesh pressed against him, she could probably feel his heart thudding hard and reciprocating her passion.

But when she yanked her mouth from his and stepped out of his arms, she took him by surprise. Her lips might be swollen, her eyes might be glazed, but her tone was firm. "No."

This time she meant it. "No?" He tamped down his simmering blood and escalating anger. If he hadn't known her better, he would have thought she was playing games, but Alara's demeanor was too serious. And he dug deep for patience, reminding himself that she came from another world and from her point of view she likely thought she was being quite reasonable. "Are Endekian women forbidden to mate unless they are in *Boktai*?"

She shook her head, swallowed hard, then raised her eyes to his. "You haven't thought about you and me."

"What's to think about?" For a moment, pain fluttered in her eyes, and then she banished the shadow so quickly, perhaps he'd imagined it. "I want you. Isn't that enough?"

She gave him one of those "I can't believe you can be this dumb" looks that reminded him of Tessa rolling her eyes at Kahn when the man was being reasonable and she thought otherwise. Tessa would then proceed to tell Kahn exactly what was wrong—but Alara was more reserved and polite.

"Sex isn't enough," she told him, her tone as prim as a virgin's.

"Sex isn't enough because you aren't in *Boktai* and your cells don't require regeneration?" He was trying to understand, but in all likelihood his blood going south had deprived his brain of too much oxygen to think clearly.

She released an aggravated sigh on a breath of air.
"Dregan hell. My saying no has nothing to do with
Boktai." She fisted her hands on her hips and glared at
him. "Last time we made love, we had no choice. This
time we do. And you haven't thought further ahead
than a sand gnat."

"You're comparing me to a sand gnat?" he growled.

"Why not? They mate on instinct with no thought
about the future, either."

She was worried about the future? Ah, she feared
getting pregnant. "I adjusted my suit. You won't have a
child from our union. And since we've gone back in
time, you won't adapt to me if we mate just one time."

"That's not the point," she muttered with a toss of
her head.

"Well, you clearly want me, so I don't understand
your objection."

"My objection is that you seem to have no idea how
you *feel* about me—other than as a sexual partner."

"That's not true. I like working with you."

"You like working with Vax and Cyn and Shannon,"
she countered.

"I like touching you and talking to you and sleeping
with you."

She cocked her hip, challenging him. "Is only one
more time enough for you?"

He shrugged. He didn't know what to say because
she was right, he hadn't thought past the moment. Ever
since she'd adapted to him, he'd simply assumed she
was his. The damn temporal changes had altered . . .
everything.

"And have you thought about what kind of future
you'd have if we were once again bonded permanently?"

she persisted. "It's unlikely I could accompany you on every mission. And we could not be separated for long because of the *Boktai*. Are you willing to give up your career?"

"I haven't thought that far ahead."

"You haven't thought at all."

"I still have a mission . . ."

"I understand. You're focused on your objectives. So I think we should keep our options open until you have time to think about what you really want."

She was refusing him, sending him away; and it sounded as if she really meant it. "Are you giving me an ultimatum?"

"I'm giving you the freedom to choose your future. That freedom is a privilege that shouldn't be taken lightly. You owe yourself that much. You owe me that much."

Thoughts swirling chaotically, his heart pounding against his ribs, he stared at her, angry, hurt, and confused. "What about you? What do you want?"

Pain shadowed her eyes. "I don't want to be trapped like my mother was, with a man who ultimately didn't care."

Pain slapped him and he started to turn away. "I guess that says it all then. You don't need me any longer, so there's no point in continuing—"

"You idiot." Her voice cracked, and he pivoted to look at her. She'd staggered as if her knees had buckled and she had to catch herself on the counter to prevent a fall. The pain in her eyes combined with the defiant tilt to her chin told him she was suffering, but he didn't understand why, when it was she who was sending him away.

Slowly, she straightened and squared her shoulders. Her voice sounded both strong and raw. "I don't need you, but I want you."

"What?"

"That doesn't mean I'd willingly tie myself to a man who doesn't have feelings for me."

"Stars." She had feelings for him. She'd bravely admitted that she did, putting pride on the line with a courage that rocked him to his core. And she deserved the same honesty from him. "You're right." He shot her a sheepish smile. "I haven't thought things through."

"You've been a little busy saving the galaxy and everything."

Now she was making excuses for him, and he realized he'd taken her for granted. He'd just assumed she was his. But now he had a choice, and for both their sakes, such a momentous decision required clear thinking.

"You've become . . . very special to me."

"I'm glad . . . and no matter what, I will always think kindly of our time together."

She was gently letting him off the hook and regret flowed through him. Everything had been simple when they'd had no choice. She'd been his . . . and now she wasn't. And the idea of losing her clashed with his clear-cut ideas of right and wrong. He'd been content with their arrangement. Having her had been more than convenient. Exciting. Exhilarating. Exotic. He'd come to care deeply for her. But was that enough?

He didn't like the fact that if they bonded permanently again, every time he risked his life, he'd be risking hers. They might pass the Endekian biology to a daughter. Before meeting Alara, he would never have chosen an Endekian wife, and he couldn't help but see many conflicts and difficulties in their future.

And yet, the idea of never waking up next to her again saddened him. Alara had seen what he had not. He had to search his heart, because anything less wouldn't be fair to either of them.

21

While Alara tended her experiments, Kirek holed up in his quarters to think about the equations and Xander busied himself with piloting his ship to Earth. Although Alara still deeply believed that research to discover a way to free Endekian women from *Boktai* was important, the need to find a solution no longer drove her with the same urgency.

Xander had her distracted. Baring her soul, telling him that she had feelings, had been the single most difficult conversation of her life. She'd never expected to want a man—except under the influence of her hormones.

But she couldn't blame *Boktai* or cell adaptation or any facet of her biology for her reaction the last time Xander had kissed her. She hadn't responded like an Endekian female driven by blind lust. Instead she'd felt genuine emotions that had developed from their time together, and those emotions had switched on her hormones.

She hadn't expected Xander to respond immediately to her declaration, and he hadn't. He would put thought into his choice and that was exactly what she wanted—only she hadn't anticipated that the waiting would be so hard, or nerve-racking.

And now that Xander was avoiding her, she missed him. She missed the comfort of his powerful arms, the sound of his compelling voice, the simple sharing of daily conversation. Perhaps she shouldn't have revealed her feelings to him. But nothing would be worse than falling in love with a man who didn't love her.

She'd prefer sex with a stranger rather than end up like her mother—a woman who'd been reduced to begging her indifferent husband for a scrap of affection. Despite the pain of knowing she might lose Xander forever, Alara was perfectly capable of being happily single. She had friends, and her work. While her life was fuller for Xander's presence, she'd never expected a man to make her happy. If he didn't want her the way she wanted him, eventually she'd heal.

However, having a man to share her happiness had been unexpectedly wonderful for the short time they'd been together. And her impatience, plus her constantly trying to guess when and what he'd decide, was giving her spaceship fever. She longed to be outside, not cooped up in the same ship with Xander.

Afraid to get her hopes up for fear he would dash them by rejecting her for all time, she'd tried to stay busy and failed. So when Shannon stopped by the lab, Alara welcomed the interruption.

In her saucy way, Shannon unpacked a basket of wine, cheese, sweetmeats, and Terran chocolates, then came right to the point. "Are you avoiding all of us or just Xander?"

"Just Xander."

"Thought so." Shannon poured the merlot and offered her a glass. "We're landing on Earth in a few hours."

"Are you looking forward to seeing your family?" Alara asked, uncomfortable talking about Xander with Shannon, who was part of his crew.

"We're planning another reunion. And you're invited."

"I'll be there." Alara sipped the rich red wine and savored the warmth as it slid down her throat. Perhaps the company would lessen her impatience.

"You know, an Earth woman wouldn't hide." Shannon could be forthright and interfering, but Alara knew she meant well.

But perhaps she'd misunderstood. "Excuse me?"

"She'd go after what she wanted."

Alara raised a speculative eyebrow and put aside her discomfort. "How?"

Shannon laughed, the wrinkle lines around her eyes crinkling. "A little flirtation. A neck massage. A candlelit dinner."

"Ah, you're talking about seduction. We're way past the seduction stage."

"Men need reminders of what they're missing. Hiding in here makes it easier on him."

"If he can forget me so easily, then we aren't meant to be together." Alara recalled her father going off to work, her mother phoning him on the holovid, and her father's nasty chuckles. No, she wanted better—even if that meant living alone, even if that meant going to strangers.

"So you intend to sit on your ass and do nothing?" Shannon shook her head, unwrapped a chocolate bar, broke off a corner and savored a tiny piece.

"I want him to decide with his head—the one on his shoulders." Alara shrugged. "I want his decision to be made with all the facts and—"

"Oh, puh-lease. No one ever has all the facts. The Zin could invade and you could die tomorrow. The *Verazen* could explode. Or—"

"I know you're trying to help," Alara said softly, "but on my world, marriage is decided by lust. I don't want that. Lust is not enough."

"And neither is deciding with just your brain."

"What else is there?"

"Heart and soul. When my Frankie was alive, it didn't matter that I was educated and he'd quit school to become a fisherman. He was my other half—the one for me." A faraway look softened her eyes and wistfulness entered Shannon's tone. "Together we were complete. Oh, don't get me wrong, we had our fights— our families disapproved."

"Why?"

"We came from different religions, different socioeconomic backgrounds, and Frankie believed he should always tell me what to do." Shannon winked. "Sometimes, I even let him think he was in charge. Times were often hard. Sometimes we didn't have enough credits to keep on the lights, but we didn't starve and our kids grew up fine. We had lots of love and that counts for a lot."

"Love has to go both ways. I won't settle for less."

"You think that Xander doesn't love you because he hasn't said so?" Shannon shook her head. "Likely he doesn't know it himself."

"That's why I'm giving him time to think."

"But he shows his love in the way he glances at you when you enter the bridge. And the way his tone lightens when he says your name. Or when he was worried sick about the Lapau hurting you. He risked his mission to rescue you."

"He rescued *us*. He would have done the same for any crew member. Duty and honor are bred into his Rystani genes."

"You're missing the point. He loves you—he just hasn't admitted it to himself. Sometimes a man needs a little help to acknowledge his own feelings."

Alara drained her wine. "I won't seduce him. There's got to be another way."

As if determined to get her tipsy, Shannon refilled her glass. "You could flirt with Vax."

"I'm not interested—"

"If Vax understood you were trying to make Xander jealous, he'd flirt back."

"No, thanks. I'm sorry, but that sounds juvenile."

"It would be effective. Have you ever seen a Rystani warrior go into protect-his-woman mode?" Shannon grinned. "It's enough to make any woman's heart leap into overdrive. Those magnificent muscles tense. Testosterone pumps the ego. It's a beautiful sight to behold."

"I don't think so."

"Then what do you plan to do?"

"There's nothing I can do. He'll make up his mind when he's ready. Until then . . . I'll wait."

For Kirek, the days on the ship passed in a blur as he worked feverishly on the formulas the Perceptive Ones had given him. During breaks, he'd sent holovid messages back to his parents on Mystique to reassure them he was all right, but he'd spent the majority of the time running equations through Ranth, trying to figure out exactly what needed to be done to blow up a wormhole. The balance of forces had to be exact. A miscalculation could rip Earth apart. And then there was the problem of time. Wormholes tended to distort time in ways both nebulous and complex.

"Ranth." Kirek rotated his tense shoulders in an effort to release tension. "Run the last simulation again, but change the vector to three and a half meters."

The holosimulation depicted a twisted cone that touched Earth's middle continent at the equator. After days spent configuring where to place the glow stones for best effect, Kirek knew he could blow up the wormhole—however, he didn't want to blow up the planet in the process.

"Perhaps if we explode the glow stones in a controlled chain reaction, instead of all at once, we won't have to decimate the planet," he suggested to the computer.

"I'll make the adjustments and run another simulation," Ranth said.

His gut in knots, Kirek watched the explosion begin; the wormhole bulged, twisted, and exploded, but once again, Earth split into a million fragments. And he slammed a fist onto the console, his frustration mounting. Certain the Perceptive Ones didn't want him to annihilate a planet, certain there must be a way to accomplish the task without sacrificing billions of innocent lives, he racked his brain for answers.

"There has to be a way to turn the explosion in on itself—like those buildings that fall in on themselves during demolition."

"Why does there have to be a way? Because you—"

"Because I won't be responsible for the deaths of billions of Terrans. Even if an empty world nearby would hold them all, there's no time to evacuate."

Ranth spoke as if the problem didn't involve the lives of everyone on Earth. "Just because you want to save them doesn't mean that it's possible. You've exhausted every viable physical combination of resources and—"

"That's it." Kirek excitedly adjusted his psi to move him into position, until he was hovering over the holosimulation.

"What?"

"Physical measures aren't enough. But if we use psi forces to hold the glow stones within the wormhole— we might force the explosion to curl in on itself."

"An interesting theory, but to employ your psi, you'd have to be inside or so close to the wormhole that when it blew, it would take you with it. For safety, you'd have to maintain a distance of thousands of miles from the explosion. Your psi won't reach that far."

"I don't see another viable option." Kirek leaned forward, knowing sacrificing a few people might be the right plan to save Earth. Yet even as he spoke to Ranth, he sought and failed to see other alternatives. "Run another simulation to see if our combined psi will strengthen the shielding enough to succeed."

"Psi is not a force I can calculate. There are too many variables. How does one measure willpower?"

"But it's possible?"

"Anything's possible."

"Ranth, computers aren't supposed to hedge their answers. What's your best guess?"

"I don't guess. I estimate."

"And your best estimate is . . . ?"

"That it might work."

Kirek hit the com switch. "Captain, I have a plan."

Several minutes later Xander joined Kirek in his quarters and he explained what he thought might work. "There are no guarantees that we can save Earth when we close the wormhole, but I'd like to try."

"Agreed." Xander studied the simulation. "Ranth, if we astrally extended inside the wormhole to steady the forces, would that increase our chance of success?"

"By a factor of four."

Kirek slapped his forehead. For a genius, he sometimes missed the obvious. While he hadn't astrally extended, he'd heard about the others' experiences on Saj. But he'd failed to factor their new abilities into his equations, proving once again the Perceptive Ones' faith in him might be misplaced.

Kirek frowned at Xander as he mulled over the idea. "Captain, right now you, Vax, Cyn, and Alara can project yourselves into the wormhole. If you don't get out before the wormhole implodes, your minds will be trapped in another galaxy while your bodies remain in this one."

"We plan to leave right before the explosion. Astral extension is as quick as thought. Although the farther we are from our bodies, the longer we will take to return. I have no idea what would happen if we were blown into another galaxy—I'd rather avoid that scenario."

"The problem will be having all of you release the forces at the exact same nanosecond. If the timing isn't right, the last person out will be the one sucked away."

"Understood. We can link into two entities as we did before to make the extraction easier."

"I don't think that will work. One of you needs to hold steady in each quadrant—and that's already spreading yourselves too thin."

Xander clapped Kirek on the shoulder as if he'd found a perfect solution, instead of suggesting a plan that would likely get them all killed. "Good work. You've given us and Earth a chance."

"Captain, five people inside the wormhole would double our chances of success."

"But only four of us know how to astral-extend."

"Then I suggest you teach me how to leave my body before we reach our final destination." Kirek knew Xander wouldn't like his request. The captain still considered him a boy. However, he'd left any remnants of his childhood behind on Endeki.

"I promised your parents I'd keep you safe." Xander tried to protect him as Kirek had known he would.

But Kirek's psi was stronger than everyone else's and most people thought it due to his birth in hyperspace. However, Kirek had joined a healing circle with his mind before he'd been born. Even then his psi had been extraordinarily strong, and from all the talk by those who'd met Clarie, Kirek suspected the Perceptive Ones had configured his birth pattern and helped him to evolve.

The idea disturbed him and excited him. Sometimes he felt this burning urge to try new things. And yet he also feared a change that would set him apart from his family and people. Convinced that he had a lifetime to explore new possibilities, he'd never been in any particular hurry to test his skills. But pitting himself against a wormhole seemed . . . awesome . . . and disturbing . . . not to mention insane.

However, it was the only option that appeared to

have any chance of success. So they would take it. And Xander must accept his help.

He spoke lovingly of his parents. "Miri and Etru would not want me to seek safety when I might be the difference between Earth's continued existence and the planet's turning into an asteroid belt."

Ranth interrupted. "Captain, Kirek has always been modest. But his psi is more powerful than any other being in the Federation. It would be foolish not to accept what will be a significant contribution."

Although Kirek appreciated his gifts, contrarily, he didn't always like being different. Children his own age had always thought him weird. Adults hadn't accepted him easily—all too aware of his differences. Although he'd done his best to hide his forceful psi, the universe seemed to conspire against him. And now, in light of what he'd recently learned about the Perceptive Ones, he wondered if he had free will, or, instead, he was their tool—and if so, would they ever free him to live his own life.

Xander's eyes pierced Kirek, but he refused to show the swirling emotions that made him conflicted about his skills. Finally, Xander nodded. "I will teach you to leave your body. If you can learn, I will gladly accept your help."

Only Kirek has any understanding of the forces they are trying to stop. Delo glowed brightly. *The others have no comprehension of—*

Oh, stop your whining, Clarie muttered. *Is it necessary for a butterfly to understand aerodynamics to fly? Is it necessary for a salmon to know why it swims upstream to spawn?*

Don't you ever tire of manipulating them into doing what must be done?

I tire of your negativity. They have come a long way in a short time. The mental leap to using psi to stabilize the explosions was brilliant and it came from Kirek, who has yet to comprehend all he is capable of. But Xander came up with the idea to astrally extend to deploy their psi.

Likely your choice pupils are going to blow themselves up.

And would you applaud?

Quite so. I'm ready for the next act.

So you welcome the invasion of the machines? You would have us give up to the Zin?

Why waste effort holding on to a galaxy we no longer need?

Because we can. Because we seeded the Milky Way with life and they may evolve enough to join us one day. I for one would like some new company. Your arguments grow tiresome.

Did you just insult me?

Take my comments as you wish. The young one is genius material, and when the time comes, he will lead the others forward.

Even if they close the wormhole, the Zin will try again.

And we will stop them again. Now go away. I have work to do.

Alara knew Xander had been busy teaching Kirek how to astral-extend, coordinating the efforts on Earth so their arrival would go smoothly, as well as seeing to it that Federation forces kept the Endekian war fleet from pursuing them to steal back the glow stones. So when Xander finally sought her out, she didn't expect him to have come to a conclusion about their relationship.

When he entered the lab where she'd been eating, sleeping, and working, he still walked with a Rystani swagger. He still kept his head high and his shoulders back, but one look into his eyes told her he was under enormous pressure and her heart went out to him. She had no right to press him on personal issues while so much was at stake.

"Hi." Her greeting sounded lame, even to her own ears, and she firmly shut her mouth. But she'd missed the sight of him and eagerly drank in his every feature from his thick black hair that she longed to thread through her fingers to his muscular calves encased in soft boots.

"We have a plan to blow up the wormhole." He came straight to the point, and it took her a moment to switch from the personal to business.

"You need my help?" she guessed. And from the worry on his face, it didn't take a mind reader to suspect that he didn't like the fact that he needed her. Not a good sign for their personal future.

Put it on hold, she thought. From the look on Xander's face, they might not have a future.

"I'm hoping you'll volunteer."

It wasn't like Xander not to come straight to the point and her tension heightened. "What do you need?"

"Kirek's plan requires us to astral-extend into the wormhole and use our psi to hold the contours steady until the implosion. If we don't, Earth and its inhabitants will be ripped apart."

He was asking her to help save the people who had killed her parents. Yet Shannon had taught her Earth, like every world, had beings both good and bad. "Of course I'll help."

"The chances of success are not good. The major problem is that timing is critical. We have to stay until the very last moment, then you, me, Vax, Cyn, and Kirek must all depart at precisely the same instant. If anyone delays, the forces will suck them into the Zin galaxy. If that happens, even if we survive, we won't be able to return to our bodies before our hearts stop pumping. So we could be doomed to spend eternity wandering the universe without our bodies. Or without bodies to anchor us, our spirit might die. No one really knows."

"I understand. I'll help."

"You're certain?" His gaze searched hers, as if he had doubts about her reasons for going along.

"I'm not doing this for you." She told him the truth. "Or for us. I'm agreeing because it's right."

"I know." He nodded and almost choked on his next words. "I need more time."

She realized he'd switched the conversation to the personal. And his admission stabbed and burned. "If the decision is that difficult, maybe I already have my answer."

He couldn't meet her gaze. With a quick nod, he left her and her aching heart alone. He didn't want her. He'd rejected her.

A tear escaped and rolled down her cheek. A shudder shook her but she refused to give in. She had her answer. And despite the pain, she was glad she wasn't tied to a man who couldn't reciprocate her feelings. Better to know the truth before she risked more than her heart. Her heart would heal, but her pride could not survive the battering it would take if she became trapped like her mother. It might take a century or two but she would get over him. Somehow . . .

Telling herself they might both die in the imploding wormhole didn't alleviate the harsh pain of rejection. And it didn't help that knowing if she'd been Rystani, his response would likely have been different. She was . . . what she was.

And perhaps it was her fate to remain tied to her physiology, her fate to continue her research, until she freed Endekian females. Only, she wished she could have continued her work and had Xander, too.

Her sorrow reverberated through her. At the moment, continuing her work wasn't possible. Instead, she stared out at the stars, her hands clenched into fists, tears streaming down her cheeks, wondering if she even cared whether she survived the wormhole.

22

They'd set down in the middle of a desert on a Terran continent called Africa and the air was dry enough to suck the moisture right out of Alara's lungs if she hadn't worn her suit. Even worse, a sandstorm could shred the skin off unprotected flesh. And she'd seen no sign of life since the shuttle had set down at the coordinates Kirek had specified.

Kirek had postulated the wormhole would open in the remote area and cause a tremendous sandstorm. In theory, since no one lived here, the Zin could keep open the wormhole and send their deadly viruses through it without detection. The huge windstorms would eventually carry the virus to populated areas on giant wind currents that passed through the tropics and then out to sea where it would spread across the oceans and over every land mass. Even with a planetwide quarantine, solar dust would spread destruction across the galaxy.

If not for the filters and cooling in her suit, Alara wouldn't have lasted long under Earth's blistering sun. A dull orange sand that rolled from horizon to horizon under a listless blue sky presented few visual distractions from her thoughts.

Every awkward encounter with Xander had been brief and impersonal and never seemed to get easier. Each time she saw him, she was struck by how much she missed his company. Avoiding him didn't help because she couldn't escape her own thoughts and memories. Although she knew she couldn't change the past, she kept wondering what she could have done differently to have changed the outcome of his decision. Each time, she came to the same conclusion—she would have changed nothing. But that didn't make the consequences easier to bear.

As the countdown to the wormhole's appearance began, bots unloaded the precious cargo of glow stones. Kirek carefully measured the distance between the stones, positioning them according to his calculations, then rechecked them repeatedly, making certain they would be within the confines of the wormhole once it formed.

Determined to do her part, she returned to the shuttle and flew back to the orbiting *Verazen*, where the crew would do their best to keep their bodies alive while they projected to the site where the wormhole would appear. Alara supposed she should have asked more questions about the coming event, but not even Kirek could tell them what to expect. So her thoughts kept drifting to Xander. Each time she saw him, his face appeared more haggard, his features more finely drawn— as if he weren't eating enough.

Perhaps Shannon had been right and that he was

suffering over their separation, too. Maybe he did love her—but obviously not enough.

She was almost eager for the wormhole to arrive so she could stop thinking about him and what had gone so wrong. She understood she was mourning the loss of him, much like she had after her mother died. While she couldn't rush the process, she could use relief—and welcomed it—even in the form of the wormhole, the greatest threat to the Federation since the Sentinels had required reprogramming.

At least she'd had a period of respite from her biology. Due to the timing of their travel backward in time, her cells had been fully regenerated. She estimated she wouldn't have to deal with *Boktai* until after they'd dealt with the wormhole.

Finally, the waiting and preliminary planning was done. Xander gathered them together in the *Verazen's* cargo bay. As Ranth flew the ship out of harm's way of the coming explosion, within the shuttle bay Cyn, Vax, Alara, Xander, and Kirek placed their bodies in the same positions they would hold on the planet. Kirek reclined in the middle. The others took their places around him and began the meditation process that led to astral extension.

Alara had a little trouble forcing her muscles to relax, but finally floated free of her body and joined the others. Within moments they soared out of the shuttle bay and left the ship in orbit behind. Astrally extended, they flew through the atmosphere and down to the desert to take up their positions, floating a mere body length above the sand. Apparently, the lower they hovered, the more grid stability they could create.

Alara didn't pretend to understand the equations. Theoretical math had never interested her. It still didn't.

Except now she was about to risk her life on the basis of Kirek's calculations.

Extending her psi, she touched Kirek's psi in front of her, Vax on one side, and Xander on the other. Cyn was exactly opposite and Alara couldn't touch her directly.

Kirek at the focal point was directing them all. *Alara, extend forward. Cyn a little to the left. Vax and Xander, hold position.*

Kirek tried to lock them into place around the glow stones. His theory was that the mental grid would keep them in place, allowing them to maintain their positions when the wormhole opened—but no one knew for sure. Their task was to maintain the pattern, give the glow stones time to explode, waiting until the chain reaction was well under way so it would destroy the opening between galaxies. Kirek believed the explosion would collapse the wormhole on Earth and travel back through the wormhole, causing cataclysmic destruction on the Zin's end, ultimately destroying them—or at the very least discouraging them from ever again attempting another attack through a wormhole.

And of course, the five of them had to escape at the very last moment.

With Xander on one side and Vax on the other, she suspected her portion might be the weakest. Kirek may have sensed that and bolstered her effort by extending support.

Is this enough linkage? Xander asked.

I don't know. Brace yourselves. Kirek's thoughts flashed at them. *According to my calculations, the wormhole is about to open.*

Space rippled. There was an initial whoosh, like a stone breaking a pond's surface. A rushing sensation followed by swirling light. She couldn't tell up from down. She lost sight of the desert and the sky. Sand swirled around her, creating chaos.

Hold tight, Kirek ordered.

She focused on the astral bond to anchor herself in the maelstrom.

The ripples swelled, increasing in frequency, building in power, threatening to tear them apart. Buffeted by a vortex, she struggled. If she hadn't locked onto the others, the jagged rush would have blown her apart like scrub brush in a tornado.

She sensed the opening widening, thickening, solidifying, until she became one with it, their astral meld, straddling the wormhole.

Brace for explosions.

The first glow stones exploded, the flare bright enough to blind. But her astral eyes had no difficulty adjusting to the brilliant flashes that would have mushroomed like atomic weapons if they had not been contained by the wormhole. But inside the wormhole, the flashes elongated and flattened. The explosions shot lightning bolts of spiraling light back through the wormhole—triggering the next glow stone and then the next.

And each explosion ripped the fabric of space, tearing irregular gaps in their psi grid. To maintain the link with one another, they each reached out, thinning themselves, stretching over the holes to maintain control.

Don't let it collapse, Xander warned.

The force sucked at her. Battered and lashed at her. Drained her. She poured more psi into the gap. But it was like a dam that had sprung a leak. As soon as they plugged one hole, another sprang up. And another.

Explosions ripped through the wormhole, the chain

reaction awesome in power. No way could they match the forces of the wormhole. The grid wobbled.

I'm losing the link. Alara sent out a plea for help.

Kirek extended his position, anchoring her with psi intensity and capacity that boggled her mind.

Cyn was also having trouble on her end. *Help.*

Hold on. As one they shifted and repositioned, Kirek taking the brunt of the stress, although Vax and Xander also did their share.

Once again she was spread too thin.

Hold on. Hold on.

If she let go, she would die. They would all die. Earth would die.

Hold on.

She couldn't let them down.

Finally, Kirek signaled. *GO.* His mental shout roared in her mind.

The final pile of glow stones ignited. The sandstorm slashed with orange and streaked with hot yellow bursts across the vortex. At the same time another blast from the inferno clawed the grid apart. She flung herself away.

But she was too exhausted. Too slow. Too late.

The explosion caught her, pummeled her. And then there was no more pain.

Xander awakened slowly. His head pounded and every muscle ached as if he'd fought a physical battle, not a mental one. Just cracking open his eyes proved to be a challenge. But once he did and he glimpsed Cyn's worried face looming over him with concern, his heart staggered.

They were alone in his quarters on the *Verazen*. Cyn held his head up and offered him a few sips of water.

"Take it easy. You've been out about one Federation hour."

He swallowed with effort. "Report."

"The wormhole is gone. Earth is safe. The Federation is safe. And we're in orbit above the planet."

Thank the stars. Too weak to get out more than a word at a time, he whispered. "Crew?"

"Vax is coming around in the same condition as you. When we released the grid, I was on the good side. The blast shredded from Kirek and the center toward Alara. They are both in a coma. Kirek took the worst of the blast and his coma appears deeper."

"Prognosis?"

"Unknown. Ranth says their life signs are steady, but he doesn't know if they made it back to their bodies. Ranth says we shouldn't enter hyperspace. He's suggesting we leave their bodies in a shuttle orbiting Earth—just in case they make it back."

Xander flung an arm over his eyes to hide his distress. And at the thought of losing Alara, Xander felt as bleak as a Rystani winter. Although she was Endekian, although he'd tried to walk away from what they had together . . . he loved her. She might have biology that was all wrong for him and his career, but he loved her anyway. It wasn't logical. But there it was. He loved her. And he'd been stupid not to tell her.

Now, he might never have that chance.

As regrets lashed at him, he forced himself onto an elbow. Instinctively, he knew better than to use his tender psi. He had to go to her and Kirek.

The Federation couldn't afford to lose Kirek. He had a mind and abilities like no one Xander had ever met. The kid and his psi had almost single-handedly held that grid. Even if the rest of their forces had been combined, they couldn't have come close to matching Kirek's power. And besides all that strength, the kid was well loved. Miri and Etru would have Xander's head— no they wouldn't. Kirek's parents wouldn't blame Xander. They were good people. But they would grieve for the rest of their lives over the loss of their precious son.

Cyn protested his attempt to get up and placed a hand on his shoulder. "You're too weak to—"

"Help me up." Xander stood, leaning heavily on Cyn for support. "Take me to them."

"They're in Alara's lab."

Xander concentrated on placing one foot in front of the other. He ignored the pounding in his head, the tightness in his throat, his fear that he'd never talk to either of them again.

As a captain, he'd lost members of his crew. But never had the bodies lived on—with the spirits elsewhere. Was Alara alone and lost in the Zin galaxy? Was Kirek with her?

Or had the imploding wormhole destroyed them along with itself? Xander didn't know.

As they slowly made their way to the lab, Ranth brought Xander up-to-date. "You have messages awaiting you from Kahn and Tessa, from the Federation Council, from Drik and from Kirek's parents. None are urgent."

"I have kept Miri and Etru up-to-date on Kirek's status, although there has been no change since you woke up," Cyn told him.

Xander grunted an acknowledgment. As they walked, his muscles seemed to remember how to hold him up. And by the time they'd reached the lab, he could remain upright on his own, although his heart was so heavy he thought it might crack. "I'll go in alone."

"All right." Cyn seemed reluctant to leave him, but she also recognized his need to grieve. "Call if—"

"Thanks." He stepped into the lab and immediately saw Alara across the chamber, lying too still. Kirek, just as still, was closer to Xander.

The kid—no, he might not be fully grown, but there was no denying he was now a man—was on a pallet, his eyes closed, his breathing shallow and steady. Xander kneeled beside him and grasped his hand.

"You did well." He cleared his throat. "I'm proud of you. Your parents are proud of you. And the Federation needs you, but it's good for you to rest. You've earned a respite. When you're ready, we will all be here for you." Leaning forward, Xander placed his hand on Kirek's forehead in an ancient gesture that preceded the *Rystani* healing circle. "Take your time, my friend. I'll see to it your body is still here whenever you return."

Saddened, Xander stood, blinked away tears, and headed across the lab to the woman who had come to mean so much to him he didn't how he could go on without her.

Alara didn't look quite as pale as Kirek. Or maybe that was hope making him see things that weren't there. She also lay on a pallet, her eyes closed, her hands by her sides. He'd never seen her so still, silent. Even when asleep, she had more life in her than she did right now.

A lump rose in his throat as he sat beside this woman whom he'd come to know so well. From the first moment they'd seen each other, sparks had flown. The tension between them had been a connection he hadn't wanted to acknowledge. But when had his admiration and respect turned to love? Had it been when she'd accepted him for a lover? Or when she'd agreed to join their mission? Or when she and Shannon had been taken prisoners on Lapau?

Or had it been when they'd merged their psi or their bodies? He certainly couldn't pinpoint a time when his feelings had turned to love. He hadn't even recognized that losing her would be akin to losing part of himself—perhaps the best part.

Another woman might have pressured him for answers. Instead, she'd told him her feelings, laid them bare. And she had a sense of honor that allowed her to give him space to decide their future. He couldn't stand to see her lying so still and hated the helplessness that prevented him from doing something, anything, to help. If her mind was lost out there, he wanted to send out a beacon to help her find her way back.

But how?

Without much effort, Xander drew upon the pain of loss, the pain of sorrow, and astrally extended. Within moments, he left the *Verazen* far behind. He dipped down to the desert, but sensed no sign of her or Kirek. Where were they? Had they been caught in the blast, been sucked into the wormhole? Were they now lost in the Zin galaxy, far from home, far from their bodies, far from him?

Or had the blast shot them someplace closer? Vax crisscrossed the desert. He stretched across Earth's southern continents. And found nothing.

And he called to her, mentally projecting his thoughts. *I did a lot of thinking, like you asked. And I'd concluded we weren't right for each other. You are Endekian, ruled by an alien biology. And if we'd bonded, if your cells had adapted to mine once more, my death would have brought about your own.*

Who would have thought he would be safe—and she

the one dying? He circled the globe's northern continents, grief and fury spurring him onward.

I didn't like the responsibility that went with being with you. I don't like your biology. I want my wife to come to me because she wants me, not because her hormones are at the high point of a biological cycle.

He paused over the northern snows, sensing nothing but emptiness. *So I made the intellectual decision that we shouldn't be together. And yet . . . despite my careful logic—I was wrong. Do you hear me, Alara? I was wrong. Because despite everything—I can't imagine a future without you.*

Are you sure?

Stars. She was alive. Hope gave him strength to keep searching. Although her mental communication sounded weak, she'd responded.

Where are you?

Here! Her aura rose straight from the Earth's core. She'd never looked so beautiful, all golden and alive and shimmering with spirit as she joined him.

Are you all right?

The blast was about to catch me but Kirek shielded me or I'd never have survived.

He's with you? Xander didn't see him. But perhaps Kirek had been thrown into the Earth's core like Alara.

Her sorrow wound through their mental link. *The blast shot Kirek in the opposite direction. He might not return, because he saved me.*

Let's get you back to the ship and your body. Ranth says you're in a coma.

I'm fine. I'll be fine. She tried to reassure him through the link but Xander wouldn't believe her until he could hold her in his arms.

Together they soared into orbit, through the ship's

walls, back into their bodies. Her eyes flickered open to gaze into his.

And he swallowed hard as love squeezed his chest so tight he could barely speak. "Stars. I thought . . . I . . ."

"Is everyone else safe?" she asked.

He told her about Earth, about the wormhole. Once he recovered his strength, he intended to astrally search for Kirek. Meanwhile, he enjoyed holding Alara's hand, staring into her eyes, happy she was recuperating so quickly.

Ranth interrupted. "Captain, Kirek seems to be coming out of his coma. His prognosis is improving."

"Great." Xander prayed the boy would make a full recovery. He'd grown quite attached to Kirek and sensed the Federation still needed him. "Please inform Kirek's parents of his progress."

Alara turned to him. "Did you mean what you said when you were searching for me?"

"You heard?"

"How could I not? She grinned. "Your mind link bellowed loud enough to reach me through the planet's core."

He drew her head into his lap, helped her to sip some water. "I meant every damn word. You see, I've figured out something. You aren't the woman I would have picked. You aren't the woman logic says I should want. But you are the woman I must have to be happy."

She eyed him warily and he supposed he couldn't blame her. "What will your family think?"

"If my Rystani people could accept Tessa, a warrior from Earth, if my people could accept Dora, a computer who transported her personality into a female body, we will accept an Endekian."

"And what about your career?" Her eyes searched

his as if afraid he hadn't considered all the ramifications. "During every other year, we can't be separated for long."

"I don't want to live apart—ever." He smoothed back her hair. "After what you've done, my world will either allow you to continue your research aboard my ship, or I will seek an assignment in Mystique's space defense. Either way, we'll be together all the time."

"And what about all your logical arguments that say we shouldn't be together?" she asked, her eyes dancing with laughter.

"Logic isn't as important as my love for you. I shouldn't love you, but I do. I don't seem to have a choice." He said the words with conviction. And then he gathered his woman close to his heart. "I love you, Alara. Even when I didn't want to love you, I couldn't help myself. I've loved you for a long time. And I always will."

Epilogue

Clarie carefully lowered Delo to the floor of their ship. *I told you they would succeed.*

No need to gloat. Delo plugged into the ship and fed. *They have merely won an insignificant battle in the coming conflict.*

Insignificant? Not only did the Zin lose the wormhole, not only can the Zin no longer send their deadly viruses into the galaxy, the Verazen crew blasted them to atoms.

They'll recover faster than your crucial player, who is damaged.

Kirek will heal and he will go on to meet his fate.

Why? Because you wish it?

Because it's his destiny.

Pfft. It's your will. Delo glowed as he absorbed power, his brown skin turning a burnished, glowing orange. *And we already know that will alone is not enough to defeat the Zin. The future—*

Enough. The future of the galaxy always hinges on a few critical beings. There's a stubborn Terran female salvage operator who requires a nudge to spacejack Kirek. Let me work.

Haven't you meddled enough yet?

Clarie hummed contentedly. *I've merely begun.*

A Preview of Susan Kearney's upcoming novel

The Quest

Chapter 1

"Captain, we aren't alone."

Angel Taylor peered at the *Raven's* viewscreen and frowned. Another starship had just exited hyperspace, their heading a straight vector toward the Vogan ship she was after. Apparently, the *Raven* wasn't the only scavenger ship on a salvage foray. "Raise engine speed ten percent."

"We're already redlining," Petroy, her first officer informed her, but just as she knew he would, he increased their speed. The *Raven's* engines vibrated up from engineering, pulsed through the deck of the bridge beneath Angel's feet, reverberated through her bones.

Ignoring the assorted rattles and moans of her equipment, Angel gritted her teeth and peered at the viewscreen where a panorama of stars served as a backdrop for the asteroid belt that had trapped the abandoned ship she intended to salvage. "Just once, I

wish the information we purchased could be both ac-
curate and *confidential*."

Yet, despite the competition, she had to secure the
Vogan ship first. Losing the salvage to a rival wasn't an
option. Due to lack of funds, her ship's safety inspection was five months overdue. In fact, the *Raven's* engines needed a complete overhaul, and if Angel failed
to procure the derelict ship, she faced the humiliation
of being grounded—a fate she'd avoided for the last
eight years since she'd won the *Raven* in a gambling
joint back on Earth.

When she'd first acquired the *Raven*, it hadn't been
safe to fly out of orbit, but Angel had patched the holes
in the hull and reprogrammed the computer systems
herself. She'd lucked out on her first run, finding and
securing the salvage rights to a wrecked Venus-to-
Earth transport ship, which she'd sold back to the mining company that had built her, earning enough profit to
take on a crew and enough fuel to leave the solar system. Since then, Angel had never looked back, roaming
the galaxy in search of abandoned space vessels, in
hopes of one day finding the mother lode, a haul so rich
she could afford to buy a ship that wasn't older than
Petroy. Meanwhile, she enjoyed the hunt. The freedom
of space and being her own boss suited her—even
when her ship's system was falling apart around her.

Leaning eagerly over the vidscreen, Angel increased
the magnification. The abandoned ship ahead tumbled
like a glinting piece of quartz among lumps of coal.
She wasn't the mother lode, but was still a prize all
right, rotating and over end in space, its once shiny hull
now pitted and partially charred at the stern. The bow
appeared undamaged and perfect for salvage. Angel
could scrap the hull for metal and the tonnage alone
would keep the *Raven* in fuel for several months. If she

got lucky, the hulk still possessed its old engine intact and electronics in the bow section that might bring enough to pay her small crew their back wages, too.

But her competition surged forward across the starscape in a streaming ribbon of light, making a bee-line for her prize. Space laws were clear, albeit not always obeyed in the vast reaches between civilized worlds where enforcement tended to be sketchy. Yet, according to Federation law, the first salvage operator who attached their clutch beam to the hull possessed retrieval rights.

"Turn on recorders to verify the clutch and grab." Angel was too experienced to risk arriving first on the scene, only to later lose a court battle.

"Recorders activated."

The *Raven* had to secure the other ship—or Angel and her crew might end up dirtside slinging hash to keep their bellies full. If only she could have afforded to purchase those new hyper drive engines she'd seen on Starbase Ten. But due to her perennial lack of funds, she'd had to settle for a retro fitting instead of a complete overhaul.

"They still have the edge, Captain. At current speed," Petroy her first officer spoke crisply, "they'll beat us to the Vogan ship."

"No, they won't. Inject the booster fuel into the engines."

Petroy's squat body shuddered and his sturdy shoulders shrugged. "Captain—"

"You want to spend the next year dirtside?"

"Better to live on a planet than blast ourselves into the ever after."

"That's where we disagree." She'd spent the first twenty years of life on Earth and had had enough of their perfect society to last a lifetime. Angel's father had abandoned her mother before she'd been born, and her mother had been too sick to work, leaving them at the mercy of her mother's family. She'd learned early that charity from her aunts and uncles came attached with strings, like obeying every societal rule. Not only did the necessity of depending on others deplete her mother's self esteem, it sapped her will to live. After her death, Angel felt as though she couldn't breathe on Earth without violating some ordinance or other. Stars, she couldn't even listen to the music she liked without some botcop knocking on her door and handing her a ticket for violation of noise control.

"I'd prefer to live another five hundred years," Petroy spoke dryly.

She ignored his sarcasm. During her childhood on Earth, Angel had learned that money could be made from what she'd found tossed in the garbage. Over the years she'd retrieved books, restored furniture, and repaired a bicycle. Broken toys often needed just a bit of glue to fix and those she couldn't sell, she'd donated to a nearby orphanage—the scary facility where her relatives had threatened to send her if she'd caused trouble. As much as she'd hated obeying rules and depending on the charity of family, she'd seen first hand that life in the orphanage was to be avoided. Space salvage had been a natural extension of her childhood, and now her fingers danced over the console to check on the condition of a volatile mixture of fuel she'd found on a dead space station last year and had saved for an emergency. "The booster fuel should get us there first."

"But its chemical formula has destabilized. Will we still be in one piece after you—"

She didn't have time to argue. With a quick flick of her hand, she coded in the sequence that would open a valve to mix the dangerous propellant with their normal fuel.

"Captain, I must protest."

"Sorry, Petroy." She spoke cheerfully, thoroughly enjoying the race. "If you don't want to stay, eject in the shuttle pod and I'll pick you up on the return."

Petroy showed all his teeth, the Juvanian attempt at a smile. "I wouldn't miss the ride, Captain. I only felt it my duty to—"

With the booster fuel in her tanks, the *Raven* burst forward like a junky with a fix, her renewed energy increasing their speed that would have flattened Angel if she hadn't been wearing her suit. Every Federation citizen wore a suit, made by machinery left by an ancient race called the Perceptive Ones. Directed by psi power, the suit protected her from high acceleration, filtered her air, clothed her, bathed her took care of all wastes and translated the many different Federation languages. Her suit allowed her to move, in short bursts, at the speed of thought and could induce a state of null grav.

When the *Raven* accelerated, Angel automatically used her psi to adjust her suit. The soles of her boots locked onto the deck. She also strengthened the shielding against the tremendous G forces.

The *Raven's* hull rumbled in protest. The deck plating arched below her feet until she feared it might buckle. The viewscreens moaned and vibrated.

She held her breath and clenched the console. "We're gaining on them."

"Preparing to engage clutch beam." Petroy laughed, a high-pitched sound that had once grated on her nerves but now she'd learned to enjoy. Petroy was an acquired taste, usually appearing all staid and severe but at heart, yet he loved taking risks, although he'd never admit it.

She tensed. "On my mark."

It was going to be close. But in her heart, she knew this salvage was hers. The abandoned ship was calling to her like a first lover bent on a reunion.

Timing would be critical. If she waited too long to activate the beam, the delay could cost her the prize and the other ship would beat them to it. But if she deployed too soon, the beam would disperse, lose power and fail to grab the spinning hull.

Her computer could calculate the particle density of the asteroid belt, the ships' speed and the vectors, but no computer could estimate her competitor's accuracy without knowing the individual captain, the make and model of the other starship or how much risk they were willing to take to capture the hulk themselves. Angel used her instincts, instincts that had won her the *Raven* with a pair of fours when she sensed her opponent across the card table was bluffing, instincts that had told her to help a stowaway Terran singer instead of turning her over to the men hunting her during her last run, instincts that told her that the Vogan ship was meant to be hers.

"Captain?" Petroy prodded.

"Not yet. The Vogan ship is heavy. She's spinning. And we're still at the outermost reach of the clutch beam."

"The other ship just deployed their beam. They locked on target."

Angel bit back a curse. Her competitor's beam flashed across space like skimmer headlights in a foggy storm. And just like a fog that dimmed, distance scattered the clutch beam's power. The derelict ship kept tumbling.

"Stay ready. They don't have her locked in, yet."

Angel held her breath, searching for signs the spin

was slowing. But like an out-of-control top, the hulk kept tumbling. "They're losing her."

"Now?"

"Wait." Her competitor would have to recharge their beam, which would buy the *Raven* extra time. And at their speed, every extra second narrowed the distance by thousands of miles. "Load the beam."

"Beam loaded."

"Lock on target."

"Locked."

"Steady. Steady. Now."

Their clutch beam shined through space, a bright beacon of good timing and skill. The *Raven's* force field captured the spinning ship and slowed the wild rotations.

"Got her. She's locked and latched."

As her competition jumped into hypespace and departed, leaving the prize to Angel, satisfaction flowed through her like sweet *frelle*, a rare spice manufactured on only one world in the galaxy. And now she looked forward to her favorite part of her work, boarding her prize to see exactly what she'd taken.

"YOU SHOULD WAIT to make sure our competition has truly left for good before venturing out of the *Raven*."

"Keep watch, in case they return." Petroy's warning had come over the com system as she'd headed to the shuttle bay, but she could hear the excitement in his tone and knew he'd trade places with her in a heartbeat if given the chance. As captain, she sometimes allowed him to have the first right of inspection. But this time, she wanted to go herself. The tight race had fired her imagination, the urge to board her prize so strong that her blood hummed with excitement. She climbed into the shuttle and ignited her engine, shooting away from the *Raven*, pleased to see the Vogan ship caught in their clutch beam like a macro fly in a Debubian spider web.

Her second team, Frie and Leval, still slept, but would awaken soon and take over for her and Petroy on the next shift. But first she intended to take an inventory of their catch. Angel loved the adventure of space. She adored not knowing what awaited around the next band, or on the next planet. As a child at her mother's sickbed, she'd read many books about space and had always dreamed of escape. Life on the *Raven* suited her.

"How's she look?" Petroy pretended to be worried, but his tone of impatience told her he was as eager to hear good news as she was to give it.

"Good. The metal alone should keep the *Raven* flying for a few more months." Even better, when she hauled the salvaged ship into Dakmar, a moon orbiting a gaseous planet with no life forms, she doubted the former owners would quibble over ownership and she could sell it immediately. Back in the central Federation, she'd have to fill out endless computer forms and wait for the authorities to track down the original owners to ensure she hadn't attacked the ship just to gain salvage rights. But Dakmar existed in a less traveled region of the Federation, where the laws encouraged free enterprise. The strongest and the fittest and the smartest ran Dakmar—an efficient system that would allow her to turn a tidy profit without a long wait for authentication of salvage rights. She might eventually earn more on a Federation world, but the down time would erode the extra profit.

"And?" he prodded.

She flew a slow perimeter check. "From the char

marks, it looks as if an explosion took out the stern. Perhaps they lost shielding and collided with an asteroid."

"What's wrong?" Petroy asked, perhaps sensing her tone wasn't as jubilant as he'd expected. Or perhaps he just knew how to read her better than she wanted to acknowledge.

Although the evidence of disaster had occurred a long time ago and likely the ship had been tumbling for years, she still hoped the Vogan's had escaped unharmed. The ship had obviously been abandoned, yet the hair on her arms prickled, as if in warning of danger.

"Any sign of our competition?" she asked.

"None. But it's possible a small ship could be hiding from our sensors behind some of the local asteroids."

"Are sensors picking up any contaminants on board?"

"She's as clean as a hyper drive engine."

"Recheck."

"Nothing. There's not so much as a nano enzyme clinging to the food processors. Why?"

She tried to shrug away the tightness between her shoulder blades. "I don't know. But I feel . . ."

"Go on."

". . . as if something's waiting for me in there."

"Then don't go in."

She appreciated his concern, but they both knew she wouldn't turn back now. And luckily she was the captain and no one could order her to turn back. Even though adrenaline had kicked in and she could taste sweet success, she remained wary. "I'm armed. And the sensors are well calibrated."

"Machines can make mistakes."

"My instincts might be wrong," she countered.

"And when was the last time you were wrong?"

"Point taken." Angel was rarely incorrect about recognizing trouble, except when it came in the form of the opposite sex. Twice married, twice divorced, of late, she'd kept her relationships short, her expectations confined to sating her physical appetites. She now looked for men who fit her lifestyle, those who wanted no more than good company for a short time and who didn't mind when she left without a backward glance.

Angel flew under the belly, taking extra care to look for any details that appeared out of place. Giant mawing holes in the hull and ports gaped where the crew had popped safety pods and abandoned ship, a sign they'd safely escaped. Most damage had probably occurred after they'd left and when tiny asteroids had collided with the hull.

While inspecting every exterior inch, she tried to calm her racing pulse. Her instincts were extraordinary. She had a knack for finding trouble. Of being in the exact right place at the right time—where things happened. If she'd been into sports, she would have been the star player, the one who always seemed to be around the ball during a critical play. If she'd been in the military, she would have been the general on the front, in the exact location where the enemy attacked. And as a scavenger, her success rate was phenomenal, considering the equipment she had to work with.

However, when her scalp prickled and anticipation rolled in her gut, when her fingers itched on her blaster trigger for no damn reason that she could discern, like right now, she'd learned to be extra careful. Angel had even read up on the phenomena. Supposedly, her subconscious picked up signals her brain couldn't interpret—tiny signals that her conscious mind didn't see or hear or notice, but ones that could still broadcast loud and clear to her subconscious.

"Talk to me." Petroy's voice pulled her from her thoughts.

"I'm taking the flitter through a blast hole in the belly." She came through the damaged hull in a cloud of dust. Her exterior landing lights revealed an empty dock and she sat down with no problems.

"I've landed and the shuttle bay if full of wreckage."

She'd expected no less. Still she couldn't keep the disappointment from her tone. It would have been wonderful to find a stash of cargo, starfire gemstones from Kenderon IV or ice crystals from Ellas Prime or even a case of Zenonite brandy. But the bay had either been picked clean a long time ago or the Vogan ship had flown empty.

Angel kept her blaster handy and popped her hatch. "I'm going for a look. "Engaging vidcamera."

Now Petroy could see what she saw, which wasn't much. Lots of twisted gray *bendar*, a metal manufactured to protect starships against hyper drive forces. She placed a portable light on her head, another on her wrist.

As well as clothing her, her suit allowed her to breathe in space, kept her boots on the deck with artificial gravity and encased her body in normal pressure. She didn't have to worry about solar radiation, but the possibility of her competitors returning was always a concern. While Petroy would notify her if they reappeared and she should have plenty of time to fly back to the *Raven*, she sensed the danger coming from within, not outside.

Straining to listen for any strange noises, she forced air into her lungs. Absolute silence closed around her like a tomb. She couldn't open her suit to sniff the air, but from the charred hull, she imagined the odor of old dust and the lingering scent of burnt metal.

Reaching an interior hatch, she popped the handle.
The massive door creaked open. She shined her light
into a corridor, expecting more wreckage. But it was
empty, the only sign of problems, a buckled floor.

Advancing with care, she passed by the empty gal-
ley and crew quarters and, in search of electronics,
turned toward where she estimated the bridge to be.
Along the way she admired the heavy metal plating of
the interior walls that would bring a tidy profit on Dakmar. The cargo ship had been built like a fortress, and
she suspected only a total systems failure could have
left her so vulnerable to disaster.

A flicker of movement out of the corner of her eye,
a shade or shape that didn't belong, caught her attention. Instantly, she shined her light, raised her blaster
and peered into the gloom, but saw nothing, not even a
shadow.

Her mouth went dry as moon dust. "Who's there?"

Petroy's tone lowered in concern. "No one's on the
vidscreen. Sensors aren't picking up any sign of life,
but be careful."

She appreciated that he didn't think she'd lost her
mind and that he'd fed her data that should have been
useful. Although angel had boarded dozens of ships,
never before had she felt as though she was being
watched and judged.

Angel squinted past the reach of her lights and saw a
dark gray shadow move in the blackness beyond. A
very large, very humanoid shadow.

"Come out. Now. Or I'll shoot." Her suit translated
her words.

The shadow moved and advanced into her light.

"Keep your hands where I can see them."

He was tall, very tall, broad-shouldered and bronze
skinned with bright blue eyes and dark hair. But it was

his carved cheekbones and full lips that curved into a confident and easy smile that made her think of a Viking warrior, one of Earth's ancient races. No, not Viking, a Rystani. She hadn't met any Rystani, the infamous battle-driven warriors from the planet Rystan, but she'd seen holopics. However, the holopics couldn't convey this man's massive size or his casual, self-assured attitude that would have been sexy under different circumstances.

"How did you know I was here?" he asked, ignoring the blaster that she aimed at his chest.

"Captain," Petroy spoke over the con, "a Rystani just showed up on our sensors."

"No kidding." She scowled at the man standing before her. "Since this is my ship, I'll be the one asking the questions. Why didn't our sensors pick you up?"

He shrugged his broad shoulders. "Perhaps your systems are faulty."

The stranger's deep voice matched his powerful chest and the sound lapped against her like waves on a white sand beach, solid, gentle, all encompassing. He wore his masculinity with the same ease as he wore his smile, as if it were so much a part of him that he had nothing to prove.

He might intrigue her, but she wasn't taking his word, especially when their sensors had been working perfectly when she'd left the *Raven*. She invoked privacy mode in the comm so the stranger couldn't hear her or Petroy's replies. "Petroy have the computer run a self-diagnostic."

"Already did, Captain. And we have one hundred percent efficiency."

She kept the Rystani in her blaster sights. "There are no computer malfunctions. So, what's your story? Why are you here?"

Just because he didn't appear to have a weapon didn't mean he wasn't dangerous. On muscle-size alone, he could overpower her. Since one generally had to work out regularly to sport such a toned physique, she assumed he could also best her in a hand-to-hand fight. Her advantage was her drawn weapon and she kept it front and centered.

"I'm Kirek of Rystan. Take me to your captain," he demanded.

Kirek hadn't tried to lie about his planet and every word sounded sincere, aristocratically arrogant, but he also evaded her questions about how he'd avoided their sensors and why he was here. Instead, he acted as if he hadn't expected her to find him. Interesting.

"I'm Angel Taylor, *captain* of the *Raven*. From Earth. Now, what are you doing here?"

At her announcement of her rank, Kirek's facial muscles didn't move, but flickers of purple darkened his eyes. "I'm looking for transport to Dakmar."

She arched a brow and kept her trigger finger poised to shoot. Obviously, he didn't think the derelict ship would take him to Dakmar, so he knew her plane. "Who said I was going to Dakmar?"

"Any salvager worth their oxygen would sell this wreck of a ship on Dakmar." His tone remained confident and easy, just short of charming. But she noted he kept his hands away from his body and didn't make any sudden moves that would risk drawing her blaster fire.

"The *Raven* is not a civilian transport ship."

"I will stay right here." Kirek's tone remained patient, confident, as if he were very accustomed to giving orders. "You should pretend you do not know of my existence—"

"—like you planned?" she guessed. If she'd depended only on her sensors, she wouldn't have found him stowing away on the derelict. But no way in hell was she sneaking Kirek onto Dakmar. Those folks were quite particular about who boarded their moon. She did too much business there to risk bringing in a stranger and being banned because he wanted a free ride.

"I do not wish to cause trouble." Kirek's casual tone implied truth. Yet, his bold stance suggested that he was a man accustomed to handling whatever came his way.

"You've already caused trouble. And I want answers. Who dropped you off? How did you know—"

"Captain," Petroy interrupted. "The other ship has returned and the captain is demanding that we turn over Kirek or prepare to be blasted from space."

The other captain had asked for Kirek by name.

She narrowed her eyes on the Rystani. "Who are they? Why do they want you? How do they know your name?"

Kirek rubbed his square jaw. "My calculations seem to have gone awry. I'll have to think about . . ."

He seemed genuinely puzzled, but she wasn't buying his innocent act. Yet she didn't have time to interrogate him. "Petroy, is the other ship in weapons range?"

"Not yet."

"Do we have time to return to the *Raven* before they can shoot us?"

"Maybe."

"Stall negotiations until I return. Tell them I haven't found anyone named Kirek. Yet."

"And then?"

"Ask what they're willing to pay for this Kirek, if I find him."

"Aye, Captain."

Kirek's eyes flared with a heat that burned hotter than a solar flare. "You trade in slaves?"

Her instruction to Petroy had been automatic. But she'd obviously touched a sore point, and maybe it would make Kirek more agreeable to answering her questions. While she'd never deal in the slave trade, he needn't know that right away.

She intended to drop the Rystani off on the nearest habitable planet—but she also wanted to know how he'd avoided her sensors and how he'd learned her destination. She told herself she would have made the same decision not to turn him over to her competition if she'd found a slimy, eight-tentacled Osarian aboard, instead of the finest male specimen she'd seen this side of a holovid screen.

"You," she waved her blaster at Kirek. "Come with me."

He planted his feet, crossed his arms over his massive chest and spoke with calm contempt. "I will never again be a slave."

Kirek presented one awesome picture of Rystani stubbornness, and she realized he'd called her bluff. This proud warrior would clearly rather die than give up his freedom. She couldn't imagine him ever having been anyone's slave and regretted her threat since she could most definitely sympathize with his principles.

From the rock hard tension in his muscles, from the angry heat in his glaring eyes, he was a man bent on dying before he yielded his will to anyone. Oddly, she didn't feel threatened, but sympathetic and admitted, "I do not buy, sell or keep slaves. Not ever." She cocked her head to one side. "But if you want to live, I suggest you answer my questions. Who's after you?"